Jessica R.... ....ttlement worker. She has rece.... .... MA in Creative Writing at Canterbury Christ Church University, and her stories have been shortlisted for the Kimberly Chambers' Kickstarter Award, Wordsmag and the Val Wood Prize for Creative Writing. When she's not scribbling away, Jessica can be found meandering through the woods, reading stories that pull on the feel-strings and eating yoghurt-covered skittles. Jessica lives in Dover with her husband, two children and their high-spirited springer spaniel. *The Extraordinary Hope of Dawn Brightside* is her debut novel.

🐦 @Jessryn1

www.jessicaryn.com

KU-050-062

The Extraordinary Hope of Dawn Brightside

Jessica Ryn

ONE PLACE. MANY STORIES

This novel is entirely a work of fiction. The names, characters and incidents portrayed in it are the work of the author's imagination. Any resemblance to actual persons, living or dead, events or localities is entirely coincidental.

HQ
An imprint of HarperCollins*Publishers* Ltd
1 London Bridge Street
London SE1 9GF

This edition 2020

1
First published in Great Britain by
HQ, an imprint of HarperCollins*Publishers* Ltd 2020

Copyright © Jessica Ryn 2020

Jessica Ryn asserts the moral right to be
identified as the author of this work.
A catalogue record for this book is
available from the British Library.

ISBN HB: 978-0-00-836461-8
TPB: 978-0-00-836462-5

MIX
Paper from
responsible sources
FSC™ C007454

This book is produced from independently certified FSC™ paper
to ensure responsible forest management.

For more information visit: www.harpercollins.co.uk/green

This book is set in 11/15.5 pt. Bembo

Printed and bound in Great Britain by
CPI Group (UK) Ltd, Croydon, CR0 4YY

All rights reserved. No part of this publication may be reproduced, stored in a retrieval system, or transmitted, in any form or by any means, electronic, mechanical, photocopying, recording or otherwise, without the prior permission of the publishers.

This book is sold subject to the condition that it shall not, by way of trade or otherwise, be lent, re-sold, hired out or otherwise circulated without the publisher's prior consent in any form of binding or cover other than that in which it is published and without a similar condition including this condition being imposed on the subsequent purchaser.

For Patrick and Jack and Emilie.
My tribe and my world.

PROLOGUE

THEN

Dawn

THE PROBLEM WITH MOVING trains is, they are tricky to exit without causing rather a lot of fuss and bother. Dawn could do without the fuss and bother, especially with *him* in the carriage behind. It's the fourth train she's boarded today, and she'd been hoping to have lost him by now. Even ducking into the station loos to change her clothes hadn't helped. Maybe she should have chopped off her hair like they do on the telly.

'Anything from the trolley, love?'

Dawn jumps as a cart comes clattering into carriage B, pushed by a young man with a proud smile and a modest collection of beige cookies. Perhaps he could help. She could whip out her eyeliner and scribble a note on one of his napkins… *Help, I'm being followed by the man in the Metallica T-shirt. The one with the huge shoulders and the red hair.*

But then what? He'd just say it wasn't him and that there's no proof.

Dawn needs to hide; start again.

'No thanks,' she smiles at the trolley boy, regretfully pinching at her belly fat, knowing it will make him grin, tut and leave her the hell alone. It does.

If only laying off the cookies would get rid of the heaviness sitting on the inside of her stomach. She can deal with the flab, it's a reminder of motherhood, of how her body had stretched and strained and carried. That the past fourteen months had been real. She's been having some trouble with that lately: reality. That's why she'd spent the previous week trying to convince the staff at the Barton Wing that she was fit for discharge. They'd agreed after the paint-by-numbers piece she'd displayed of her recovery. Of her nearby friends, all on hand to help. How they'd rally around with their cuddles, cups of tea and daily reminders to take the medication that's lodged in the bottom of her rucksack under Rosie's cot blanket that still smells like her. Of course, she'd had to lie, there was no way anyone could be there for her, not after everything she's done.

The overhead lights on the train flicker on in response to the early winter's evening, illuminating the grubby floor and the empty crisp packets strewn across the stained fabric of the seats. The approaching darkness also means Dawn can see more of the inside than outside through the window. She looks away from the glass, wishing she could close her eyes for five minutes. She daren't though, she needs to keep her wits about her.

Four young women occupy the table at the front of the carriage. The curly-haired one says something witty about their sociology lecturer and they all laugh. Self-assured laughs. Aren't-we-clever laughs. Dawn can't work out whether it feels an age or a minute since she was the one on the train on the way back from uni, snickering with Mel and her other student midwife buddies. It's still less than two years ago. Two years since her twenty-year-old self had plonked her springy backside on a train, carrying her dreams, an engagement ring and a glint in her eye.

How the mighty can fall.

The girls grow silent and Dawn inches herself downwards, easing her shoulder blades against the back of her seat. She needs to stay calm. Relaxed. This is the only way. A clean slate with all the old stuff rubbed off. None of the memories, none of the people. A new place.

Step one – get off the train and onto the next without *him* following. If she can't get that one right, the rest is pointless. Step two – start new life. Get herself and her rucksack somewhere safe, dry and not too fussy about references.

She distracts herself from the reanimated group at the front by imagining what her new flat might look like. Her new job. Obviously, she won't be able to do what she was doing before; she no longer has the required paperwork. But something. Something good.

How can she even hope for good things after what she's done? Happiness can't happen, not without *her*. Not *until* her.

But that's step three, and she can't start that until she's sorted the first two.

That's why she's spent all day riding rails that span the length of England, from north to south and back up again.

He may have followed her onto this train, but the next station is soon, and she reckons she can lose him at that one. Then there's just one more journey to take. The one that leads back to Rosie.

CHAPTER I

NOW

Dawn

WHEN LIFE SENDS YOU right to the bottom, sometimes it helps to climb a hill and look at the world through higher eyes. Dawn catches her breath and decides what to do as she stands at her thinking spot by Dover Castle. From here, all of the town can be seen, its edges drawn around by hills of green. The stone harbour wall cuts a semi-circle through the sea, making space for ferries to come and go between Calais and the cliffs of Dover that stand like sparkling white teeth bared from England's biggest grin.

She can't stand there all day though, she's got problems to sort, people to see. She walks the winding road to town as the school run rushes past, taking bleary-eyed children home from days of times tables and silent reading and towards their summer holidays. Adults scurry across pavements, skiving the last two hours of the working week. Friday afternoons don't count, and every one of them knows it as they propel themselves towards their kettles or their glasses of Prosecco. Dawn expects they've earned it; it's been one of those weeks.

She cuts through the park and past the line of boarded-up

shops until she reaches the council building. She nips inside and joins the queue, smiling her usual thousand-watt smile. Disarming or alarming, no one can ever agree which.

'It's Dawn Elisabeth Brightside, Brightside one word,' she tells the woman behind the Perspex-encased desk, before rattling off the numbers of her date of birth. She waits to be told that she doesn't look like a woman in her forties. She must be thirty, maximum.

'Address?' The woman has barely looked up at her though, so there's still time.

'That's why I'm here. I don't actually have one.' Dawn's laugh makes the woman jump but at least she stops tap-tapping on her computer. Everyone else in the room must have heard too as they're all looking at Dawn with varying degrees of curiosity. She would too if she were them. They're thinking she doesn't look like someone who would get themselves in such a pickle. She peers back at them, one at a time, wondering what they're doing in the rows and columns of itchy seats.

She bets the man in the corner has just been let go from his job as an encyclopaedia salesman – not much call for them anymore, what with the internet and asking Siri. And her with the Marks and Spencer's jeans; well, she probably just wants to complain about a late bin collection.

'Miss Brightside?' The desk woman, name badge; *Tracey, here to help*, is staring as if she's waiting for an answer.

The reception area is nicer than you'd imagine. The desk goes around in a big circle with all the people behind it facing outwards behind their screens, ready to catch all the problems. It's light and airy, and the walls are almost entirely made up of windows so all the regular people out doing their shopping can stare in and make up their own stories about the misfortunes of those inside. Dawn gives a quick wave towards the panelled glass on her right, just in case.

Tracey-here-to-help is still watching. 'I was asking you if you have an appointment. There's nothing showing up on the system?'

'Oh, the system.' Dawn make a *pfft* noise and bats her hand away towards the floor. 'The system never shows anything; happens all the time. Just tell them Dawn Elisabeth Brightside is here, I'm sure that will be fine. That's Brightside all one word.'

'For homeless applications, we do need to set up a proper appointment, Miss Brightside, so you can speak to the right person in a private room.'

'It's Mrs.'

'Sorry?'

'It's Mrs Brightside. My husband's no longer with us.' Dawn lowers her voice.

'I'm very sorry to hear that.' Her head is cocked to the left at a thirty-degree angle, the universal gradient of sympathy. It makes Dawn feel warmer for a moment. Nice lady, that Tracey.

'We could actually squeeze you in now, Room 2 appears to be free.'

Dawn should ask her why she didn't just say that in the first place and no wonder it always takes so long to get through to the council if they're always dilly-dallying about like this, but there's no time to fit the words in before she's ushered into a small pine-coloured room with purple-cushioned chairs.

'There's several factors we need to consider whilst we assess your application. First we need to assess whether or not you've made yourself intentionally homeless.'

This Tracey has an odd sense of humour. It's a good job it's just Dawn she's asking; she can always see the funny side of most things. But if she was to say this kind of stuff to the wrong person, well, perhaps that's what that security button on the desk is for.

'Maybe this will explain things. It's from my last landlord.' Dawn gives Tracey the crumpled letter that's been lurking in her bag for the last few months. She looks at the posters on the wall whilst Tracey reads it. They're mostly about support groups and food banks.

'This letter suggests you were given notice to leave over six months ago. Were you in arrears with your rent?'

'Oh no, she just wants the house back. Something to do with her daughter, she...'

'Could you not have arranged further private rented accommodation for yourself during this notice period?'

Perhaps Tracey doesn't know how much landlords want paying upfront nowadays. All those deposits, a few hundred quid to fill out a form and a few more for the credit check people to tell her she can't 'pass go', can't collect two hundred pounds, and it's straight to the council for Dawn. She's always sucked at Monopoly.

'I was a bit short of cash. Lost my job at Reg's Reptiles – couldn't afford me any longer, they said.'

'Where have you been sleeping?'

'Here and there. Dover really is a beautiful town. I've got to know it really well.'

'Do you have family who could help?' Tracey has stopped banging on her keyboard, her voice softer now.

Dawn wonders how many people must come in here who have no family at all, alone in the world with no one to turn to. It must really suck, knowing if anything happened to you, no one would actually notice.

'There's Rosie, my daughter. She's abroad at the moment, Spain. She's project-managing a… project. A very important one, I wouldn't want to worry her. They're trying for a baby, her and Mike. Imagine it, me a grandmother at forty, wouldn't that be something?'

Tracey still doesn't say anything. Maybe it's company policy not to make remarks about how young people look. Dawn wishes she would say something though, anything, just to distract her. She's still thinking about all those poor, lonely people with no one, and how if they died, people would only realise once their bodies started to decompose. That's if they had a home of course. At least they'd be found quicker if it happened in a shop doorway or in the park. It's a good thing she has her Rosie to speak to every day. If the worst happened to Dawn, Rosie would wonder why she hadn't answered her calls and she'd alert someone. Yes, of course that's what she'd do.

'Are you suffering from any of the following: physical health problems, domestic abuse, disabilities of any kind and do you take any medication?'

The window on the left is open, leaving a path of warm and heavy air between the room and the arse-end of the park where all the ramps are kept. Children are performing tricks of impressive complexity on their boards, especially taking into account what it smells like they're smoking. Dawn fights to remember the list Tracey's just sprinted through.

'No,' she says after a moment.

'Any mental health issues that may class you as being vulnerable?'

Is she more vulnerable than anybody else? She looks out again at the kids. One of them has just cracked open a can of Strongbow.

'Nope. I mean, I've always been a bit up and down, but no. I'm fine.' She remembers being asked a minute ago about medication but can't think what it is she's supposed to be taking.

'I can place you on the list for social housing, but as it stands, you don't qualify for emergency housing. You're not classed as a priority.'

Ouch. Dawn glances up at Tracey's 'Investors in People' award that's fixed to the wall behind her. She tries her best, she supposes. It must be hard having to spend the day telling people they aren't her priority. I mean, it's fine for Dawn, she's used to it, she hasn't been at the top of anyone's list for a long time, but for some people, well, that sort of thing could be hurtful.

'There's a list of phone numbers in this booklet for hostels who can sometimes take in people who we're not obligated to house. It may be worth giving them a call, but they often have waiting lists. St Jude's is the nearest, on Dover cliffs. I can give you some vouchers to take along to the food bank until your benefits are instated. Any questions?'

She has plenty.

Dawn forces the booklet and the vouchers inside her

over-flowing holdall, £12.99 from Primark. 'Thank you for your help. I'll give that St Jude's place a try.'

Tracey holds an arm out towards Dawn when she gets up to leave. Dawn is already hugging her when she realises she'd probably just been going in for a handshake.

CHAPTER 2

Grace

'I AM STRONG, I am confident and I am brave,' Grace Jennings mutters to the blank computer screen in front of her. 'I do not fear Mondays… ' Grace's phone bleeps its eight-forty reminder to make her green tea (with ylang-ylang) and to complete today's meditation in her *Six-Minute Meditation* app.

Mondays are especially busy at St Jude's homeless hostel and Grace is in its cramped, cluttered office exactly twenty-two minutes before her shift starts. As her *Work–Life Balance* book says, it's important to start the week as she means to go on and every minute spent wisely before nine o'clock is an investment in the rest of the day.

She flicks on the kettle and presses the lotus icon on her phone screen. Nothing happens, and the display freezes as she taps it several times in quick succession before it flashes back at her, *Application is not responding. Would you like to close Six-Minute Meditation?*

Stupid, cheap, crappy phone. It's eight forty-three now and that's not enough time to do her sun salutations before Peter gets in at eight fifty. Eight fifty is the time for checking emails and the day's to-do list.

'Morning,' she beams at Peter as he walks through the office door wearing his usual cords-and-green sweater combo.

He grunts a few syllables back at Grace as he shuffles past her desk. That's another reason to be twenty-two minutes early: the acquisition of prime position in front of the office hatch. As hostel manager, it's rightfully Grace's spot but Peter, twenty years older than her twenty-five, seems to think he should be the one putting out all the fires when it comes to the residents. 'I'm well aware you know what you're doing,' he always snaps when she says anything about it. 'It's just that I know what it's like to be the other side of this hatch and you don't.'

It's an argument he uses for most things and each time he says it, Grace gets closer to wishing she'd never suggested to head office that they should take on an ex-resident as a staff member. She taps in her password at lightning speed, so he doesn't have the chance to suggest they switch places, and then logs into her emails.

'Wait till you see the interview list head office have emailed us. Tons of names. Don't they know we only have one room to offer this week?' Peter pulls off his crooked glasses and wipes at them with the corner of his sleeve.

He must have read his emails before he'd even come into work. Grace shakes her head. Some people are so competitive.

Monday is interview day at St Jude's. Each week, the staff meet with prospective residents in the hope of hacking away at their ever-growing waiting list. Grace mentally reaches for the first breathing exercise from her 'Breath of Zen' app and tries to follow it whilst she stares at the names on the list in front of her. Peter's not wrong; there are a lot to get through. Monday is also transaction day, so the residents will be queuing at the hatch to pay their rent top-ups and chase late benefit payments. That's why she always opens up at eight fifty-eight. Two minutes of quiet… just to look out into the empty foyer before the storm begins.

It's an entrance hall like no other, the other side of that hatch. A gateway between people's lives and the big wide world; residents come and go through it, for the first time and the last, often reappearing months or years later. It's a place where tenants come for help, to read the noticeboard and to pick up their post. It's the hostel's hub.

The shutters roar as they retract upwards and Grace dashes to the kitchenette in the corner of the office to pour the drinks before nine o'clock hits – she will start tomorrow with the whole giving-up-caffeine thing. She'll just have to reset the goal date on her phone calendar. That way it won't count, and she won't have failed. Grace doesn't like to fail – it's like her parent's always said, *It's not what Jenningses do.*

'Tea for me, ta,' Peter says, without turning away from his computer. 'And none of that flowery shit.'

Grace clinks the teaspoon with some extra force against the inside of the cups as she stirs the drinks.

'They've arranged a relief worker to man – or woman – the office for us today, so we can concentrate on the interviews. It's her first time, so one of us will need to show her where everything is. Then I thought we could use the residents' lounge downstairs for the interviews. It's homelier,' Grace says, carrying the hot mugs back to their desks.

'Homelier?' Peter splutters after he's swallowed his first gulp of tea. 'Most of them have come from the streets or other people's sofas. I'm sure any room we use will feel *homelier.*'

She ignores him while she scans through the rest of her emails. Quite a few today, all from head office. Why couldn't they just put everything in one message? All this reading will throw her even further off-schedule. She's about to start at the bottom of her unread list when a subject line from halfway up catches her eye.

And it makes her want to throw up her low-calorie granola bar.

'Listen to this,' she hisses to Peter. '"Please be aware that Supporting Futures are carrying out rigorous inspections across all supported housing hostels under their funding schemes. Over the last month, *ten* projects have been forced to close as a result of having their funding pulled…" Oh, this is bad, I'm not sure I can read any more of it.' Grace rests her forehead in her hands and counts to ten. Well, she manages to get to five before she looks back at the screen. '"These checks are sporadic, but each project will receive a letter approximately two weeks before each inspection."'

'Ah.'

'*Ah*? Do you realise how behind we are on some of our paperwork? And the laundry room is falling apart. Then there's the incidents we've had lately with the… '

'Grace. Stop. We've not had a letter yet. Might not even get one till the end of the year. Let's just focus on the interviews – who's first?'

'The first one's due at eleven thirty. A young lad, Shaun Michaels?'

'You always say that like you think I know every homeless person in Kent just because I used to be one. It's as bad as someone telling you they're from Australia and you saying, "*Oh, my Auntie Karen used to live there; perhaps you know her?*"

The office phone rings as soon as the clock strikes nine. Grace answers it, forcing her mouth into a wide smile. People can tell over the phone if you are smiling; it says so in her *Women in Leadership* magazine. The same issue that had inspired her last week to chop her blonde hair into a sleek bob with an edgy fringe, just like the woman on the front. '*There's more to maintaining a successful image than the right hairstyle,*' her mum would have said. Then in the same breath, '*Be the best version of yourself, Grace. You really should make more of an effort, it's important to create the right impression.*' It's always been a bit tricky, getting the balance right. Enough make-up to impress, but not so much that she looks shallow. Professional clothes – not too expensive (she shouldn't look as if she's trying too hard) but not too cheap either (she has the family name to uphold after all).

It's head office on the line and they want to add yet another name to today's interview list. Head office oversee St Jude's as well as four other hostels across the south-east, but they always seem to find the time to give them extra work to do.

'Absolutely. The more the merrier,' Grace sings, ignoring Peter's eye roll. She puts the phone down and concentrates on helping him with the small queue that's formed behind Teardrop Terry from Room 3.

Teardrop Terry has been a resident of St Jude's for almost three months following many years of spending his life between prison cells and shop doorways. It hadn't taken Grace long to notice that – despite his colourful rap sheet, bulky frame and tear tattoo below his left eye – he is, in fact, the least intimidating person you could ever meet.

'Peter.' Teardrop Terry pulls the front of his baseball cap

down a smidgen as if showing some sign of respect. He'll take that back in a minute when Peter tells him he's already three weeks in arrears with his rent top-up.

'But they've suspended my jobseeker's again. I can't pay you nothing I ain't got yet, can I?' Terry says at double speed, trying to squash his hat back into place over long voluminous curls that look like they've been cut from an eighties band photo.

Grace's eyes are drawn to his tattoo as they always are. Peter had scoffed when she'd asked if teardrops were inked onto people's faces in prison to signify remorse for their crimes but Terry had chuckled and told her she was right.

'You could always do a couple of shifts in the café?' she offers. St Jude's has an adjoining café for the residents to work in, and they're short-staffed this week.

Peter picks the phone up and keys in the number for the job centre before handing it to Terry.

'That was head office,' Grace whispers into Peter's ear. 'They've added another one to the list for this afternoon. A woman called Dawn something-or-other. They're emailing over her referral.'

Teardrop Terry has got bored with holding the receiver to his ear and has left it on the desk on loudspeaker whilst he stands in the open doorway rolling a fag.

'Wonderful,' huffs Peter. 'As if I hadn't already spent a million hours of my life listening to Vivaldi's *Four Seasons*. I don't think the job centre has changed its on-hold tune in ten years.'

Grace rushes downstairs to get the room ready at eleven twenty-eight. She rearranges the cushions on the sofas and switches on the lava lamp to provide a *psychologically enhancing environment* for the interviews. She glances at the time. Eleven thirty-one. Not only is Shaun late but so is their relief worker. If he turns up before she does, they'll have to close the office.

She bounces back upstairs to join Peter as he collects the clipboards and interview paperwork from the office cupboard. She peers out of the window onto the long driveway to see if anyone is on their way. St Jude's sits up on the clifftop, and its entrance is around the back, facing away from the sea and towards the twisty road that leads back to the high street. It's fifteen minutes' walk from town and accessible by a quiet road that leads only to the hostel, the café and the cliffs.

Two figures appear at the bottom of the track and are walking towards the building. At least they've arrived together and Grace won't need to put the shutter back down.

'Are you here for the interview?' Peter asks the boy after Grace has buzzed the two people into the foyer. His referral form says he's eighteen, but with his short, skinny frame that's drowning in that XL hoody, he looks at least four years younger. 'Shaun Michaels? Is that right?'

The boy nods and blushes as he studies the posters on the noticeboard, avoiding the eyes of the crowd around the desk.

'Grace,' she introduces herself as she shakes the young man's hand. He may be anxious, but it's a good handshake and there's a glimmer of a smile in his eyes. Good start. Putting people at ease is important when interviewing potential tenants. As is, according to Peter, doing a proper background check and switching on one's bullshit radar.

The woman with the wild curly hair who'd walked in behind him, skips around Shaun and sidesteps to the front. 'Mrs Brightside,' she says with a smile, huge dark eyes and a handshake Jean–Claude Van Damme would be impressed with. 'Your head office said you'd be expecting me?'

'So glad you're here, we really need an extra pair of hands today,' Grace answers with a smile. She asks Shaun to take a seat for a few minutes in the foyer so she can show their new relief worker where everything is.

'Have you worked in places like this before?' Grace asks her. She shows her the code to the fire panel and the filing cabinet where the resident's files are kept.

'Umm… yes, a few. Not for a while, mind. I don't think I'll need to see those files though. Other people's lives are none of my business.'

Grace wonders if head office has checked this lady's references. Most new staff members like to have a quick scan through the files so they know what to expect to be dealing with.

'Okay, if you're sure. We'll be downstairs if you need us. There's an alarm button you can press if you're worried about anything. Don't look so panicked, they're a lovely bunch here at the moment.' Grace picks up a pen and her cold coffee, ready to leave.

'Don't you want to ask me any questions?' Mrs Brightside asks as Grace is walking out the door.

Honestly, the staff getting sent to this place just keep getting stranger, Grace decides as she downs her drink and heads back down the stairs, two at a time.

CHAPTER 3

Grace

SHAUN MICHAELS IS PULLING hard at Grace's feel-strings. Most interviews in this place err on the side of sad. Stories that have broken people's lives apart. This boy though, life has dealt him so much shit she's surprised he's not leaving a trail of it everywhere he walks.

'Do you have any contact at all with your mum?' Grace asks Shaun in her gentlest voice. She shuffles forward on the lumpy sofa and leans towards him. They should really think about getting some new furniture in the resident's lounge if they're going to be inspected. And some fresh wallpaper. The wall behind Shaun is peeling in several places. Perhaps paint would be better. She'll grab a colour chart next time she's in Homebase.

'I go to her flat sometimes, but only when *he's* not there. He pretty much broke my jaw last time. She don't remember when I visit anyway. Too pissed.'

According to Peter, Grace is too easily shocked and needs to work on her face during client interviews, as if she needs to plug it up with some sealant to stop all that pesky emotion leaking through. It's because she's led a sheltered life, he always says. And she has in way; growing up in a nice bungalow with just her nan for company. Her parents had been around for the odd summer and almost every Christmas. As cosmetic surgeons, they used to turn up with harrowing stories about botched boob jobs and free scar-cream samples from their many cosmetic enhancement clinics scattered around the globe. Most parents brought sticks of rock or lame postcards when they came to visit. Or even better, didn't leave their kids behind in the first place.

Still, Grace tries to be patient with Peter. *Patience is the highest form of wisdom*, it says on the canvas plaque on the wall behind her. And it must sting for Peter, being answerable to someone twenty years younger than his forty-five. Even if she does have a social work degree.

Grace makes some notes on Shaun's 'Social and Family Network' section of his interview form, already knowing that this is the client she wants to offer this week's room to. Peter will insist they stick to the scoring system and wait until they've gone through today's list. Grace can't help but wonder about what would have happened to Peter this time last year, if she'd done that when it had been him lying in the corner of Tesco's car park in a puddle of his own piss.

'Where have you been sleeping?' Peter asks Shaun.

'Sofa-surfing. I'm staying with a mate at the moment, but I can't much longer. Landlord said he'll kick him out.'

Damn. He has shelter. That will mess with his vulnerability score. Grace glances at Peter as he scribbles away and thinks of ways to bump up Shaun's numbers. Peter's bound to notice though, and then she'll have to put up with him accusing her of being a do-gooder and wanting another pet project. He'd do well to remember how well her last pet project had gone. The one she now has to share an office with every bloody day. At least the residents love him. Grace thinks it's because he always seems to know what to say and do when it comes to them, and he's never fooled by people's smokescreens. He says it's because 'you can't bullshit a bullshitter'.

'Thanks for coming,' she says to Shaun as she shows him out, hoping she'll be able to call his pay-as-you-go with good news at the end of the afternoon. 'Keep your phone charged – the library can help with that – and don't lose those food bank vouchers.'

As she walks back through the foyer, Grace starts thinking again about that email. Where would people like Shaun go for help if St Jude's wasn't there anymore?

She joins Peter back in the office to find the poor relief worker still dusting the spotless desk as if she doesn't know what else to do with herself.

'Thank you for holding the fort for us today. It's a massive help that you could cover at such short notice. Don't worry about doing that, I'm sure you've had enough to do dealing with this rowdy lot.' Grace grins at Teardrop Terry, still at the hatch with the office phone against his ear, and she prises the cloth from the woman's chipped nails.

'I've met a few of your residents,' Mrs Brightside says. 'I helped one of them fill out a form to register at a doctor's surgery. I hope I did it right, I'm not too good with things like that.'

Grace and Peter share a quick look at each other before she carries on.

'I hope all this won't go against me getting a room. They didn't tell me I'd have to do any role play.'

Leabharlann Contae na Mídhe

Grace's mind starts to wobble, and the question falls slowly out of her mouth. 'What did you say your name was again?'

'Mrs Dawn Elisabeth Brightside. Brightside, one word.'

The office hatch is now closed, and head office have been notified about the absent relief worker. Grace and Peter have ten minutes to squeeze in Dawn's interview before the next one arrives.

'You got family?' Peter asks that one this time.

'I'm a widow,' she tells them and stares out of the window. 'I have a daughter but she's living in Saudi Arabia at the moment. She works in finance. She'll work herself into an early grave, I always tell her.' One of Dawn's clasped hands has gone white in the areas pressed tight against her fingernails.

'How old?' asks Peter.

'Twenty-two and two months,' she answers without missing a beat.

Grace tells her she looks too young to have a daughter that age and Dawn reaches across and squeezes her wrist.

'Thank you,' she beams.

Grace had mostly just been being polite, but when Dawn smiles like that the years do fall away from her face. The date of birth on her referral form places her at forty-two. She's dressed like someone younger; her clothes too big for her angular frame. Her dark brown eyes are overpowered by the thick smudges of eyeliner beneath them which draws attention to the sharp hollows of her cheeks.

'I'm sorry about your husband,' Grace says. 'How long ago did he pass?'

Dawn gets up out of her seat and walks towards the glass,

staring down the driveway as if she's expecting someone to arrive.

'He was murdered,' she announces. 'And the police have no suspects.'

Grace can't think of anything to say that doesn't sound wildly inadequate and Peter is busy cleaning his scratched-to-bits glasses. They've been like that for months but he won't go to the opticians. Peter doesn't 'do' appointments as they tend to include two of his pet hates: small talk and waiting.

Grace leaves a respectful gap of silence, looking at Peter every now and again for clues about when it's the right time to go back to the questions.

Dawn tells them she's slept in the park, the seafront and a few bus shelters since her landlord chucked her out. Apparently, he'd been dealing drugs from the address and wanted rid of Dawn because she knew too much. She'd lived in Dover for almost a year, and lots of different towns before that. 'I like to travel,' she says. 'Travel is good for the soul. Staying in one place can be... dangerous.' Dawn shudders. 'So, I've slept in lots of places of varying qualities. Quite a few shop doorways too, but we can't have everything.'

Dawn's score creeps up as she lets them know what medication she's prescribed and that it's been a while since she's seen the nice people from the mental health team; she expects they've been very busy.

Dawn gives them both unexpected hugs before she leaves, and Grace suppresses a smile at Peter's pale face. Peter's not fond of physical contact, too many germs. She often wonders how he'd coped when he'd been a surgical doctor, working in humanitarian aid mission fields in less-than-sanitary environments.

The afternoon of interviews passes by, churning with stories and answers to questions they hadn't asked. There's half an hour to go until they hand the shift over to the evening staff. Thirty minutes to decide whose life they can pluck from the streets and patch up with paperwork, a tiny room and an Argos duvet cover.

They add up the scores from a pile of papers. Grace had already worked out the answer.

CHAPTER 4

Dawn

THE EVENING IS BEGINNING to cool even though it's July and only one minute to five. The park is holding all the evening sunshine in its top corner where the swings are, leaving none for its other inhabitants. People enter through one end and leave through the other, scurrying home from work to watch *Neighbours* and order a Domino's.

Dawn slips her phone out of her jeans pocket (Topshop, £25.99, and getting a bit baggy). She makes sure she has signal and that it's not on silent. Not that she's expecting St Jude's to call; there's plenty of people needing that room, probably more than she does, which is why she hadn't contacted them before now. It's just if they don't call, she'll need to pick a corner of the park to set up home in for the night. Which is fine; she has her sleeping bag and she's managed perfectly for the past month. She's tried lots of different parts of the park and it's tricky to decide which is best, under the trees where the bins are or behind the toilet block.

She leans back on the park bench, pushing her aching back muscles into the cool slats, and glances towards the skate ramp.

Shaun's still there, fiddling with the wheels on his board, no dinner to get home for. Perhaps there will be two beds available at St Jude's soon.

'All right?' she asks him, realising she's got back up, crossed the large stretch of browned lawn between them and now he's right in front of her.

'How did your interview go at St Jude's?' she asks him.

'Not sure. The woman said she'd let me know this evening.'

Dawn nods and notices the large sports bag bulging at his feet. 'You not staying at your mate's again tonight?'

'Nah, he's got people coming over.'

She watches him as he meticulously constructs his roll up, only for it to leap out of his hands when the phone rings. Neither of them moves, they just look at each other's frozen faces. It's Dawn's; she can feel the vibration against the top of her thigh.

She whirls around and walks along the path a bit further. It takes her a while to turn back again once she's put her phone away, and he's not on the ramp anymore. She can just make out the back of his head, disappearing into the lane that leads out of the park.

'Take care of yourself, Shaun,' she whispers under her breath.

Dawn's room at St Jude's is number six and at the back of the building on the second floor. It looks right across the sea and she can see the ferry leaving the docks, heading for Calais. Although the room is tiny, it's bursting with sunlight and has an en suite, a fridge, microwave, a dented chest of drawers and a small single bed. On the bed sits a new duvet cover and pillowcase set, still in its wrapper, £14.99 from Argos (20 per cent off). Dawn has moved into countless rooms over the past twenty years. Bedsits. Squats. Flats. So many towns, so many different places she could never call home. She came close a couple of times… but then she'd catch sight of a particular shade of red hair and have to move on. The cold hard ground of parks or shop doorways had become regular pit stops between addresses. As time crawled on, these pit stops became longer than the brief stays between them. Anything not to be trapped. Being hemmed in must never be an option.

Never again.

Dawn looks around the room and prays that this time it will be different, that this time she will stay. She could even get herself a job nearby. She'd almost left Dover when Reg's Reptiles had let her go, but something about the town kept her from leaving. She's had loads of experience – a ton of different jobs. It would just be tricky tracking down references. That's the problem with changing your life and starting again so many hundreds of times. Still, a change is as good as a rest, they say, and maybe this could be the life she's been heading towards all these years.

There's a sound outside the door, and Grace is standing behind it holding groceries and wearing a big smile.

'We always provide a welcome pack for new residents,' she says, balancing carrier bags on her wrists as she struggles through the door. She blows the wisps of blonde hair away that have fallen across her face. 'Just basics. Toiletries, bread, milk and pasta type stuff.' She starts unloading her cargo onto the top of the fridge. 'Oh, and tea and coffee, obviously.'

Dawn swallows the ball in her windpipe and tries to suck

the tears back into their sockets. She's not sure where they came from, but she doesn't have time for all that nonsense. She has unpacking to do.

'Welcome to St Jude's,' Grace says, and she brushes Dawn's shoulder with her fingers. It's the briefest of touches but it's enough to reverse all her hard work.

'Hey,' Grace whispers as Dawn sinks to the bed, water freely flowing everywhere from her cheeks, staining her top with mascara-ridden teardrops.

'I don't deserve it,' Dawn blurts out just as Grace is leaving. 'So many people out there need this more than me – I shouldn't have gone to the council, shouldn't have come here. I put off trying for ages because of that. A few more months on the streets wouldn't have made much difference. I should have stayed away – who was next on your list?'

Grace turns back from the door and hands Dawn a booklet of house rules from her carrier bag. She doesn't answer the question but gives Dawn's shoulder another quick squeeze before she leaves. Shaun's face swims into Dawn's mind and a plan begins to form alongside it as she looks at the booklet. Rule number three pulls her eyes towards it. *No Overnight Guests.*

Dawn pulls the clothes from her holdall and places them in the drawers before popping the toothpaste and shower gel onto the tiny shelf above the sink. She leaves the food bits where they are; she can't remember the last time she ate. She doesn't really get hungry anymore.

She puts off going to bed for as long as she can, but quickly runs out of things to distract herself with. She switches off the light and guilt hits as soon as she's under the duvet. The darkness squeezes tight around her, keeping the sleep away and forcing out those age-old pictures that can be drowned out by daylight but never the night. Tonight, it's not just Rosie's face Dawn sees. She blinks again and again but she can still see Shaun Michaels between her eyelids. Tomorrow, she promises herself. Tomorrow she'll save him.

But you couldn't save me, she hears, right before sleep catches her.

Dawn's room is already drenched in light when she wakes up, just before six. Her bed is directly underneath the window, so she lies for a while, watching the seagulls soar in the air above the sea. Local people always moan about the racket they make but she likes it. It reminds her she's there now. Near the sea and away from the city. Not many seagulls in Manchester. They call out, letting each other know which roads have rubbish collections this morning and which houses never do their bin bags up properly.

After enduring a lukewarm shower (a notice on the wall tells her that temperatures are capped for health and safety reasons), she pulls on a pair of light leggings and a long floaty top from New Look, £19.99, buy-one-get-one-free. She picks up her key and clicks the door shut behind her.

The staff flat is across the corridor. According to the information booklet, the night staff take it in turns to sleep in it in case there are 'incidents'. Dawn can't decide if she's comforted by this or not. The office shutters are still down, so it must be too early for a natter. She decides to take herself on a little tour and pads about in her pumps as quietly as she can. The top two floors appear identical and the ground floor is mostly just the office and the foyer. The basement is home to the resident's lounge and the laundry room; *only to be used before 8 p.m.*

The lounge is empty of people but the TV is still on low and Lorraine Kelly is smiling down from the wall. Maybe it's screwed on in case anyone nicks it. Two worn sofas frame the room and there's a patio door that leads into a small, walled garden that's littered with fag butts and dandelions. The coffee table in the middle of the room is covered with torn boxes of board games that look like they've been there since the eighties. At least they're trying. Dawn was always quite good at playing Frustration; she likes the satisfying clunk of the push-ey down bit in the middle.

Lorraine's gone from the telly and now there's a local news bulletin. Someone's been found dead, probable overdose. Dawn swipes the remote from the arm of the sofa and switches it off. No point wasting electricity.

The muffled roaring sound of the shutter from upstairs makes her jump, and she runs upstairs to see the office is now open. She's looking forward to having someone to chat to – she'll go and make a cuppa for the staff to say thank you for letting her stay. As Dawn strolls towards the office, she wonders if Grace is working today. She stops when she reaches the hatch.

Grace is hunched over a newspaper on her desk, tears falling down her cheeks. Peter's arm is placed awkwardly across her.

'It's all my fault,' Grace says.

Dawn will leave quietly. She won't intrude; Grace probably isn't allowed to cry in front of the residents.

30

She can just about see the headline in front of Grace. It has the word 'overdose' in it. Underneath is a photo of a toilet block in a Dover park. Dawn stares at the paper and back at Grace's heaving shoulders.

And then she runs.

CHAPTER 5

Grace

GRACE'S TEARS HAVE MIXED with the ink on the page and she dabs at the newspaper with the sleeve of her cardigan, smudging the article and making it worse. Not that it could get any worse, each word is drilling a hole straight into her heart and she has to look away from the featured photograph as it smiles back at her. It must've been taken some years ago before life had come along and stolen all the sparkle.

'It's not your fault,' says Peter as he hugs her shoulders, reading over the top of her head. 'We can't save them all.'

'But he was on our waiting list.' She swipes a man-size tissue from Peter's freckly hand and blows hard into it.

'You couldn't have known,' he says, pulling a chair towards her and sitting down. 'We interviewed seven people yesterday for one room. This could have happened to any one of them. And they're not saying it was definitely deliberate. People accidently overdose all the time. Even if he was living here, it still could have happened.'

'Yes, but at least it wouldn't have happened on the floor of a grotty public toilet in the park.' She thumps the desk in front of her and realises that she's shouting. She tries to still

32

her thoughts and then closes the paper. She shouldn't take it out on Peter, it's not his fault and his night shift finished half an hour ago.

'Lorna should be here any minute, it's her day to run the activities. I'll wait until she gets here,' he says when she tells him to go. 'I can't leave you on your own like this. You'd be better taking the day off, you've had a big shock. Why don't you take yourself off home?'

Home sounds appealing. She could have a big wardrobe clear-out. She'll do some yoga – that one on YouTube led by the woman with the weirdly long toes. Exercise always calms her. Yoga, running, stretching. *Just keep yourself moving,* her mum would tell her. *When life goes to shit, it doesn't mean you have to.*

'I can't, the police are coming up soon to take statements. We might have been the last people to speak to him as he phoned the office yesterday to check on his application.' Her voice wobbles again. 'And you've been here all night already.'

'I'm fine,' he assures. 'It was a quiet night. I slept. No incidents.'

Peter is still in the office even after Lorna has turned up, twenty minutes late as usual. Beads of sweat cling to her grey spiky hair and she peels off a layer of her signature high-spec sports gear before disappearing downstairs with Peter to put on an activity for the residents so Grace can speak to the police in private.

'A large amount of heroin was found in his system,' they tell her once she's written her statement. 'Probably too much to be considered recreational, unless he'd been a regular user for a considerable amount of time.'

'It wasn't on his referral form that he had a drug issue.' Grace shakes her head. 'We always ask and let them know they can be open with us; that it wouldn't stop them from getting a place here. We only ask so we know how to support them best when they move in.'

'People aren't always honest, Grace,' Detective Jeffries says, glancing at her statement. 'Sometimes people just get trapped inside the lies they tell themselves, and the truth can't squeeze back in.'

Grace opens the shutter after he's gone, and pokes her head through the gap, listening to the silence of the foyer. Everyone must still be downstairs playing 'backwards-bingo', a favourite group activity whenever Lorna's working.

'Have you been crying, Miss?' Jack from number four appears in front of the hatch, making Grace jump. He always calls her Miss, even though he's two years older than her twenty-five. She keeps telling him she's not a primary school teacher. Peter says it's because he spent his youth in detention centres and has never got out of the habit.

'I'm fine,' she smiles. 'Just a touch of hay fever. What can I do for you?'

'I can't face spending another day of my life playing backwards-bingo.'

Grace laughs at his scrunched-up face. 'Can't say I blame you.' The sunshine hits her shoulder blade from the office window, reminding her of the sunny morning and the cloudless sky outside. 'How about a walk along the cliffs when Lorna comes back up?'

Jack grins and his bright eyes twinkle. Before Jack moved in, Grace had always thought of dark eyes as being the most soulful. But his light green ones always look like they have stories in them that will make her laugh.

'I'll go and get my trainers,' he says, flashing a cheeky dimple.

Grace begins to feel lighter as she whips her scarf on and clips her pedometer into place around her wrist. Daily steps are daily steps after all, and every one of them deserves to be counted. She says goodbye to Lorna, assuring her that her phone will be on if she needs anything. She blinks away the image of the park toilets and steers her mind towards the people she *can* help. Jack has been with them for a few months now and not once has he had a letter or a phone call from anyone who wasn't the TV licensing people.

'How are things going?' Grace says to Jack as they wander down the footpath. She keeps glancing back at St Jude's and wondering how the outside would look to the inspectors. The building had once been a fisherman's cottage and it's been stretched and strained, built upon and extended to accommodate the ever-growing waiting list of Dover's needy and without. It proudly sprawls across the very top of the cliff, surrounded by a low pebbledashed wall that could do with a bit of TLC.

'All good, ta. Best I've been in a long while. Peter reckons I'll be ready to start viewing flats and moving on soon.' He stops walking and there's a note of panic in his voice. 'I know there's loads of people waiting to move in.'

'We don't want you to feel rushed,' Grace says, briefly touching his forearm in reassurance, before retracting her hand. They're supposed to be careful with showing physical affection, but she forgets sometimes. 'We usually suggest anywhere up to a six-month stay before resettlement into more permanent accommodation – and even then, we wouldn't kick you out until we'd helped you find somewhere to live. I just wanted to check you were doing okay?'

'Mostly,' he says after walking in silence for a few moments. 'Peter's been a great keyworker. I'm starting that course tomorrow – the one he helped get me signed up for. When I've finished that I should be able to get some building work. Put these muscles to good use.' He grins as he flexes his arms as well as the dimple in his left cheek.

'That's great.'

He flops to the ground and stretches his long legs out in front of him. The breeze blows his sandy-blonde hair across his face. 'I'm just a bit freaked,' he admits, pushing it from his eyes. Grace resists the urge to tell him he needs a haircut. She'll suggest to Peter that he adds it to Jack's to-do list. Grace has one for each of her key clients and gets them to tick off the tasks with her at the end of each day. That way they can all share the satisfaction of productivity.

'This course will be the first thing I've stuck to in a long time. It will be so great to actually have something to fill my days up properly. Boredom's not good for me and I can't end up back inside. Not now I've come so far. I can't let Peter down after all he's done.'

'Well then don't,' she shrugs. 'Only you're in charge of that, no one else. We only get one life—' Grace breaks off as the image from the morning's newspaper pushes its way back into her mind.

Jack hauls himself back onto his feet and they walk further along the clifftop, enjoying the quiet, broken only by the sound of sea on shingle, far below. An array of orange canoes are lined up near the shoreline and the ferry is on its way in from France. Grace looks to the castle, its stone walls shimmering in the sunshine, and her shoulders relax.

'Drink?' Jack asks. They've reached the pub already. The White Stag is kept spotless on the outside; its front always gleaming Daz-ultra white as it looks over the clifftop and across the sea. Inside is another matter, with its sticky floor and dubious graffiti on the toilet doors. Grace doesn't go in there very often as the St Jude's residents tend to frequent it and staff are discouraged from socialising with them outside work hours.

'Just a Coke and a game of pool?' Jack seems to sense her hesitation.

'Go on then.' Grace can't resist a game of pool and there's always a table free in there.

The pub is empty except for a couple of old men at the bar reading the paper, and they zoom through game after game of pool.

'You're pretty good,' says Jack, wiping his forehead with his forearm. It's boiling in there and Grace checks her pocket for some change to buy another Coke.

'From my uni days, probably,' she says. 'We used to play all the time between lectures.' Grace would have preferred to have played pool during them too, if she's honest.

'Bloody social work?' Her mum had yelled when Grace had shown her the details of her first-choice course. 'You'll be signing up for a lifetime of paperwork and helping people who don't want to be helped. Do something profitable. Medicine, perhaps, if you really want to be a do-gooder.'

Social work was still the obvious choice when it became apparent that she wasn't cut out for medical school, but she'd still spent all three years waiting to feel like she belonged between the pages of her social policy handbook.

'I haven't played pool for ages though. I lost touch with most people around here whilst I was studying, then all my uni mates moved back home. I don't have anyone left to do this with anymore. I even used to bring my nan for a game before she went and died.' The lightness in Grace's voice sounds false, even to her. 'You're not bad yourself.'

'When you've stayed in as many Young Offender Institutions as I have, you get a lot of practice,' he winks. 'I'll get these. I got my jobseeker's money yesterday, and I'm feeling flush,' he grins. 'How about a proper drink and we can sit outside?'

Grace eyes up the lager taps and tries to remember the last time she'd enjoyed a pint of Foster's with another human being. There are so many reasons this would be a bad idea. It's against the rules to even be in here with Jack, let alone drinking with him. It doesn't feel right to let him pay, but then she might hurt his pride if she doesn't. And she's supposed to be the manager. And she's not supposed to be drinking alcohol. Too many calories and it's on her list of things to cut out – the laminated version.

'Pint then, please,' she finds herself saying. 'Foster's. I'll grab us a table out the back.'

CHAPTER 6

Dawn

DAWN STUMBLES INTO THE park, legs and lungs burning with the effort of processing oxygen and lactic acid. Running all the way from St Jude's has numbed her brain, but her eyes are working overtime as she searches for Shaun, her throat getting tighter with each passing second.

She stops when she reaches the police tape that's cordoned off the area around the toilets. A horde of people are standing around it, talking in low voices. Dawn scans the crowd, still looking for an oversized hoody and a Converse baseball cap.

'I can't believe what happened to that guy,' a voice says from behind her. 'I've seen him around here a few times. Even got a light off him once. It's messed up.'

'Shaun.' Dawn's shoulders sag, and she squeezes him tight, almost lifting his skinny frame from the ground. She's left a mascara-stained tear on his left shoulder but hopefully he won't mind.

'What the hell was that?' he mutters, dusting off his arms as if she's ruffled his feathers. 'I only saw you yesterday.'

'I just thought it was you who... Never mind. You're right. Terrible thing to happen.' She shakes her head. 'I heard something about it on the news.' Then she stops because of course he wouldn't have seen the news, on account of having no walls.

'Fancy a coffee?' She nods towards the café that's squeezed between Poundland and the bookies in the row of shops that faces the park.

'Don't really drink coffee,' he says. He somehow looks even younger than he did yesterday. He's taken his hoody off and his ribs show through his faded blue T-shirt. 'I only drink hot chocolate.'

'Brill. You can have it like my daughter always likes it if you like. Whipped cream and marshmallows?'

'I'm eighteen, not eight,' he says as he swings his bag over his shoulder and saunters off in front, leading the way.

The café is jam-packed with shoppers and hungry toddlers. It's noisy, so Dawn has to shout if she wants Shaun to hear her. A couple of times, she thinks she may be overshooting volume-wise because the pretty lady behind the counter keeps looking at her, but she keeps talking anyway. It's nice to have someone to chat to for a change; to have a drink with as if they're just two normal people. Plus, the more she speaks, the easier it is to push that uneasiness back into its box where it belongs.

'You have cream all over your nose,' Dawn laughs, grabbing a serviette. She leans over to wipe it off him, just as she used to with Rosie. She asks Shaun about his family and what sports he's into.

'What's this, twenty questions?' he says. He does tell her he supports Arsenal and starts going on about seasons and players and how much they're all worth. It's nice hearing his voice, but most of the words evaporate inside the steam from her hot chocolate before they reach her brain. The woman sandwiched between their table and the counter is with a baby in a sturdy stroller that's designed to take on the Himalayan mountains. The little cutie drops a pink bunny from her chubby little fists. Dawn picks it up from the floor and waves it in front of her face.

Rosie always did her best belly-laughs when Dawn used to do her special teddy voiceovers, so she tries it now. The baby screws her eyes up in preparation for a big bawl. Dawn brings her performance to a halt, but not before she sees the mum's face. The woman pulls the stroller away, only an inch, but it's enough to let Dawn know what she thinks.

'She was only trying to give her back the frickin' toy,' Shaun explodes, making Dawn jump. 'Does she look like a baby-stealer?'

Dawn gets up out of her seat, spilling hot chocolate all over the table. She needs to get out of there. All these years and she still can't bear to hear the cry of a baby. It's both the best and the worst sound in the whole world.

She moves quickly along the pavement. She's grateful that Shaun has followed, and he holds her elbow to steady her as she sways all over the place.

'Thanks for standing up for me. That was kind of you,' she whispers.

'Shit. Did you pay?' he asks, once they've reached the other side of the park.

Oops. Dawn checks her handbag, £7.99 from Claire's Accessories. Just big enough to hold her phone, a tampon and her last crumpled fiver. Some shops won't miss the odd item here, the odd piece of clothing there. Cafés are different though, especially when they're not from a chain. The first thing she'd borrowed from a shop was a baby-gro for Rosie. She hadn't even meant to; it was hiding in the bottom of the trolley. Lots of expectant mothers do it.

Apparently.

It was sort of difficult to stop after that, especially when she started needing other things later on. Food, blankets. She will never steal though, only borrow. Items and prices are all noted down in her special book and when her luck turns, she will pay it all back. Life could get better at any minute, who knows what could happen? Or perhaps she just needs a few lucky hands.

She looks behind them at the café. No one is following them. Then her eyes turn a couple of feet to the left of it. She knows she should look away. She's managed to stay out of the betting shop for months but today feels like it needs a certain something to lift it higher as it's starting to sink.

Can't let that happen. Must keep her spirits up.

'Dawn! We've been wondering what happened to you. We've missed you, it's not the same in here without you,' Barney says from behind the desk. Well, that's what he would say if he wasn't busy fiddling with the CCTV monitor above his head. Hard worker, that Barney. It's quiet for a Tuesday. Good old Bert is in the corner, chewing on a biro and moving his eyes from his paper to the screen in front of him. It's usually the dogs with Bert.

The fruit machines stand in a trio; the middle one whistling out sounds for a lanky lad with a man-bun. He looks like a Steve, Dawn reckons. The machine takes it down a few octaves and Steve punches the side of it three times, one for each bad word he spits out.

'Maybe we should get out of here,' Shaun whispers in Dawn's ear. 'You might need that fiver for something else.'

Dawn has already smoothed out the creases and fed her note into the hungry gap; her heart beginning to thump in line with the satisfying clunks of money turning into coins. The day around her is lifting already. Five pictures to match in any direction. Parrot, parrot, parrot, skull, pirate.

Damn.

Shaun shuffles about on his feet next to her, bored. Irritating really, kids have no attention span nowadays. Too much screen time, probably. One skull, and four pirates. Nearly. The machine sings and dances with her, joining in with her celebrations as the five parrots chirp at Dawn from the screen display. Clink, clink, clink.

Now you're talking.

Dawn steals a glance behind her. It's quite a bit busier now, and she catches Barney's eye. He gives her a little nod before getting back to his paper. Dawn expects he's really pleased for her that her luck is turning. Today's going to be a good day. Dawn keeps playing and wins again and then again.

'Maybe we should stop now.' Shaun points to her fistful of eight-pound coins. 'I could pop back next door and pay for our drinks.'

'Great idea.' Dawn feels like hugging him. Such a lovely, honest boy. Not many around like him these days. 'Let me just have a quick go over there, then we can double it and I'll treat you to a Maccy Ds.'

'Why did you do that?' Shaun groans as they stumble back out onto the pavement. 'Everyone knows roulette's for losers.'

Dawn may be five pound lighter after losing the last of her

benefits for this week, but she doesn't feel like a loser just yet. She can't find the words to explain to him. It's such a small price to pay for the buzz inside her head. She wants him to understand how the blood's now pumping through her veins with that extra bit of enthusiasm. She just needs to keep it going.

'Where now?' Shaun asks, making her smile. It's exactly what Rosie always used to ask when they went out shopping together. She's pleased he wants to stay around to have some more fun. She doesn't want to go back to St Jude's yet, and the day is a beautiful one, bursting at the edges with sunshine.

There's a large poster with its own frame on the wall next to the hairdressers. She takes in the pictures of the beautiful wedding dress, the flowers and the small words at the bottom: *Complimentary champagne and cream teas for two at Dover Castle.* Dawn quickens her pace towards the traffic lights.

'Where are you going?' Shaun is having to break into a jog to keep up with her.

'We, young man, are having a trip to the castle. They're putting on a wedding fayre and I have a consultation to attend regarding my upcoming nuptials.'

Dover Castle always takes Dawn's breath away. Partly because of its beauty and the way the sunshine bounces from its stone walls and turrets, and because it's at the top of a bloody great hill. She and Shaun trundle up to reception and Dawn feels sorry for Shaun having to carry that heavy sports bag as the beads of sweat appear on his forehead. She would offer to hold it for him, but she can't have the castle staff thinking she's there to steal stuff. If they ask, she'll tell them they've come straight from her son's football match. Perhaps he could play for Dover FC. She looks again at Shaun's face. Maybe the under 16s team, let's make it realistic; the boy still doesn't have a single strand of facial hair.

'It's Dawn Elisabeth Brightside, one word. For now, anyway,' she adds with a girlish giggle, ignoring Shaun's eye roll. 'I have an appointment for the wedding consultation? My son's joining me.'

'You don't need an appointment, it's an open event,' the girl says, each word as flat as her ghd-smooth hair. She points to the right. 'Just go back out and up the hill a bit more to the next entrance.'

The view from the top of the hill fills Dawn's chest up with goodness as the sparkling sea winks back through the gaps in the lush green hills that surround the town. She can even see the park from here, the roped-off toilets are just a tiny dot. She looks away and tells Shaun to hurry up.

Dawn had thought there would be more people there, but there's just one couple sitting at a desk chatting to someone with an *Event Coordinator* badge on. An elderly woman is stapling photos to a display wall of various brides and grooms, smiling as they throw their vows around over the top of a tower.

'Maybe we're a bit early for the champagne,' she mutters, disappointed.

'Can I help you?' the woman with the stapler asks.

Dawn tells her all about Hugh: millionaire property tycoon who couldn't get out of London this week after all on account of being so busy with work. The woman nods so she carries on, letting her know every detail of his romantic proposal at the top of The Shard. Right down to the cello player he hired to play One D's 'What Makes You Beautiful'.

'So, he told me to go ahead and get the prices for all the available packages and he'll join us next time,' Dawn finishes.

The woman looks a little relieved and Dawn wonders if she'd gone too far with the part about Hugh hiding the ring inside an oyster that she'd almost choked on, and how Daniel Radcliffe who was sitting at the next table had to perform the Heimlich manoeuvre. Sometimes she gets a little carried away.

To Dawn's delight, a thin flute filled with sparkles is placed in her hand as soon as it's their turn to sit at the special table with the coordinator lady. She wraps her scone up in its napkin and covertly passes it under the table to Shaun for him to put in his bag for later. He's already eaten his, and Dawn's not that hungry.

'Will this be your first marriage?' the woman asks over a pair of rimless glasses.

'The first one that matters,' Dawn says with a light laugh. It's pretty rude of her to ask, really. It's like she thinks Dawn looks old enough to be wearing a string of failed marriages around her neck like boulders, holding her down under the water when all she wants to do is rise to the top and be free.

Her chest starts to squeeze all the air out and doesn't seem to let enough back in, making everything seem further away as it whirls around. Dawn can feel Shaun's hand on her elbow, anchoring her to the present. She closes her eyes, focussing on his touch for a few seconds.

'Are you feeling unwell, madam?'

Dawn mutters something about having to leave for a dress fitting and pulls Shaun with her until they're behind the display wall. She puts her index finger over her mouth to signal for him to be quiet and wait for a moment whilst she peeks around the side. The women are busy giggling with each other over something and she's spotted the door she'd been looking for.

'Follow me and stay quiet,' Dawn whispers to Shaun. 'If we sneak out that way, we can get into the rest of the castle without paying.'

He looks unsure, but nods as he pulls his bag higher up on his shoulder.

Twenty seconds later, they are laughing their butts off inside the chamber of King Henry the second, who built the castle, 'No, not by himself,' Dawn chuckles at another one of Shaun's ridiculous questions.

After they've browsed through some of the grand rooms, playing imaginary games about being various kings and queens of England, they flop down in a beauty spot on the castle's grounds so that Shaun can eat his mushed-up scone.

'What was the matter earlier, when that lady asked you about being married before?' Shaun asks through a mouthful of jam and cream.

'I just don't like remembering,' Dawn answers after a minute.

Life had felt like one big promise in the months leading up to the wedding. A future filled up with love and each other. Bridal magazines. Home-made invitations. It had been a small ceremony at a registry office in Urmston on the outskirts of Manchester. The two of them, and two of Dawn's midwifery colleagues as witnesses. He'd looked at her in awe when she'd walked into the room to sit behind the registry desk, a long white dress covering up the modest bump around her middle. Light-hearted jokes about shotgun weddings. A romantic honeymoon at Butlins in Bognor, followed by what was supposed to be the first few months of wedded bliss in their flat above the British Heart Foundation charity shop.

They'd been so very young, but they still would have got married eventually, even without the baby, Dawn was sure of it.

She hadn't believed her luck when Rob had first spoken to her. He'd worked behind the counter at the university café and had served Dawn a sausage roll and a shy smile during her first week. He'd asked Dawn what she was studying and seemed interested when she'd told him she was training to be a midwife.

'You must be dead clever then,' he'd said in his thick Mancunian accent. 'I've heard it's hard to get into, that. Way more people apply than there are places.'

Dawn had noticed his blue eyes, dark hair and the cute mole on his left cheek and prayed that he didn't have a girlfriend. She'd been almost at the end of her first year by the time he'd asked her if she wanted to go and see *Twelve Monkeys* at the Odeon. She hadn't had the heart to tell him she'd already seen it with the girls from her cohort and hadn't understood much of it then. If she was being honest, she still didn't really get it the second time around either, but at least she'd had Rob's Lynx-infused arm around her shoulder.

But that was all before. Before the trips to the hospital and the unit. No one believing that someone was after her. Her midwifery career snuffed out so soon after her graduation.

That life belongs to someone else now. Someone long gone.

'If you don't like remembering,' Shaun says as he wipes cream off his chops with the jam-encrusted napkin, 'perhaps coming to a wedding fayre wasn't the best idea.'

He's sharper than he looks, that one.

CHAPTER 7

Dawn

DAWN IS WAITING BEHIND the door of the resident's lounge. Staff at St Jude's hold an *Equip* session each Tuesday evening and judging from the noise from the other side of the door, the room is already full. At least this way she can make an entrance and meet all her neighbours at the same time.

A hush falls across the room when Dawn walks in. Several tenants are squeezed onto the sofas and others are taking up most of the green swirly carpet. Grace and Peter are standing in front of the TV either side of a whiteboard.

'Before we start our session, please can we give a St Jude's welcome to our newest resident, Dawn,' Grace says in a bright voice.

The responses vary. Some clap, one person cheers and others mutter words towards the floor. Dawn expects they're just shy. She's sure they'll all become great friends by the end of the week. Then they could have sleepovers and pillow fights and midnight feasts. *This place has been such a fun place to live since Dawn moved in,* they'll all say.

Grace introduces the tenants one by one. There's Terry with the huge shoulders and a curtain rail of rings across his eyebrow. His frizzy hair is sticking up at all angles, making his teardrop tattoo look almost clown-like.

'Pleasure,' he grunts as he shakes her hand with his very hairy one.

Jack has the most welcoming smile in the room; he'd been one who'd cheered. His hair falls to just below his chin and he keeps trying to tuck it behind his ear. His eyes are light and bright and he has a dimple that has probably got him out of trouble a few times.

Cara wants to know why Dawn had been allowed in the office to help her with her GP form and looks unconvinced when Dawn explains that it was a roleplay exercise to ascertain whether she was ready to move into St Jude's.

'Well, I'm never allowed in the office, and I've been here almost a year,' Cara grumbles as she pulls at the locket around her neck. The chain has left green patches on her skin. She scrapes her straight black hair into a tight ponytail and pulls down the sleeves of her hoody.

'These sessions are designed to equip our residents for when they move on and to hopefully prevent future cycles of homelessness. Sometimes we invite past residents to come and speak to us about how they are doing now. Tonight, we have our very own staff member and former tenant, Peter.' Grace has put her bright voice back on again and gives an enthusiastic clap. 'He's leading a session on budgeting and dealing with debt, then afterwards, he's going to tell us his story.'

Dawn keeps her eyes to the front, enraptured as Peter draws an 'income and expenditure' chart on the whiteboard. She listens as he explains how to prioritise rent, bills and living expenses and what to do if you owe money you can't yet pay.

'Debt is one of the leading causes of homelessness,' he says. 'And one of the worst things you can do is ignore it and hope it goes away.' He explains how to contact companies, what forms to fill in and gives out phone numbers for organisations that can help.

'Before Peter speaks to us again, I just wanted to finish off the last discussion point on the itinerary.' Grace holds up a colour-coded chart. The first two points on it have been discussed and ticked off. 'We need to discuss the rota system for the café. Quite a few of our workers have moved on, so we could do with some more volunteers. Working just three hours per week will pay your rent top-up as well as growing the amounts you have in your resettlement funds without affecting your current benefits.'

Excitement rises inside Dawn. She sees herself with a nice, neat pinny and a winning smile. Her scones will be out of this world and people will come from far and wide to sample them. The tip jar will need emptying several times per day – Dawn will probably be promoted to café manager by the end of the month.

'I'll do it.' Dawn throws a hand in the air, feeling like a pupil who desperately wants to shout out an answer to a question that none of the others know. 'I'd love to help. Baking is my *thing*. I taught my daughter to bake when she was little and she went on to win prizes for her cakes and pastries.'

Grace throws a glance towards Peter and he nods his agreement. She promises to show Dawn the café tomorrow and suggests that Cara shows her the ropes if she wants to help out. 'Peter's asked me to leave him to it, so I'll be in the office if anyone needs me.'

Peter launches into his story and Dawn kicks herself for not putting a tissue up her sleeve. He tells them about his missions as a surgeon abroad with Doctors Without Borders. About his breakdown and the drinking and losing his job, his identity and everything he thought he was. The long nights in a soggy sleeping bag on the streets of Dover.

'You all have a story, and each of us, by being here, has been given another chance. My road to recovery wasn't a straight one. I was so angry when I first got here – *Every journey begins with a single step,* Grace used to tell me at the beginning of our keyworking sessions, and it pissed me off every time. I felt sick every time I thought about how much I owed her. It wasn't easy being a hot-shot surgeon one minute and being hauled from the gutter the next. Sometimes gratitude sucks. Some days, I just wanted to tell my keyworker where she could stick her inspirational quotes.'

Chuckles are heard from all corners of the room. Peter looks different when he talks to everyone at once, it's like he comes alive. He doesn't even fiddle with his glasses or his grey speckled hair.

'But learning to accept help is important. Yes, it was shit at the time. But I've been sober for a year, I live in a cottage nearby and I have a job that means something to me. Don't tell Grace this or she'll get a big head, but if wasn't for her, I might not even be alive today.'

The only sound in the room is from the dripping tap in the corner.

'Working in the café helped me get my confidence back. Going to a support group with Grace helped me tackle my drinking. I sorted my debts, learned how to cook again, on a budget. I just want each of you to make the most of being here and to see that there is a way out the other side.'

Dawn gets to her feet and claps and claps, tears in her eyes.

Peter takes a step back and takes off his glasses, clearly overwhelmed by her support. 'Anyone got any questions about that or any hostel-related stuff?'

The rest of the meeting consists mainly of people complaining about one another's taste in music, Jack requesting a second-hand pool table for the café, and Dawn asking for clarification on the rules about guests.

'During the day is fine as long as we've seen their identification, but for safety reasons, they must be gone by 9 p.m. There's often vulnerable people staying here, and we have a duty of care,' says Peter.

Teardrop Terry 'pffts' when she says 'vulnerable' and shifts his very solid weight from one side to the other.

'What happens if someone breaks the rules about visitors? Do they get kicked out?' Dawn asks Cara in a loud whisper. Cara's eyes dart towards Peter, and Dawn wonders if she'd spoken too loudly. Most of the residents begin to file out of the room with their coffee mugs and Dawn watches Peter as he fiddles with the TV remote. Why had she mentioned overnight rules? She should have kept her mouth shut.

What if Peter decides to check the CCTV outside number six?

On her way back to her room, Dawn stops when she sees a tall man in a grey raincoat coming out of number one. He gives her a nod and holds out a hand.

'Paul,' he says. 'You just moved in?'

Paul's hair is thick and red. The same bright shade that either lets those images from the past back in or sends her running for the next train.

'Yes,' she says, and keeps walking, pretending she hadn't seen his outstretched arm. It's not him; why would it be? But it's better not to take any chances. She'll keep her distance and stay put. She can't keep running, not anymore.

Shaun needs her.

CHAPTER 8

Dawn

DAWN STRETCHES OUT HER leg until it finds Shaun's shoulder at the bottom of the bed. She's slept surprisingly well considering the two of them had top-and-tailed in that tiny single bed. He'd offered to sleep on the floor, informing Dawn that it's 'weird' to share a bed with a woman old enough to be his mum. She'd told him to *shh* and that it was just like having a sleepover.

'Yeah. With your own mum,' he'd complained as he'd climbed in over the duvet. Dawn had flicked the base of his foot pretending to tell him off, but it had been nice; him more or less saying she was like a mother to him.

He's still asleep, his cheeks flushed with warmth and his wispy blonde hair slicked to his head. It must have been wonderful for him to sleep in a bed away from the cold hard ground of the park. Dawn wonders if his actual mother has even missed him or noticed that he hasn't been to visit. Dawn could help him in so many ways whilst he stayed there with her. Starting with putting some meat on those skinny bones of his. She could pop over to Canterbury on the bus; there are still some clothes shops she's allowed in there. She could get him some new T-shirts.

Dawn almost can't bear to wake him but she's spending the day in the café today, learning how everything works, and she needs to brief him on how to stay unseen. Can't have them both turfed back out onto the streets.

'I'll be careful, I promise,' he assures her. 'If anyone tries to unlock the door, I'll hide in the shower, and if I need to get out, I'll use the fire escape.'

'Only leave if it's absolutely necessary though,' Dawn warns him. 'I don't want you to get seen and not be able to get back in.'

Dawn thinks she may have interrupted something when she arrives at the café for her trial shift. Grace and Cara are behind the counter; Cara's dark hair scraped back and hidden under a net. They both stop talking and turn towards Dawn when she closes the door behind her, setting off the 'ding' sound. Grace places a hand on Cara's shoulder, which Cara shrugs off before stomping towards the fridge.

'Morning, Dawn,' Grace sings, painting a bright smile across her face. 'Why didn't you come through the resident's entrance, through the hostel?'

'I thought coming through this way would make me feel as if I was coming to work. You know, more like I have a real job.'

Cara slams the fridge hard enough that Dawn can hear the contents rattle around inside. 'Trust me, this feels like real work.' She makes bunny ears with her fingers over the last two words and Dawn thinks she might have pissed her off.

'I didn't mean that. I know it is, I've worked in cafés before. I just meant… ' she stops speaking as it's clear Cara's busy stabbing rolls and spreading butter on them with the vigour of an angry Zumba instructor.

'Don't mind her, she's having a difficult morning,' Grace says as soon as they're out of earshot and standing in the café's sun-drenched tea garden. The view across the sea is similar to the one from Dawn's room but it feels even more majestic with the warm wind slapping against her arms. There are several small garden tables with matching chairs placed strategically under small trees and a pretty water fountain in the centre, surrounded by geraniums.

'It's beautiful,' Dawn says, watching an obvious burst of pride pull Grace's lips into a smile.

'The tea garden is my baby.' Deep blue eyes shine back at Dawn. 'When I first came to work here, the outside areas were in a right old state. Took me a while to raise the funds for it of course, but now Terry does most of the upkeep. He's a fantastic gardener.'

'Terry with the tear tattoos on his face?' Dawn asks, surprised. Anyone could enjoy digging around in soil she supposes; it's just that Terry looks more like the type to be burying someone beneath it.

Grace shows Dawn around the spotless café area that holds the dark green tables and shabby-chic painted wooden chairs. The walls are heaving with artwork of varying tastes and qualities. 'The ones next to the window were donated by a local artist and the pictures on this wall are from St Jude's residents from our very own art group,' Grace says. Dawn likes the sound of an art group, even though she hasn't drawn anything since she was a child. She does have those special drawings that Rosie drew her as a child on her first day of school. They're glued inside her photo album that Dawn still sleeps with under her pillow every night.

'What other groups do you have?' she asks Grace who is chewing on her lip and watching Cara as she stacks the rolls up so high, they could probably have a game of Jenga with them.

'We have cooking night, after hours in the café on Friday evenings. Peter normally runs that. Cooking-on-a-budget-type stuff usually. Saturday mornings we have Hazel in to do a creative writing workshop. That's usually well attended, and often the group go down to the library together afterwards to get books out and chat about what they've been reading.'

Dawn's mind dances with all the possibilities that could arise from attending those groups. She imagines John Torode granting her an apron on MasterChef or topping the bestseller charts as an award-winning novelist. In either of those scenarios, she'd give a heart-wrenching interview on a daytime TV show about her climb from the streets all the way up to fame and success, allowing nothing to hold her back. The presenters would have tears in their eyes but will carry bravely on with the programme before coming to find Dawn personally in the dressing room afterwards. 'Such an inspiration,' they'll say. She'll wave their comments away with a modest wave and tell them she couldn't have done it without all the amazing people at St Jude's. Then she'll donate a large sum from all of her new riches to the hostel and they'll change the name of the place to 'St Dawn's'.

'This is where we keep the cleaning supplies,' Grace is saying. The cupboard squeaks as it opens, yanking Dawn away from her thoughts. 'Any questions?'

She stands next to Cara as she fills the pile of rolls with a selection of sandwich fillings and waits to be shown how to use the coffee machine, as instructed by Grace before she'd been called back to the hostel to deal with a blocked-toilet emergency.

'You could help you know, instead of just standing there,' Cara mutters as she slops egg mayonnaise all over the counter with the force of her knife.

'Of course, it's just that Grace said I wasn't allowed to prepare food until I'd got my food hygiene certificate… '

'It's a sandwich,' she says, staring Dawn in the face. 'My three-year-olds could do it without messing it up; I'm sure you'll be fine.'

'You have twins?' Dawn asks as she shoves her hands under the tap, *Caution Hot Water,* and spends a long time rubbing in the soap. 'Boys or girls?'

Cara cuts several slices of mild cheddar before she answers. 'Boys. Three years and two months. I see 'em every Friday morning in a room down the community centre. They live with their gran.'

Dawn steals a look at the side of her face as she chops the onions. Years of hurt are etched deep inside the soft lines around her mouth and under her eyes, making her look older than she said she was on her GP form. She decides not to ask if she's really only thirty-five as some people can be sensitive about things like that, and she's holding a very sharp vegetable knife.

'That's to say I see them every Friday except this week. Just found out the bastard social worker has gone on leave and their gran's messaged to say she's not bringing them. So that's that.' Cara throws her knife across the worktop and it clatters across the whole length of it before falling to the floor. 'Bastard onions,' she says, wiping at her red, streaming eyes with the tops of her arms.

Dawn doesn't think it's the onions.

'What are their names?' she asks as she begins to stack dirty plates and cups up next to the sink.

'I don't tell people from here stuff like that,' Cara says. 'Some people use things as leverage, you'll see.'

A mug slips out of Dawn's wet hands and splits into pieces on the shiny floor. She looks up at Cara, expecting her to tut but she's already got a dustpan and brush and is ushering Dawn out of the way so she can clear it up. Dawn's grateful for that as she's just noticed how much she's shaking.

'I have a daughter. Rosie,' Dawn says, wondering why her voice matches her wobbly hands. 'She's twenty-two and lives in Florida. She's a fashion photographer. I miss her every day. I know what it's like.'

Cara gives her a small nod before emptying the dustpan into the bin. Her sleeve rides up as it catches on the corner of the lid, and Dawn sees that her arm is marked with angry red holes across her veins, the same as the ones on her neck.

'Curtis and Kyle,' Cara says after putting the dustpan away. She pulls at her locket, twisting it between her fingers before popping it open to reveal a tiny photograph. 'My boys.'

'Beautiful names,' Dawn smiles as she opens her eyes wider, so the tears stay in them rather than falling down her face. Must be the bastard onions.

As the morning rushes past, Dawn is surprised by the number of people who come in for cups of tea and coffee and scones.

'It's cos we're so close to the cliff and the cycle path – and we're the only café around here that allows dogs,' Cara tells her.

Dawn follows Cara as she strides across the seating area,

collecting empties and cleaning tables before rushing back to the kitchen to stack and to clean. 'Does everyone work as hard as you in here?' Dawn asks. 'You keep it spotless, even when it's busy.'

Cara nods. 'Have to. We get inspected every week. Grace does it. Which reminds me,' she lowers her voice. 'None of us are meant to know this yet, so keep your trap shut in front of Grace and the others, but Terry told me something earlier and it ain't good.'

Someone scrapes their chair across the café floor, making Dawn's teeth rattle. Something in her gut flutters. 'What is it?'

'It's them people who give hostels the money to stay open. They're inspecting them all and closing loads of them down. Let's hope we're not next, eh?'

The front door dings and Dawn turns away from it when she sees Paul from Room 1 with the red hair. She busies herself in the cleaning cupboard out of sight, hoping to find a paper bag to breathe into. *Lots of people have red hair,* she tells herself. *It doesn't mean it's him.*

'Hi Paul,' Cara says. 'Didn't see you at the session last night. You really should join in with stuff. Ain't it boring stuck in your room all the time?'

'I'm off out now as it happens. Run out of coffee at mine, so I'll have one to go, please.'

'Coming right up. Dawn?' Cara bellows, obviously not noticing her backside hanging out the cupboard three feet away from her. 'Perfect time to show you the coffee machine.'

Dawn keeps still, willing Cara not to see her. She tells her heart to beat slower and quieter; it's making quite a song and dance in there. It's not him. His voice isn't right, and she's spent

62

enough time replaying his words to know what he'll sound like when he finds her.

Cara clatters about making a racket with the coffee machine. The door dings again.

Paul has gone.

'How do you know? About the inspections?' Dawn squeezes the Cif onto her cloth and attacks the counter with it. Surely St Jude's couldn't close – she's only just got here. And where would they all go? She couldn't let Shaun sleep out in the park again, she just *couldn't*.

'Teardrop heard them talking. Told me not to tell anyone cos people might panic, but he thought we could help out a bit without 'em knowing. Tidy the place up and that. Shit, you look worried, sorry. It probably won't even happen for ages.'

Two St Jude's residents arrive to take over from them in time for the lunchtime rush and Dawn has an idea as she grabs her handbag from under the counter.

'There's someone I want you to meet,' she whispers to Cara. She feels like Cara would understand about Shaun, and she doesn't seem the type to grass.

Cara agrees to come to Room 6 with her, and Dawn smuggles a chocolate brownie from the counter into the pocket of her hoody. It would be rude to invite her over and not give her anything to eat, and she might be hungry after all her hard work.

'You have to promise you won't tell anyone,' Dawn says in a low voice as her key turns in the lock. 'He's just staying with me until he gets back on his feet—' Dawn breaks off as soon as they are in the room.

Shaun has gone.

Dawn remembers what she'd told him to do and runs to the en suite, yanking the shower curtain across. The cubical is empty.

'Hey, what's up with you? Who's gone?' Cara dabs at Dawn's cheek with her pinkie finger, making her realise she's crying. Dawn is about to tell her all about him, and how he can't leave because he needs her. But then she sees them.

Three thick metal bars across her window. She clutches at her mouth with both hands and sinks down onto the bed. A hundred locked doors appear in her mind, one after the other. They belong to the flats she left behind. The squats she escaped from. Her room at the Barton Wing. The other door with the lock she couldn't quite reach, the tiny toilet cubical and the smell of posh soap. Dawn gags into her fist and closes her eyes.

'Someone's after me,' she says in a quiet voice close to Cara's ear. 'Someone I know from a long time ago. I think he might be dangerous.'

'Who?'

'I don't know his name,' she whispers. 'He's put bars across my window. He's sending me a message. I'm trapped, and he won't let me leave.'

'Course you can bloody leave, it's not a friggin' prison. It'll be some health and safety crap or something. They should've warned you before barging into your room, though. Stop shitting yourself,' Cara adds when she looks back at Dawn's face. 'Do you want me to see if they've put them on mine too?'

Dawn nods, grateful that she's at least pretending to take her seriously.

Cara glances at the blister pack of tablets on the top of the

64

chest of drawers on her way out and Dawn wishes she'd thrown them away. Now she definitely won't believe her. It's not as if Dawn even takes them anymore, they were old ones that had fallen out of her make-up bag.

Cara had only been gone a couple of minutes when she knocked at the door again, only opening it wide enough to stick her head through.

'Can't come in now, I've got keyworking with Grace, but the answer's no. I don't have any bars on my window.'

Dawn lies face down on the bed and screams into the pillow, bunching the duvet cover tightly between her fists until her throat hurts and her knuckles have turned white.

She needs to leave. It's not safe here. Dawn flies from the room and down the corridor to the office. Grace and Cara look out at her from the other side of the hatch.

'If I want to leave, I can, can't I, no one can stop me?' Dawn blurts towards Grace.

Grace opens her mouth and closes it again. She disappears from the hatch and Dawn feels crushed until the office door falls open and Grace walks through it.

'You are completely free. This is your home, not a prison. That being said, I really hope you choose to stay. Cara said you were a natural in the café today.'

Dawn's pulse rate begins to slow to normal. She nods at Grace and tries to walk as normal and casually as she can back to number six.

She's still trying to will herself to pack everything back into her holdall when there's a knock at the door.

'I'm busy at the moment, Cara. Come back later,' Dawn croaks.

The door opens slowly and Shaun slips through it, banging it behind him.

'What the hell are you doing?' Dawn hisses as she pulls him close, squeezing all the air from his lungs. 'You weren't supposed to come in or out unless you had to. What if someone had seen you?'

'I had to get out, I'm sorry. This room's so tiny, I was going off my head. I came up through the fire escape, like we said. No one saw me, stop worrying,' he says, wriggling out of her tight grasp. 'I'm friggin' starving though. Got any food?' The corners of his mouth turn upwards when Dawn presents a brownie to him from her pocket. 'You are a legend,' he says, spraying crumbs all over the duvet.

Dawn is staying put. Whatever that man has in store for her, she'll risk it. Shaun, Cara; they both need her, and she's never going to let them down.

CHAPTER 9

Dawn

DAWN WAKES UP THE next morning with Shaun's foot in her face. Bright light filters through the curtains, and the clock on her wall tells her it's still early.

'Do you wake up thinking about them, Shaun?'

'Eh?' Shaun's voice is thick with sleep as he turns over.

'The people we left behind. The ones still outside.'

Shaun stays quiet. Dawn wonders if he's gone back to sleep.

'I've had an idea,' Dawn says. 'I'm going to wake Cara up and get some supplies first. Meet me outside at the bottom of the hill in ten minutes.'

'Do you know what time it is?' Cara grumbles from the other side of her door. 'It's not my day to work. I was looking forward to a lie-in.'

'Do you have the keys to the café?'

'Yes. Why, what you planning?' Cara's eyes narrow into two suspicious hyphens.

Twenty minutes later, Dawn is trundling down the hill towards the seafront with Shaun and Cara, armed with flasks of coffee and packets of biscuits.

'I'm glad they didn't catch us nicking the coffee.' Cara sounds breathless.

'I'll talk to Grace later,' Dawn promises. 'The biscuits are from my room and we'll put the flasks back later. She'll understand when I tell her who it's for.' They decide to go along the sea shelters before they head to the park. When sleeping outside, the first minutes of waking are the worst. The aching joints and frozen limbs. The absolute alone-ness of waking to the sound of other people on their way to places where they're needed. Thinking of those starting their days with morning coffees in sun-drenched kitchens.

The sea is calm and blue with only the smallest of waves dancing against the shingle. Pigeons waddle across the promenade, beaks to the ground in search of breakfast, and seagulls call to each other in surround sound. Behind the seafront shelter and across the road is a row of hotels, B&Bs and tall houses bearing paintwork that's been mercilessly eroded by salt air and neglect.

Bill is in his usual spot under the middle sea shelter. Guilt snaps at Dawn when she counts how many days it's been since she last saw him. She'd slept beside him many times before he moved from the park and she always checked on him each day afterwards. He is already awake and rolling up a stained, coverless duvet.

'Dawn.' Bill's already crinkled face creases up into a smile when she enters the shelter.

Dawn pulls him into a hug, feeling his bones through his beige anorak and his coarse grey beard against her face. She wishes she could take him back to St Jude's. 'How've you been? How's the foot doing – you seen a doctor yet?'

'You haven't given up your ruddy fussing, then?' Bill's eyes are twinkling but his hands are shaking, and Dawn knows they will do so until he can get hold of something stronger than what's in their flasks.

'Sit for a minute and have a coffee with us before you go wandering,' she says. 'Then I'll call the surgery for you. I can see with my own eyes you're still not putting any weight on that left foot.'

'Who's this then?' Bill nods towards Cara, ignoring her words but holding the cup she'd given him whilst Dawn pours the contents of her flask into it.

'Cara and Shaun. They live with me at St Jude's.'

Cara and Shaun shake his hand and say 'hi' in choral unison.

'So, that's where you've been – St Jude's. We wondered where you'd got to. Maisie reckoned you'd left town.'

'Where is Maisie?' Wherever Bill is, Maisie isn't usually far away. She's better at being homeless than anyone else Dawn has ever met, and most of the locals are frightened of her.

'Woods behind the park. Got sick of my company, I reckon,' he chuckles. 'She managed to get a tent from somewhere. She'll probably tell you to piss off.'

'I'll take my chances.'

Footsteps pound the pavement behind Dawn, and she turns around to see Jack jogging towards them along the promenade.

'What's he doing up this early? Did you ask him to help?' Cara says.

Dawn shakes her head and watches Jack's face break into a smile.

'Bill!' Jack slows his pace to a stop and hi-fives Bill.

'Young Jack's one of the gooduns.' Bill slaps Jack's back.

'Brings me hot chocolate every night just before it gets dark. Same flasks as them, I reckon.'

Jack coughs. 'Umm… those from the café too?'

Laughter bubbles inside Dawn. Jack must've had the same idea but had been carrying it out at the opposite end of the day.

'The surgery can fit you in at ten past nine,' Dawn says, putting the phone back in her pocket. 'You really must make sure you go. You might need antibiotics.'

'Aye. I'll be there.'

Dawn can tell by the light tone of his voice that he won't.

'I'll go with him. We'll go via the off licence,' Jack adds when he sees Bill's face fall. Bill wouldn't even get through a doctor's appointment without something to take away those shaky hands.

'Come up to the café afterwards,' says Dawn. 'It's writing group day. I'm sure Hazel wouldn't mind a few extra. Might even be a scone in it for you.'

Bill lets out a wheezy laugh. 'Not my thing. Ta for the coffee and biscuits. You're a good woman.'

Dawn, Cara and Shaun make their way to the park and distribute their coffee amongst those waking up on benches or huddling against the large oak tree by the river. Dawn squeezes as much information from Cara as she can about the workings of the hostel. She dishes out phone numbers and drop-in days for St Jude's along with the biscuits, hoping to get every homeless person in Dover on the waiting list. Buoyed up by the success of getting Bill packed off to the surgery, she finds herself dispensing copious amounts of medical advice too. Really, with her background and all this intuitive knowledge, she really should consider becoming a doctor. She could tend to the wounds of the sick and needy of Dover. She would heal them of all their afflictions and after she's died, they might erect a marble statue of her in the middle of the park. *In Memory of Dr Brightside*, it would say. *She Transformed Dover with the Healing Power of Hope.* Or something like that.

Heat rises from the tarmac as they climb the hill to the next park, the one with the woods behind it. The park at the top of the hill is awash with flowers and smells of honeysuckle rather than dog poo and stale pot.

'What if she doesn't even want to see us?' grumbles Shaun. 'Maisie can be pretty scary if you get too close to her sleeping bag.'

'No one should have to go more than a day without anyone speaking to them,' says Dawn. 'If Maisie wants us to leave, we'll leave. But she should have the choice.'

The tent is easy to find. It's small, torn and bright blue and sits in a small clearing between a cluster of trees. A sizzling sound is coming from behind it and a pleasant smell is wafting up Dawn's nostrils.

'What are you lot doing on my property?' Maisie swings her head away from the frying pan she's precariously holding over some eager flames. 'I'm not putting my fire out. I'm sick of you lot telling me what I can and can't do. Bloody health-and-safety this and environmental-that. You council people should go and get yourselves a real job.' Maisie wobbles on the sideways cider barrel she's somehow managing to perch on. Her waist-length dreadlocks are tied into a knot on the top of her head. They look too heavy to be able to hold up for too long at a time without needing a lie down.

'We're not from the council. It's me – Dawn. I stayed in the sea shelter for a few nights with you and Bill.'

'Ugh, that feckin' man.' Maisie shivers. 'I came up here to get away from him. Snores like a bloody rhino. Need my beauty sleep, I do.' She rubs at the skin under her right eye, smearing several inches of melted make-up onto her fingers. A lopsided heart drawn in lipstick, sits across her left cheekbone.

'Would you like a cup of coffee?' Dawn starts to unscrew the top of her flask.

'Why would I want your coffee? Got a whole tub of Nescafé in my tent. It was in the bin behind Morrisons. Right next to these eggs.' She points towards the sizzling pan. 'Why don't you sit down, and I'll make *you* a cup of coffee and an egg sandwich. Might have to pick the mould off the crusts, I know how fussy people can be. Health-and-safety-this, environmental-that,' she mutters as she pulls the pan away from the flames and sets it down on an upturned Quality Street tin.

'Not for me, ta.' Cara sits on the ground and starts pulling daisies from the ground.

'Ah. My food not good enough for you? Well, in that case, why don't you just f—'

'Egg sandwiches and coffee would be lovely,' Dawn smiles. 'Wasn't expecting a nice picnic in the sunshine now, were we?'

Cara and Shaun mumble some words and Dawn bites into a sandwich, focussing on the gloriously runny egg yolk and ignoring the green speckles. The mould might even do her good. There's so much waste in the world. Really, Dawn is probably helping her own health *and* helping the environment. That sicky feeling in her tummy is just psychological.

'Mmm. Delicious. Thanks, Maisie.'

'What are you really doing here?' she suddenly snaps. 'I'm not moving my tent. I've already told the council that. Did they send you instead? I'm staying put – if they don't like it, they can stuff it up their arse.'

'Quite right too,' Dawn says. 'Now if you aren't too busy later, we have a writing group up at St Jude's café. Free cakes and it starts at two o' clock.'

The skies have clouded over by the time the three of them are walking back down the hill towards the town.

'There's no way she's walking all that way to a writing group,' says Cara. 'I don't know why you even invited her. Can you imagine what a nightmare she'd be if she turned up?'

'I thought she was funny,' Shaun shrugs. 'Bloody good egg sarnies too.'

'You've invited how many people?' Hazel says as she slides two of the café's tables together. Hazel runs the writing group at St Jude's and looks like one of those kind librarians you see in films. The ones that inspire troubled kids to read books that go on to change their lives. A mousy brown cloak of hair frames a lightly lined face and cheerful eyes. At least, when Dawn had first walked in, they'd looked cheerful. Now they look a little nervous and keep darting from chair to chair whilst she counts up numbers under her breath.

'Grace told me you like it when there's a good turnout,' Dawn says. 'Think of all those creative minds you'll be able to guide with your expert teaching. One of us could write a bestseller and then everyone in Dover would want you to tutor them.'

'Well, I guess that's true,' Hazel laughs. 'I did always say the sessions were just for St Jude's residents, but if it helps the community, I suppose we could make room for a few more.'

73

'Umm, a few?' Cara nods towards the front window of the café at the unwieldy queue that's gathered outside.

Hazel glances at her watch and flings the door open with a welcoming smile. Jack and Bill are the first ones through the door. Bill is still hobbling but his hands have stopped shaking.

'Didn't want to leave him out there on his own,' Jack explains to Hazel in a low voice. 'He was a bit distressed after his doctor's appointment so I said he could come back with me.'

The seats in the café fill up quickly, and Cara darts off to borrow some extra paper and biros from the office.

'I'd like to start with a warm-up exercise,' Hazel says to the room. 'I'm going to give you a sentence, and I'd like you to include it somewhere within your story or poem.'

Dawn takes the lid off her pen and waits with excitement.

'She remembered every lie.'

Dawn drops her pen and it clatters across the laminate floor. She dives under the table and then sits back up too quickly. The blood rushes to her head and the café spins around her, fast and loud. She holds her rescued pen over the paper and waits for the words to come. Not the first ones to arrive, they're too painful. Too intrusive.

Dawn doesn't want to remember any of the lies. She doesn't really want to remember the truth either. She closes her eyes but she's not quick enough. She still sees the red hair. Just a glimpse, it's only ever a glimpse.

Tell anyone, and I will kill you.

The words play on repeat and she realises she's written them down instead of the sentence she was given. She's pressed hard on the page and made a hole in it. She turns the paper over and shakes her head.

The story comes to her in the end. She bases it on Rosie, and the time she stole the last biscuit from the tin in the cupboard. She left it in her back pocket and crushed it into a million pieces when she sat on the kitchen worktop. She cried because she'd forgotten it was there and now, she'd never be able to enjoy it.

'Okay everybody, would anyone like to share their work with the group?' Hazel looks around the room.

'That's what happens when we're dishonest,' Dawn reads her last line out after entertaining the group with her story. 'We miss out on the good things in life, like the truth. And biscuits.'

Hazel leads the group with polite applause. Dawn knows they don't get it. She doesn't either, really, but it sounded good in her head.

It's Bill's turn next. Dawn keeps her eyes on the table and listens to the lilt of his voice. She closes her eyes and tries to hear the words between his slurred ones. After a minute, she finds herself totally immersed in his story. She starts rooting for Sigrid, the Viking princess on the run from the evil king who is intent on stealing her baby. Sigrid is hiding in an underground cave, holding her daughter close and praying for her to stay quiet whilst the king's army storms past, when Bill stops.

'That's it. Run out of time after that,' he says putting his pen down.

Dawn sneaks a peek at his paper across the table. No words, just a beautiful drawing of a baby. She swallows and blinks away a tear. 'Did you tell that story right from your head?' she whispers.

'Aye. I'm always making stuff up. It's what I do when I'm trying to sleep or it's too cold and noisy. I tell them to myself again and again, I don't write 'em down. Can't write. Can't really read, neither.'

The café door swings open and everybody looks up. Maisie has brought a Morrisons shopping trolley with her, piled high with her possessions. She parks it in the corner and heaves herself between the tables, plonking herself down at one, taking up two seats as she peels off three jacket layers.

'Aren't you hot with all that on?' a woman on her left asks her.

Maisie glares back at her. 'Have you been out there today? It's bloody stifling, of course I'm hot. Sweating me tits off. It's easier to wear them when me trolley's full. Satisfied?'

The woman shrinks back in her seat.

'What have I missed?' Maisie shouts. She starts scribbling noisily on her page with her tongue sticking out whilst everyone reads their pieces.

Dawn takes a deep breath when it's Maisie's turn and braces herself for angry sentences and expletives. Instead she reels off pretty words of poetry that tell of the majesty and beauty of Dover, of the cliffs and the castle and the hills, of the park and the woods that she sleeps in. When she's finished reading, Dawn peeks at her face. There's a peace in her eyes that wasn't there before. A softness in her voice when she says, 'Thanks for listening, everybody.'

Dawn goes straight to Maisie's table when the session is over and Hazel starts collecting the pens. 'Your poem was beautiful. I'm so glad you came. I really hope you'll come back next week.'

Maisie pulls on her three jackets and looks back at Dawn. 'I'll do what I flippin' well like, if it's all the same to you.'

Bill is still chatting to Jack, long after all the other visitors have left. Dawn watches them both before turning to Hazel.

'Do you think we could add some other learning to the creative writing days? Maybe start a bit earlier and do some basic writing and reading? Not everyone can, you know.'

'Wonderful idea. You'd be great at that.'

'Me?'

'Why not you?'

Excitement begins to stir in Dawn's belly. She imagines word getting out and people coming far and wide to learn to read. She'd be responsible for getting hundreds of people back into education or work. Universities will hear about it and offer her free training to become a senior lecturer in literacy.

'Aye,' Bill says when she asks him about it. 'You can try. Can't promise I'll pick it up quick. But it would be nice to read the paper in the mornings.'

Dawn pulls Cara, Shaun and Jack into a huddle when Grace walks into the café.

'There's something we'd like to do each day,' Dawn says after calling Grace over. 'I'll be honest with you – I stole from the café this morning. Only some coffee,' she adds when Grace takes a step backwards. 'And I borrowed some flasks, but I've put them back already. Jack's been doing it too.' Dawn points a finger towards him.

'Is this true?' Why?' Grace has a strange look on her face and Jack is looking down at the laminate.

'He's been going out every night and giving hot chocolate to people sleeping outside.'

The strange look softens and becomes something else entirely, but Dawn still can't work out what it is.

'Just wanted to do something,' Jack shrugs. 'Bedtime's pretty shit out there.'

'And Cara and I thought we'd give out morning coffee and biscuits.'

'I see.'

'We were wondering if we could make it a regular thing – ask all the residents from here if they want to help, maybe on a rota. And we could use the money we get in the tips jar in the café to cover the cost of the biscuits and drinks?'

'That's usually used for days out for you lot.'

'Nah. We don't need days out. We've got this place. They haven't. Not yet anyway,' Cara says.

'Lots of them are on the waiting list. And loads of them came to the writing group. Hazel's taking some of them to join the library next week. We just want to share some of the help we've had,' says Dawn.

'It's a brilliant idea. You're all brilliant. Just brilliant.'

Dawn likes being called brilliant. She'd feel the weight of the compliment more if she'd been looking at all of them when she gave it, but she can see that Grace's eyes are all for Jack.

CHAPTER 10

Grace

WORKING A HALF-DAY ON a Friday is supposed to be something to feel good about. Before her gran died last year, Grace used to zoom out of the office door, excited to eat her twice-weekly lunch with her in front of Gran's fireplace. It was always corned beef and jacket potatoes on a Friday. She's still having the same today, her single potato is already wrapped in foil on the kitchen side of her tiny flat. It just never tastes the same without Gran.

Her phone bleeps, letting her know her shift is over. She waters the office plants and gathers her bag and cardigan. She's almost out of the door when she remembers she hasn't checked next week's staffing rota. As she pulls it from the filing cabinet, an envelope falls from behind the folder and flutters to the floor. It's addressed to 'The Manager', so she pops it into her handbag to read over lunch. Taking work home is usually a no-no, it says so in her *Work–Life Balance* book that she got from the library last month, but it might be important, and the corned beef is calling.

Grace strolls along with the sun on her left and the sea on her right, watching as the English Channel folds its waves over to kiss the chalky toes of Dover's cliffs. She slows her pace as she strides past the mid-terraced townhouse she used to live in with her nan, and glances through the ground-floor kitchen window. She can almost see Gran and herself sitting down in their usual places at the table and tucking in. She remembers that last lunch they had together, six months and two weeks ago, before Gran got the diagnosis that changed everything.

'Pass me that blanket, will you please, pet?' Gran had put her fork down and wrapped the thick fleece around her shoulders, not showing any attempt to get back to her meal. She'd left three potatoes and a whole slab of corned beef.

'You okay? It's already warm in here, you've got the heating up much higher than usual.'

'You start feeling the cold more as you get older. You'll see.'

Grace poured them both a tea from the pot, pretending she hadn't heard what she'd said. Gran hardly ever spoke about aging and Grace liked it that way. For most of her life it had been just the two of them whilst her mum and dad spent her childhood in various corners of the world, busy stuffing collagen into the rich and famous of Hollywood or New York. It had been decided that Grace would be better off with stability. A life of staying put with Gran. Her parents had graciously decided not to be selfish. It wouldn't have been fair to expect Grace to traipse around with them when they were so busy working.

Grace's gran wasn't someone who needed to worry about aging, not for a long time, anyway. She didn't dress like an old person either, with her brightly coloured tracksuits and the latest trainers from JJB. She even swam in the sea every day, regardless of the weather. Her gran was the one constant; aging was just not allowed.

The journey from her gran's old house to her bedsit is a short one. She walks past the harbour and crosses the busy road to a multi-coloured row of once-smart townhouses. The peeling paintwork and rickety stairs make it possible for Grace to afford a penthouse bedsit with sea views. She'd been warned about the racket before she'd picked up the keys and the family noise from the overcrowded flats below and beside her draws circles around her aloneness with fluorescent pen.

Her bedroom/living room/kitchen is a rectangle of white and purple. Everything matches and everything gleams with clean. She flicks the kettle switch and roots for her mobile phone. As Grace rams her hand into the zipped compartment, she touches the letter from work at the bottom of her bag.

It's not a good letter. It's one of those ones that pull your heart down lower with each word. By the time Grace gets to *Yours sincerely,* hers has travelled along the length of her gut. The inspection from Supporting Futures will be taking place at St Jude's anytime from two weeks onwards. There are also several warnings about the likelihood of decreased funding following unsatisfactory visits.

In an effort to distract herself from the panic, Grace reaches for her phone. She'll try some whale songs or one of her meditations. The text message icon blinks back at her. It's from her mother.

Hello, Grace.

Grace rolls her eyes.

I am taking leave from clinic in two weeks' time. I'll make

> my own way to your house from the airport. You'll have
> to text me your address as I don't seem to have it. I will
> let you know my ETA nearer the time.

Grace's mum hasn't visited since Gran's funeral. Why now, when the inspection is looming? Surely that's enough stress to be dealing with at one time. Grace enjoys a challenge; she sends it an invitation, welcomes it in and climbs aboard. Usually. But this is different. This affects everyone, and it's down to her to sort it. Everything could just come crashing down in as little as two weeks.

And now her mum will have front row seats.

She flops herself down, supine on her king-sized bed, sur-rounded by her childhood teddies and starts to count the swirls on the ceiling. She needs to make plans. She needs an A, a B and a C at the very least. She'll do a mind-map, a spreadsheet. Be methodical. It will be fine.

She runs out of swirls to count. Exercise is her next go-to distraction technique, so she jumps up to begin her daily stretches. Quads first, then calves and glutes. Upper body work doesn't start till seven; it says so on the colour-coded chart above her bed. *Exercise is key,* her mum would say. Grace is *lucky* to have a healthy body, she should look after it, keep it in tip-top condition, *never take it for granted.*

Perhaps she should call her mum and tell her to postpone her home visit. Let her know how busy she'd be at work, that she wouldn't have time to see her. Might be nice for the shoe to sit on the other foot for a change. She won't, though, she already knows what she'll say. *Lack of time is just an excuse, Grace. We all get given the same number of hours each day. It's our job to worry about how to use them.* Or something along the lines of: *I can't mess my clients about; it would be selfish to change my plans.*

Selfish has always been her mum's favourite word and it's tattooed onto the front of Grace's mind for quick access during any decision-making process.

The rare contact Grace does have with her mum tends to unearth the memories; the hidden ones that lay otherwise shrouded in her fifteen-year-old mind. A rare visit home from both parents. Her dad clutching at his arm and his chest in the back garden. Sirens. Blue lights. Then the initial recovery in the stuffy hospital. 'If anything happens to me, it's down to you to make your mum happy. She's a strong woman, but you'll be the only family she has left, so make her proud,' he'd said, right before the machines went crazy and a million nurses rushed into the ward to silence the high-pitched beeping. It had taken a while, but it turned out silence was louder.

Obviously, she'd said yes, of course she will do everything she can to make her mum proud. Partly because Dad had thought he *was* dying (who can say no to a dying person?) and partly because she thought he *wasn't* dying, so she wouldn't actually have to worry about it.

Ed Sheeran sings from Grace's phone as the office number appears on the display. Lorna is due to work the sleep shift, but she's called in sick and no one is answering at the agency the hostel uses for back-up staff, Peter tells her.

'No worries, I'll cover,' Grace says to him, waving goodbye to a good night's sleep. She never settles properly when she sleeps in the staff flat; each noise a potential incident. At least it will give her mind some time to come up with a masterplan.

Grace's plans to calm her mind into action have so far been

unsuccessful. As soon as she'd got there, she busied herself with tidying the office. *Tidy room, tidy mind.* She takes a notebook and a set of highlighters up to the staff flat, hoping for inspiration to hit whilst she relaxes in bed. A killer to-do list could take the hostel to new and heady heights within two weeks. After separating her goals into colour-coded columns, she decides that all she needs to do is convince head office to take on more staff (despite already being over-budget for the year), find landlords that will take on those residents who are almost at the end of their allotted stay, get the client files up to scratch and repaint every room. Easy, right? Putting her pens away, Grace concedes that sleep may be a better plan. *Early to bed, and early to rise, makes a man healthy, wealthy and wise,* Benjamin Franklin had said. Clearly, he'd forgotten about the women.

After fidgeting onto her left and right sides and throwing the duvet off and on again, she gives up and creeps downstairs to the resident's lounge, stopping off at the office and opening her secret box from the back of her locker. It's a box she hasn't opened for six months and she curses herself inwardly as she slips out the sealed packet of Golden Virginia and half a packet of Rizlas. The building has a strict 'No smoking inside' rule, but no one's about and the lounge always has a slight pong of stale tobacco so she's pretty sure some of the residents partake in there overnight anyway.

Grace swings open the patio doors once she arrives in the sanctuary of the lounge. The cool air rushes in and she sinks down onto the sofa; hands shaking as she fiddles with the packet and starts to roll up.

'Well, well, well. What have we here?' Jack uses his best mock-policeman voice as he appears in the room, clicking the door shut behind him.

'Urgh, why are you always around when I'm doing something I shouldn't,' she grumbles as she chucks her lighter at him in mock-frustration.

He catches it in one hand with a flourish and Grace can't help smiling. 'What are you doing down here past your bedtime?' he asks as he flops down next to her, putting the TV on low with the remote.

'Couldn't sleep,' she mumbles. She wants to tell him how worried she is about the inspection, but she knows she can't. She's supposed to be there to support him. It's important to be strong, and if the news gets out, everyone living there will start to panic. That won't help anyone. She needs to *be the change she wants to see in the world*. As her *Women in Leadership* mag says; *you can't light a fire with a wet match*.

'Back in a minute,' Jack says. His room is on the basement floor, right next to the lounge and he appears a few minutes later with two steaming mugs of hot chocolate. He finds some space between the battered board games on the coffee table and places them down before disappearing again. When he returns, he has a duvet wrapped around his shoulder that he shakes off and places over Grace before handing her a warm drink.

Swallowing the lump in her throat caused by the deliciousness of someone looking after her for a change, she raises an eyebrow and looks straight at Jack. 'Spiderman, really? Don't think I've ever seen a twenty-seven-year-old man with one of those. We do have brand new ones in the linen cupboard, you know.'

'Hey. It's my favourite duvet cover. It's pretty old but it was on my bed in my last foster home before I went away for the first time. It's been washed plenty since then, obviously. Just sleep better with this one, I suppose,' he shrugs before plopping down next to Grace. He pulls the duvet over both of them, swinging his legs underneath him and briefly poking her calf with his toe.

'Peter seemed even more pissed off than usual tonight at cooking club. Didn't even have a cake,' he says. 'Do you think he's okay?'

Grace hesitates before replying. It's unprofessional to speak about other staff members with residents. 'Did you tell him about the other day?' she asks in the end.

'What about the other day?' he pretends not to know what she's talking about, but she sees a flash of dimple by his mouth. Some of the tension melts from her shoulders. She's relieved Jack hasn't told him about their impromptu drinks in The Stag. Especially as they'd extended into three pints and several more games of pool.

She sips her hot chocolate, trying to ignore the implied intimacy of huddling together like that on the sofa. She glances sideways at Jack. If he feels awkward, he's certainly not showing it as he scrolls through the channels looking for a film to watch.

'Ha. *Sharknado*'s on if you fancy a good laugh.'

They spend the next hour laughing at the ridiculous film and critiquing the skills of the scriptwriters. Grace begins to feel her muscles unclench, one by one.

'It makes a change watching a film with someone else,' he says. 'Teardrop comes in at night sometimes, but he'll only watch *The Godfather*, *Scarface* or *X Factor* re-runs.'

Grace nods. After a lifetime of watching TV with Gran, she still turns around as if to catch her eye when something funny happens on *Coronation Street*. Laughing alone is never the same.

86

'What did you used to like watching before, when you were a kid?' Grace asks. Hearing about Jack's Spiderman duvet reminds her that he'd had a life before prison and Young Offender's Institutions; one that he probably has no one to talk about or reminisce with.

He doesn't answer as he runs his fingers over the letters on the empty mug he's still cradling. The letters spell out 'Best Dad Ever'.

'It was my dad's,' he says when he catches Grace looking. 'I gave it to him for Father's Day. Kept it all this time. Stupid really. This is the first time I've drunk from it. I don't usually need to make more than one drink but I only own two mugs.'

'I'm sure he'd be glad you kept it,' she says, imagining a six-year-old boy snuggling up and drinking hot chocolate on a sofa with his dad; blissfully unaware that he was about to lose him to cancer three months later, despite the fact that he was the only family he had.

According to Jack's file, his mum had died from a post-natal infection only hours after Jack was born, and his grandparents had never been in the picture. According to Jack, his parents had met each other as teenagers in a children's home. Perhaps they'd dreamed of becoming the family they'd never had.

Grace shakes her head and bangs her cup down on the table, harder than she'd meant to. Life is a right bastard sometimes.

'You okay, Miss?'

'Stop calling me Miss. How many times do I have to say it?' Grace forces out a grin as she flicks his elbow. 'I'm twenty-five, not ninety and it's the twenty-first century.'

The film comes to end. Grace hasn't got a single clue what's been happening for the past ten minutes, but she still wasn't ready for it to finish.

'What were they like, at the foster home you brought your duvet from?'

'Nicer than most of the others,' he says, his eyes not leaving the screen even though the credits are still rolling. 'But by then it was too late, I was already a little shit. Too many months in the kids' home hanging out with wrong-uns who were older than me. No excuse though; by the time I got there I was old enough to know better.'

'You still in touch with them?'

'Nah. Too much damage done. Doubt they'd want to hear from me.' Jack switches off the TV with the remote, shuffles out from the duvet and stands up to collect the cups, making the space feel colder beside Grace.

'What's up? You look all stressed out again,' Jack says, pausing by the coffee table.

Grace doesn't know if it's tiredness or the fact that she wants to keep Jack with her for longer, but the words come tumbling from her tongue. 'We're having an inspection.'

'What kind of inspection?'

Jack sounds so calm. She shouldn't be worrying him with this. It's unprofessional and he has enough going on. 'Our funding body is conducting it any time within the next two weeks. They've been dropping the funding from several hostels across the country by constantly raising the expected standards of performance, so they can judge them more harshly. There's just not enough money in the pot to keep all of them open.'

'Right. But you guys are awesome. You've got it under

control, I know you have. You'll ace it.' Jack slaps her shoulder with a confident grin.

'Course.' Grace brightens her face. 'Course we will. I'm just tired, you're right.' She folds up his duvet and carries it behind him towards his room. 'Oh, and Jack?'

He looks back at her, holding his hand out for the duvet.

'Could this stay between us? You know – the inspection and… well, everything?'

'No worries,' he says from his open door. 'Ain't you forgetting something?'

'Umm,' Grace falters, suddenly realising that Jack is wearing nothing but a pair of shorts and had been the whole time they'd been in the lounge. That would have raised a few eyebrows if someone had seen them.

'Your baccy?' Jack grins as if he can read her mind.

The packet of Golden Virginia is still on the arm of the sofa, along with her untouched roll-up. She picks them up and lobs the whole lot into the bin behind the door.

Jack's door is shut by the time she's left the lounge. Her eyes begin to droop; the milky drink warm and settled in her stomach. She only has one thought left in her head as she climbs the steps to the staff flat. She's got to get St Jude's into the best possible shape.

And nothing is going to get in her way.

CHAPTER II

Dawn

DAWN HAS ARRIVED AT the office clutching her keyworking appointment letter from Grace. She's been at St Jude's for one week, and today's the day to start setting her goals. There's a small queue at the hatch and Peter is glowering over the top of it, whilst Terry and Cara shout over each other like two pupils in the headmaster's office after a scuffle in the playground. Dawn takes a seat on the worn leather armchair in the foyer. They look like they're going to be there for a while, so she may as well enjoy the show.

'But it's not your bike, it belongs to the hostel,' Peter is saying, his face turning red with a hint of purple, matching Dawn's outfit for today: a jumpsuit and light cardigan combo, H&M, £24.99.

'I know that, it's not like I just let him have it.' It's as if Cara's voice is being pushed through a pencil sharpener, each word becoming more pointed than the last. 'It wasn't exactly fun for me either, you know, being mugged in the street.'

'Pfft,' Terry snorts. 'I've been here a while now, and if I had a fiver for every time a resident gets "mugged" for the hostel's bike, I'd have the deposit for my own flat already. Everyone knows that's what the dealers round here have off you when you can't pay.'

Cara steps back from him and exhales so hard out of her mouth that Dawn wonders if she's trying to blow him over.

'I haven't touched that shit for two months, and you know that, Terry. How bloody dare you even suggest that when you know how hard I've been working,' she hisses.

'Okay, okay. Let's all calm down and talk about this downstairs where it's quiet.' Peter opens the office door, beckoning the two of them to follow him downstairs, his face now returned to its normal shade.

Dawn pokes her head through the gap to look for Grace. She's sitting at her desk, staring out of the glass and holding a biro between her fingers like a cigarette. Her face looks pinched together and someone's stolen the smile from it.

'Everything all right in there?' Dawn asks her, when it's clear her eyes might stay stuck to the window if no one says anything to unglue them.

'Sorry. What?' she jumps, dropping her pen on the desk in front of her. She turns towards Dawn and screws up her forehead as if trying to remember something important. Dawn's sure it's not their meeting that she's forgotten; she's probably been looking forward to that, excited to hear all Dawn's stories.

'Of course.' Grace slaps her forehead. 'We have a keyworking arranged, don't we?' She gets a file and a pile of papers from the filing cabinet and wheels a stool around for Dawn to sit on across the other side of her desk.

'Usually we use the first meeting to get to know each other a little better and to put a support plan in place for you. Identifying your goals and what-not,' she says, writing

Dawn's name across the top of the page. 'At St Jude's we like to encourage *smart* goals – do you know what I mean by that?'

'Umm, something to do with office wear?' Dawn throws out a guess. She hopes she's right; she can smash that goal. Debenhams have a sale on for their office clothing line at the moment and she's never been banned from Debenhams.

'It's an acronym,' Grace explains, pointing her biro at large, capital letters on the page between them that spell out the word S.M.A.R.T. 'It stands for specific, measurable, achievable, realistic and timely.'

'Oh.' That doesn't sound as fun as she'd thought it would be.

'So, what sort of goals do you think you may like to make that fit into these brackets?' Grace is watching Dawn's face, waiting for answers, but Dawn's not sure if she's ready for them. Her goals are pretty epic, even if they do tend to change from day to day.

'I've always fancied being a TV presenter. Probably a morning one as I'm up early most days. I don't need much sleep, not lately anyway.'

Grace chews hard on her biro, leaving little tooth marks on the end of it. 'I suppose we could say that definitely ticks the "specific" box,' she says, slowly. 'How about we think about the smaller steps first? The more immediate issues, such as finding permanent housing, sorting your benefits, getting some training in to help you get back to work. That sort of thing?' she says. 'What jobs have you done in the past?'

'I was a midwife,' Dawn says, but it comes out as a croak.

'Wow, that must have been exciting,' Grace says brightly.

Dawn wonders if she believes her. She probably wouldn't if she was Grace.

Grace explains that the only people who will see her file are auditing inspectors or staff members, so it's fine to be honest throughout their keyworking meetings.

'How well do you know all the residents?' Dawn asks.

Grace gives her a reassuring smile. 'I interviewed every one of them personally. But if you have any problems with anyone, just let me know.'

'Are they all, um, safe?' Dawn wants to ask her about the bars on her window but doesn't know where to start without sounding paranoid. She'd been tempted to sleep with her door open for the last three nights, just so she knew she could get out quickly if she needed to. There had been too many times in the past when she couldn't and when there's somebody after you, it's important to always have a clear exit.

'They are one hundred per cent safe. All been police-checked,' Grace promises. 'Shall we get back to your goals? Are there any family members you feel like you may want to begin building bridges with?'

Building bridges. It's a section on the support plan; Dawn can read the words from where she is. Lego bridges, from house to house, built across the top of a Formica coffee table. Her dad's eyes smiling behind horn-rimmed lenses, proud of her architectural prowess. Her mum coming in, complaining about the mess and knocking them down with clenched fists. The memory feels fresher than it should; a cup of tea that's still warm.

'Not applicable,' Dawn says. 'Just write N/A, those inspectors will know what you mean.' She wants to carry on speaking, so she can soundproof the memories by wrapping them in sentences, but Grace's whole face twitches when Dawn mentions inspectors and her mask slips off. She's paler than usual under that layer of foundation and worry is written between her rows of neat eyelashes.

'What are your goals? Do you have smart ones?' Dawn asks her.

Grace puts down her pen and closes the file. 'I want to help people get their lives back and keep this place going strong for as long as I can,' she says, her voice wooden enough to get splinters from.

'And what else?' Dawn asks. There's always more, the first wishes people come out with are almost never their real ones. Grace might as well have just asked for world peace.

'Perhaps I should fill out one of these for myself.'

'Perhaps you should.' Dawn pats her hand before getting up from the stool. Maybe then she'll see how tricky it is to plot all your dreams and regrets on a matrix that won't spit out the answers. 'You can make anything happen if you hope hard enough.'

Dawn is walking back downstairs after her meeting when Cara runs past her, water running down her cheeks. Cara's door bangs shut, and a loud thump tells Dawn that Cara has kicked it from the inside.

Terry is alone in the resident's lounge, cursing under his breath about, 'that bloody woman'.

'Anything I can do to help?' Dawn asks. If the staff are busy, perhaps someone else needs to put out the fires in the other corners.

'Not unless you have a plan to steal back a bike from Dover's finest pharmaceutical reps,' he mutters. 'Stupid, *stupid* woman.'

'Did you use the bike a lot then?'

'It's not about that,' he says, his voice rising to greater heights before he stops to take a deliberate breath. 'It's about her kids.'

'Aren't they a bit small to ride a bike?'

'Urgh, no, it's not about the bike. Cara's trying to sort herself out, so she can have her kids back with her when she gets her own place. Staff from here go to meetings with people to speak about how she's been and if she's stayed off the gear.'

'Right,' Dawn says, beginning to understand.

'If she doesn't get that bike back, the staff will think she's used it to pay her debts to the local, erm… businessmen. Then what are they supposed to tell the social worker?'

'How much does she owe?'

'Depends how much she's slipped off the wagon. She's not telling me shit right now, and you can bet your arse they'll be adding on interest.'

'We'd better leave now then,' Dawn says. 'Wait out the front for me and I'll go and get my raincoat.'

'What the hell do you think you'll be able to do, lady?' he calls up behind Dawn.

It's spotting with fine raindrops as they wander down the hill; the type that feels like tiny electrical tingles on your skin and don't show that you're getting wet until you're drenched and need wringing out like a sponge. Steam rises from the ground as the warm path is dampened, making the air smell like fresh earth.

'These aren't the type to negotiate with,' Terry says, watching his boots making steps as he walks, 'and it's not like I'm scared of them, cos I'm not.'

Dawn looks at his enormous shoulders, his inked teardrop and his curtain rails of rings running up the length of his ears. 'No, I don't suppose you are.'

'It's just I'm on probation still. Can't afford to be getting in trouble.'

'That's what I'm here for,' Dawn grins. 'Watch and learn.'

Terry shakes his head the rest of the way into town until they reach the park.

'Whereabouts did you say they'd be?'

'They usually hang about around there,' he nods towards the hut by the skate ramps.

'Stay here for now,' Dawn says.

'No way,' he hisses and grabs her arm. 'You can't go in there on your own.'

She looks around the park at the parents walking about with pushchairs, older teens playing football and a couple sitting on the bench holding hands.

'I'm just going to walk past and see how many there are,' she says, shrugging out of his grip.

There are just two of them; lanky and sunken-faced. They may have chunky chains hanging from their jeans and enormous baseball caps balanced on the very tips of their heads, but they don't fool Dawn. They're talking fast at each other and looking over their shoulders several times a minute. There's a bike lying on the ground by their Reebok-clad feet. Dawn sinks to the ground, pretending to tie her shoelaces whilst she has another scan around, checking there's no one else on their way to the hut.

No one is looking. Dawn holds her head higher and braces herself for action.

'S'cuse me,' she slurs as she stumbles inside. 'The guys from the skatepark said you could sort me out?' She fumbles around in her shoulder bag as they glance at each other.

'What you want?' the one with the skinhead asks after the other lad nods at him.

'Depends.' Dawn sways to her left before sinking down onto the wooden-slatted benches, only inches from the bike. 'There's a young lad up near the loos who says he'll sell for two quid less than what you are, and I'm a girl who likes to shop around.'

The boys play a frenzied game of verbal tennis, batting expletives back and forth, some of which Dawn hasn't even heard before, and then they set off towards the toilets. 'We'll be back, don't go anywhere,' the non-skinhead one says over his shoulder.

'I'll be here,' Dawn sings out.

As soon as the boys' backs are turned, she pulls the bike up by its handlebars and leaps aboard, her heart skipping with excitement. Now *this* is the kind of thing she was made for – bringing justice and righting the wrongs for those around her.

It's been a while since she's ridden a bike, especially at this speed, but they do say you never forget and they're right; she probably won't forget this in a hurry.

'Get on then,' Dawn winks at Terry as she scrapes her feet across the damp and dusty grass, coming to a stop next to him. She feels a little bit like Batman. Next time she'll make a cape for the occasion.

'I told you not to go in there,' he says into her ear as they swap places and she squeezes behind him, holding onto his substantial frame as they zoom off again. She looks behind her as they're leaving the park and sees two baseball caps bobbing up and down after them, both balanced on the heads of two angry men. Dawn whacks Terry's back to make him go faster, forgetting he's not a horse.

It somehow works and within seconds they're hurtling around the one-way system. Dawn had forgotten how much she loved riding a bike. A pink and white one with a wicker basket cycles into her mind's eye, taking her back to that first ever one she'd got for her eighth Christmas. She throws her head back, allowing the wind to blow loudly into her ears, drowning out the memories. Laughter bubbles up inside her, and she whoops and cheers, using all the air in her lungs, spilling out her relief. She can't wait to tell Cara she has the bike back and that she's in the clear. This is exactly the reason she needs to stay at St Jude's.

People need her.

'That's interesting,' Peter says when Dawn wheels the bike in through the foyer, breathlessly telling him that Cara had got it wrong; they'd found it at the bottom of the path. 'It's very interesting, and it's a very nice bike. But it's not ours.'

CHAPTER 12

Grace

IT'S ALMOST THE END of the day shift and Grace is still thinking about that damn inspection letter. Peter's been quiet all day, and she's barely said two words to him either. The spreadsheet she's supposed to be working on just feels like a blur of numbers and words. The more she panics about how much there is to do before the inspection, the harder it is to get anything done.

'All right, Miss?' Jack appears at the hatch with the top-up money for his rent. His eyes sparkle when he smiles, and Grace tries so hard not to look at them that she tears his receipt.

'You look happy,' Grace says.

'I've just been writing my speech.'

'Speech?'

'Peter's helped me arrange to give some school talks about homelessness. I thought it might help other kids in the care system. If I'd been given some advice about when to ask for help, I might not have ended up in the mess I found myself in.'

Grace's heart swells. 'That's an amazing thing to do. I'd love to come and support?'

Jack looks towards Peter, uncertainty etched on his face. 'Actually, I've already kind of told Peter he could… '

'Good idea, Grace, you go. School's aren't really my thing.'
Peter shudders. 'I'm sure it will be great for Jack, having you
there. Plus, it's at the high school up near the castle – didn't
you used to go to that one?'

Grace opens her mouth to say, yes, she'd love to be there.
But something jolts between them when her eyes meet Jack's
again. He's holding her gaze, something Grace remembers
he was never able to do with anyone when he first moved in.

'Love to,' she sings as soon as she can trust her voice again.
'I'll be there with bells on.' *Seriously? With bells on? How old
is she, seventy?*

'Great.' Jack nods and walks off with a grin.

'Well, that seems to have put a smile on your face, at least,'
says Peter.

'Hmm?'

'Finally getting Jack's rent top-up. At least he's up to date
now. He'll be ready to move out soon – he's really got his act
together that one. I don't think he needs much support from
us anymore, especially now he's got the hang of budgeting
and getting his rent top-up paid. That will look better on our
records for when we… '

'When we what? Get inspected?'

Peter bolts up out of his seat and springs across to the
kettle. 'Tea? Ylang ylang?'

Grace carries on typing slowly with one finger. She's
really just pressing the space bar and there's nothing in
front of her except for her screensaver: a picture of a dog.
Not even her dog, just a random one taken from the Dog's
Trust website.

Grace stays silent, even after he's put her tea, no sugar, in front of her. Then she thumps the table, making her tea slop over the side of the cup and onto some half-completed paper-work. 'We're never going to get our paperwork up to scratch in time.'

Peter doesn't answer. He probably has a pretty good idea where this is going by now.

'There's never enough hours in the day. One of the residents always needs us, and we definitely don't have enough staff anymore. Maybe I'm just not up to the job.'

Peter sighs and takes a large gulp of coffee. 'Grace. That's not true and you know it.'

'Now we only have a few days to show that our move-on success rate has risen since last time, and I can tell you without looking, Peter, that it hasn't.'

'The move-on targets are bullshit anyway,' he says. 'The people that set these thresholds from their glass offices have no idea how this stuff works in the real world. We can't just move people on before they're ready; it sets them up to fail and they'll be right back here again within six months.'

'That's if we are still here in six months,' she mutters.

'And where do they think we'll find all these magical land-lords, willing to rent to people with bad credit histories and on housing benefit? It takes time. These funding people need to be told.' Now it's Peter's time to thump the table.

'Do you think we should let the residents know in advance? They could help get the place looking a bit fresher. Plus, they might want to interview some of them,' Grace says, her gaze falling through the gap in the hatch.

'No. It's not their problem to worry about, and it wouldn't look good if they've been prepped on what to say. We can manage it between us. Just tell me anything you need me to do and I'll do it.'

'Thanks, Pete,' she says, squeezing his shoulders as she takes her mug back to the sink. 'And I'm sorry for screeching at you. I just can't bear the thought of a single one of our residents losing their beds and having to sleep on the streets again.'

'There is one thing we've forgotten though,' Peter says. 'We arranged that client interview for today and she should be here in ten minutes. I think her name was Maisie?'

Grace tuts. 'I know we need to interview everyone on the waiting list, but sometimes it feels cruel to get people's hopes up when we still don't actually have any beds to offer them – especially when we already have so many people waiting for one.'

'Yep. But as you're always telling me – policies and procedures are policies and procedures,' says Peter.

Twenty minutes later, Maisie McDowell is sitting in the office, already taking a breather from answering her interview questions. She's enjoying a swivel around on Grace's chair. 'So – about the perks.'

'Perks?' Peter looks up from his clipboard.

'Of living here. You know, like – do we get a morning paper each day, a wake-up call, room service – sell it to me.' Maisie slouches back in the chair and places her arms behind her head as if she's about to sunbathe.

Grace shoots a look at Peter. 'It doesn't quite work like… '

'The last homeless hostel I stayed at in Birmingham had a spa.'

Peter drops his pen on the floor and the thud of it landing on the carpet is deafening in the silence of the room.

'Pah! I'm kidding. The looks on your flippin' faces.' Maisie roars as she shakes her head. 'Seriously, though,' she starts up again once Grace and Peter have joined in with the laughter, 'I will need a bit of help. I haven't lived inside for a while. Last time I tried to live with other people it didn't go so well.'

Grace smiles back at Peter. 'We'll be here to help with that. St Jude's is so much more than just a roof to live under. You'll see.'

After the three of them have rattled through the rest of the questions, Maisie gets up from the chair. She takes up half the office when she stands, mostly because she appears to be wearing about six layers of clothing. 'Easier than lugging them around in a bag and my trolley's already bursting,' she'd explained whilst parking her Morrisons shopping trolley outside. Her bedding is on the top, hiding the multitude of food she's collected from the food bins and bakeries. 'It's criminal what them shops throw away,' she'd said. 'So, I take 'em and give them out to the ones that sleep in the park. Them lot are always getting thrown out of the soup kitchens for bad behaviour, so at least this way, they'll get something down 'em.'

Grace smiles as she pictures Maisie moving into St Jude's when a room becomes free. She will fit right in. She wishes they had more bed spaces and a shorter wait.

Grace and Peter work in silence after Maisie has left, in a desperate attempt to make their paperwork gleaming and error-free.

'Wow, it's like a morgue in here. Who's crapped on your cornflakes?' asks Lorna when she arrives for her sleep-shift. She looks tanned and extremely well for someone who has called in sick for the past few nights.

'One of those days,' Peter grunts. 'Too much paperwork and not enough time.'

Lorna is waving around that sort of smile people wear just to invite you to ask about it, but even Grace is too tired to fake enthusiasm for whatever her answer may be.

'Me and the Mrs have set a date,' she says. 'Five months from now at Dover Castle. They've had a cancellation. You're both invited, of course.' Lorna rubs her hands together.

'Wonderful news. Congratulations.' Peter puts his jacket back down on his seat.

'That's what you need to put a smile back on your face, Pete. The love of a good woman.'

Grace winces inside as Peter turns away, pulling down the shutters bit by bit so Lorna doesn't see the pain she's just chucked straight at his chest. Peter's only ever spoken once to Grace about the first and only love of his life: Jenny. He told her that Jenny's face haunts his mind whenever his eyes are closed for longer than a minute and that he could never imagine being with another person.

'You should get on that Tinder,' Lorna says, breaking into Grace's worries about Peter. 'Tons of women on there. If you get a match this weekend, you might have someone to bring with you when I tie the knot. Or the noose, as they say.'

'Oh, I'm not sure that's really my thing.'

Lorna is already sitting at the computer tapping away. 'Here we go, you just need to set up a profile.'

Peter picks up his coat again, pulling his arms into the sleeves.

'Come on, I'll help you. It's how me and the Mrs met, after a few false starts. What's the worst that can happen?'

'Right, we need a photo,' she says after a few more minutes of clicking. 'Which one do you have on your Facebook?'

Peter shrugs.

Grace gets a calculator and types in random numbers, pretending not to listen. She'd deleted her own account after a string of horrible dates. She'd only created it in the first place out of pure loneliness. She'd had one boyfriend before, at uni, and he'd slept with three of her friends by the second semester. Much better to be alone. No time for all that, not when St Jude's needs her.

'Doesn't matter, I'll do a search from mine,' says Lorna. 'Gotcha,' she says before throwing Peter a wolf-whistle. 'And in scrubs. Great photo, we'll use that.'

'I really don't think… '

'I'll put you down as a social worker rather than a support worker. It sounds more impressive,' she says. 'You practically are one anyway and it shows you have a caring side. That ought to go down well.'

Peter flicks the kettle on, staring wistfully at the jacket on the back of his seat.

'What would you say your interests and hobbies are?'

'I like reading. Crime novels mostly.'

'Nah. They might think you're a serial killer. I'll change it to, you "like reading French literature".'

'But I can't speak French.'

'Pfft,' she waves her hands over his shoulder as if swatting away a fly. 'Just wing it, it probably won't come up anyway. Ohh, you can put more photos up on here now. You definitely should post one of you with your dog.'

'Lovely. Will do,' Peter says, downing his drink and picking up his phone from the desk. 'Thanks so much for your help, but I really should be getting home. I have selfies to take with my dog,' Peter adds when Lorna looks like she's going to protest.

'That's my man,' she grins.

After being rinsed of energy by a double shift, Grace had been expecting sleep to grab her as soon as she got into bed. No such luck. She keeps imagining strangers rifling through the client files and digging through the hostel like evil foxes, searching for prey and admin mistakes.

In between fidgeting and getting her feet twisted about inside the bottom of her duvet, Grace dreams. Broken dreams where her mum arrives to inspect St Jude's and pulls away their funding because Peter had done the paperwork wrong for Lorna's wedding list. Then she snogs Jack in the office right in front of everyone before saying, 'See? Jack appreciates French literature.'

Grace is back in the office her usual twenty minutes before her shift is due to start. She's finished her sun salutations and has just opened her morning meditation app when Peter arrives.

'I'm sorry about yesterday,' she blurts out before he's even sat down. 'I've just got a lot going on, and I can't stop worrying about what will happen to this place if we fail our inspection.'

'So, we won't fail.' Peter says, using his most supportive voice. He slides behind the keyboard, and Grace can feel him watching her whilst she chips her way through the 'client outcome' forms. 'Have head office sent you next month's activity budget yet?'

'I've forwarded it to you, didn't you get it?' Grace says, turning her head towards him.

Peter's computer makes a loud 'ding' and a box appears in the middle of the screen, saying, '*You have four matches!*'

'Oh – let's have a look,' Grace says with a mix of excitement and nosiness.

'I meant to delete the profile. But I suppose there's no harm in having a quick look.'

One of the photos looks as if it had been taken in an old people's home and the 'match' looks as if she's at least ninety. The other two have photos that are so grainy that Grace can't even tell what they look like. The remaining one though, she doesn't look terrible at all. Nice straight teeth; sleek, shoulder length hair.

'She looks a bit like Jenny. Same hair,' Peter says.

The screen pops up with '*You have a message*'. Peter clears his throat and glances again at Grace before clicking on it. The message is from her; the one with the good teeth. She's called Caroline and she's from Whitstable. There are four words next to a little bubble containing her photo. *Hi. How are you?*

'How to even begin to answer that,' mutters Peter.

CHAPTER 13

Dawn

'I'M SORRY I CAN'T take you with me,' Dawn mutters to Shaun as she stuffs everything she might need for the day into her new shoulder bag: £14.99 from Accessorize. A cardigan in case it clouds over, which it probably will do. Sunscreen in case it doesn't.

They're having a hostel day trip to Samphire Hoe, a local beauty spot and nature reserve at the foot of one of Dover's white cliff faces. It's at the end of a steep tunnel and there's remnants of World War Two bunkers and a wildlife centre to look around. Grace feels they would all benefit from some 'team bonding'. She'd also mentioned something about having something to tell them all, but then Peter had shouted over her, rather unnecessarily in Dawn's opinion, that there was no need to save an announcement about changing the hostel's toilet paper until they have their picnic. She'd gone quiet after that, so Dawn had whispered to her that she thought it was a great idea; the current brand was rather abrasive, and she'd heard you could buy 'word of the day' toilet roll paper online which sounded very educational.

'But there's nothing to do in this place when you're not

around,' Shaun grumbles. 'Maybe I could just bump into you there? It's only a forty-minute walk, I don't get why you're all going in the minibus.'

'Someone's donated it to St Jude's, so Peter said we should use it. We aren't allowed to go too far away as it may break some of the resident's bail conditions.'

Dawn clicks the door to number six behind her, leaving Shaun sulking on her bed. His top lip always curves over his bottom one when he's peeved about something, just like Rosie's would. Dawn wonders what she'll be up to today. Perhaps she's in a board meeting, wearing a power suit and making compelling arguments about why the company should be going in a particular direction. She'd give a rousing speech before throwing a heavy notebook down on the table in front of her after her concluding sentence. All the other suits sitting around the large oak table would slowly stand to their feet, one after the other and begin to applaud. The person opposite her concedes defeat, telling her she was right after all and then offers her a promotion. Rosie would flick her shiny hair over her shoulder before graciously accepting. *'It's all because of you, Mum,'* she'd say when she calls to tell Dawn the news. *'You've always believed in me, which is why I always believe in myself. I love you,'* she'd add after Dawn tells her modestly that her success is nothing to do with her; it's down to Rosie's hard work and that she makes Dawn proud every day.

The minibus is bulging with bodies by the time Dawn gets in, but Cara's saved her a seat next to her.

'Someone's nicked my meth,' she whispers when Dawn sits down. 'It's gone from my room so now I'm gonna be rattling all day unless I can get hold of something. Don't think I'll be able to find much on a friggin' nature reserve.' Cara's face is whiter than usual, the lines of her face look deeper and have clumps of pale-biscuit foundation trapped inside them.

Dawn lifts her index finger and rubs it in gentle circles across the tops of Cara's cheekbones in an effort to blend it in.

'Thanks,' she says, and her shoulders relax downwards from her chin. Dawn wonders how long it is since someone has given her a hug. The poor girl needs mothering. Dawn hasn't had a mother at all since her mum died during her first year at uni, and she hadn't had much of one before that, so she knows what it feels like to need a little TLC.

Everyone on the bus has started to sing, 'What a Feeling', all in different keys and tempos but with equal gusto. It's difficult to imagine any of them slipping into Cara's room and stealing her medication.

She'd explained to Dawn why she needed it the other day when they were in the café. How it keeps her withdrawals at bay, so she's not in agony with stomach cramps and vomiting. If she doesn't have it, she might get desperate and go back to heroin, which might put a stop to her having the boys back – she gets tested every week by the drugs and alcohol team. Cara had told her how she'd just been allowed to start taking her methadone home from the chemist; before that she used to have to go and drink it in a special room. 'People always know what you're going in there for,' she'd told Dawn. 'And they look at me when I'm leaving as if I'm responsible for every piece of shit they've ever walked in.'

'Have you told the staff?' Dawn asks. 'They might be able to check the cameras and see who it was. Plus, you might need medical attention.'

'I'm not a grass.'

Dawn glances towards the front of the bus. Peter is driving and the muscles from the back of his shoulders look bunched together like stones, weighing him down and hunching him forward. Grace is sitting next to him and staring straight ahead; her mouth has folded itself into a thin, straight line. Perhaps she already knows they have a thief in their midst. She's certainly preoccupied about something.

'I'll take care of you today,' Dawn promises Cara, squeezing her skinny hands as gently as she can. They look as if they could snap in half at the slightest pressure.

Cara gives her a weak smile. She needs Dawn, that much is obvious. Good thing she arrived at St Jude's when she did. Who knows what would happen to them all if she hadn't come along?

Terry and Jack are sitting behind them, swapping stories about their cell mates and pretending they're not trying to out-do each other with shocking tales. All the other residents fall silent as they emerge from the long, dusty tunnel and the glistening sea and lush green hills come into view.

The bus swings into the car park, exactly eight minutes after they'd left St Jude's, including the time it had taken Grace to remember they'd left the drinks box and they'd had to turn back for it.

The sight of the sparkling waves causes Dawn to take a deeper breath or two, as if she could suck up the beauty that way and store it inside herself for a while. It's the same body of sea she can see from her window in number six, but down there next to the majestic white cliffs and large navy faux lighthouse it looks more vibrant, as if a billion different torches are shining on it at once, making the water glitter like precious jewels.

'And that was when they realised he had a bag of coke and two phone chargers stuffed up his arse.' Terry's voice reverberates around the bus.

The group decide to take the grassy route across the nature reserve, so they can eat in the picturesque picnic area in the middle and still look at the sea. It means they are also a little too close to the cows for Dawn's liking. She's never trusted them. They may have large, sad eyes, but they use them to lure you in before they teach you a lesson for every quarter-pounder-with-cheese you've ever enjoyed.

Everyone is tucking into cheese and pickle sandwiches and cheap bottles of Aldi lemonade when Dawn sees Shaun's silhouette ambling down the grassy hill towards them through the blazing sunshine. She glances around at everyone as they laugh and chat. Some are gazing towards the sea, using their hands to partially shield their eyes from the brightness of the day. No one seems perturbed when Shaun parks himself next to Dawn on the bench.

'You look out of breath. Did you run all the way here?' she asks him as he mops up all the bubbles from his forehead with the sleeve of his T-shirt.

Shaun gets out his most boyish grin. 'Told you it doesn't take long to get here on foot.'

A few of the residents flicker their eyes towards them both but look away before Dawn can introduce him. Cara and Terry had met him two nights ago and have agreed to keep quiet about his existence at number six. Her shoulders relax, and she offers Shaun her other sandwich. It makes her smile to see the enthusiasm with which he stuffs it into his mouth.

'My Rosie's a good eater like you,' she tells him. 'Even as a child, she always ate her vegetables without me having to nag. She's a vegan now of course, and gluten-free… most days.'

A wash of silence ripples around Dawn and she pauses, trying to decide which part of the conversation people are finding interesting enough to stop scoffing their Quavers for. Probably the vegan thing, everybody likes to have an opinion on that.

She's about to launch into some interesting facts about surprising things that aren't vegan-friendly such as several types of wine and how you can even buy vegan-friendly tattoo ink. That should spark some lively conversation; people love to go on and on about other people's life choices, even if they have no effect on their own lives whatsoever.

'When's your daughter back from Afghanistan?' asks Jack. 'Someone said she's in the forces?'

Oh. It was the bit about Rosie they were interested in, not the vegan thing. Never mind.

'I thought she was in Ibiza?' someone says.

They're all looking up at her now, sitting crossed-legged on the floor in front of her bench, like school children waiting for story time on the classroom carpet. Dawn has many tales she could tell them, but her mind is whirling around too fast to catch hold of one.

'She travels a lot, does a lot of things.' She waves her arm around with some vigour, trying to illustrate the vastness of Rosie's life experiences, but as she does so, she sends an economy jam tart through the air that lands inches away from the nearest cow. The cow looks right back at her as if she can see into her soul and through every fib she's ever told.

'You know what; I think I'll walk home. It's not far and it's a lovely day.' Dawn uses her happiest voice as she collects up her rubbish and puts it in the bin. It's only as she's walking away towards the tunnel that leads back to the road that she remembers her promise to help Cara through the day. It will look odd if she turns back now, but her tear-stained face is lodged right at the front of Dawn's mind.

Shaun's long strides match Dawn's own. She'd known he'd follow her and keep her company on the walk home.

'Would you mind doing me a favour?' she asks. 'Could you go back and join the others for a while and stick close to Cara? She needs a friend today.'

He agrees and turns around immediately. Lovely boy, that Shaun. Dawn would like to think he gets his helpfulness from her. She's obviously a good influence on him. Rosie's probably the same. Wherever she is today.

CHAPTER 14

Dawn

IT'S COLD IN THE tunnel and it's longer than Dawn had realised. Dusty square bulbs give off just enough brightness to see about a metre in front. People always go on about light at the end of tunnels but the end of this one looks rather dim and is still miles away even though she's been walking through it for ages.

She gets out her phone and sends out a little message to Rosie, wherever she is, telling her she's thinking of her and she hopes she's having a good day. Maybe she'll get an answer back from her once she reaches the light; the reception is sure to be better out there. People always say that girls in their early twenties are terrible at keeping in touch once they get wrapped up in their own lives. Dawn never stops thinking about her though, not since the second she'd discovered Rosie existed.

'Are you sure it's positive?' Rob had said, snatching the stick out of Dawn's hand, presumably forgetting that she'd peed all over the end of it. Time had slowed, the sounds around her slurring like music on a Walkman that's running out of battery. Rob's face made the beginnings of several different faces before breaking into a smile that Dawn had tried to copy.

'Shit. We've got a *lot* of stuff to sort out. Where we're going to put him for a start,' Rob had laughed.

'Or her. And we'll manage.' Dawn clutched at her flat belly and stared out of the kitchen window of their shared student house, imagining rows of baby clothes pegged to the washing line.

How had her own mum felt when she found out about Dawn growing inside her like an acorn?

The first time she'd wondered what her mum had been like when Dawn was a baby had been on a Christmas Eve, many years before.

She'd been sitting on Daddy's knee, wondering if eight was too old an age to be doing so. All the other children's heads were lined up along the pew in front, whispering secrets to each other about Santa.

Don't call him Santa. We're not American. Call him Father Christmas, Dawn's mum would have said if she had been there. She wasn't though; she was at home in bed propped up with her flowery pillow and empty bottle of grown-up drink. Well, it probably would be empty by then, Dawn reckoned as she smeared her finger across the watch face on Daddy's hairy arm.

'You okay there, Dawn-light?' Daddy untangled the curl that Dawn had wrapped tightly around her thumb before sticking it in her mouth. Her hand smelled of oranges from the Christingle she'd been squishing in her hand.

'Mmm. Just worried about Rudolph. Mum said she didn't buy carrots. What are we supposed to leave out for him?'

Daddy had snuggled his soft, woollen arms tighter around her. Eight couldn't be too old after all. Dawn leaned back, resting her cheek against his snowman jumper that smelled of soap and cigarettes.

As the man in the black dress told them about the real story of Christmas, Dawn watched the display in the corner of the stage. The crib holding the Tiny Tears baby Jesus was stacked high on milk crates in front of Mary and the Angel Gabriel.

If Dawn was Mary, she wouldn't have wanted to leave her baby stuck in a draughty milk crate; she'd have held him close in the crook of her elbow, away from the grubby hands of shepherds and wise men. Had Mummy ever held her like that when she'd been that small? She wished she could remember.

'An angel of the Lord appeared to him in a dream and said, Joseph, do not be afraid to take Mary home as your wife… ' The man behind the wooden box stopped reading and looked up from his big leather book.

Why would Joseph have been afraid to take Mary home? Perhaps she was a scary wife, like Mummy sometimes was. The angel seemed to think Mary would be up to the job though. Perhaps if Mummy had an angel looking out for her, she might find things easier.

'Hark the herald, angels sing,' the girls and boys in red and white had sung from the front.

When Dawn became a grown-up, she'd look out for people like that angel had. She'd keep her baby wrapped up in her arms and kiss her every day, so she'd know she was loved by both her mummy and her daddy. She'd try not to be a scary wife.

'Glory to the newborn king,' the choir trilled to a close.

And she'd remember to always buy carrots for Rudolph.

Dawn had occasionally wondered during the years that

followed about what sort of grandmother her mum might be. At least her baby would have a wonderful grandfather.

She hadn't considered that by the time she would see two lines on a clear-blue stick, neither of them would be around to tell.

Dawn emerges from the other side of the Samphire Hoe tunnel and feels disappointed that there's still no answer from Rosie. The air is no warmer than it had been inside. The Dover skies have clouded over, leaving the blistering heat of the St Jude's Samphire Hoe picnic firmly behind. It's like someone has turned off the light. Goosebumps pop up across her lightly sunburned arms and she shivers as she crosses towards the ring road.

Frank Sinatra's 'My Way' blares out from St Mary's Church as she passes. The doors are still open and she takes a step backwards to have a peep inside. There's a coffin at the front and only two people are sitting in the audience. Perhaps audience isn't the right word. She's still trying to work out what would be, when she realises she's entered the church and is already halfway down the aisle.

'Is this seat taken?' she asks the two mourners. They both look back at her and then around the room at the empty pews. The younger-looking of the two – the man with a huge hole in one of his earlobes that looks as if it's been plugged up with a saucer – gives Dawn the slightest of nods and she lowers herself down next to them. The woman next to the man with the ear-thingy is slightly older, probably in her thirties and is dressed a little more like you'd expect for a funeral, but also not like someone who really cares very much. The vicar is standing in the pulpit looking at his notes while Frank continues to sing from the music system.

'Did you know Brian very well?' Dawn whispers to the two beside her, after glancing at the name plaque beside the large photograph on top of the coffin.

'We knew him from Lakeside – his care home,' says the woman. 'Well, I've met him a couple of times. I'm on nights, you see, so he was normally asleep by the time I got there, and he always insisted on laying in until half past eight after I'd gone. The day staff didn't like that at all; messed with their morning hygiene routines. Max here hasn't actually met him, he only started there yesterday, but none of the other staff could make it.'

Max is staring at the programme in front of him as if he expects to be tested on the content of the hymns afterwards.

'Are no family coming?' Dawn asks, and they both just shrug.

The vicar begins to speak about Brian's life. Except it can't be about Brian's life, not really. He's only giving out information about the day he moved into Lakeside, the music he liked to listen to in the dayroom and how Battenburg was his favourite cake. Dawn tries to picture her own funeral and wonders what Rosie would say about her. Would they be able to reach her, and would she make it back in time to even say anything? Otherwise Dawn supposes it would be down to Shaun, Cara and maybe Grace. There's no one else. 'She made good muffins in the café,' they'd say. Or, 'Once she stole a drug dealer's bike by accident.'

Dawn looks again at Brian in front of her and studies his face. She likes the fact that he'd refused to get out of bed at the time the staff had wanted him to. The 'I did it my way' lyrics from his opening song seem as if they suited him. His wrinkled face looks back at her and she can see the pride in his eyes as well as the strength, born out of a lifetime of being Brian.

'I'd like to say a few words.' Dawn stands to her feet and walks onto the stage. She stands beside the pulpit and holds her hand out towards the vicar for the microphone, although why they're using a microphone when there are only four of them in the room, five including Brian, is beyond her.

'Of course,' the vicar's head jolts backwards a few centimetres. 'Are you a relative or?'

'His niece,' Dawn says loudly into the microphone, smiling at the front row. She takes a step forward and another one immediately back again when the music system makes a screeching feedback sound. 'My Uncle Brian was an inspirational man; one that I wish I'd taken more notice of when I was growing up.'

The Lakeside staff are now looking at the floor, but the reverend is smiling at her, encouraging her to carry on.

'He was a strong man who lived his life on his own terms. He travelled to many different amazing places, collected stories that would be fascinating, if only people had bothered to listen. He worked hard all his life so that he could buy himself a lovely home. Well, I suppose he must have had to sell it if he'd had to pay the extortionate fees for residential care,' she chuckles.

No one else does, but in Dawn's mind's eye, Brian is roaring with laughter and clutching his stomach. 'To sum up, his life really mattered, and I just want him to know that. Oh,' she adds, 'and actually, he bloody well hated Battenburg. He only used to eat it because that's all there ever was apart from the stale custard creams.'

One look at night-staff lady and earlobe-Max tells Dawn she's got it spot on and she winks at Uncle Brian as she walks back past his photograph.

She can't be certain, but she's pretty sure he winks right back at her.

CHAPTER 15

Grace

AS THE ST JUDE'S residents finish their picnic at Samphire Hoe, Grace pulls her cardigan from around her waist and pushes her goosebumped arms into the sleeves. She stands to her feet, jumping from one to the other to warm herself up and wake up her metabolism. All around her, St Jude's residents are layering up against the plummet in temperature as newly arrived grey clouds join forces to cordon off the July sun from the grass banks of Samphire Hoe.

They swallow their last mouthfuls and shove the rubbish away, some into bins and some into pockets but Grace is pleased that no one leaves any on the ground. If only they could keep the hostel as tidy, she might not have such a huge task on her hands. Perhaps she shouldn't have left the office and brought them out today, not when so much needs doing before the inspection. On the other hand, teambuilding is important. It's at times like this that people need to work together. *Teamwork makes the dream work.*

'They have some interesting displays in the Samphire Visitor's Centre. It's just behind where we parked the coach,' she says, watching as Dawn gets swallowed by the tunnel in the distance. 'There's a lovely one about some local butterflies.'

Once they're all inside the centre, Teardrop Terry and Peter begin a big debate by the beetles and rare insects stand about who would win in a race out of a wart-biter bush cricket and a leaf-beetle.

Jack is looking at the noticeboard but keeps glancing back at Grace and smiling. He knows Grace is still on edge today and she throws him a grateful nod, trying to forget that last time they'd seen each other alone, he'd been in his boxer shorts. And how he'd no longer looked like a lad who'd lost his way, but like the grown man he was. With his sharp wit and interesting opinions – and just the right amount of chest hair... Grace turns back to the display, hiding her pink face from the others. It's probably just sunburned. Should have put on some factor fifteen.

Only after she's immersed herself in the wealth of information regarding six species of butterflies, does Grace allow herself to rejoin the group in the middle of the hall. After all, *the only fence against the world is a thorough knowledge of it,* she'd read somewhere.

'Where's Cara and Jack?' Peter asks as he peers through the gaps in the heads of their huddled group.

A commotion is brewing outside. Grace yanks open the door and strides across the grass until she has a clear view of their missing residents. The ones having a huge barney by the tea and coffee kiosk.

'Why the hell did you think you could steal from some woman's handbag and get away with it?' Jack's voice is several octaves higher than usual and Grace can see his jaw twitching from eight metres away.

'You know why. I've told you,' Cara blots at the tears on her pale face, 'I can't cope no more and it's only gonna get worse if I can't sort something.'

'But you could have just asked me, I could have helped,' says Jack.

'Pfft, yeah right,' Cara spits on the ground next to her and Grace prays that no one outside of their group is watching them. 'Not if you'd have known what it was for, you wouldn't 'ave.'

'What's going on?' Grace asks once she's reached a respectable speaking distance.

Jack is watching a middle-aged couple in the queue for the drinks kiosk beside the visitor's centre. The man whispers something in the woman's ear and she throws back her head as she laughs, causing her wide-brimmed sunhat and Louis Vuitton handbag to wobble about. A pair of sunglasses falls from her bag and the man picks them up and puts them back before doing up the zip.

'You should be more careful,' the man says with a smile.

'Thank goodness you noticed,' the woman laughs, 'I'm sure it was zipped up though.'

Both Cara and Jack's eyes are following the same path from the handbag, back to each other, and then at the floor.

'Nothing's going on,' Jack says, leaving his gaze where it is.

'It's not as if they can't afford it,' Cara mumbles.

'That's not the point. If I hadn't stopped you… '

'Then maybe I'd be okay later on, and now I won't be, thanks to you,' Cara snaps back at him.

Grace watches in silence as she begins to work out what's happened. This needs sorting, pronto. But having the two of them sniping at each other is not a good look for the hostel.

'Pete, could you take Cara and everyone else back to the hostel? Jack and I will be fine to walk back. Just keep an eye on her,' Grace adds in a lower voice. 'We'll separate them for a bit. I'll talk with her once she's calmed down, but she really doesn't look well.'

Peter starts rounding everyone up for the bus journey, and Grace walks towards the sea, nodding at Jack to follow her.

'You did a good thing back there from what I can work out,' Grace says when they've reached the strip of concrete that spans the water's edge. The sky is beginning to clear again, making the coast of France just about visible on the horizon. She adjusts her pedometer and checks the display.

'I just hate it when people from St Jude's give people exactly what they expect from us,' Jack bursts out. 'Everyone already looks at us like we're scum in our town. Maybe lots of us deserve it, including me. But it's hard when you're trying your best to change and prove them all wrong and then someone goes and acts like a junkie.'

'Don't call her that, Jack,' Grace says softly.

'I'm sorry. I don't mean it, I know she's trying, and I know she's had a shit life. I just look at some of the others that stay at St Jude's and feel bad that they're all marked with the same pens. Like Rory from Room 8 – do you think people even know he used to be the head of the whole history department at some university? Or that Karen from Room 11 owned her own café and used to run a soup kitchen from it on Sunday afternoons? People never see any of that, they just see a load of crackheads who want to get off their faces and waste their taxes.' Jack's voice cracks apart as he speaks, spilling out hurt through the gaps.

'Most people just fear what they don't understand. They don't realise most of us are only ever three steps away from homelessness. Two pay packets, in lots of cases, it said in *The Big Issue* the other week. Often all it takes is a break-up or a lost job.' Grace places her hand on his arm and leaves it there this time. He covers it with his own and blinks several times before turning his face towards her.

'Good thing we have St Jude's and people like you,' he says, his dimple creasing beside his smile. 'At least some people give a shit.'

Grace is interrupted from her brief thoughts about Jack's full mouth as his words about the hostel hit her right in the chest.

'That's why I can't let anything happen to it,' she says, watching as two seagulls fight over a crust of bread.

'And it won't.' Jack looks back at Grace and she can see the concern leaking out.

'I shouldn't have said anything in the first place, I'm sorry. I certainly shouldn't be worrying you with it.' Leaders should be strong. *Don't spill your weakness and leave it for others to mop up,* her mum would say.

'Course you should've. I might be a resident, but I'm not a child. I want to help.' Jack takes his hand away from Grace's, causing hers to feel immediately colder. She removes it from his arm, feeling awkward that she'd left it there.

Within seconds, he's beside her, his arm slung around her shoulders, guiding her to walk along the path towards the beach. An elderly couple walk past with their Highland Terrier and they smile as they pass by. With a jolt, Grace realises they probably think they're a couple. Surprised by the thrill this gives her, she fights to keep her face impassive and her eyes on the sea as Jack pulls her closer, stroking his thumb across the skin on the inside of her elbow.

'So, tell me,' he says once they've reached the beach and flopped down onto the shingle next to the large, grey rocks. 'What can I do for you?'

Grace laughs, forcing herself not to answer his question the way her mind first tells her to.

'To help, I mean. With the hostel. Whatever it is that's happening.' He's blushing, and Grace straightens her face. She hadn't meant to make him feel uncomfortable, it's just the proximity of his thigh to hers is making her feel giddy. His arms have caught the sun, and his T-shirt is damp with sweat across his chest. And those shoulders... Stop it, Grace. *Duty of care.*

He is moving out soon, though, Grace reasons with herself. He has worked through his issues and is definitely no longer someone who she would class as 'vulnerable'. Would she still feel guilty about noticing his shoulders if they'd met in other circumstances?

Jack pushes himself up to a sitting position and starts lobbing small stones into the sea in front of them. 'I could have a word with the others, we can help get the place spruced up and work out some things to say to make you look good. Not that you don't look good already. I mean, you definitely do, but that's not the point I was trying to make.' He breaks off as his cheeks return to his previous shade of pink. 'We'll pass,' he adds. 'You, Peter, all of you; you do a great job.'

Grace turns over as Jack lays back and turns towards her at the same time. There's barely an inch between them but neither of them moves back. 'I don't want everyone to worry,' she continues, covering her embarrassment. 'And Peter doesn't want us to say anything.'

'You're the boss though.'

'Mmm.' Grace doesn't feel much like a boss right this second and she can only imagine what the other staff members would say if they could see her lying on a deserted beach almost toe to toe with a *service user* – a shit term and crappy label to stick on someone, in her opinion. People couldn't just be residents or clients or patients anymore. 'I probably shouldn't discuss Peter with you. It's not professional.'

A smile arrives on Jack's face before he can cover it and they both chuckle. The dimple by his cheek disappears after a minute and his expression falls into something more serious as he looks into Grace's eyes. Grace holds his gaze, hoping he can't see that she's shaking. Must be the cold. His arm snakes around her waist and Grace closes the inch between them, leaning her head on his shoulder; her cheek against the light stubble of his face, resolutely keeping her mouth away from his. Some places are tricky to come back from. Grace can feel Jack's heartbeat against her chest and it's thudding as fast as hers is.

'This shouldn't be happening,' she murmurs.

'Neither should lots of things,' he says. 'But we're not doing anything wrong. Can't friends hug anymore?'

'Uh-huh.'

'On an empty beach, where no one would see them anyway.'

Grace smiles but stays exactly where she is. They lay in silence, listening to the crashing of the sea as the wind gets up and the waves get higher and louder. Every part of him that's touching every part of her feels warm and electric.

'I suppose we'd better go soon, Miss.' Jack's grin seeps

through into his voice and he laughs as Grace swipes at his chest.

'How many times have I told you not to call me Miss?'

'I promise I won't say it ever again,' he smiles as he tucks her hair behind her ear.

Grace's mind falls to the staff handbook. She'd read it cover to cover on her very first day (to be successful at work, it's important to know the rules and essential to keep them), and she'd committed it to memory. This morning, she'd glanced again at page six, paragraph two, just in case it had changed. It hadn't. Personal relationships between staff and service users are *forbidden*. Not discouraged, not frowned upon. *Forbidden*.

Be a good girl, Grace. It's the way her mum used to end every phone call to her and has done since she was first old enough to hold the receiver in her tiny chubby hands. What would she say if she could see inside her mind right now?

Grace knows it's only a matter of time before she kisses that mouth.

CHAPTER 16

Grace

GRACE MAKES A BIGGER space between her and Jack as they make their way up the hill to St Jude's.

'Finally,' says Peter when they reach the foyer, 'I was starting to worry. It's pissing it down and I felt bad we took the minibus.'

'Sorry we've been ages. Traffic was terrible.' Grace peels off her soaking wet cardigan.

'But weren't you on foot?' Peter asks.

'Yes, but that was what made it terrible,' she says, knowing she's making no sense whatsoever.

'Do you need me to stay on any longer?' Peter glances at the time in the bottom corner of the computer screen.

'No, it's fine. How's Cara been?'

Peter waits until Jack has left the hatch before answering. 'She's not well – looks as if she's withdrawing. She's out of methadone way before her next prescription is due. Probably best to let the night staff know when they get here and ask them to keep an eye out.'

'Will do.'

'Also, erm, before I go, I'm just going to pop to the staff flat

130

for a shower. I'm going straight out from here and don't have time to go home first.' Peter picks up his bag. He's almost out of the office when Grace remembers the message he'd showed her from Caroline.

'You're going on a date, aren't you?' she grins. 'I knew it. How are you feeling?'

'Shitting myself,' Peter admits. 'We're meeting at Francine's, the Italian place on the seafront. She might not even turn up. She could be doing something Lorna's told me is called *catfishing*. Hell, she may not even be a *she*.'

Grace smiles and pats his arm. 'You will be fine. What's the worst that can happen?'

'I know I'll run out of stuff to talk about, which is likely to happen before the starter appears. I never had to worry about this stuff with Jenny. She'd always been happy either to natter into the gaps or to leave them be. Maybe I should just cancel,' he adds, looking panicked.

'I'd come with you if I had someone to bring – take the pressure off you a bit.' Grace chews the inside of her mouth, depressed that the only person she can think of bringing is her nan and she can't even do that anymore. An alternative occurs to her and her heart thumps a little faster when it does. 'How about Jack and I come with you? We won't sit with you or anything, but at least I can be there for moral support.'

'Jack? Resident Jack? I don't think that would look right at *all*.'

'Obviously, I don't mean as a date.' Blood rushes to Grace's face until even her scalp feels hot. 'I was planning to take him somewhere away from the hostel to go through his school speech – he wanted me to look over it.'

'But I'm his keyworker — surely it would be bloody inappropriate to have him accompany me on a date.'

'We'll arrive separately and sit on the opposite side of the restaurant. It will help me as well — this way I can help Jack with his speech somewhere nice without breaking any boundary rules if you're there too — and he deserves to go somewhere nice after all his hard work.' Grace injects as much casualness into her voice as she can. Peter looks closely back at her. Maybe she overegged it. She fights to hold her head up and doesn't look away.

'Fine. Go on, then. But separate tables and don't do anything embarrassing like trying to *help* me.'

'Deal,' Grace triumphs and shakes Peter's hand.

'I've never been anywhere this posh before,' Jack whispers as he and Grace arrive at the entrance to Francine's. It's a warm evening and there are still straggles of people splashing about in the sea and several more marching along the promenade heading for their dinners. It's as if the wind and rain from earlier in the day had never visited the town.

'Table for two?' the waiter asks. Grace tries to ignore the thrill this gives her and does a quick scan of the restaurant. The place is packed-full and she can't see Peter anywhere. 'We only have one table left — if you'd like to follow me.' The waiter takes a path through the seating area and waves them towards a small table. One that's inches away from one that Peter is sitting at.

'Wow. Hi. I didn't know you were going to be here.' Jack's face lights up.

Guilt pulls at Grace. She should have just told him the truth. 'Peter's meeting someone. We're here for backup.'

Peter gives Jack an awkward grin before pulling off his glasses to clean them.

Grace sits at the table next to Peter and Jack slides in opposite. His knees graze hers and she fidgets backwards in her seat.

The waiter brings over a jug of water and Grace forces herself to relax as Jack pours her a glass. She breathes in the aroma of cooking and wine and listens to the hum of conversation around her.

'Thanks for bringing me here,' Jack says. 'It will be good to hear what you think about the end part of my school speech.'

'Absolutely. And I'm so sorry.' Grace lowers her voice and places a menu between her and Peter. 'I really did want to take you out to go through your talk anyway, then I thought Peter could use some support and it just made sense…'

'Hey.' Jack puts his hands up towards her. 'You've nothing to be sorry for. It's just good to spend more time with you.'

'You mean you haven't already seen enough of me today?' she laughs, but then stops when she sees Jack's eyes change.

'No,' he says softly. 'Not enough by far.'

Grace's stomach flips and she glances at Peter. He's busy studying his menu from various angles. That man really does need to see an optician about those glasses.

A woman is walking past Peter's table, her gaze firmly fixed on the door to the toilets. She turns her head to the left and catches Peter's eye, smiling at him with an instant recognition. Perhaps that's because Peter actually looks like his picture. She looks nothing like hers. Several years older in fact, and she's shuffling towards his table with the help of a walking stick.

'Arthur!' the lady says when she finally reaches him. 'You haven't even ordered my drink yet, that's not like you,' she laughs. 'Oh, don't look at me like that, I'm only having a giggle. I don't mind really.' She looks at the stick as if she doesn't understand what it's doing in her hand before balancing it against the table and fumbling to pull the chair out from under it.

Peter jumps up and pulls the chair back for her. She lowers herself into it with a mixture of effort and grace. It's only when Peter has sat back down that Grace realises he hasn't told her he's not Arthur.

'How was your day, my love?' she asks, looking at him as if she really wants to know.

'It was rather stressful actually,' he says. 'Tricky day at work. It's hard knowing the right things to do to help people very often.'

'I'm sure you always do your best,' she smiles, patting his hand that's resting on the table. She then covers it with her own and leaves it there. Peter stares at their pile of hands and stays silent.

Grace catches Jack's eye and suppresses a chuckle. 'Should I do something? I'm supposed to be wing-woman-ing.'

'He's a big boy. And she's got great chat. Why break into that?' Jack breaks off a chunk of bread from the plate between them and grins before putting it into his mouth.

He even makes eating bread look sexy. 'So, was there anything particular about the end of your speech you wanted to discuss?'

'Mmm,' Jack nods before finishing a gulp of water. 'I really want to share my experiences of the care system with the kids. I want to be able to reach out to the ones who might be going through similar stuff and help the ones who aren't to have a better understanding of them.'

'Absolutely.'

'But what I don't want to do is make excuses for the things I've done. There are kids in the care system who don't go off the rails. I want to explain the ways that my experiences contributed to my homelessness without suggesting that's what will happen to any of those who are already in foster homes or struggling.'

Grace briefly covers one of Jack's fingertips with her own. 'It's great that you're being mindful of your message. The fact that you care about what the kids will take from it can only mean you'll do a good job. What's the one most important thing you want to leave them with?'

'That they're not alone. That they should always ask for help, even when they think they can't. That life can be full of so much shit but doing the wrong things won't put any of it right. And that we shouldn't judge each other so harshly. We don't always know what others are going through and people won't ask for help if they think they're just going to get blamed.'

Jack is fiddling with the handle on his spoon, his face flushed with emotion.

Grace swallows. 'That's definitely more than one thing,' she says lightly.

The restaurant door opens and Hazel, the writing group leader, rushes through it, scanning the seating area with panic in her eyes until they settle on the older woman who is still talking away to Peter.

'Mavis! I thought you were only nipping in to use the loo. We're going to miss the bus if we don't hurry.'

'Why were you worrying? I'm with Arthur. Where else would I be?' Mavis rolls her eyes at Peter and nods towards the woman as if she's had a lifetime of trying to be patient with her and it's begun to wear as thin as the soles of Peter's decades-old shoes.

'That's not Arthur, dear, that's Peter from St Jude's,' Hazel says, removing the sharp edge from her voice and cushioning it with concern and a manufactured brightness. 'Why don't we go and get a cup of tea and we'll get the next bus instead? Then when we get back, we can have a game of scrabble.' Hazel turns to Peter and lowers her volume. 'Mavis lives next door to me. Her husband, Arthur, died years ago, but she gets confused.'

'I see,' Peter says.

'Haven't seen you at the café for a while,' Hazel carries on. 'The writing workshops are going really well. I'm always surprised by how many of your residents show up every week.'

'I think they probably don't have much else to do,' Peter says.

Grace cringes at Peter's clumsiness and braves a glance at Hazel. There is no sign of offence in her kind eyes, which always look like they hold the punchline to a clever joke.

'You should come along one day. To one of my sessions, I mean. You might like it.'

'Indeed.' It's all Peter seems to be able to manage.

Mavis jumps out of her daze. 'Hello there,' she says warmly, as if Peter had only just sat down with her. 'Have we met?'

'You thought he was Arthur. You were doing that thing again,' Hazel says, with neither tact nor malice.

'Ah,' Mavis says.

This time, Peter is saved from thinking of something to say by a very loud and deliberate clearing of somebody's throat.

'Are you Peter?'

A small queue appears to have formed behind Mavis. The question was from a familiar-looking woman standing behind Hazel. Grace realises as Peter tells her that yes, he is indeed Peter, that the reason she recognises her face is because it matches the photo of Caroline, the woman he is *supposed* to be meeting.

Mavis jumps up with impressive speed considering the time it had taken to lower herself into the chair in the first instance. She shuffles off with Hazel and they take a newly vacant table in the far corner.

Peter watches them go before glancing back up. Caroline is still standing there, staring at the back of the chair with a straight mouth. It seems she's refusing to get in it until someone is gallant enough to come along and pull it back for her. By the time she is seated, Caroline's lips are pressed even more tightly together.

'Who was the old lady?' Caroline asks.

'I'm not entirely sure,' Peter chuckles.

Hazel looks his way at the same time as he looks at hers and she waves. Peter waves back. Caroline makes a strange sound, something between a sigh and a hmmppff.

'Why was she sitting with you if you don't know who she is?' Her voice is stiff, making her sound older than he thinks she is.

'To be honest, the woman that was sitting in your seat — Mavis. I thought she was you.'

Caroline's face changes to a few shades paler as she spins her head around to stare from Mavis and back to Peter. 'You thought she was me?' she repeats back to him. 'Do I look like an eighty-year-old woman in my photo?'

'To be fair, there was no information about your age on your profile.'

Jack snorts and turns it into a cough. Grace chews on her lip and prays for the waiter to come back.

'Shall we just order?' Peter asks.

Grace sneaks another look at Caroline over the top of her menu. Red, wavy hair falls to her shoulders. Ice-blue eyes, empty of sparkle and lined with carefully applied make-up.

Peter orders steak. Caroline orders a vegan pasta dish. Neither of them asks for a starter and Grace suspects they both want to leave. She should really try to get Peter out of this but she has no idea how, and she's having far too much fun with Jack.

'So, what is it you do for a living?' Peter asks.

'I don't like to talk about work.'

Mavis and Hazel are giggling over in the corner and pointing at a humorous quote on the wall. Peter catches Hazel's eye and smiles. Hazel waves back at him.

'Am I keeping you from something?' Caroline's face is expressionless, closed for business, but her tone gives little room for misinterpretation. Peter doesn't answer, he just glances at her phone, still on the table. Caroline has already checked it several times since she sat down.

'So, how old do you think I look?' Caroline obviously doesn't want to let this age thing go.

'Fifty-three and a half.'

Now it's Grace's turn to suppress a snort. It's probably Peter's best guess, but it turns out he's wrong by over a decade, and not in the socially acceptable direction.

Peter later blames this blunder for his shaky hands that knock over his glass of orange juice.

Caroline's phone enjoys a little swim across the tablecloth, buoyed up by three quarters of a pint of Sunny Delight, Florida style.

'Which is a shame,' Peter says after Caroline has left. 'Everywhere else seems to have stopped selling it.'

CHAPTER 17

Grace

DESPITE ARRIVING AT WORK early, the phone is already ringing as Grace jangles the keys in the lock of the office door. The room is a shit-tip. Lorna was working the late shift last night and she always leaves chaos in her wake, but this is worse than usual. Grace has to lean over piles of scattered files in order to reach the phone.

'It's Myra from head office,' a cut-glass voice projects itself through the landline. 'I know it's early, but we've had a call from Supporting Futures? The ones who are due to do an inspection?'

Grace's heart drops right through her, landing somewhere near her size five ballet-style pumps.

The voice continues. 'They're coming to see you today. They said they'll be at St Jude's around lunchtime, and then they will be visiting our other Kent hostels tomorrow and Monday.'

She's only just put the phone down amongst the masses of paperwork when the door opens and spits Peter into the office.

Grace opens her mouth and gives him the news of impending doom, before ranting and raving about the state of the office whilst stomping about, gathering up papers and wiping the desks.

'It's fine, stop panicking. We have at least three hours to tidy up and get things ready. Stay calm,' says Peter. 'At least we've been given a heads-up. Be far worse if they just turned up out of the blue.'

'Anyone working today?' Teardrop Terry's booming voice travels through the tiny gap under the closed hatch.

Peter tells him they're just about to and puts the kettle on, and Grace hides the overflowing office bin behind the door of the staff toilet.

The front entrance buzzer sounds as soon as Grace has finished opening up.

'Are you in the habit of opening up late to residents?' Boris the inspector says after introducing himself and heaving himself into the foyer, beads of sweat running from his freckled brow.

Damn. They'd forgotten to remove the *Office Closed* sign from the door.

'No, no, not at all,' Grace blusters, as the man peels it off himself and hands her a lump of balled-up blu tac. 'I thought you weren't coming till lunchtime. It's only ten past nine.'

'We always arrive early. Don't worry,' Boris adds. 'Just wanted to make sure your sign was gone before my colleague gets here. She's parking the car and she's not as understanding as me.'

The entrance buzzer sounds again, right on cue. Grace's heart squeezes tight when she looks at the woman on the other side of the heavy glass-fronted door.

Wavy red hair, frosted blue eyes and a 'Supporting Futures' badge. Wearing the same scarf she'd worn on her date with Peter.

'Good morning, Caroline. Fancy seeing you here,' Peter sounds as if he's being strangled.

Shit. Now they're already off to a bad start.

'Hello Mr Andrews,' she says, peering at Peter's ID badge. 'And Miss Jennings, lovely to meet you.' Her tone sounds as if she means anything but, and more like she's addressing a pubic hair she's found in her lasagne. 'Shall we go to the office first?'

Grace nods and prays for someone to set the fire alarms off before Caroline sees the state of the desks.

During the two hours Caroline and Boris spend going through the files, they ask what seems like five hundred questions, many of which Grace doesn't know the answers to.

'So, how about the percentages on the outcome forms; what have you done to improve them since last time?' and 'How have you utilised the training budget to best optimise the service user experience?'

'I'm sure I would be able to email most of the answers to your enquiries once we've checked with head office,' Grace says, looking towards Boris and hoping he'll step in and throw her a lifeline or an inflatable armband at the very least.

'I see from your rota that only one of you is on shift on some days during the week,' Caroline remarks. 'I'm surprised you allow lone-working in a high-needs project this size. I imagine it would be next to impossible to deal with emergencies or give adequate support to clients this way.'

'The residents we have here at present are fairly stable,' Grace says smoothly. 'Incidents have been kept to a minimum.' She sends a silent prayer of thanks that things appear quiet and drama-free from the resident's side of the hatch this morning.

Teardrop Terry chooses this time to reappear. 'Just to let

you know that the bike's been nicked again and someone's broken into the shed.'

'He's at it again, that bloody man, whoever he is.' Dawn joins Terry at the hatch and thumps her fist down onto it. 'You need to run better background checks on your residents. Somebody's been in my room and chucked all of my tablets down the loo. I know they're trying to scare me, but the joke is on them – I don't even take them anymore. Maybe whoever it was took the bike too.'

Peter bumbles around trying to provide some reassurance, and Grace is acutely aware of two pairs of eyes boring into the back of her skull. Terry and Dawn wander away from the hatch and she hides a sigh of relief. She's just put the kettle back on and begun hunting for biscuits to try and sweeten up the inspectors, when she gets her wish granted, two-and-a-half hours too late.

The fire alarm screams out around them.

'That'll be the new lad in number five having a spliff in his room too near the smoke detector again,' shouts Terry over the obscene volume. 'Oh, and about that bike… Cara's just thrown up all over the downstairs hallway. Now, I'm not saying the two things are connected but… '

Caroline and Boris scribble something on their clipboards.

Grace shakes the stress from her shoulders as she takes a seat at the back of the assembly hall of her old secondary school. It's been three hours since the inspection finished at St Jude's, and she wants to purge it from her mind so she can focus on supporting Jack.

It's surreal being back there after all those years, as if the past ten years have evaporated. The same smell of paper and disinfectant. The scrape of plastic chairs against parquet flooring. The nudges and giggles and whispers of those in front of her. Even the thick velvet curtains at the windows are the same.

Grace remembers standing behind those curtains, running through the opening lines for the hundredth time in her head. It was the first performance she'd ever been involved in at secondary school and to open the show as a humble Year 8 was a great honour. She had to get it right, though; her parents would be out there. They'd flown back from the US the day before but had things to attend to at their London branch first. They decided not to come to Dover until that afternoon but had promised to be there in time to watch the play. The curtain swept back, and a hush had fallen across the hall as Grace scanned the rows, front to back. Gran's strained face with a painted smile, third from the right on the back row. Two empty seats either side of her. Grace pushed her lines out through a tight throat and ran off stage before anyone could see the tears.

The door to the hall slams behind Grace, jolting her back to the present and away from a myriad of memories involving countless other performances, false promises and her gran's consoling face.

Grace makes a mental note to stock up on wine over the weekend before her mum arrives on Monday. At least the inspection is over now. And who knows, maybe she and her mum might actually have a nice time together.

Jack is on stage, next to her old head teacher. The paper his speech is written on is shaking in his hands and he keeps wiping his forearm across his brow. Grace feels sick on his behalf. Teenagers are not always an easy audience and Jack isn't carrying an easy message.

Mrs Jacobs, the headteacher, introduces him and exits left, leaving him alone in the middle. He's holding a microphone with a shaking hand. He opens his mouth and closes it again. He takes a step forwards and sound feedback screeches from the speakers. Giggles and fidgets rise from the audience.

Grace stands to her feet at the back and lets out a whoop before clapping wildly. She'd hoped the kids would join in, but all they've done is crane their necks around to stare at her instead. She sees Jack take a deep breath and he grins back at her before opening his mouth again.

'Thanks for the warm welcome from… one of you in particular.' Jack's amused voice sounds clear and strong. His hands are no longer shaking. 'I'm here this morning to talk to you about what it's like to be homeless. And what it's like to feel homeless even before it happens.'

Grace listens with a tight throat as Jack speaks about his struggles as a teenager; his overwhelming need to fit in and be wanted.

'My parents were both dead by the time I was in junior school,' he says. 'I went from foster home to foster home, hoping for someone to adopt me, but nobody ever did. I thought there must be something wrong with me. Then I tried to make the older kids like me instead. I started doing favours to help them out. Small things to start with, like nicking cakes out of shops. Then cakes became clothes and clothes became cars. I didn't know how to stop.'

He tells them about his other mistakes, his time in young offenders' programmes. How he'd got older, with no one there to catch him when he fell into homelessness. About how he once longed to be surveyed about his energy-supplier needs, just so he could have a conversation with someone who didn't want to pee on his sleeping bag.

'There are so many points in my life where I could have asked for help. I could have turned my life around just by taking a different path. I wish I hadn't left it so long and wasted so many years. I can't change that now. Instead, I'm choosing to start my life again at twenty-seven years old. The staff at the hostel I'm living in have helped me to get onto a training course that will get me back to work. I've learned the life skills I need to live on my own again and I'm learning to drive – legally this time.'

Uneasy chuckles fall across the room and everyone sits up straighter.

'I may not be able to do much about my past. But I can shape my own future. And if getting up here to talk to you guys helps just one of you to think about reaching out before you do something damaging, or to change the way you might treat a homeless person, then the stuff I've been through will be worth it. Has anybody got any questions?'

Hands shoot up around the hall and Grace watches with pride as Jack tackles their questions with humour and sensitivity. Mrs Jacobs and two other teachers have misty eyes and Grace begins making a mental note of other schools in the area. Resettling homeless people is vital work for St Jude's, but helping to prevent homelessness in the first place could only be a positive thing. Perhaps once the others have heard about Jack's success, some of the other residents might be happy to get involved.

'You were amazing,' she says to Jack on the way home in her car.

'I thought I was going to blow it before you got up and clapped. The head teacher asked afterwards if I'd go in once a week and help with the football coaching. She said the kids seemed to like me and she remembered me mentioning all the five-a-side I did at Young Offenders.'

Grace can't stop the smile from stretching across her face. 'What did you say to her?'

'I said yes. Maybe my life's shaping up to be less of a waste than I used to think it would be.'

'Have you only just realised that?'

Jack nods. 'Before I started my course last week, my days were just filled up with trips to the job centre or playing backwards bingo in the residents' lounge. Now I'm learning stuff all day and studying most evenings. Between the driving lessons and the football coaching, I might have to actually start using a diary.'

'Hope there's some room in it for me,' Grace finds herself saying as she puts on the handbrake. She punches his shoulder and covers her words with a high-pitched laugh, turning her reddening face away from him before getting out of the car. She locks it and rushes up the hill, keeping two paces in front of Jack all the way to the top.

CHAPTER 18

Dawn

CARA LOOKS AS IF she's got seven different kinds of flu and is shivering so hard she's making her bed shake. It's been two days since the picnic and she's told Dawn that it's three days since she's had any methadone.

'Please help me, Dawnie,' she says as she grips her stomach. 'I've been waiting all night for someone to wake up and come and see me.'

A sicky feeling settles in the place where Dawn's chest joins her stomach. She knows the kind of help she means, and she'd guessed all along that Cara was going to ask. It's what had kept her from coming into Cara's room yesterday when those strangers were wandering around the hostel with Grace and Peter about half an hour before the fire alarm went off.

Dawn looks around the bedsit and studies Cara's belongings, partly to stall whilst she thinks of an answer and mostly to distract herself from the overwhelming stench of Cara's furious stomach contents coming from the en suite bathroom.

'You were right about the bars on your window. You don't have any,' Dawn says. 'That means mine were put there for a reason.'

'That's very helpful, Dawnie. Can we please get back to my shitty situation now?'

'Why do you keep calling me Dawnie? You never usually do. Is it because you want me to do something I'm not going to like?'

'I can't go out like this and I'm short by a stinkin' fiver. Kong said he won't let me have stuff on tic anymore after last time.' Cara interrupts herself to heave into a dirty saucepan next to her purple flowery pillow. 'But if you could lend me a few quid and go and meet him then I'll be able to sort myself out. Start going back to group and stuff.'

Dawn's eyes land on a cuddly white unicorn at the foot of her duvet. The duvet cover is a faded lilac, 'Bang on the Door' one. Dawn remembers having the exact same set when she was nine. Her dad had bought it for her, right before he upped and left forever.

Dawn lowers herself onto the bed beside Cara and holds the unicorn on her lap, as if clinging to it for solidarity.

'Why don't you just explain to the chemist that your meds were stolen and you need more? Wouldn't that would be easier?'

Cara gathers the corners of her cover inside her tightly wound fists and pulls it higher over her shoulders, despite the sweltering heat of the airless room. 'They never believe that kind of shit,' she mumbles into her pillow. 'I've said that loads of times before when I've sold it or got through it too quick.'

'And what about this time? Are you sure it was definitely stolen? You couldn't have… misplaced it some other way?' It feels strange saying 'misplaced' as if she's lost a pen or the remote control.

'I might have run out a bit quicker than I meant to,' she mumbles into her fist. 'And I have been buying other stuff. Teardrop was right about what happened with the bike.'

Dawn gives her a nod. 'Whose unicorn is this? Is it one of your boys'?' She strokes it like a well-loved pet.

'Yeah. Her name's Rainbow-Sparkles. Curtis lent her to me to look after so I wouldn't miss him so much. I pretended I'd forgot to take it back last time. Couldn't bring myself to part with her. S'pose we can add that to the list of crappy mum-points I'm collecting.'

'I'm sure they miss you very much too,' Dawn whispers. 'And of course, I'll help you. I'm also going to find two extra special teddies for you to take to give to your boys to hold onto whenever they're sad.' She pulls Cara's head onto her lap, takes out her hair bobble and gathers up her long dark tangles, fashioning them into a fresh ponytail and ignoring the faint whiff of vomit. How had she coped on the streets? She's heard stories from the others about Cara from before she'd moved into St Jude's – enough to know that Cara *needs* this place to stay open. That closure stuff is probably just a rumour anyway, and Dawn's not one to listen to rumours.

'Thank you,' Cara murmurs as her eyes begin to close.

Dawn strokes her forehead, green-tinged and covered in a film of sweat, and wills her to stay asleep for a while, so Dawn can think. The universe has clearly brought her to this very hostel to help Cara and the others. She has a duty of care. What would she do if Rosie asked her for help? She'd move heaven, earth and every other bloody planet, that's what. If only she'd been given the chance. Dawn swallows hard and forces her mind back to Cara. She is going to help her, of course she is. But not the way Cara wants her to.

Cara's eyes flutter open for a moment at the faint knock on her door, but she closes them before the handle begins to move slowly downwards and the intruder creeps into the room.

'Shaun!' Dawn hisses. 'You shouldn't be sneaking around the hostel, you're not signed in. We'll both get kicked out if they see you.'

'Sorry. I just wanted to check Cara was okay. And you've been gone ages.'

'I didn't realise how late it had got.' The light outside Cara's window has begun to dim; the sea has swapped its daytime blue for dusky-grey. Dawn gently guides her dear friend's head back onto the pillow and pats the top of her duvet. 'Could you stay with her please? I've somewhere I need to pop out to.'

Dawn's footsteps echo in the hallway and on the stairs to her room. It's quieter than it usually is at half past nine on a Saturday night. Dawn hopes Terry will be easy to find; her mission will be a trickier one without his contacts and expertise but she *has* to get hold of some of that methadone. She'll stop Cara from going down a darker path. She'll be her rock – the one to lean on when she's tempted to stray. She'll help Cara to see the kind of mum she could be for her boys, and she will rise to the challenge. Then Curtis and Kyle will grow up strong and well adjusted and visit Dawn every weekend. They'll probably call her 'Auntie Dawn'.

As soon as she enters her room to get her purse, something feels different. She can smell something sweet and cloying and it's not the same deodorant Shaun wears. She closes her eyes and sees the familiar flash of red hair that always accompanies the smell of patchouli and lavender.

Tell anyone, and I will kill you.

Dawn shakes the voice from her mind, closes the door behind her and slides the bolt across before tiptoeing to the bathroom to check no one is lurking behind the shower curtain. They're not. Life is rarely like TV or books. It's never the monsters hiding in dark corners that people need to worry about; it's the ones that bash into them in the middle of the day with a phone call or a knock at the door.

It's then she notices the fire blanket has been ripped off the wall and draped over her bed as if it's trying to suffocate whoever could be sleeping on it. *It's a sign.* She knows it is. A packet of pasta gets knocked from the shelf, spreading its shells across the floor as Dawn grabs clumsily at her purse.

She is rushing towards the office, but still has no idea what she's intending to do once she gets there. What exactly can she say to them? 'Someone's put bars on the windows to show me I'm a prisoner? That they've put a fire blanket over my bed to make me think I'll die if I stay?' Even Dawn knows that doesn't make any sense, and believe it or not, she's struggled with things like that in the past.

Low voices hum from the office hatch. Dawn flattens herself against the wall next to it, so she can hear who they belong to. One of them is Grace and the other one belongs to Paul from room one.

'Dawn? Is that you?' Grace's voice squeezes through the hatch and Dawn realises she can probably see her on the camera.

Dawn spins around on one foot and skips sideways so she's

face to face with Grace. She runs her finger up and down the side of the hatch as if checking for dust. Really, she's looking for *him*. She needs to see if he has forced his way into the building and found her, like he promised he would.

'You've been here for a couple of weeks now, and things seem to be going well,' Grace says to Dawn. 'I know you've had an initial licence agreement for your room, but that runs out soon and we'd like to offer you a short-term tenancy agreement? It won't change very much about your stay here, but it does offer you more protection.' Grace is waving A4 paperwork at Dawn and smiling as if she'd arrived at a surprise party Grace had thrown for her.

'Thanks,' Dawn mumbles. And she does mean it. More protection sounds good.

'I'll just get you a pen. Ugh, Peter must've moved them again,' Grace says as she rummages around in the drawer.

Paul has disappeared to his own room opposite the office.

'I'd like to report a break and enter,' Dawn says in a loud voice, fighting to keep the wobble out of it. 'Someone has been going into my room when I'm not there and doing things to try to frighten me. It's someone who managed to steal a key so it's less of a break and more of just an enter, I suppose.'

Dawn braces herself for the voice again, the one that threatens her whenever she sleeps in the same spot for too long. Usually she packs up and leaves as soon as she hears it.

Should she be signing a form to say she wants to stay? What about all those others out there on the streets needing beds? And even if *he* hasn't found her already, he might if she stays in one place. She must try to keep the gate to that part of her mind closed; she has important things to attend to. People who need her. But those pesky memories keep peeping through the bars.

'What was all that about your room? I can check the CCTV if you're worried about something?' Grace looks up from her paperwork.

Another thought crashes into Dawn's mind and runs around with the rest of them. The CCTV will prove that someone's been going into number six, but it will also show Shaun coming and going too. Allowing him to stay overnight and not having him signed into the building will mean Dawn has already violated the tenancy agreement she's meant to be signing. The ugly nights on the cold, hard ground of the park and those other ones, a while back in Poundland's doorway, fall around Dawn like a curtain, making her remember and stopping her from seeing anything else. She thinks about Cara, shaking on her bed downstairs with poor Shaun who needs a mother's love like a duck needs water. Do ducks need water? Dawn expects they do. All living things do.

'Just sign and date here, please.' Grace is still smiling but she looks puzzled and as if she's been holding that pen out towards Dawn for a while.

Dawn takes it and stares at the page. She never signs anything without reading it thoroughly first and she needs time to weigh up her decision.

What will *he* do to her if she stays?

On the other hand, Dawn may be safer here with the others than out on her own.

'Done,' Dawn says when she's finished the final flourish of her signature.

Grace photocopies the papers and gives the originals back to Dawn, all held together with a bright pink paperclip. The embers of fear remain but Dawn smiles as she looks down at the contract. She may not be safe yet, but at least, for now, she has an address.

CHAPTER 19

Grace

GRACE RUSHES HOME AFTER her shift, wishing she'd taken her car. She's got lots to do at home this evening if she's going to get the flat ready for her mum's visit after the weekend, and she has to be back at work again for a sleep shift tonight. She'll give the place a thorough clean, then drive up to Homebase to pick up an inflatable mattress and some nice new linen for her own bed. Her mum can have that of course; Grace will sleep on the airbed.

'Ah, what beautiful bedding. Such exquisite taste you have, my darling,' perhaps her mum might say. They've never really had a 'fun visit' before; the two of them have precisely zero in common. But perhaps this time will be different. The inspection is out of the way and Grace has taken two whole days off work to spend with her mum. Maybe her mum will make more of an effort now that Gran's no longer around. She might even get a hug when she arrives. They'll have a glass of prosecco together and her mum will tell her how much she's missed her.

A renewed sense of energy and purpose fills Grace as she jogs up the stairs of her building, which is surprising given she's just had the shift from hell. Apparently one of the other residents had 'helpfully' sourced Cara some street methadone to ease her withdrawals in an effort to stop her from buying heroin. Which was all very well and good, except it was a dodgy batch and it had sent Cara completely loopy. Which wouldn't have been *so* bad if it hadn't happened on the day of her child protection meeting. Needless to say, she'd cocked it up on an epic scale and would not be allowed unsupervised access to her boys for a very long time. Then had come the hospital visit to get her checked over, and then she'd had to fill out an incident form after settling her back into her room at Jude's for fluids and rest. At least Cara now has her chemist-sanctioned prescription sorted, although she'd had to commit to taking it at the pharmacy each day instead of being allowed a takeaway.

Grace's phone buzzes with a text alert. She walks through the door to her flat, gets out her phone and throws her bag on the armchair. The message is from her mum.

Hello Grace, I've cancelled my leave. One of last year's Big Brother contestants has had an emergency. She's got a part in a film and she wants me to do her lips tomorrow. I did them last time, so it wouldn't be fair to expect her to see someone else – continuity of care and all that. I'll be in touch soon!

Grace tries to swallow down the anger. It tastes nasty. She'd known, really. She shouldn't be surprised. *An emergency.* It always is. This is good, she tells herself. It's what she wanted. She's been dreading having to see her anyway. Now she can concentrate on work. Perhaps she could start a Masters in

157

housing management and do it from home, then when her mother finally decides to arrive she'll be able to show her how well she's doing.

Grace stomps past the sofa and through the kitchen area before attempting to fling the window open. Only it's locked, and she can't make the key go in the right direction, so she just keeps yanking it, harder and harder, ignoring the drips of water from her eyes as they drop onto the inside of her forearm.

Why is she getting upset? It's not like this is the first time this had happened. And she's a grown-up now, not seven years old – it's hardly the same as the time they had to cancel their Malta holiday, two days before they were due to go, because her parents had to perform emergency liposuction for an A-lister. She wasn't supposed to cry then either. *Lots of kids had never been on holiday.* Most kids didn't have half of the financial security she had. *Selfish, Grace. You're always so selfish. We have to think of our client portfolio. This is a valuable life lesson. Work comes first.*

Grace picks up her overnight bag and throws in her PJs and toothbrush before galloping down the stairs of her building and slamming the door behind her. She tries to push back against the overwhelming feeling of aloneness as she walks towards work for her sleep shift. Sometimes, she just wants someone to put their arms around her and tell her it's all going to be okay. A face falls across her mind. One she wants to see and touch and be near to. And it sure as hell doesn't belong to her mother.

Covering her Winnie the Pooh PJs with her longest cardigan, Grace keeps her head held high and her gaze straight ahead on her way down from the staff flat, ignoring the wobble in her knees.

She tiptoes towards the lounge, holding her breath when she hears the TV from the hallway. Her heart picks up pace and she stops moving so she can slow it back down. If he is in there, she wants to be cool and calm and casual. Can't have him thinking she's going in there on purpose to see him. She creeps further towards the door. She just wants to watch another film with him, that's all. Have a chat, a giggle. Maybe snuggle under that Spiderman duvet and drink hot chocolate.

The room is empty. Grace stands in the middle of it, staring at the mindless talk show that's blaring from the screen as she swallows down her disappointment. She swipes the remote from the arm of the sofa and rams her thumb down on the off button before turning to leave.

A door creaks open somewhere from the corridor. Grace's shoulders sag when she hears Dawn calling goodnight to Cara. Cara's door closes, and Grace lets out a breath as Dawn's footsteps get gradually quieter as she pads back to her room.

The silence feels thick and cold and the need to not be alone almost overwhelms her.

Grace stands outside Jack's door for several minutes. She zips up her cardigan. It's one thing to sit in the lounge in her PJs but quite another to knock on someone's door after midnight in them.

Concentrating hard on the force with which she raps on number four, Grace checks behind her that no one is watching. If she's too quiet, he won't hear her, and she'll lose her nerve. Too noisy and Cara might come out to see what's happening.

Grace is still trying to decide between knocking again and slinking away when the door opens.

Jack's eyes are pink from sleep and they flicker as they adjust to the light behind her. He takes a step backwards and flicks on the lamp.

'Umm. You want to come in? Or did you need me for something – has something happened?'

She steps into the room. She had planned to ask if he wanted to watch a film in the lounge, but the words sound like a lie, even in her own head. She ignores that inner whisper, the one accusing her of needing someone to want her.

That sounds far too feeble.

Jack takes a step towards her and stops, confusion written in his eyes.

'I've just… just had a bad day and couldn't sleep,' Grace stammers. 'I didn't want to be on my own.'

Jack fixes his gaze on her face, blush marks springing up on his cheeks. He doesn't look tired anymore. 'Erm – of course. You're always welcome.' He holds his arms out towards her, concern written in his eyes.

She closes the door behind her and walks slowly towards him. He opens his mouth to speak again. Grace closes it with her index finger and presses her forehead against his.

They stay like that for several seconds, their lips millimetres apart. Jack's full lips look soft and plump and his breath sounds as shaky as hers. Grace moves her hands to his chest and inches her mouth closer to his.

Jack covers her hands with his own, keeping them still and moves his face further from hers.

'What's brought this on?' he asks in a low voice. 'What's happened?'

'Nothing I want to burden you with.' Grace can hear the wobble in her own voice.

'I just don't think we should… ' Jack peels her hands from his chest and drops them before taking a step backwards. 'You're crying,' he says, peering at her face.

Grace wipes her wrist across her face. It comes away slick with tears and clumps of black mascara. Her face burns with humiliation. He obviously wants her to leave. She wants to run far away from his concerned face and his Spiderman cover, but her legs won't move.

She watches in silence as he opens his wardrobe and gets out a scratchy-looking blanket. He wraps it around her shoulders, guiding her onto the bed until she's lying on top of the duvet and pulls the blanket tightly around her. Plumping up his pillow, he sits up next to Grace and scoops his arms around her, guiding her head to his shoulder. He smells faintly of sleep, toothpaste and Lynx Africa.

'I'm sorry, I shouldn't have assumed,' she says with a hollow laugh. 'It was unprofessional. I completely understand if you want to report me.'

She doesn't dare to look at his face as the seconds tick by, she's afraid of what she might see written all over it. Disgust? Pity? She's not sure which would be worse.

She's so preoccupied with waiting for his answer that his sudden laughter makes her jump.

'Report you?' he sounds as if he's choking on his own chuckles. 'Yes, officer, I'd like to report this really hot woman I know. We've been flirting for a while now, had a few cuddles, I very obviously fancy the socks off her and she has the cheek to knock on my door. Can I have a complaint form please?'

'I still shouldn't be doing this. Not in my position.' Grace blushes and bats his shoulder with the back of her hand. 'Why did you stop me, if that's what you really think?' She snuggles down further into his arms, immediately feeling her body sag and her eyes begin to droop.

'Because I want something to happen with us, and I don't want it to start with you crying or using it as a way to escape whatever other shit you've got going on today.'

Bingo. He has her there, she supposes.

Grace wakes to the delicious smell of coffee and Egg McMuffins. Jack is perched next to her on the bed, his dimple on proud display beside his smile.

Grace sits up as she feels beside her for her phone. It's not there, she'd left it in the staff flat. 'What time is it?' Panic sets in and her stomach drops.

'Hey, don't panic. It's ten to ten.'

'*What?*'

'You'll be fine. You said you weren't working today?'

'Well, no, I'm not, but I didn't mean to fall asleep in here. Peter must've wondered where I was when he got to work. I was supposed to be in the staff flat. What if something bad happened last night in the hostel and no one could find me?'

'Relax. Nothing happened. Besides, I hung around the hatch this morning and told Peter you'd only just left for a dentist appointment. He didn't bat an eyelid. Then I went for a run and picked up our breakfast.'

Grace's stomach growls and she sniffs her hash brown, her face breaking into a smile despite her nerves. 'Smells delicious.'

It tastes just as good. Grace closes her eyes and savours every mouthful, feeling her shoulders relax with every bite.

'Do you like escape rooms?'

'Eh?' Grace laughs. 'Can't say I've ever been in one.'

'Neither have I.' Jack wipes ketchup from the side of his mouth with his finger. 'But they've just opened one up in town. They have loads of rooms to choose from – all different themes – they lock you in and you have to solve clues to get out in under an hour. It's half price today, so I thought we could go. Have some fun away from this place.'

Grace opens her mouth to say no, and then wonders why the hell not. She's already sitting on a service user's bed in her PJs on her day off. How could a fun day out be any worse?

Jack goes to the office to keep Peter busy and Grace holds her cardigan tightly around her and runs on her tiptoes to the staff flat, praying that no one sees her, and that Peter isn't watching the cameras.

She pulls on her day clothes, puts her PJs in her bag and picks up her phone. Footsteps and voices move past the door and Grace stands still until she thinks they have gone. Then she inches the door open and creeps down the back stairs to the fire exit until she's beside the bins at the back of the building. A quick survey of her surroundings confirms she's alone, and she hops over the back fence, using the bin to step onto.

'I can't believe we just did that.' Grace bursts out laughing as soon as Jack appears around the corner. 'Now run before anyone sees us!'

They are still laughing when they arrive at the escape rooms. Grace feels like a naughty schoolgirl and can't remember the last time she'd felt so free.

They are both hopeless in the escape room. The room is supposed to look like a witch's cottage. They are supposed to find clues, but they keep getting distracted by their own conversations.

They cover everything from music to celebrities and politics. Grace is just about to say how great it feels to be talking about things other than her problems, when Jack throws her a curveball.

'So, what *was* the matter last night?'

Grace sits down on the wall along the side of the room. She tells him the truth. She lets him know about the inspection being a disaster and that they are waiting for the verdict from head office. She even tells him about her mum cancelling.

'She's a pain in the arse. Not a nice person at all, if I'm being honest. But she's my mum, and I wanted to see her. I wanted her to see me and just for once, be proud.'

Jack nods. He looks as if he's going to say something when a man wearing a *Dover Escape Rooms* T-shirt rushes through the door.

'Are you two all right in here?' he says, breathlessly. 'It's just that your time is almost up and you've still got seven clues to find. We haven't even sent Hansel and Gretel in yet.'

CHAPTER 20

Dawn

TONIGHT'S EQUIP MEETING AT St Jude's is supposed to be about CVs and interview skills. It appears to be very well attended, which is surprising to Dawn when she notices the lack of biscuits. Not a rich tea or a custard cream in sight.

Every sofa seat and hard-backed chair is filled with the behinds of St Jude's residents and most of the scratchy carpet is covered too.

People are staring at the empty space on the coffee table where the biscuits usually sit. Not Dawn though, she can't quite tear her eyes away from Peter and Grace's faces and the looks that pass between the two of them every few minutes. Grace keeps opening her mouth and then closing it again, fiddling with the clip from the top of her board. Peter looks as if he wishes he could be anywhere but there and keeps staring around the room, looking for an exit or someone to save him.

'Have we still got the bike? Only I wanted to borrow it next week for a job interview. It's in Deal and I hate going on buses.'

'Good thing I got it back again then,' mumbles Cara.

Dawn waits for Grace and Peter to congratulate Terry on his interview and begin discussions about progress and increased

165

self-worth etcetera. But none of it comes, just another weird expression between them that seems to plead with each other to say something.

'What's happened?' Cara pipes up. She looks a normal colour today and is managing to hold her head up higher on her shoulders. She even looks as if she's washed her hair.

'We've received an email,' Grace says, glancing sideways at Peter. Peter just looks straight ahead, refusing to meet anyone's eyes. 'It's from Supporting Futures, the people who give us the majority of our funding.'

The room is silent now, most people are sitting up just a little bit straighter.

'They came to carry out an inspection, as many of you are aware. There were a few issues that were highlighted, which have dropped our rating, meaning that they are pulling a significant amount of our funding.'

The silence deepens, rooting itself into the ground and thickening, filling up the room and taking all the air out of it.

'Can't head office do something?' Jack asks.

More furtive glances between the staff and Dawn's stomach takes a downwards dive.

'They've spent the past few days looking at the figures and trying to secure finance elsewhere. Unfortunately, there's nothing more they can do.'

'What does that mean?' Terry always has the biggest balls in the room, and almost every resident looks at him gratefully. No one wants to ask a question that no one wants to answer.

'We're now facing a shortfall of ten thousand pounds. It means we can only operate for a further four months.'

The silence is punctured by sixteen separate gasps and almost as many different swear words.

'During that time, Peter and I and the rest of the staff team will be working closely with each one of you to work towards relocating you to more permanent housing.'

One by one, each face in the room drains of colour. Dawn's must look the same. Four months is so soon. Even if they do all get relocated, what will Dawn do then? Who would be left for her to look after? It would be tricky to watch over them if they weren't all in the same building. St Jude's is so much more than just a roof over their heads.

'No.' The word falls out of Dawn's mouth before she even knows it's in there.

Every face is pointing towards her as something stirs deep inside her belly.

'We can't give up on this place. I won't. There's sixteen of us who live here as well as staff. Am I right?'

Grace gives Dawn a nod.

'You read about it all the time, and there are definitely films about it… you know, where a group of people band together to raise money for some good cause? We could be those people!'

A cluster of blank faces stare back at Dawn. They don't get it, not yet, they've had too many years of 'no' and 'can't' and 'move the hell on, you're not allowed to sleep here'.

'We have four months,' Dawn carries on. 'At any given time, there are plenty of us in this building. If we do it in shifts, we could use all of that time to try and make money for St Jude's. That's a lot of man-hours.'

'People-hours,' corrects Grace, but she does look intrigued. 'Say we could do this,' she says, excitement poking out between syllables. 'What would that look like? Has anyone here got any fundraising experience?'

Silence is back again as people throw glances to and from each other around the room.

'I do.' Terry puts his hand halfway up for the briefest of seconds before using it to scratch his head, as if that's what he'd meant to do in the first place.

'What, legally?' Cara screws up her face. 'I'm not sure you're talking about the same kind of fundraising.'

'I used to work for the RSPCA. Door to door and down the high street, jiggling the boxes, giving out stickers. Not too different from sleeping on the street actually, people still speak to you like shit or pretend they haven't seen you.'

'That's settled then. Terry, you are head fundraiser,' beams Grace.

'Cool,' he nods.

A warm feeling begins to spread inside Dawn's stomach as people start to smile and shout ideas out to the front. This is the kind of thing she was made for. Inspiring people. Solving their problems. Being the wind beneath their wings. Years from now, some of these residents would be telling this story to their grandkids over a home-cooked spag bol. *We almost lost our rooms. Our hostel. We were facing being back on the cold, hard streets. We were about to give up. Do you know why we didn't? Because of Dawn. She's why I'm still here to tell the tale. Good thing too, otherwise you wouldn't have even been born…*

'We could have a charity run, like those Races for Lives?'

'Cake sale?'

'Sponsored walk? Scavenger hunt? We could get the mayor involved!'

'We could do car washes, painting and decorating.'

'Artwork! There's some great stuff in the café, we could paint some more and have a gallery night; sell some of the work?'

'You're all amazing.' A tear falls from Grace's eye and the room waits in silence as it makes the journey down her cheek before pooling in the corner of her mouth. 'Let's do it.'

Applause breaks out, mostly from Dawn as she stands in the middle of the room doing slow claps, but she can tell everyone else is sufficiently moved. Perhaps they are less used to public displays of emotion or they've just not seen as many films as she has.

Everyone begins talking at once, sometimes addressing the room and other times just the people beside them. Grace disappears then reappears with an A5, leather-bound notebook, her personalised parker pen and a selection of highlighters. Dawn senses that things are about to get wild, and sneaks back to number six to get three multipacks of melted Wagon Wheels from underneath her bed. They all deserve a treat and they were three-for-the-price-of-two from Aldi. Plus, the security guard who works the morning shift is a little lacklustre during the lunchtime rush.

By the time she's arrived back in the residents' lounge, the conversation has moved on to methods of collecting sponsors and the potential use of social media.

'I've heard that Facebook is always the way forward for fundraising,' Cara says, her face more animated than Dawn has ever seen it.

'When exactly have you ever done any fundraising? Selling

stuff that doesn't belong to you to cover drug debts doesn't count,' chuckles Teardrop Terry with an edge of revenge.

Dawn holds her breath and watches for another storm to brew, but Cara bats his knee with the back of her hand and chuckles. 'Okay, maybe I've not done any actual fundraising, but I can hustle pretty good. Plus, I'm great with Facebook. We need to get local people to see the page. People outside the area won't give a shit about helping some grubby hostel in Dover. Okay, I didn't mean grubby,' adds Cara hurriedly as she catches Grace's eye. 'I just mean that's what people will think who don't know who we are.'

Grace is beaming by now, obviously relishing the task of handing out people's individual tasks and responsibilities and making a corresponding, colour-coded pie chart in case of any confusion.

'Oh, yes! Dawn and I will do that.' Cara has her hand high in the air like a school child who knows the answer to a tricky question and thinks that nobody else does.

'Making the Facebook page,' she explains to Dawn. 'Don't look like that, it will be fun, and we make a good team.'

The knots of muscle at the top of Dawn's back bunch up together and her head starts to pulsate on one side. She's always steered clear of the internet and the idea of things like Facebook. It's easy to hide your face from the universe inside a grotty bedsit, a shop doorway or a stranger's sofa. But the whole world is inside a computer screen. Watching. Waiting. Knowing where you are and waiting to pounce. She grits her teeth and shakes out her shoulders.

'Fine,' Dawn smiles. 'You'll have to show me though

because I haven't used a computer since Friends Reunited was first launched.'

Everyone looks at Dawn blankly and she feels a surge of smugness about her knowledge of vintage technology.

Maybe this will work. Maybe they won't all be out on their arses in four months' time. Maybe Dawn really is there for a reason. Maybe, maybe.

CHAPTER 21

Dawn

'WHO DO YOU SPEAK to on this thing?' Dawn asks as Cara proudly shows off her Facebook page. A photo of her with Curtis and Kyle shines out at Dawn from the screen. Underneath the picture are various 'about me' sections. Under 'work' Cara has put 'full-time mummy'. Dawn swallows the pebble that's formed in her throat.

'Oh, just people.' She waves her hand around. 'Mostly people I haven't seen in forever – like people from school.'

Dawn's mind spins at the thought of old school friends trying to find her. Perhaps Matthew Jenkins from year eleven has spent the past decade typing her name in that search bar at the top, wondering what had become of her. Matthew had been the best-looking boy at Marsden High. Almost every other girl used to stare and give themselves an extra squirt of Body Shop white musk whenever he walked past. He'd never actually spoken to Dawn or even looked in her direction. He was probably trying to play it cool, so she wouldn't realise how much he fancied her. Dawn supposes he'd never properly got over her.

'What shall we call ourselves?' Cara's fingers hover over the keyboard as she watches Dawn out of the corner of her eye.

'Eh?'

'Our fundraising project. It needs a name.'

Dawn stares out the window of the residents' lounge, watching Teardrop Terry and Jack as they sweep the patio and water the geraniums in the oversized plant pots. 'Do you know who St Jude was?'

Cara shrugs her shoulders and bites her thumbnail whilst she waits patiently for Dawn to explain what she's on about.

'St Jude was the patron saint of lost causes. I guess that's what a lot of people think of us as being. It's definitely what people would view this project as.'

Cara's hands freeze in the air and her eyes light up like two full beams on the motorway.

'St Jude's Last Cause,' she says slowly. 'It's perfect.'

Dawn watches over Cara's shoulder as her fingers spin over the keys, putting details in the boxes and attaching links to places where people could donate.

'We could get people from here to be interviewed,' she says, seeming to warm more and more to the initiative. 'They can talk about different ways that St Jude's has helped them. Oh, and we need some photos of us all, of the café, everything!'

Cara almost trips over the computer stool in her hurry to round everyone up to help with photos. Not everyone wants to be in them; many people have lives to hide from.

Seeing Cara come to life makes Dawn's heart squeeze with pride. She's come so far this week. She looks around at the semi-circle of residents, all gathered around the coffee table. These people deserve a chance. And Dawn will be the one to give it to them. Whatever it takes.

'I'll take the photo. There's no need for me to be in it. People won't want to see my ugly mug,' Dawn jokes lightly.

'Of course you need to be in it – this was your idea. You're the one who made us feel like we could do this.' Cara places a hand across Dawn's back, nudging her forward.

Cara's enthusiasm for the publicity is infectious, and somehow, for the first time ever, Dawn's need to be part of something feels bigger than her fear of being found by her past.

It's been twenty years and he hasn't managed to catch her. And even if he does, she's not alone now. St Jude's needs her, and she needs St Jude's, along with all of those who sleep between its walls.

In for a penny, in for a pound.

And that's how Dawn ends up smack-bang in the middle of a group photo between Grace and Teardrop Terry with an article underneath containing a heartfelt story of how St Jude's had rescued her from the street and pulled her back from the brink of death. Some of Dawn's answers to Cara's interview questions carried a little more creative licence but hey, it was all for a good cause.

A lost cause. A voice of negativity whispers inside her mind. Dawn wishes it would shut up.

It's difficult to get to sleep after all the excitement. Adrenaline continues to trickle through Dawn's veins as she thinks about all the plans they've made; ways to help save the hostel and what will happen to everyone if they fail. She also keeps thinking about her face on the profile picture of that Facebook page. If she had her own account, how many people would she be able to search for? People she's always wondered about.

Shaun kicks her shoulder as he turns over in his sleep and she listens tenderly to his gentle snoring. He probably has a profile himself she could look at, with pictures of his family or photos from the childhood he never seems to want to speak about. It might help her understand him. She may even be able to help him better.

Dawn shrugs off the duvet and pads quietly across the floor. She heads downstairs to the residents' lounge, closes the door behind her and gently presses the power button on the communal computer, jumping when it roars to life in the stillness of the room.

Fortunately, Dawn has somehow managed to remember her log-in details for the email address the nice lady at the library had helped her to set up. She uses the email address to make herself a profile and copies the photo from the St Jude's page to her picture. Her face is already strewn across the internet on the St Jude's page, so having her own profile surely couldn't make much difference now.

A frisson of excitement fizzes through her as she stares at the page. She's a real person. She exists. Dawn Elisabeth Brightside, one word, has a place in the world. Now she just needs to make sure it stays that way.

She 'joins' and 'likes' the St Jude's last cause page and 'adds' Cara as a friend. It's a long time since she's had one of them and it's nice to see it in writing. Makes it real. Official.

Dawn tentatively puts some names in the search bar – just out of curiosity. Who knew there were so many Matthew Jenkinses in the world? She gives up the quest to find her first schoolgirl crush after clicking on at least ten profiles that probably don't belong to him. Or maybe they do, who knows?

When she thinks about it, she can't even really remember what he'd looked like anyway.

There are a few others. Jane Davis from across the road; they had spent every day of the summer holidays playing in the fields behind their houses, making dens under trees and daring each other to eat various unknown species of berries to see whether or not they were poisonous. Mr Griggs, her piano teacher with the dodgy breath; she's often wondered what happened to him. Dawn had walked in on him cuddling her mum in the kitchen once. She said it was because his cat was poorly and he was sad. He never came over for any more lessons after that – Dawn had suspected back then that poor old Pickles must have popped his clogs. Shame though; Dawn never had finished learning how to play Beethoven's Fifth Symphony.

There's others of course. Those who left her and those she had to leave behind because of *him*. Her midwife buddies, her best friend, Mel. And of course, Rob. But she won't go there.

Even as Dawn types in the names of people she used to know, she's aware she's doing so to keep her hands busy, so she can't type in the words that her fingers want to. The letters that spell out her dad's name. She could have a tiny look but why should she?

He could never be found before, and he's the one who left her alone with Mum for all those years after promising to protect her forever. *That* hadn't worked out too well, had it?

Of course, there's the one other name that sings loud and proud around her mind above all the others. Dawn doesn't type her name in the search bar; she knows there is no point. Instead, she sets up a new email address – rosiebrightside@hotmail.co.uk – and attaches it to another profile. She adds details. Rosie's favourite book (*Alice Through the Looking Glass*), her favourite film (*Titanic*) and what she does for a living (editor-in-chief for a major publishing company.) After browsing through Google Images, Dawn finally settles on a picture that best represents Rosie. A young woman in her twenties, light-coloured hair threaded with highlights. Her brilliant smile zaps the camera lens from the sandy-white beach she's standing on barefoot, in a light, floral sundress.

Before logging out, she searches for Dawn Elisabeth Brightside and 'adds' her as a friend. Dawn's heart pounds with pleasure when she logs back into her account and sees the words: 'Rosie Brightside has sent you a friend request'. A tear rolls unbidden down her cheek and plops onto the semi-colon on the keyboard. Brushing it off with her little finger, Dawn briefly wonders if there's ever been a time in her life when she's used one before. Probably not. Perhaps she could make use of it now. Rosie would like that, she'd be proud that Dawn takes care with her presentation and punctuation. She'll realise that she gets her high standards from her mum.

Hello my darling Rosie!

It's so lovely to hear from you, and what a lovely photo of you. How is Fiji? You look like you are having the time of your life! I hope you are wearing plenty of sunscreen and eating properly? I miss you so much. Thank you for your friend request; at least we can stay in touch better from now on.

Love you always!

Mum

Xxx

Dawn notices the faint, metallic taste of blood and realises she's been chewing too hard on her lip. She busies herself with logging out and changing accounts again.

Hi Mum!

Yes, I'm wearing plenty of factor 30 – I always do, it's like I can hear your voice every time I'm on the beach lol. And yes, I'm eating well, but missing all your home-cooked meals. Work is going well, I'm so thankful you always taught me to follow my dreams.
   Miss you too and love you very much,

Your Rosie.
Xxx

Dawn's own account welcomes her back with a message alert. She clicks onto the icon through misty eyes and feels her shoulders heaving as she reads the whole message three times, each time as if it's the first.

It's almost getting light and the seagulls have begun their morning chatter by the time she prints out the photo she's chosen for Rosie's profile.

She'd better get back to bed soon, they are kicking off their fundraising with a Dover-wide roaming bake sale tomorrow and Grace would be up and about making preparations in an hour or so.

The hostel is silent as she creeps back into her room and Shaun stirs only slightly as Dawn rummages in the drawer of the bedside table until she finds what she's looking for.

It's such a beautiful book, despite the years of being packed up and unpacked, squashed into bag after bag, the corners dog-eared and creased. Dawn holds it with reverence and flicks through till she finds the next blank entry. Slipping the latest image of Rosie between the pages, she sets a mental reminder to borrow some Pritt Stick from the office tomorrow.

As the day's sunshine begins to bleed between the gaps in the curtains, Dawn flicks carefully backwards through the pictures already glued in. The photo of Rosie graduating from Oxford. Rosie's first and last days of secondary and primary school. One of them even shows the price of her school skirt, £4.99 from Woolworths, so it shows how long ago that was. Dawn used to love her piles of Woolworth's catalogues, even before Rob started working there, and the back-to-school issues were always the best.

She continues to look back through the book, admiring the toddler pictures of Rosie taking her first steps and sitting up on a shiny new potty, one shaped like a real-life miniature toilet, £18.99 from Mothercare. She can't think why she'd have spent so much on a potty, but it must have been worth it. Anything for her Rosie.

Then she gets to the first page. The one of Rosie only hours after Dawn had given birth to her on the bathroom floor. It's the proudest she'd ever been of anything in her life, and as she'd held her in her arms, she knew she'd never felt love like it.

Dawn closes her eyes and in an instant she's back there, in the flat above the British Heart Foundation, cradling her baby. She runs her finger over the photograph in front of her and gives into the sobs that remind her this photo is the only one that matters.

Shaun sits up and swivels back from the foot-end of the bed, pulling Dawn into his arms. She allows herself to cry freely; the sound muffled by his young chest.

'Shh,' he whispers. 'You have me now.'

CHAPTER 22

Grace

THE STAFF FLAT IS hot and sticky, and Grace's feet are tangled in the sheets from hours of fidgeting. Telling the residents that they might have to leave St Jude's had been one of the hardest things she's ever had to do.

Watching the sprinkles of hope gather in the lounge as they'd made plans to make a stand against closure had lit an ember of possibility deep inside and now she can't switch her mind off. Her fingers itch for paper and pen, a colour-coded chart and a ten-step plan.

Grace hauls her legs from the bed and pulls on her clothes. She'll make a warm drink in the office and get some work done. Anything's better than lying there counting down the hours until she has to start prepping for the fundraising bake sale.

'Why wait?' Cara had gabbled with excitement at the meeting last night. 'We have plenty of ingredients in the café. Let's get up early and do a bake sale tomorrow? No time like the present, my nan used to say.'

Every one of Grace's footsteps echo through the silent corridor. Everyone must be asleep. She unlocks the office door and walks through it, jumping when she sees she's not alone.

'What the hell are you doing here?' Grace hisses.

Peter is sitting at his desk, slumped over his phone, the only source of light in the dark office. He puts his phone on the table but doesn't look up.

'It's four in the morning. Have you been here all night? Didn't you go home?'

Still nothing. Peter's shoulders move up and down. Grace places a hand across them and Peter shrugs it off, keeping his eyes down.

Peter's phone screen is still lit up with a message and Grace has read it before she can stop herself.

Not seen you at group for a while – you okay? Don't be a stranger.

The display says it's from **Sponsor/Dave.**

'I tried to go home,' Peter mumbles. 'But I couldn't walk past it. The off licence.'

Memories of Peter's old life come flooding back to Grace. The state he'd been in those first few weeks after he'd moved in and how hard he'd worked to get rid of those jittery limbs each morning. He's been sober for eighteen months; how had she so quickly forgotten to watch out for the signs?

'Did you buy any?' she asks.

Peter switches the desk lamp on and leans back into his chair. 'Walking past an off licence or a pub hasn't been an issue for ages, but the last few days… since the inspection really, I just keep hearing that whisper again. *Just have the one, it will help you relax.* I can even taste the whisky.'

'Did you buy any?' Grace repeats.

'Why should I get a second chance at life when the people in this building are about to lose their beds? It's my fault. It was my stupid date with that bloody woman that cocked up the inspection. Soon as she saw me, she probably made up her mind to mark us down.'

'It was nothing to do with that, I'm sure. Much more likely to be because of the fire alarms and the million questions I couldn't answer. If anyone's to blame, it's me.' Grace points at Peter's phone. 'Are you going to message your sponsor back?'

'I was going to. That's why I had the message open. It's an old one, though. I've left it too long – support is supposed to be a two-way street, that's what they always say at group. I haven't been the best partner. Wouldn't blame Dave if he's paired himself with someone else by now. Right now, giving up feels like a good option.'

Grace wheels a chair around beside Peter and sits in it. 'You can't give up now. Not after all your hard work. We all need you.'

Peter pulls off his glasses with force and swipes at his eyes before returning them to his nose. He looks briefly at Grace and she can see from his face that his shutters are back down. Closed for business. She had forgotten how prickly he can become after opening up.

'What are you doing out of bed this early, anyway?' he says.

'Couldn't sleep after that meeting. Kept thinking about some of those fundraising ideas the residents were coming up with and thought I'd come down and do some research. See if I could come up with something to help.'

Peter's jaw visibly stiffens. 'Uh huh.' He plucks a file from the filing cabinet, opens it on the desk in front of him and picks up a pen.

'What does that mean?'

'Nothing. Just think it's bloody cruel, that's all. Letting them think they're in with a chance of raising ten thousand pounds in so little time. How the hell are they going to do that?'

'Not *they. Us.* We all need to work together.' Grace pulls Jack's file away whilst he's still writing, and a long line of ink gets struck across his 'Smart Goals' section. 'What are you doing, anyway?'

'Just getting Jack's files up to scratch. I've got a bit behind,' Peter mumbles. 'If I leave or this place closes down, it's only fair on Jack that all his notes are in order.

'I wish the inspectors could have seen how dedicated you are to your clients. When the files aren't up to date, the work we do doesn't always show through.' Grace's voice is quiet but the wistfulness in it echoes across the room.

He snatches the file back from Grace and stomps to the filing cabinet, flinging it open. The metal door crashes loudly as it bounces back against the office wall and Peter and Grace stand still in the silence that follows.

'Peter, I'm sorry. I didn't mean… '

'Just forget it. Okay? Just – forget it. I know my client files weren't up to date, and I know that didn't help.' Peter slams the cabinet shut again, swipes his phone from the desk and heads for the door. 'This fundraising shit, though – just keep me out of it. You might be happy keeping everyone's heads in the bloody clouds with yours but I'm not interested.'

'I just think we can buy them some time.' Grace's eyes sting with tears. 'Having something practical to do will keep their spirits up,' she carries on. 'It will stop them focussing on the problem and get them focussed on the solution.'

'For once, Grace, would you just stop with all that positive thinking bullshit and come back to earth,' Peter snarls before storming out of the office.

It's just getting light when Grace heaves herself out of the office chair and makes her way to the café. Her mind is full of worries about Peter. What if he has a slip and buys alcohol after all?

He wouldn't have meant to speak to her like that; the struggle with addiction can play havoc with a person's mood and she remembers how he had been when he first moved into St Jude's.

Has Grace just made everything worse? She can't even go after him as there's no one to watch the hostel and there's too much to do in the café.

She tries to find calm in the quiet of the morning as she starts the prep for the day's bake sale. She's still weighing the flour when she hears the door open behind her, the one that stands between the hostel and the café.

'Thought you'd be up early today.' Jack looks tired but carries his smile and his dimples along as he walks towards Grace.

Heat floods her face and she turns back to her mixing bowl, slowing her breathing in an attempt to look normal. Grace's heart thumps faster when Jack's arms fall gently around her waist and she leans back into him, still not trusting herself to look him in the face.

'I was worried about you after the meeting yesterday,' he murmurs into her ear. 'You looked so upset when you told us about the funding, even though I know you half expected it. Thought you might come and see me last night. I kept listening out for a knock on my door.'

Grace covers Jack's hand with her own. 'I wanted to.

I thought about it. But I couldn't – not after last time, I'm still so embarrassed.' She tries to laugh but it comes out as more of a squeak. 'I feel like I've done enough off-loading onto you, you've got enough going on without listening to my woes all the time.'

Jack moves his fingertips over her forearm in long, gentle strokes. 'I came to see if you needed an extra pair of hands. With getting all this ready,' he adds, still not letting go of her. 'It's great that you're trying. It's the right thing to do, whether we raise the money or not.'

'Thanks, Jack,' she whispers. She twists herself around in his arms and puts her arms around Jack's shoulders. His body is warm against hers and his mouth is only inches away. Without taking her eyes away from his, she begins to close the gap between them as the café fades away.

Until the door handle squeaks.

Grace jumps away from Jack as if he's made of needles. Her head darts towards the door as Peter enters the room. He doesn't smile.

'Jack, would you mind popping back in half hour? I need a word with Grace.'

'What do you want?' she asks once Jack has left the room. The edginess from earlier has left her voice and so has the pleading. Now she's just drained. What *does* he want? To apologise? To confront her about Jack? Grace tries to still her racing mind, frazzled from lack of sleep.

'I just came to see if you wanted a hand – with the baking.'

Grace looks at Peter for a long second before handing him the packet of flour. He takes it and gets another mixing bowl from the bottom cupboard. He walks to the larder and starts pulling out cake ingredients.

'I don't blame you, you know. For the inspection,' Grace says in a low voice, not taking her eyes away from the dough that she's kneading.

Peter puts a bowl on the scales and starts scooping caster sugar into it. 'I'll help,' he says. 'With the fundraising. Whatever you need.'

Grace turns her head around and nods at him. 'You can hold the fort and clean up the kitchen whilst we're out selling today. Hazel will be here later to do the writing workshop and I don't want her walking into a mess.'

'You're the boss.'

'Yes, I am,' Grace says, and she almost smiles.

CHAPTER 23

Grace

GRACE IS ATTEMPTING TO coordinate the pastry production line with military precision. Not an easy task when the café is bursting with bodies. Almost every resident is up and about and squished around the worktop; kneading dough or sprinkling cakes in preparation for part one of the *Save St Jude's* initiative. Energy levels are high as they discuss the day's plan to corner all the hotspots of Dover and tempt the locals into buying their delicious home-cooked goodies.

'Mmm. That smell is incredible,' Jack grins as he swivels back into the kitchen, lightly brushing his fingers across the small of Grace's back as he passes.

She flinches and throws him a warning glare from the side of her face. Her nerves are still recovering from earlier. Peter had come so close to catching her with her arms draped around Jack and her mind has been spiralling ever since.

'I've just had a phone call,' Jack says, his eyes shining. 'The interview I had with that building company. I only went and got it!' He catches hold of Grace's hands before dropping them again as if they were made of lava.

Grace's chest squeezes with pride. She wants to fling her

arms around him and jump up and down with excitement. 'That's great.' She beams at him, instead. 'We're *all* so proud of you, and I'm sure you will be excellent at it. Can you tell me the rest later? I really do want to hear more about it, but we just need to get today sorted.'

The sparkle fades from Jack's eyes as if he'd had a power cut. He steps back and starts fiddling with the zip on his hoody.

'Finished!' Dawn triumphs after she's added a strawberry slice to the cream topping of her last cupcake. 'We're going to rake in a fortune. Where are we all going to start? I think each team should have a competition to see who flogs the most… like on *The Apprentice*.'

Grace feels a pang of self-hatred for shutting Jack down but she can't help but smile. Dawn's enthusiasm is always infectious, she has a way of making people feel like anything is possible and she's grateful to have her on the team – if only for the boost to morale, she adds to herself as she glances at the precarious slants on the tops of Dawn's cakes.

Grace pairs Dawn with Cara. They get on well and Grace has seen for herself how much Dawn tries to keep the younger woman out of trouble. She decides to keep them away from the park for obvious reasons and stations them down at the harbour.

After most of the other staff and residents are partnered up and allocated patches to sell on, Grace puts herself with Paul who's just sauntered through the door and agreed to be involved in something for once. She suggests they try the bottom of Market Square to catch the Saturday morning shoppers. Today needs to go well, and they need to sell, sell, sell.

'So, I'm suddenly not good enough to be partnered with?' Jack mumbles into her ear. He says it with a chuckle, but it's a hollow one, and the pink stains above his cheekbones let Grace know he's super pissed off. Grace's throat tightens and her limbs tingle as the reality of the fire she's been playing with continues to seep in. Jack has played a main part in almost all her thoughts this week, co-starring only with the hostel and how the hell to keep it open. It feels like an arm is missing when he's not around. She wishes he wasn't the one person who could make her feel better through the shiny shit-show that appears to be her life lately.

Silent accusations call from the darker parts of her mind and she tries to drown them out by scoffing a cherry Bakewell. No, she isn't using him – is she? Yes, she has a duty of care towards him. Yes, he's still a resident, but does that even matter if he's leaving soon? No, she hasn't been clinging to him just to make herself feel better.

What if his feelings towards Grace are as real as hers are for him? It's not as if this thing they have, whatever that might be, could ever actually go anywhere, at least not until Jack has moved out. She'd lose her job for one thing, not to mention her reputation. And then what would Mother Dearest think? Dad would have been appalled too, if he was still alive, but he wouldn't have been able to get any words in between Mum's repetitions of *I'm just disappointed, that's all. Just disappointed.*

She shivers and tries to shake out some of the negativity. No time for wallowing today; there's too much at stake. What is she thinking, standing around fretting about her love life? *Selfish, Grace, Selfish.* More important things are at stake. People die each week on the streets without shelter. From the cold, from the heat and from illness. From drugs and from violence and poor nutrition. She can't let that happen to their lot.

She tries to push away the quieter voice. The one that reminds her how much money they actually need to raise. Peter's words from the night before ricochet around her mind. He may have apologised – in his own way – but maybe he was right. Perhaps this is all a massive waste of time and custard pies. But it might just help her to claw back some precious time before she thinks of something else.

The hostel needs to be saved. And for that to happen, she needs to believe that it can. As Pinterest had told her several days ago, *Negativity is the enemy of creativity*.

'Right you lot, grab your goodies and let's go, let's go, let's go,' Grace yells like a football coach right before a premiership game.

Jack picks up a tray of gingerbread with a little more force than is necessary, sending a man-shaped cookie hurtling to the floor, snapping off one of the legs on impact.

'Three-second rule.' Teardrop Terry scoops it straight up, shoving it right into his mouth.

Jack doesn't look back at Grace as he strides out of the door followed by Terry, who leaves a trail of gingerbread crumbs in his wake.

Grace looks around for the others. Dawn and Cara are just specks on the horizon. Dawn had been keen to go and get started as quickly as possible and had left only seconds after Paul arrived.

It's a busy morning in Dover town centre, and to Grace's amazement, she and Paul have completely sold out after only an hour and a half.

Grace takes out her work mobile phone and calls St Jude's café. She wants to show off and rub it in Peter's face. He'd been wrong to say it would be a disaster.

There's no answer. When she hangs up, a text from Jack/ Room 4 appears on her screen, making her stomach twist. Jack shouldn't be sending messages to her on the work mobile. What if Peter or one of the other staff members had seen it?

Sorry I stomped off. I really need to speak to you. I'll be in the White Stag. Ps: We sold all our cookies. Mostly good feedback but some of the park customers requested space cakes next time.

Grace slides her phone back into her pocket and turns to Paul, trying to think of a polite way of losing him so she can go to the pub without him trailing behind.

'Better get back to the ship!' She opens her smile up as widely as possible.

Paul mock-salutes her before turning to go. Just as Grace's fingertips find her mobile to tell Jack she's on her way, Paul has swivelled back around again and taken a step towards her.

'Before you go,' he says as a frown falls across his freckled face. 'I was hoping we could have a quick chat about that Dawn in number six. I probably should have mentioned this before, but she seems really frightened of me. The other day she said something about my red hair. How it had been following her around for over twenty years. She said I'd been getting away with it for too long, but she was onto me.'

'That's odd. I'll talk to her. I think she sometimes gets a bit confused.'

'Well, yes. Twenty years ago, I was two years old. The only person I followed around then was my big brother.'

Grace is dizzy by the time she arrives at the White Stag. Her head has been spinning the whole way there with thoughts of Jack. His lips, his arms.

His support plan. Her duty of care. How close they'd come to being caught by Peter.

By the time she finds Jack sitting in the back of the pub in the darkest corner, she's struggling to string a sentence together.

'You managed to tear yourself away then.' Jack sounds agitated, his face is paler than usual and his hand wobbles, spilling drops from his drink on the table in front of him as he lifts half a pint of Pepsi to his lips.

'I'm sorry,' she says as she sidles in next to him on the wooden bench, an instant spark jolting between them as her thigh brushes against his. Grace shuffles back again a few inches. She won't go into the ins and outs of why she's kept him waiting. It's her job to worry about Dawn and the others, not his, and blurring the professional boundaries between them is exactly what has got them into this mess.

'I shouldn't have stormed off like that in front of everyone this morning,' he says, peeling at a beer mat. 'It's just you didn't even look at me earlier, not even when I told you about my job, and then you jumped away from me every time I went anywhere near you – like I had something you didn't want to catch.'

'Jack,' Grace begins.

'I know it's complicated. I know about the rules and that you could lose your job. I don't want that to happen either, but I don't want to ignore what we have between us.'

Grace remembers the two mugs from Jack's room and how only one of them was being used until that first night they spent together in the residents' lounge. She thinks about how far he's come since he moved to St Jude's. How his defences and his anger has fizzed away, dissolving bit by bit. And now he even has a job. She shouldn't distract him from rebuilding his life.

But he's been left so many times by people who had promised to love him. Grace knows what that tastes like. How could she make him go back to one mug?

Because if she doesn't do it now, it will be so much harder later on. *For both of them.*

'We need to put the past couple of weeks behind us,' she says in a low voice, as if the whole of St Jude's board of trustees is standing in the next room, listening through pint glasses they've pressed against the wall. 'It's for the best. I'm your hostel manager. Your point of call for housing-related support along with Peter. And that's the way things have to stay.'

Jack shakes his head and stares intently at the ice cubes at the bottom of his glass. 'I know you feel this… thing we have between us. You're just too scared to take a chance on it, because, God forbid, it just might make you happy.'

Grace winces as Jack slams his empty glass back down on the table. She sucks back the tears that are stinging her eyes as they stick to her mascara. *The hostel must come first.*

'I'm not even going to be a resident forever. If you can look at me, straight on without blinking and tell me you don't want us to be together, I'll drop it. I'll go back to being the resident in number four and never bother you again unless it's to tell you my toilet's leaking, the laundry room is still locked or that I'm moving out.'

Grace locks eyes with the only man who's ever made her feel like she matters.

'I do care about you, Jack, but in a professional capacity. I care because it's my job.' The coldness in her voice ricochets from the corner of the walls in front of her and freezes her in place.

She watches the wall rebuild itself in front of Jack, rendering his eyes dull and empty. He shakes his head, gets to his feet and walks away for the second time that day.

The afternoon heat must have pulled every spare bead of sweat from Grace's back. She peels off her sticky summer cardigan and ties it around her waist as she strides up the path to the hostel, still swallowing back the tears. She'd taken the long way around. *More steps equal less stress.*

Apparently.

The creative writing workshop must be running over time, as Grace can see the back of Hazel's head and an outline of two other bodies huddled around a table in the café through the window. She looks back across the sea, willing it to wash away some of the guilt and disappointment. The cover of her diary says, *Better to regret something you did than something you didn't do.* Actually, regret seems to come and bite you on the arse either way.

Grace feels her work smile crawl across her face as she opens the door to the café. 'Hi everyone.' Her voice sounds normal. Happy, even. How long had she been putting on this mask that now moulds to her so easily?

'You're back!' Peter sounds excited. Peter never sounds excited. His face is flushed and his eyes are sparkling behind his thick lenses. Grace remembers his anger from last night and worry pricks at her as the word *relapse* flickers across her mind. But he looks focussed and his speech is clear. He and Hazel are bent over a sheet of A3 and a set of marker pens.

'Now, this looks like my kind of party,' grins Grace before slipping into an empty chair next to Teardrop Terry. 'I didn't know you went to writing group.'

'Writing group's over,' Terry says. 'We just thought we may as well crack on with the fundraising.'

'Hazel's agreed to give us a hand,' Peter explains.

Grace sees the glint in his eye and suppresses a knowing grin.

'Wait till you hear what we've all come up with.' Terry's teardrop looks at odds with his wide, cheesy grin.

Grace looks at the three of them, pens in hand, and hopes they'll forgive her for wasting their time when it's all over. She's pleased they want to help, and that they're excited, but whatever their ideas are, it just won't be enough to raise the kind of money they need.

'Thanks for stepping in,' she says to Hazel.

'This was a group effort,' Hazel waves her words away. 'And it's my pleasure. Holding my workshop here is the highlight of my week. Such a creative bunch. Even Peter joined in earlier.'

'I did!' Peter rubs his hands together. 'And I'm coming back next week too. I don't know why I've never taken part before.'

'What do you think?' Terry slides the paper across the table so it's in front of Grace. A long list of ideas is written in black marker pen, and one of them has been bubbled in with squiggly pink ink.

'We thought we could do a midnight walk around Dover – all the way up to the castle and back. We're going to advertise on Facebook, link it to our JustGiving page… '

'Amazing. Love it.' Another image comes into Grace's mind

as she pictures the residents hiking round the very streets they used to sleep on. She sees them lined up in sleeping bags under doorways.

'And I've got another idea,' Grace says, slapping the table. She thinks about the mountains of paperwork, the red tape, the risk assessments she'll have to get written up. She looks at Dawn's smiling face from across the table, remembering what she'd said in her keyworking meeting. *You can make anything happen if you hope hard enough*. She picks up the marker pen and writes it down as everyone crowds around the table to watch what she adds to the sheet of paper.

Sponsored Sleepout.

Cheers and whistles break out and everyone starts talking at once as they throw and catch ideas between them across the table. Grace looks out through the glass at the vibrant colours of the tea garden; the pinks and purples of the hydrangeas. Getting the outside areas up to scratch had seemed like an impossible task too before they'd got started. As the sun's rays shoot through the window and rest across Grace's shoulders, she realises her mask has melted. And it turns out there was a real smile under there after all.

'Well, I'm off to find some sleeping bags,' Terry announces before getting up from the table. 'I think there's a few of them in the storage cupboard downstairs.'

Peter and Hazel both thank him before rushing to get back to their conversation. They're onto books now. The ones they love, the ones they hate. Grace didn't know Peter even liked reading. She slips out of her chair and heads back to the kitchen. It's sure to be a right mess from the bake sale prep and Peter's clearly been otherwise engaged.

'How about Francine's again?' Grace hears Hazel say behind her. 'We could meet there on purpose this time – I'm free tonight? Or a curry? Curry's my favourite, but either would be fine.'

'Actually… ' Peter begins.

Grace's heart lifts as she reaches the counter and plonks herself behind it. The nosy part of her had wanted to stay and listen, but she'll leave them to it and squeeze the gossip from Hazel another time. A twinge of envy pulls at her as she imagines having the freedom to ask Jack on a proper date without worrying about who could be watching.

Peter, though? Grace can't help smiling again as she fills the sink with washing up. If grumpy Pete can find love, there's hope for anyone.

She's getting a tea towel from the drawer when Peter walks past, knocking over a stack of recyclable takeaway cups on his way to the coffee machine.

'So. Date night then. Where are you going to take her?' Grace sings in a teasing voice. She can wind him up for days with this one.

Peter struggles with the coffee filter and bashes the side of the unit. 'Bloody machine. I only want a bloody coffee.' He mutters. 'And there's not going to be a date. Told her I'm too busy.'

'You… you did what?' Grace whips around from the draining rack, towel in one hand and a dripping mixing bowl in the other. 'What did you tell her that for?'

'You're getting that everywhere.' Peter points to the soap suds swimming across the floor around Grace's feet. 'It's just not a good idea, that's all. You saw how I was last night. I just don't think I'm ready for another relationship after what happened with my Jenny. And then there's the fundraising. What if we go out and it all goes tits up? She might not want to help us then, and it'll be my fault.'

'Listen, Pete.' Grace dabs at the floor with the soggy dish-cloth, ignoring Peter's disapproving glare before chucking it across the room to the laundry basket. 'You need to grab happiness whenever it comes past, otherwise it just keeps moving, leaving you cold and empty.' The tap's still dripping, they must get that fixed. Jack's face appears at the front of her mind. His face in the pub when she'd told him they were over. Grace gives herself a shake and tightens the cold side until it plops more slowly. 'The point is, you deserve love. Hazel deserves love. The fundraising is important, and so is this place. But you have to think of your happiness. Of a future with love in it. Go after her.'

Peter stares back at her with a blank face. 'You don't half talk some shit sometimes, Grace.' But he unplugs the coffee machine and runs from the café, banging the door behind him. Grace watches through the window as he catches up with Hazel along the clifftop, all the way up by the lighthouse. *Looks like your boat's come in, Pete.*

CHAPTER 24

Dawn

FOR THE THIRD NIGHT in a row, Dawn strolls along the clifftop at midnight. It had been too hot to lie in bed and her thoughts were far too loud in the silence of her room. She can manage them better out here. They feel smaller against the expanse of the sea, the lights from the boats below.

It's been a busy day, and it's hard to switch off sometimes. As soon as she'd got back into her room after the brainstorming session and the bake sale this morning, she'd given a sample selection of the day's cakes and pastries to Shaun. He told her he liked Dawn's the best. Lovely boy, that Shaun. She'd then sent another Facebook message to Rosie before leaving, telling her all about the bake sale and how next time she saw her, she'd make her one of her special scones; she's getting quite good at them now.

She's almost reached her favourite bench, but someone is sitting on it.

'Peter – I thought it was you!' Dawn had heard him and Grace talking earlier about Peter taking Hazel on a date tonight. Looking at the state of him, it looks as if it didn't happen or it didn't go according to plan.

Peter is shivering in his corduroys and keeps shuffling from one side to the next.

Dawn plonks herself next to him. They sit in silence for a long time. Dawn enjoys the peace for a little while, but then it gets awkward, especially when he gives up on hiding the drink inside his coat and is now holding it out in front of himself like a bomb.

'Are you going to drink that?' Dawn asks, breaking into the silence.

The wind is getting up. The sound of the waves slapping the rocks below has been switched to surround sound.

'I'm not sure,' he says.

Dust from the ground below is being blown all over the lenses of Peter's glasses. He removes his frames with his one free hand.

'You want me to take it?' Dawn asks, looking at the bottle. She throws him a smile, just a small one, and Peter releases his grip as she takes it gently from his hand.

'One of those days,' he says as he wipes his scratched-up glasses and returns them to the bridge of his nose.

'Yup. Guess we've all had them,' Dawn says. 'Looks like it's been a bit more than that for you, though.'

'Just been on a date with Hazel. Only she wanted to go to the pub. I'm not good with pubs and I ended up telling her why. That I'm an alcoholic. Thought she'd understand. I think I was wrong.'

'I'm sorry. Least you were honest. What did she say?'

'Not much. She didn't get up and leave or anything – she just went quiet. I'd forgotten how much this shit hurts when you give it an inch and let it rise to the surface. It's all my fault, that's all.' His voice sounds shaky. 'The inspection, the hostel… all of it. My fault.'

'How do you work that out? Grace told us they're taking money away from loads of places like St Jude's, all over the country. That your fault too?'

'No… but dating the inspector and managing to offend her in a hundred different ways probably didn't get us off to a good start.' Peter pushes his cold hands deep into his coat pockets.

'You dated the hostel inspector?' Dawn shouts over the wind as it blows past their ears.

'Not intentionally, and only once. Right before she assessed us. Stupid of me to even think about getting involved with a woman again. Especially after… well, before.'

Dawn shuffles back and settles further into the bench, pulling her coat tighter around her middle. 'What happened before?'

'I shouldn't really be talking to you about it, it's inappropriate. I'm sorry.' Peter shakes his head.

'I'm still holding the Jack Daniels that you were about to drink straight from the bottle on a freezing-arse bench on your own in the dark. Bit late to be worrying about your professional image if you ask me. Which I realise you didn't,' adds Dawn.

A chuckle falls from Peter. He starts slowly at first. Telling her about his early missions as a surgeon with Doctors Without Borders. The stress of working under pressure in dangerous situations with minimal resources. The buzz and the pride that came along for the ride with every soul he helped, every shift that made a difference. He tells her about meeting his fiancé, Jenny, for the first time and the fierce joy he'd felt when she joined him out in the Congo as a nurse on his team.

'Jenny was kidnapped?' Dawn asks, leaning forward when he gets to that bit. 'What do you mean, kidnapped? Did she come back?'

'Some of the local military groups didn't like it when we helped the enemy. DWB is impartial – they have to be. Sometimes people did extreme things to send the message that we weren't welcome in the area.'

Dawn lets out a long whistle as she breathes out.

'Luckily we found her alive – just. And she recovered in the end. She left nursing. I didn't blame her one bit. I stayed on for a while, but I kept getting these flashbacks. I couldn't stop them taking her, see, and I should've... I should've.' His breaths are getting jagged again. 'Things just went to shit after that,' he carries on. 'I got discharged from DWB and went back to working in Kent. General surgery. Just like before, except this time I had all these memories for company. And the only thing that could switch them off for a while was the booze.' He stops and looks at Dawn.

'That's when I really screwed up,' Peter plunges back in, telling Dawn about his memories. The flashes that come to him out of nowhere each day. The inside of a girl's chest cavity. Her hospital notes; the claret smudge in the corner by her name. Miss Leah Moat aged nine. His shaking hands. The severed aorta; blood can travel so very far.

'Some things you never come back from,' he whispers.

He describes the grey of Mr Moat's face. *They did every-thing they could.* The meetings and the hearings in the days that followed. The alcohol concentration in Peter's blood. *Just routine.* BAC levels point zero six three. *Increased impair-ment likely.*

'Hey,' Dawn says. She places her coat over Peter's thin jacket, and her arm across his shivering shoulders. Wheezing with tears, he surrenders his forehead to the crook of Dawn's shoulder and heaves against her with guttural sobs.

The ferry is making its way through the stone arch of the harbour now, the lights from its windows casting patterns on the inky waves below.

'Shit, I'm sorry.' Peter sniffs as he sits up, hooking his index finger under his glasses and poking at the skin below his eyes, soaking up the tears. 'You must be frickin' freezing.'

'I'm giving this back to you now,' says Dawn. 'I know you know what to do.' She leans over to her side of the bench and hands him the bottle she's retrieved from the ground.

The cap pops as it opens, and the dirt below makes a fizzing sound as it receives the first few drops of the bottle's contents. The rest is poured on the grass, an oaky smell filling the air as droplets splash back onto Dawn's shoes.

'Thank you,' Peter says, quietly. 'Think I'll go back to my support group at the community centre tomorrow morning. I've not been for months.'

'Want me to come with you?' Dawn hopes he'll say yes. Her and Cara have usually finished with their morning coffee runs on the seafront and the park by 9 a.m. and she likes to fill her mornings with interesting things to do.

Peter shuffles his feet and stares at his shoes. 'Normally I'd say no thanks. You're a resident and it doesn't feel fair for you to have to listen to all my stuff. But Grace is working and you've already heard the worst of it.'

'Count me in. And if being at St Jude's has taught me anything,' says Dawn, 'it's that you need to find your tribe.

The rest of the journey's not designed to be a solo one. Group tickets always offer the best value.'

After speaking with Peter on the cliffs last night, Dawn had gone to sleep with the type of glow that comes along whenever she's helped someone. She'd woken feeling refreshed and is enjoying the warm sea breeze on her skin as she trundles down the hill from St Jude's to meet Peter.

Peter is already standing outside the community centre when Dawn gets there, shuffling his feet and cleaning his glasses.

'Ready to go in?' Dawn asks him.

The hall is just as draughty as it had been the last time Dawn had set foot in there with Cara, this time last week. A few of the faces are the same but there are plenty of new ones. The circle of people around her is larger and even more eclectic than before. It's rarely like the films or the TV documentaries about crack addicts who experience miraculous religious conversions and become vicars or self-help book authors. Mostly it's just people like Pat from the post office.

Dawn takes a sideways glace at Peter. His eyes keep flittering around the circle, probably sizing up the newbies and see what they're about, but without making any actual eye contact. He's already admitted to Dawn how terrified he is about being asked to blurt out his name and addiction of choice, especially after so many months away from them.

The woman opposite Dawn is blabbing through words that are difficult to decipher. Grey circles sit under her eyes in stark contrast to her pale face. Lank hair falls to her underweight shoulders.

'Thank you so much for sharing with us, Candy.' The facilitator serves her a sweet smile, albeit with a side of patronising.

Candy? There's no way that's her real name. Dawn bites into the stale rich tea that had been thrust upon them when they'd first sat down.

'And it's wonderful to see you back again. Would you like to introduce yourself to the group?'

Dawn has a mouth full of cloying crumbs that she can't seem to swallow, and even if she could, her mind had gone so blank she can barely remember her name. Maybe she should make one up too. She could call herself Destiny or Chlamydia. Perhaps she could be a famous rock star who turned to Class As when the pressure of success got too much. After all she probably *would* have been hugely successful in the music industry, had she been able to carry on with her piano lessons.

Peter nudges her, causing her to choke violently on a biscuit crumb that somehow catapults out of her mouth and into the circle along with a glob of her saliva. Dawn realises through her red-hot flush that the leader-woman hadn't even been speaking to her, but to Peter.

He clears his throat and Dawn steals a glance at him, a proper one. He looks terrified and is studying the shiny parquet flooring of the community centre as if it holds the words he's supposed to say.

Dawn gives Peter's hand a squeeze and watches as he stares sobriety in its ugly face and takes his first step for the second time.

'My name is Peter,' he starts, before talking about his life before he got sober. About how Grace had been the one to get him there a year ago. He describes the chaos that his life had been in, and how he'd begun to ache for feelings that hadn't been manufactured in a countryside brewery. He explains how much it had sucked at first, baring his soul to a group of strangers. But it had got easier over time, he'd even started to look forward to it. Then he'd got his job at St Jude's and that had taken over his time and his energy. His sobriety, now, he admits, is on borrowed time. He's tried to play solo but the road through recovery is narrow and oh, so slippery.

'Thank you for sharing this morning.' The group leader smiles at Peter and Dawn during 'tea and biscuits' time after the meeting. 'It's great to have you back.'

'Well, I might be a screw-up and I've caused no end of shit to fly from my life and land across everybody else's. But if I keep myself on the straight and narrow, I can at least make up for just a tiny part of it.' Peter smiles at Dawn. 'Plus, one of my good friends has dared me to believe there might be hope on the other side.'

CHAPTER 25

Dawn

AS SOON AS DAWN arrives back at St Jude's from the community centre, Grace rushes out from the office door and hovers in front of her.

'I tried to catch you yesterday after the bake sale, but then we all got distracted with the fundraising plans and you seemed in a rush to leave this morning.'

Dawn says nothing. She can't let her know where she'd been going; Peter might get into trouble for allowing her to go along.

'You're not in trouble,' Grace says. 'We just wanted to check you're okay. One of the other residents mentioned you've been feeling a little anxious about things that have been happening in your room,' Grace says.

Peter arrives at the hatch beside her, he'd gone on ahead of Dawn after the group session so he could give Grace a hand in the office.

The bubble of safety and belonging that Dawn had felt since going to the group with Peter pops in an instant. Cold creeps across her arms as she remembers the fear. Who had told? Does someone want her out? She shouldn't have let herself feel safe, not even for a moment. Complacency is the enemy when it comes to hiding from danger, that's why she always keeps moving. It's not only herself she needs to keep safe – what if he finds Rosie?

A single sob echoes around the foyer, bouncing right back at Dawn. The words start sliding around in her ears again, quiet at first, getting louder and louder as they gain momentum. *Tell anyone, and I will kill you.* His red hair burns brightly in her mind. Everything in this hostel is just so damn noisy. People's voices, mixing together like an untuned orchestra. Footsteps behind her make slow clapping sounds across the cheap laminate. Heat is crawling up her body and burning her up from the inside.

'I think someone's been threatening me. Trying to show me that if I don't leave soon then I'll be trapped here and found.'

'Someone has said those actual words?' Grace says slowly as she places an armful of paperwork back on her desk, glancing sideways at Peter who continues to look at Dawn, waiting for her answer.

'Well, no. No one has used any "actual words",' Dawn says, fighting to keep the impatience from her voice by drawing inverted bunny ears in the air with her fingers. 'The man who's after me doesn't need to. He's probably one of those types of men – those *actions-speak-louder* kind. He has red hair. I did think it might be Paul from room one, but his voice isn't the same. Whoever the man is wants me gone from here so he can get me. He's been in my room, put bars on my window and laid the fire blanket over my bed.'

'Why would anyone do that?' Peter's nose is all crinkled up.

'To show me that I'm trapped. That he has control over me.'

209

'Right,' says Peter slowly, fiddling with his chin dimple. Dawn knew he wouldn't believe her. No one ever does when you have words like 'Puerperal Psychosis', 'Bipolar' and 'prone to psychotic episodes' written on the medical history section of your file.

'And the fire blanket is a death threat – to show that he could suffocate me in my sleep if he wanted to. I can prove it,' she adds, hearing the desperation in her own voice. 'I have the days and times written down. If you check the CCTV, you will see him coming in and out of my room. Then you'll know.'

Peter and Grace look at each other for a long moment as if weighing up whether or not to give into the demands of a mad woman.

'We'll go through the feeds now,' promises Grace. 'And we'll take it from there.'

Grace is merely placating her at this stage, Dawn knows, but once she sees the evidence, she'll know the truth. And then she and Rosie will be safe.

Hopefully.

'There is one more thing I need to tell you,' Dawn mumbles, looking at her Shoe Zone flip-flops. She can't recall how much they were. She tries to remember, but her memories are sleeping. 'I have been breaking a hostel rule. A big one, I'm afraid. I've been letting someone stay in my room. He's been no trouble, and I completely understand if you want to kick me out, but all that I ask is that you give the room to him. He really needs it.'

'Let's just wait and see after we've looked at it, eh?' Grace opens the office door and beckons Dawn through. The dull roar of the hatch closing reverberates around her ears and she feels as if she's at the bottom of a deep pool.

Dawn perches wordlessly on the stool next to the CCTV monitor as Grace fiddles with the controls and Peter adjusts the rows of pens in his drawer in order of size and colour. She tells Grace the dates and times to start looking for. She'd written them down, but there was no need to check her notebook as they'd permanently inked themselves onto the front of her mind.

'Here we are.' Grace presses play with a flourish, seeming to forget she's not popping on a boxset they've all been looking forward to watching.

As soon as the screen comes to life, Grace appears on it at Dawn's door armed with three metal bars. She places a toolbox at her feet and pops the bars into the crook of her elbow as she fiddles with a huge bunch of keys in her other hand.

'Head office asked me to do that, honey,' Grace says in a quiet voice.

Dawn winces at her sympathetic use of 'honey'. The girl is almost half her age after all.

'It's the new building regulations. It's for health and safety. Your own health and safety. It's to do with how wide the windows can open,' Grace carries on.

'Cara's not got any,' Dawn barks.

'Cara's on the ground floor.'

Oh.

'Is it in case I jump out of it or something?'

Grace and Peter must get so bored with each other's faces. They seem to look at each other every time Dawn says something lately.

'Well. Okay. Fair enough about the bars. But you haven't seen the next one yet – the day with the fire blanket.'

Peter picks up a remote control and Grace tells him the next day and time Dawn has given her.

It's weird seeing yourself on a TV screen. Dawn had probably had more than her fair share of chances to see herself on CCTV, but it still shocks her every time. When did her arms become like twigs? The sharp hollows of her cheeks look positively zombie-like. And when did she get so old? She's like an extra in *The Walking Dead*. Teardrop Terry had been watching that all week in the resident's lounge. CCTV-Dawn closes the door to number six behind her and looks around her shoulder before creeping past the camera.

Dawn's heart begins to skitter as she realises that any second now, Shaun will be seen on the screen. Remorse pricks at her. By doing this, she's probably increasing his chances of having to sleep on the street tonight. At least he'll have her for company this time, Dawn guesses. It's the only way though, she can't let *him* win this one. The minutes tick by one after the other until she sees the back of her lime-green top on the screen, hanging off her shoulders.

CCTV-Dawn reappears, opening the door again and entering before slamming it shut, leaving the image still and devoid of anything to look at apart from the door with the number six on it.

'There must be a mistake. You must have put in the wrong date. The wrong time.' But Dawn knows that was the only day she'd worn that green top since she'd moved in.

'There was a health and safety inspection that morning,' Grace says, suddenly. 'We always check the fire blankets as part of that. I expect Lorna knocked it down and it blew onto your bed in the wind. Perhaps you just didn't notice it until the afternoon?'

'Maybe,' Dawn murmurs.

The culprit wasn't the only one missing from the CCTV feed.

'Who was it you said you'd had staying in your room?' asks Grace.

Bugger.

'Shaun Michaels.' In for a penny, in for a pound.

Grace's eyes widen, and she switches the power off at the monitor before placing a gentle hand on Dawn's shoulder. Peter has finished lining up his stationery yet again and closes the drawer with a bang.

'I think you must have got that wrong, Dawn,' says Grace. 'Shaun Michaels is dead. He was found in the park toilets the day after you moved in.'

CHAPTER 26

Dawn

TOO MANY PEOPLE ARE crowded around Dawn's bed. She got carried there because she collapsed in the foyer an hour ago. Room 6 is small. It's not designed for staff members and people in uniform to stand in; it's only just big enough for Dawn and Shaun. Shaun. Mustn't mention Shaun again, not to these people. Grace has shown Dawn a newspaper, full of details. Too many details. Next of kin have been informed. Someone needs to let them know it was all a lie. Dawn knows it was all a lie because Shaun's still there, in her room where she'd left him this morning, behind all of all those concerned faces staring over her. Can't they see him?

There's been whispered talk about 'survivor's guilt', and lots of rummaging through Dawn's medication packets. Apparently, they are all well out of date and most of the blisters are still full.

'Ah,' Peter had said. As if that explained everything.

Grace has been speaking to the ones in uniform, using words that are to do with hospitals. They aren't proper uniforms, just the clothes of the smart–casual brigade. The ones that try to portray the right balance of being 'approachable' – *Hey, we're just like you guys!* – but smart enough to lay deep foundations for the 'professional boundaries'. If you asked Dawn, it would be far simpler if they just wore uniforms; at least that way everyone knows where they stand.

'No ward spaces at the moment,' one of them mutters. 'There hasn't been any for ages. Funding cuts, you know how it is.'

Grace raises an eyebrow. Yes, she knows exactly how it is.

Somehow, Dawn becomes part of a conversation about making a deal. She consents to an injection to help her feel better and agrees to another one in a month's time. That way, apparently, she'll avoid having to go to a psychiatric ward. She feels a little short-changed by this deal given she already knows there are no beds, but she goes along with it anyway. It's the least she can do after putting all these people through so much bother on a Friday afternoon. Other words get thrown around the room. Words about care plans, therapy waiting lists, risk management. Dawn's grateful for the concern, she really is, but all she wants is for everyone to leave so she can talk with Shaun and go to sleep as they ramble on about their days, just like they usually do.

Then everyone does leave; everyone except one of the uniforms. She opens her briefcase and takes out a syringe as she explains to Dawn about the benefits and the risks of the stuff she's about to jab into her thigh. Dawn doesn't hear much of it, probably because seeing her take the vial out of her briefcase is reminding her of a *Resident Evil* film she'd seen where the characters injected themselves with an anti-zombie vaccine.

She barely feels the 'sharp scratch' she's been warned about, but she does feel the warmth pooling in the top of her left leg.

The woman stays with Dawn for a while, and she stretches her legs out, lying on her side along the length of her bed. The breeze from the open window makes her shiver and the woman manoeuvres the duvet from under her, draping it over her body until it covers her shoulders. Her lids begin to feel heavy, and she experiences a sensation of long-ago déjà vu. Dawn's dad used to be able to make her feel safe and calm like this, whenever he tucked her in. Often, she would already be in bed by the time he'd get in from work. Mum was never the type to read stories; she would usually be in bed even before Dawn was, sallow-faced and puffy-eyed, even if she'd only been up for a few hours during the afternoon. It was Dad who had taken her to school on her first day. Dad who wiped away her tears when Bobby Carter tripped her up during her dance show.

The door clicks shut, and Dawn opens one eye, realising she must have begun to nod off. The room is empty now. She searches each corner with her eyes, hoping to see Shaun. She sees something flash by the window, but by the time she focusses her eyes in that direction she can see nothing but the sea, the sky and the trees. The seagulls are making their usual racket and Dawn concentrates on the *caw* sounds, unclenching her toes and pulling her duvet up higher until it covers the nape of her neck. Small parts of her mind are still trying to fight their way forwards for attention. Where would Shaun sleep now? What if something happens to him and Dawn's not around to protect him? She still doesn't understand why they told her he was dead.

It's happening all over again; a small voice says. *It's because of the evil. You were warned not to tell, and you did. He was taken, just like Rosie. You couldn't protect her either.*

A tear trickles across the bridge of Dawn's nose and seeps into the lumpy pillow beneath her head.

Rosie. Where are you?

CHAPTER 27

THEN

Dawn

DAWN'S MIDWIFE HAD TOLD her during their last appointment that she'd know when labour was starting. She'd believed her because she'd said it to so many women herself throughout her midwifery training. They'd sat down together on Dawn's blue and white stripy two-seater in the corner of their tiny living room, scribbling notes on her paperwork and creating a birth plan.

She could have a home birth if she'd wanted to, the midwife had told her. She was healthy, at a low risk of complications and it would mean the baby would be born in tranquil surroundings.

Dawn's not sure how their flat could be described as 'tranquil', not with all the banging about from the shop downstairs. The British Heart Foundation sells furniture as well as second-hand jeans and ancient Mills & Boon books, so there's often a delivery van parked outside with men shouting over each other as they load it up with various shades of pine, oak and fibreboard.

She smiles to herself as her little princess boots her in the ribcage. She reckons wherever she's born she's going to come out wearing a pair of Dr Martens. 'Just like her mum,' Rob had beamed when Dawn had mentioned her theory to him.

They don't know for sure they're having a girl; the baby had stubbornly refused to expose her genitalia to the sonographer at twenty weeks and Dawn hadn't blamed her one bit. But deep down, she *knows*.

Rob had been a little concerned when she'd mentioned a homebirth. 'What if something goes wrong?' he'd asked. 'Wouldn't it be better if there are doctors around in case there are any emergencies?'

Dawn had explained about the benefits of being at home; how they weren't far from a hospital if they needed to transfer. That she could put on her favourite CDs and scented candles. He'd ummed and ahhed, but Dawn could tell he wasn't convinced. He'll come around. All Rob ever wants is for Dawn to be happy. 'That boy thinks the bloody sun shines right out of your arse,' her friend, Mel, is always saying. Dawn usually tells her to shut up, but secretly thinks she's probably right.

And now she has a tiny human inside her that's half her and half him.

Hopefully.

Despite having studied the exact ins and outs of what is happening inside her uterus, she still shakes her head in disbelief every time she thinks about it. It may have happened sooner than they'd planned; they've only been together for two years, but it's a miracle, nonetheless.

Their miracle. Hers and Rob's, she tells herself.

Another kick, or possibly a punch this time, makes Dawn jump so much that she spills some milk from the bowl of her Crunchy Nut Cornflakes. She's almost ninety per cent sure that she's knocking to say she wants to come out. The twinge in her back comes back again, a bit stronger this time, and a small wave of anxiety laps at Dawn's feet. She gives herself a mental slap; she should be well prepared for this after spending all that time preparing women for what to expect during labour.

All those 'primip' women, having their first babies and worrying about whether they would get to hospital in time and what if they accidently gave birth in Tesco's or down the toilet? Dawn and her mentor would smile knowingly at each other and explain the early signs of the onset of labour and how, although it does happen, most births can take a fair amount of time, particularly first babies.

The truth is, Dawn doesn't think it's the birth itself that's scaring her. It's what happens afterwards. Is she ready to be a mother? She didn't exactly have the best role model and her own mum's not around at all anymore. A familiar stone of grief shifts in her gut when she thinks about her baby growing up without grandparents.

Rob had been in and out of care most of his life and it had been eleven years since Dawn had seen her dad. She wonders every day what her mum would have thought about Dawn having a baby. It's still only a year since her death. Liver failure brought on by years of alcohol abuse has robbed her baby of her only grandmother.

The pain has spread now; it's no longer just in her lower back, but along the bottom of her pelvis. Dawn glances at their wedding photo from eight months ago, the only one on the magnolia walls, shining in a brand new frame from the Woolworths branch that Rob manages. Perhaps she should call

Rob at work. But it's probably a false alarm; Braxton Hicks, happens all the time.

She picks her pregnancy notes up from the coffee table, staring at the number of her community midwife who also happened to have been Dawn's mentor throughout her three years of community placement. She considers calling her but she's worried about looking stupid. Dawn has trained for this after all.

The decision is taken out of her hands when the phone starts trilling away from its place on the wall at the top of the stairs.

'I think I'm okay,' Dawn tells Rob through the receiver. 'Just a bit crampy, but that's to be expected when I only have two weeks to go. Thanks for doing your daily check on me, though.' She smiles, glancing at her hospital holdall sitting patiently outside their bedroom door, plump and full, the material straining around the zip. She's checked it and re-packed it so many times that she's lost count. Another twinge makes her gasp, but it's over in seconds. Rob's heard enough and tells her he's on his way; he'll get his assistant manager to cover the shop floor. She's not phoning the midwife though; not yet. She runs herself a bath instead, pops her Norah Jones CD on loud and lights the candles she's balanced on top of the bathroom radiator.

She's leaning over to turn the cold tap on when it happens. A small pop and warm fluid seeps down the inside of her thighs. She doesn't have time to enjoy the frisson of excitement that trickles through her veins before the pain hits, almost knocking her off her feet. Dawn's abdomen has gone rock hard and she feels like she's being squeezed from every angle. It feels like it lasts forever, and just keeps getting stronger. When it does eventually begin to ease, she gives herself a wry smile, remembering how she'd been taught to use the word 'discomfort' rather than 'pain' when discussing labour with women and how some women preferred to say 'surges' rather than 'contractions'. If someone spoke to her right now about her 'discomfort', she thinks she'd want to punch them squarely in the vagina just so they could get a small idea of the 'discomfort' she was in.

A couple more tsunamis crash across the trunk of her body over the half hour it takes to hear Rob's key in the door. Another 'surge' hits her as his footsteps climb the stairs. He calls her name out as he rushes into the bathroom, finding her leaning over the basin. His hand grips hers and she sinks to her knees on the tiles, leaning her forehead against the edge of the porcelain bath. Then something changes, much more quickly than she's prepared for. The overwhelming need to push takes control of her and she's bearing down before she can stop herself. *Just breathe through it,* she can hear her own voice in her head, using words that she'd thrown in front of women countless times before. Rapid deliveries like this can happen, she just never thought it would happen to her.

'What are you doing?' Rob's voice is at least two octaves higher than it usually is, and Dawn opens her mouth to reassure him, even tell him that she probably just needs a poo, something she's never actually said to him yet, despite being two years into their marriage.

It doesn't matter in the end; she doesn't have time to say anything before she's pushing again.

'Shit,' she gasps when her contraction has ramped right back up. Dawn can feel a sudden burning down below and the pressure in her bottom is overwhelming.

'What. What?' Rob screeches, frantically pulling at her arm.

'You are going to have to get my trousers off,' she whispers, barely audibly. 'The baby's head is *right there.*'

'Oh shit.'

'Oh shit,' she manages to say before she has to push again. Somehow Rob manages to wrestle her black Mark One trousers down to her ankles and actually screams when he sees what Dawn can feel between her legs.

'Dawn, half the head's out. I can see the nose... and its top lip.'

'You. Need. To. Call. An. Ambulance.' Dawn forces the words through the gaps in her panting. Even through the panic, the pain and the knowledge that the baby's head had been in that position too long already without the chin popping out yet, she still wants to have a go at Rob for calling their baby 'it'.

'But I can't leave you on your own,' he wails. 'The phone's all the way out there.'

'Do it. Now. Now, Rob,' she says through gritted teeth.

After Rob flees from the room, Dawn places one foot up on the side of the bath as she'd encouraged other women to do when their babies' shoulders were stuck in the birth canal behind the pelvises of their mothers. She cups her hand gently over the damp curls of her baby's head and pants like a mad woman. An almighty contraction takes over her entire body and she cries out, keeping her hands ready beneath herself to catch her.

Nothing happens.

'Rob!' Dawn screams. She gingerly places her foot back on the floor before lowering herself to it. 'I'm going to lie flat on my back,' she tells him as he bursts back into the room. 'Then I need you to pull my knees right back to give the baby more room. She needs to come out and she needs to come out with this contraction. Do you understand?'

Rob has gone a strange shade of green. 'No. No, I don't understand any of it. What the hell is happening?' he shouts through tears.

'Calm the hell down, Rob, and hold my knee,' Dawn says through gritted teeth.

Rob looks around helplessly before nodding and grabbing the underside of Dawn's knees. 'Please say you're going to be okay. I'd die if anything happened to you,' he sobs. 'An ambulance is on its way. They wanted me to stay on the phone but then you called.'

'Don't worry about that. We can do this,' Dawn says as much to herself as to him. She closes her eyes tight and waits for the next contraction. She doesn't have to wait long. The new position has worked and as she pushes down, she feels her slide out. The pain is astronomical, but all Dawn can think about is her baby.

'Pass her to me,' she demands through her constricted throat, incredulous that Rob is holding their baby out in front of him like a football. Rob places her, face up on the lino, and scoots backwards until his back meets the wall and pushes into it as if wanting to go right through it and get far, far away. His face is the colour of fag ash and he won't look at Dawn, just at the child in front of them. The child who remains blue and very still.

To begin with, Dawn hadn't wanted to let Rosie go. The relief when she'd taken her first cry after Dawn had scooped her from the floor and rubbed her hard with their soft Debenhams towel had carried her through the first two days. She'd kept her close, smelled her hair and thanked God for keeping her safe. Dawn had barely let anyone near her, not even Rob. *Especially* not Rob.

Last night, though, Dawn had slept for hours. She gasps when she sees the time on the digital alarm clock on the bedside table. Day three of being a mum and she's already slept in. She looks immediately to the space on her right where the Moses basket should be and she jolts when it's not there. *She'll be fine. She's with Rob. She'll be fine,* she repeats to herself.

Dawn climbs out of bed and pulls on her jogging bottoms. She moves gingerly to the living room; her stitches still stinging as she walks, and heads straight to the Moses basket. She looks into the face of her baby. She takes in her bright eyes, her button nose, her adorable mouth.

She sees nothing of Rob.

Rosie starts kicking her legs. *Pick me up, Mummy. Play with me. Hold me in your arms.*

Dawn touches her baby's face with tenderness. She brushes her hand over Rosie's hair and pulls it away again as if burned.

Rosie's hair is turning red.

'See? She just wants her mummy.'

Dawn stays quiet. Nausea fills every part of her insides as the last nine months tear themselves into shreds like cheap ribbon in front of her eyes.

'Dawn? Earth to Dawn? I know you're still tired, but just pick her up, can't you? She wants you.'

The door buzzer smashes through the silence. Rob gives Dawn a puzzled look and goes to answer the door, leaving Dawn alone with Rosie.

He's going to know. He's going to see.

'Where's my favourite two ladies?' Dawn's best friend of three years sings out as she runs up the stairs and into the flat. Her bracelets jangle as she rushes into the living room, her long braids piled high on her head.

'I'm here to do your post-natal check. Oh, yes I am,' Mel coos into the Moses basket. 'And how is Mummy doing?' she turns around to face Dawn.

Dawn looks out of the window. Mel knows her better than anyone, even Rob. If Rob doesn't work out something is wrong, Mel certainly will. Dawn and Mel had trained and lived together at uni, experiencing the highs and lows of midwifery and recounting birth stories each morning over their toast and marmalade. Mel had been there when her mum died and her eyes tell her she'll be there again now, if only Dawn will let her.

'Mum and baby both doing well,' Rob answers when it's clear Dawn isn't going to. 'Rosie's got a bit of a rash on her leg, though, if you could take a look?'

Mel picks the baby up and walks her towards the window, inspecting her tiny leg in natural sunlight. 'Looks like a touch of heat rash. Nothing serious. Perhaps just take one layer off. Generally, babies only need one more layer of clothing that we have on in the same conditions.'

Dawn already knows this. She's told countless women the same thing. Why is Mel speaking to them as if they don't know how to look after their own child? Perhaps it's a good thing that Mel is leaving to work overseas in a few weeks. Maybe she'll take her patronising advice and judgey eyes with her.

'She's beautiful. And content. Looks like you're both doing an excellent job.' Mel lifts Rosie into the air and beams up at her.

Of course Mel's not judging her. She's Dawn's best friend. Where are these thoughts coming from? Dawn watches Rob and Mel as they chat about on-demand feeding and smile at the tiny red-haired baby. They look so normal. Mel by the window. Rob now holding Rosie.

How could they not see what was happening? Why couldn't they hear the noise that was inside her head? The voices. The threats. The accusations. The sudden knowledge that there's only one way to silence them.

'She isn't yours,' she says.

'What the hell has got into you?' Rob frowns as he carefully lays Rosie back down in her crib.

Mel had made her excuses right after Dawn's shock announcement and told them she'll be back later.

'I mean, why would you say something like that?' Rob strides towards Dawn and crouches down in front of the armchair, taking both her hands in his. 'I know you've been through a lot with the birth and stuff, but why say something so terrible just to hurt me? This isn't like you.' His eyes are full of concern and disbelief.

'I'm not trying to hurt you,' Dawn says, letting the words come out in slow motion. 'I'm telling you the truth. She isn't yours.'

Dawn pulls her hands away from Rob and grabs onto the corner of the cushion on her lap. She holds in a breath, trying to slow her heart rate.

Rob falls backwards from his crouching position and the floor vibrates under Dawn's feet. He pulls at the collar of his T-shirt as if loosening a noose from around his throat and lets out a guttural sound that sits somewhere between a sob and a gasp for air.

'It was the night me and the girls went out for my birthday.' Tears pool in Dawn's eyes and she blinks them away. Rob doesn't need her tears; he needs the truth. She opens her mouth to tell. To explain, but the words get lodged in her throat.

Tell anyone about this, and I will kill you. She can still see the outline of the man's blurred face but can never make out his features, just the red hair.

Rob stands to his feet and towers over her. 'How could you be so bloody selfish. Stupid. Cruel,' he hisses into her ear through gritted teeth. 'You let me think she was mine – you let me *marry* you. What was I even thinking, getting married at twenty bloody years old?'

He turns his back on Dawn and storms towards the table, landing a punch on the wall beside it.

Rosie starts to cry.

'And what were you even thinking that night? I just wasn't enough for you, eh?' He shifts back around, blood flooding to his face, both hands twisted into tight fists.

'It wasn't like that,' Dawn whispers.

'Who was it? Actually no, scratch that, I don't want to know.' Rob holds both hands in the air, palms facing Dawn. 'The fact of the matter is, you lied. For nine months, Dawn, nine. I can't trust another word that comes out of your lying mouth.'

'I don't know who it was.'

Rob flinches as if he's been slapped. He picks up the mug of cold coffee from the table and gulps from it, turning around to face the window. 'There's been that many? Or just the one stranger whose name you didn't think to ask?'

228

Bile rises inside her. 'I can't remember much,' she says, her voice hoarse with trying not to cry.

'So, you were drunk? That is *not* an excuse.'

'It wasn't like that.' Dawn shakes her head, trying to force her thoughts into place.

And it hadn't been. She had been drinking. But not a lot, she never did. She'd certainly never blacked out before. Not like that. Dawn gulps down some air and holds her head in her hands, resting her elbows on her knees. One minute she'd been having a drink in the bar, and the next… The tears fall, one after the other as she lets herself remember.

Waking up on the floor of toilet cubicle had not been on the itinerary for her birthday night out. Things like that weren't meant to happen in the nice bars. The wall tiles were clean and shiny. The door handles looked expensive. The overwhelming patchouli and lavender fragrance of high-end soap had got right down her throat, making her retch over the basin. The back of her head felt bruised and she tried to blink away the pictures in her mind. The man with the red hair. Her absolute lack of control over her own body. The numbness of her limbs.

Tell anyone about this, and I will kill you, he'd hissed.

The cleaner was scrubbing the sinks when Dawn emerged from the toilet cubicle. 'I think I was spiked,' she blurted out to him, fog thickening inside her head and between her words. 'I would never have let him… *touch* me.' A sob fell out and her throat felt sore and scratched. This man will know what to do, she thought. He'd help her find her friends and Mel will take her to the police, the hospital.

'Pftt. How very convenient.' The cleaner rolled his eyes at her in the mirror. 'In my day when girls got paralytic and had sex with strangers in public toilets, they didn't stand around looking for someone else to blame.'

The words hit Dawn like a blow to the stomach. Was that what people would think? *Had* it been her fault? She blinks hard, trying to slow the spinning room, trying to remember how she'd got to the toilet cubicle in the first place.

She stumbled through the empty club and out through the double doors into the cold night air.

'Dawn! What the actual hell? Where have you been – I was just about to call Rob to see if you'd gone to his place. You weren't answering your phone. We were so worried.' Mel squeezed her phone back into her tiny handbag that was as blurred at the edges as everything else was.

Through her wobbly vision, Dawn could see that Amy had her tongue down some guy's throat, Claire was tucking into a bag of chips and everyone else they'd come out with must have gone home. Not everyone was worried, then.

Dawn tried to grab hold of Mel's arm. She missed the first time and then dropped it the second; her fingers were numb and clumsy. 'I need to tell you something.' A large van beeped as it thundered past, and Dawn jolted back, her heart hammering. Mel's face and everything in her vision melted into strange shapes. All she could hear over and over were his words.

Tell anyone about this, and I will kill you.

She'd been foolish to tell a stranger. What if *he* had heard her? Could he hear her now? She mustn't tell anyone else. Too risky. And what if she told someone and they looked at her like that cleaner had?

She'd gone home, propped up by Mel and spent the next day wrapped in a duvet. Then somehow, she got out of bed, went to work and carried on with her week. It was amazing what the human brain could forget. For a little while, at least. Five weeks later, she found herself staring at a piss-soaked stick; two pink lines burning into her eyes.

It would be Rob's child, of course it would be Rob's. A tiny person; half her, half Rob. What could be more perfect?

Rob had been thrilled after the initial shock. Two days later he'd proposed and she'd accepted with shining eyes, laughing about how old-fashioned he was.

Neither of them are laughing now.

CHAPTER 28

THEN

Dawn

DAWN HAS BEEN A mother for ten whole days and six hours. She'd spent the last five days in bed. Not asleep. Closing her eyes is too painful; all she can see is Rob's face as he packed his suitcase. His gut-wrenching sobs as he said goodbye to Rosie.

'I just can't,' he'd said through his tears. 'I can't stay. Can't bring up some stranger's child who you cheated on me with. Too many people have lied to me before, and I've let them get away with it. It ends now.' Bitterness had leaked from his voice and filled the room with a sense of doom that hasn't yet gone away.

Dawn should have told him the whole truth. But she couldn't put Rosie in danger. What if the man with the red hair came after her? Does he know, wherever he is, that his baby is in this flat? Would he come for her?

After Rob left, the hours had blurred together and telling the difference between night and day became harder. Dawn clutched the duvet like a shield against Rosie's cries and the sharp, unwanted flashes that stabbed their way into her mind. The toilet floor, the shame she carried in her gut as she pulled herself up, the cleaner's face.

The man's red hair. Rosie's red hair.

It's a relief to be left alone again in her room. Mel has finally left after spending twenty minutes having a go at her for keeping her dressing gown on for nine days straight.

'And this flat stinks,' she'd said. 'Get dressed and I'll open some windows. Maybe we could even go for a walk. It'll do you good.'

Ha. A walk. She's funny. How could Dawn ever do something that takes the kind of strength required to put one foot in front of the other in a public place? It takes her hours to force herself to throw off the duvet and walk to the bathroom when she has to pee. Even then she tries to time it so that she doesn't have to see Mel or the baby. Mel has been camping in the living room since Rosie was three days old and it's become easier and easier to just leave her to it until she can hardly bear Mel to be in the same room as her. She doesn't think she could stand the blame that she knows must get lodged in her eyes whenever she looks at Dawn. Blame that tells her she's failed royally as a mother. Blame because Mel's exhausted from doing every night feed for the past week. Perhaps it's not even Mel she doesn't want to look at. Perhaps it's *her*.

A few nights ago, Dawn had actually wished, just for a moment, that she hadn't even ever been pregnant. What kind of mother did that make her? She'd kept her smile frozen in place and posed with Rosie as Mel took about a hundred photos.

As soon as Mel had put the camera down, Dawn handed Rosie to her. 'I'm going to bed,' she'd announced, her voice as flat as her mood. 'I don't think I can do this anymore today. Not sure I can do it at all.'

She hadn't even looked behind her to see Mel's reaction, she just let the bedroom door bang shut behind her before sinking into her bed. Dawn hadn't realised it would be one of the last full sentences she'd say to anyone for several days. She'd assumed that she'd feel normal again after a decent night's sleep.

She'd been wrong.

The last week has passed in a blur. Most days, Dawn barely moves from the bed and instead just sleeps and sleeps. That way, she can stay safe in that other place; the place away from Rosie. Away from Mel and her accusing eyes. She begins to lose all sense of time and her memory starts to play sneaky tricks on her.

One morning, she wakes up to sunshine streaming in through the window. There's a lightness to her brain and she gets all the way out of bed and down the hall to the bathroom to brush her teeth before she remembers that she'd ever even been pregnant, let alone birthed a child. She spits out the toothpaste and goes straight back to bed.

It feels like days before she sees Mel again. She opens her eyes to see her sitting on the edge of the bed; her shoulders heaving, her body wracked with sobs.

'What is it?' Dawn asks eventually, forcing herself to lift an arm and place it across Mel's back. 'I'm sorry,' she says after several seconds. 'I'll try harder. You shouldn't have to do all this. *I'm* her mum.' Dawn heaves herself out of bed and re-ties her dressing gown.

'I want to keep helping, I really do,' Mel says. 'But I've used up all my leave from work, and there's only a couple of weeks before I have to leave for India.'

Dawn swallows hard before nodding. She pads into the living room, pausing beside the Moses basket. She looks down at her baby, willing herself to feel the love she had on day one. 'It's just going to be you and me, Rosie,' she sings softly. 'You and me against this butt-ugly world. We're both going to be just fine. We don't need anyone else.'

Rosie kicks the blanket off her legs and stares back without blinking.

Dawn picks up the handles of the Moses basket.

She can do this.

'You go home and get a shower and some sleep,' Dawn says to Mel when she enters the bedroom. She lays the basket in the middle of the bed. 'I'll keep her in here with me whilst I get dressed and tidy up a bit. Then I might take her for a walk.' Dawn paints on a bright smile on her stiff cheeks.

'If you're sure… ' Mel looks far from sure. 'I'll pop back later — check how you're getting on.' She picks up her bag and strokes Rosie's cheek before closing the door behind her.

Dawn walks to the window and watches Mel as she walks away down the road. The bedroom feels huge all of a sudden and so silent. She pulls on a pair of jeans and a stained tank-top from a heap of clothes on the floor and creeps back towards Rosie.

A garbling noise rises from the Moses basket. It's a sweet sound like a burbling brook.

Dawn tentatively places her hands underneath her baby and pulls her onto her lap, resting her head in the crook of her elbow.

Rosie finds Dawn's finger and grips it with her tiny hand. Her bright blue eyes search Dawn's face and her mouth breaks out into an enormous grin. Dawn knows it can only be a sign of wind at this age, she *knows* this. But somehow, that smile seems like it was saved for her and her only.

A splash of water hits Dawn's forearm and she realises she's crying. She lifts Rosie up to her shoulders and buries her face in her hair. 'Oh, my baby,' she says through her sobs. 'I'm sorry. I'm so, so sorry. Mummy loves you.' Relief fills Dawn's heart as she says the words and knows they are true. Of course, she loves her baby. From now onwards they would only have each other.

Rosie's neck smells like talc and a hint of something else. Lavender.

Dawn holds Rosie further away from her, steadying her against the bed as she retches and swallows the bile back down. The lavender is overwhelming, it's filling the whole room and bringing other unwelcoming smells with it, like patchouli. Patchouli and lavender, they always seem to go together, especially when something bad is about to happen.

An outline flashes sharply in Dawn's mind. A leering, featureless face under a shock of red hair. His voice echoes through her mind, saying the same sentence over and over.

Tell anyone, and I will kill you.

The voice keeps getting louder. Dawn places Rosie back in her basket and pushes her palms against her ears, rocking back and forth in an attempt to shake the words free.

The door buzzer blares. Rattling comes from the door downstairs.

Has he found them? The rattling gets louder, and Dawn snatches the basket handles, pulling it up from the bed and as far away from the door as possible. She needs to hide Rosie. He can't find her here.

She looks wildly around the room, her eyes settling on the airing cupboard. She pulls out the sheets and the towels and dashes them on the carpet before placing the Moses basket on the empty shelf and closing the door.

Footsteps clomp up the stairs. Dawn flattens her back against the bedroom door and slides to the floor.

A muffled cry comes from the airing cupboard. The door behind Dawn's back vibrates with the force of something trying to prise it open.

'Dawn? Are you in there? It's only Mel – I can't open the door.'

'How did you get in?' Dawn manages.

'Rob's key – you gave it to me, remember? Can you just let me in so I don't have to keep shouting through the bloody door?'

Dawn lets out a breath and scoots forward across the floor, leaving enough room for Mel to enter the room.

Rosie's cries have got louder.

'What the actual… ?' Mel rushes to the airing cupboard and flings it open. 'She probably can't even breathe properly in there. What the *hell* were you thinking, have you lost your mind?' She lowers the basket from the shelf and places it on the bed, before picking Rosie up and walking out of the room.

Dawn rushes after her through the hallway and into the living room. She stops when she realises there's someone else in there. A woman with a brown choppy fringe and purple-framed glasses. She looks familiar.

'Do you remember Anna?' Mel asks. She's trying to sound casual.

The hairs on the back of Dawn's arms feel prickly.

'We both worked with Anna on our hospital placement. She's the lead mental health midwife in the area. I asked her to drop in with me and see you.'

Mel is standing next to the window, clutching Rosie. Sunlight is bouncing off Rosie's hair, highlighting a whole spectrum of different reds. Mel is watching Dawn's face, waiting for an answer.

'What are you looking at?' Dawn says. 'Come away from the window. He'll see you.'

Mel and Anna share a look.

'See what I mean?' Mel mutters. 'I was just opening the window,' she says louder, to Dawn this time. 'It's stifling in here.'

'Why are you here?' Dawn turns to Anna. 'I don't know what Mel has told you, but I am fine, Rosie is fine. We are both *fine*.'

Anna glances again at Mel before speaking. 'I'm sure you are, Dawn. Just thought you might like to see a familiar face, that's all. First few weeks are never easy, and sometimes it's good to take all the help you can… '

'We're fine.' Dawn strides over to Mel and prises her baby from her grip. 'Now, if you don't mind, the two of us are going for a nap. I'll let you see yourselves out.'

Mel and Anna have 'dropped in' to see Dawn every day since the airing cupboard incident two weeks ago. Today, though, they've brought reinforcements.

The sofa and armchairs in Dawn's living room are filled with people wearing lanyards and professional smiles.

Rosie lies in her Moses basket kicking her legs, not a single clue that life as she's known it for the past month is about to change its course forever.

Dawn doesn't look at the sofas, or the people sitting on them. She doesn't look at the Moses basket or at the window. She keeps her eyes on the TV screen in the corner. The volume is muted but the people on the daytime TV show are doing the same as them: sitting about on sofas and talking about the world as if everything is normal. Just because the sun came up, people's alarms went off and everyone got ready and went to work, doesn't mean it's an ordinary day. They can't see the evil the morning brought with it.

One of the presenters on the TV looks out of the screen. He seems to look at Dawn as if he can see exactly who she is. What she's about to do. She can still hear *him* screaming those same words in her head. For a moment, it's as if the voice is coming straight from the man on the telly. Perhaps it is.

'And what about Dawn's partner – is he aware of the situation? Has he had a chance to say goodbye?' one of the lanyard wearers asks in a low voice.

'He's out of the picture.' Mel speaks quietly too. 'There's no one else. No other family. If there really are no spaces at the mother and baby units, temporary foster care until Dawn is better is the only option. I'd help myself, but I'm off to India next week. I've already postponed twice, they won't hold the position for me if I let them down again, and someone's got to look after that baby.'

Dawn swallows. *Please don't be listening to this, Rosie. None of this is your fault. You are perfect.*

Dawn feels Mel's eyes staring down at her. She looks directly in front, avoiding her gaze. They're cooking something on the telly now. A Beef Wellington. The one they'd made earlier is cut in half, showing off just the right shade of pink and the correct amount of puff to the pastry. It's easy to make something perfect when no one is watching. If they'd shown the one made in real time, Dawn reckons it would be a different story. All those eyes watching. Waiting. It would have come out tough or burned. Inedible.

One of the lanyard wearers is telling Dawn that a nice family would keep Rosie safe for a while until she gets better. She must mean that *he* won't be able to find her there. That's good.

The living room is getting hotter. Too many breaths from too many people and the window is still closed. Dawn shuts her eyes, letting the conversations around her drift in and out of her ears. They're talking about paperwork. Signatures. Then the mother and baby unit again.

'We can't really say how long it will take. The waiting list is horrendous. Obviously, Dawn will be high priority, what with the severity of her symptoms.'

'Will they admit Dawn to the Barton wing in the meantime?'

Mel chews on her lip until she tastes blood. The Barton Wing is the adult mental health ward in the hospital where Dawn had completed her labour ward placement. It has a history of higher-than-acceptable rates of 'incidents' and of being severely understaffed.

Anna glances Dawn's way before turning back towards Mel. 'I shouldn't think so at this stage. There's such a shortage of beds and she doesn't appear to pose any immediate danger to herself. We just need to make sure this bubba is looked after.'

Mel frowns. 'But, don't you think all this points to – well, to *puerperal psychosis*.' She hisses, not as quietly as she thinks. 'Dawn thinks some random man is after her. She says he wants to kill her and take Rosie, but she can't tell me why – surely we can't ignore that?'

'I don't think that,' Dawn says. Her words come out too high, too shrill. Too loud. 'Not anymore, anyway. I was just tired, hormonal. I'm much better now.' She can't go in the Barton Wing. She just *can't*.

The psychiatric nurse beside Anna picks up Dawn's postnatal notes from the table. They'd all had a read, now it's his turn. 'I see from your notes you've had rather a traumatic birth.' His too-big glasses slip down his skinny nose and he pushes them back up as he flicks through the pages. 'Occasionally, birth trauma can trigger episodes of puerperal psychosis, particularly if there had been high levels of stress during the pregnancy.'

Dawn looks at the carpet, counting the faded coffee stains.

'Sometimes women might exhibit symptoms similar to PTSD following the birth or harbour very vivid delusions that often centre around their newborn child.'

He sounds as if he is giving a lecture to a group of medical students, and Dawn feels like his not-so-glamorous assistant.

'Of course, Dawn will need an ongoing psychiatric assessment of her progress, which we will put in place as swiftly as possible,' he continues in a smooth voice. 'How does that sound to you, Dawn?'

Dawn gets up and moves to the Moses basket. She picks up her baby and holds her close. Baby talc, warm skin, soft neck.

'Please don't take her,' she whispers.

'Hey,' Mel says. 'It's not forever. Just until you get better. They can't do anything at this stage without your permission. It's up to you, but it's the best thing for Rosie.'

Dawn nods slowly and a piece of paper is thrust in front of her to sign. Everyone seems to stand to their feet very quickly after that.

Anna holds her hands out towards Dawn, waiting for her to place Rosie into them.

Dawn takes a step forward, holding Rosie close. She shifts her from her shoulder so she can look at her face, her perfect nose. 'I can't do it,' she sobs.

Anna closes the gap between them and lays a gentle hand on her shoulder. 'You can. Let me help you.' She places her other hand around Rosie and begins to prise her away from Dawn's grasp.

Rosie grabs a handful of Dawn's curly hair and holds it tight, her tiny face wrinkled with determination, as if Dawn's hair was an anchor between them.

Anna uncurls Rosie's fist and releases Dawn's curls.

'Goodbye little one. We'll be together soon, I promise. You just need to go somewhere safe for a little while. Somewhere *he* won't find you.'

It's only after they've all left that she lets the screams out. She pounds on the door with her fists and screams until her throat's sore.

Dawn spends the next week alone in her flat. She doesn't answer the door or the phone. Letting Rosie go hasn't stopped *him* from torturing her mind. She puts chairs against the doors and keeps the lights off to try and stop him getting in. Even in the dark she can see it: the flash of red hair.

You told, Dawn. Remember what I said would happen if you told?

'I only told one person. One stranger,' she shouts. 'Not

Rob, not Mel. Not even the people who want to help make you go away.'

He's quiet for a while after that. Good.

She gets the tealight candles from under the sink and makes a circle on the living room floor. Circles are for protection. She lights each one and sits in the middle, cross-legged on the floor. She mutters words, the same ones over and over again. Words that will keep Rosie safe, wherever she is. Time loses meaning when she does this, and the candles have long gone by the time Mel bursts into the flat, knocking the chair flying.

Mel doesn't care about the incantations, she's too pre-occupied with the state of Dawn's ribcage and the mouldy food in the fridge. She moans about the stench and that it's coming from Dawn's soiled trousers. It's easy for her to say; she's not the one who has to stay inside the circle.

Mel has a crowd with her this time too. This time some of them are wearing uniforms and they're holding paperwork about the mental health act that takes away her choices. Dawn is taken somewhere with a bed and locked doors and a woman who takes away her shoelaces and the drawstrings from her hoody. Minutes bleed into hours which run into days. Dawn spends those days sitting in larger circles on chairs with other people next to her. Sometimes she manages to speak but most days she doesn't. To begin with, she still hears his voice, his threats. She has endless meetings with doctors who throw various words at her. They try one lot of meds and then another. They pile pills on top of pills until she's so numb it feels like she's left her body and is watching it walk around without her.

Her support worker comes into her room almost every day. A beaky-nosed woman with sour breath. She says the same things each time. 'Rosie's doing well in her foster home and you're going to be in here a long time. Perhaps it would be fairer to your daughter if you… well, if you *let her go.*'

Dawn had screamed in her face the first time she'd said that.

After a few weeks, though, she no longer quite had the energy. 'The other staff said they could arrange for a visit with Rosie. And there might be a mother and baby placement coming up one day soon,' Dawn says instead.

'You think this would be a good place for a baby? And even if you get a place on a mother and baby unit, you might never get well enough. Then you'd have taken her away from her foster family for nothing. Don't be selfish. Think of what's best for your baby.'

Her support worker's words stomp around and around in her mind, night and day, competing with *his* vile vitriol. He is still very clear about one thing: he will find and take Rosie if Dawn has her back with her. She'll never be safe, not whilst they're together.

The day Dawn starts on yet another new injection to 'help with her mood,' she requests a visit from a social worker. It takes her hours to force the words out between broken sobs. They're words she's already chewed on, trying them on for size.

Other professionals are brought into her room. Conversations happen around her. Things are said and then said again in different ways. All of them sewn up at the seams with 'Do you understand what this means, Dawn?' Lots of repetitions of words like *permanent, adoption* and *you-need-to-be-sure.*

Dawn hasn't been sure of anything for a long time; not since the night her future was ripped away from her inside the cubicle of a nightclub toilet.

'It's the only way to keep Rosie safe,' she says.

The days that follow are dark ones. They don't get any lighter afterwards, more that Dawn's eyes adjust to the dimness around her. She immerses herself in a different world, one where Rosie is with her and she wears the thoughts around her head like a torch, lighting a path through each day.

Almost a year goes past. Twelve months of long talks with assessment teams, with nurses and doctors. Further weeks inside sterile rooms on beds covered with NHS sheets. She learns to smile. She learns to pretend, to look like she's coping. Then comes the day. The first day of the beginning of the end.

'You're free to go,' a psychiatrist announces. He warns her of the long path ahead; that puerperal psychosis sometimes goes hand in hand with bipolar disorder which seems likely in Dawn's case. He says she'll need ongoing treatment if she's to manage her life in the long term. He gives her a smile, armfuls of leaflets and blister packs filled with dosage instructions. 'You'll need lots of support from those closest to you,' he adds.

The doctor obviously hasn't read each part of her file, otherwise he'd know she had no one.

The staff on the Barton wing check Dawn's address before she walks out of the door. Someone from the mental health team will come and visit her every other day for her first week home, they tell her.

Dawn doesn't go to her flat, what would be the point? If the discharge nurse had bothered to check, she'd know there is no way the flat above the British Heart Foundation would still be hers to live in. Who would have paid the rent? The bills? Someone else would be living there now, someone who wasn't being followed by a faceless man with red hair.

She makes her way into the centre of town. She'll jump on a train at Manchester Piccadilly. She still has money in the handbag she'd been admitted with. It wouldn't last long but it could get her across the country. Dawn can't stay around here, he's still too close, she can feel him all around her.

She'll start again somewhere new. She'll make herself strong and then one day she'll find her Rosie. She reaches the station and takes a last look at the city she grew up in before walking through the doors.

The only way is out.

CHAPTER 29

NOW

Grace

GRACE'S HEART ACHES FOR Dawn as she sits with her in room six, holding her hand as she finally drops off to sleep. It had been heart-wrenching last night, watching her fall apart when she found out about Shaun's death. The medication helped to calm her, and it was as if a wall had been dismantled from between them, brick by brick, as Dawn began to open up. The truth seeped through in dribs and drabs to begin with, until the whole, ugly story had come gushing out, drenching the room with Dawn's buried guilt. Her fear. Her longing. She'd showed Grace the photo album filled with pictures of Rosie, still intermittently believing they were all real. Grace had known the first one on the front page was really Rosie. It had made her ache all over just to see her scrunched up blue eyes as they peered at the camera.

'I can't believe you had to go through that all on your own,' Grace had said as she squeezed her hand.

'I just needed *someone* to help me. Mel was great, but she couldn't stick around forever, especially when she was offered work abroad. She wouldn't have been able to contact me after I left the psych unit, anyway. My other friends were busy with their own lives. Maybe if Mum hadn't died or my dad had stuck around, I'd have been okay, and Rosie would still be with me.' Dawn had dissolved into a fresh portion of tears which Grace did her best to wipe away with the ever-dwindling box of tissues by her bed.

'Do you know where Mel and your dad might be now?'

'Mel's still living overseas, according to Facebook. I sent her a friend request, but I don't think she's seen it. Maybe there's no internet where she is.'

'And your dad?' Grace gently pushed, wondering if she was going too far. Dawn was clearly still so fragile.

'I haven't seen him since I was ten years old. Dad was my whole world, and he just upped and left overnight. Mum said he met someone else. I always told myself I didn't need him after that.' Dawn let go of Grace's hand and pulled the duvet cover up over herself.

'And now?'

'I think I'd like to find him. He's the only family I have, apart from Rosie.'

Grace had watched as Dawn's exhausted eyes fluttered shut. She'd whispered goodnight and straightened the duvet but couldn't bring herself to leave her side for over an hour.

There is one more thing Grace needs to speak to her about, but it requires gentle steps. Following Dawn's outpouring of her story, Grace had done an internet search whilst Cara sat with Dawn. She'd searched for news stories from where Dawn had lived at the time that it happened. The search had thrown up an article saying that there had been several reports of a man spiking women's drinks in the area – he had been arrested, convicted and jailed for nine counts of rape and many more of assault. There was a photograph below the article of the man – and he had red hair.

After perching on the hard chair beside Dawn's bed for half the night, Grace feels like a spring that's been stretched and then dropped, only her coils haven't quite returned to the correct shape.

Sunlight filters through the curtains and the birds are making a racket, chirping at each other outside the window. It's five in the morning, too late to bother getting ready for bed.

Grace creeps downstairs and lets herself into the office, leaving the shutters down. She flicks on the kettle and makes a coffee with two heaped spoonfuls of Azera and sits in the quiet, thinking about Dawn. Half a lifetime of loss and missing a part of herself, never knowing where her daughter was or whether she was safe. No wonder she was always inventing stories about what Rosie was up to; she must have been wondering about it almost every waking minute of her day.

Grace will look into ways of tracking down Dawn's dad. In the meantime, Dawn's going to need all the support available and all the services they can wangle in to help. Which probably isn't many, the way all these funding cuts are going. What the hell will happen to her if St Jude's closes down? Grace feels sick just thinking about it. Dawn has done nothing but look out for everyone else since she got there. Who would be there for her if she's turfed back out onto soggy cardboard? Dawn would still find something to care for, even then. She'd probably invite a pigeon into her sleeping bag and give it her last slice of bread.

'Life is short, Grace,' she'd said to her an hour ago after spewing out her whole, sad story. 'Don't let go of anyone or anything that makes you happy.'

The words keep replaying in her head along with the image of Jack's face. His smiling one, complete with the signature dimple, and his hurt one when Grace had told him he was just a job to her and nothing more. She would give anything to take those words back.

She puts the computer to sleep and closes her eyes. She takes some cleansing breaths and reaches for a phone. If there's ever a good time for a six-minute meditation it would be now.

'Grace?'

She hears the soft whisper from the other side of the door before she hears the muffled knock. Her heart flips around a few degrees in her chest at the sound of his voice and she immediately feels guilty for her excitement after spending the last few hours processing heartache that belongs to someone else. She lets him in, willing him to throw his arms around her as the door clicks shut behind him.

'It's okay, I know you're not allowed to discuss Dawn with me,' Jack says, as he wipes the tear from her face with his little finger. 'But if it helps, I already know. Cara told me everything.'

Cara had been in and out of Dawn's room that night too, they'd been tag-teaming it. Grace can't be sure how coherent Dawn had been when she wasn't in the room, or how much she'd shared with Cara, but it's comforting to know that she's not carrying all of that information on her own.

'Thank you,' Grace whispers, stepping against him and resting her face against his chest, the warmth of his jumper cushioning her cheek.

He holds her quietly as she stares out of the window, seeing nothing but the reflection of the two of them in the glass.

Grace moves her head upwards, brushing her forehead against his chin, still not ready to meet his eyes. 'How did you know I was in here this early?'

'I heard your footsteps and the office door slamming shut. I couldn't sleep either. Stuff on my mind,' he adds casually.

'It just makes you think, when you hear stories like Dawn's,' she murmurs. 'It makes you think about how short life really is; how rare it is to find happiness alongside people you can trust.'

Jack's shoulders stiffen. 'I know my past isn't squeaky clean,' he says, pulling away from her a few inches. 'And I'm not expecting you to trust me right away, not with all the backstory you have on me, hidden away in that filing cabinet.'

'That's not what I meant.' Grace places his forearms around her waist, pulling him back to her. 'And I do trust you, it's just all so complicated.'

Jack sits down on the swivel chair beside them and Grace perches on his knee, keeping her arms around his shoulders. She leans against him and closes her eyes, mentally placing the heartbreak of others on the desk beside her, just for a little while, knowing it will soon be there for her to pick back up on her way out again.

They sit like that for a long time, Grace dozing on and off until the alarm buzzes on her phone.

'We have half an hour before Peter arrives and I'm not sure you should be alone in the office with me when he gets here.'

'Hmm. Probably won't look too good for you to be found attached to an inmate,' Jack says lightly as he pulls his shoes on a little too hard.

'Don't say that. That's not how I see you.'

'How do you see me then?' he says, tying up his lace before

turning his pale blue eyes towards Grace, his voice still even, his face just inches from hers.

The front door outside the office makes its unmistakable sound. The bleep from Peter's fob.

'He's early,' Grace hisses as she scrabbles to her feet, picking things up and frantically straightening the paperwork on the desk.

Jack flies out of the door and accosts Peter before he can put his key in the office lock.

'Just been trying to get Grace to help me with my budgeting sheet,' Grace hears him say. 'But she's been up all night with another resident. She asked me to come to you instead.'

Grace wheels the office chair into its rightful position, plastering on a smile and swinging the door open to display it before remembering she hadn't yet brushed her hair or cleaned her teeth.

'Rough night, then,' says Peter. It's not a question, he'd been there when Dawn had begun to spiral out of control.

'You could say that. Let's just say, I'm glad you're here.'

'Bloody hell. Never thought I'd hear you say that,' Peter grins. His face looks so different when he does that. 'Seriously though, I know you'd have done great. Good thing she had you to help her through the night.'

Grace blinks away her surprise. Did Peter just imply that she's good at her job?

'I'll help you around lunchtime-ish if that's okay?' Peter turns to face Jack. 'Grace needs to get off home soon and get some rest, so I'll be lone-working this morning.'

Jack nods and gives Grace a sad smile whilst Peter's not looking before disappearing from the corridor and from her sight.

'I can't leave you,' she says to Peter. 'Not with things as they are with Dawn. She's a loose cannon right now and I'm not sure how long it will take for those new meds to work.'

'I'll be fine.' Peter throws her a reassuring smile, lightly gripping her shoulder. 'She has people from the community mental health team popping round in an hour and I'm sure Cara will sit with her.'

'Let me go and see her first, see how she is and say goodbye for the day,' Grace says, acquiescing.

Dawn is lying on her side, on top of her duvet. Her glassy eyes face the door as Grace enters through it. For a split second, her stomach lurches as she thinks the worst, but then Dawn stirs.

'Thank you for listening last night,' she whispers. 'And I'm sorry if I… misled you. About Rosie.' A tear escapes and plummets down her cheek, taking Grace's heart with it. 'I feel so stupid. And I've wasted all this time – time you could have spent on somebody else. Someone who deserves it. I don't expect you to believe me about what happened with my baby after all the other stories I've told you, but I'll always remember that you listened. All of you. And I'll pack my stuff as soon as I can, I might just need to borrow a few bags for life. I've got quite a bit more baggage than I did before… '

Grace's mouth twitches as she reaches for Dawn's shoulder, although she's not sure if it's because she wants to laugh or weep.

'Don't ever say sorry. No one on earth should have to go through what you've been through and there is nothing I can say to make it any better. Of course we believe you, all of us do. Every word. All I can promise you is that I'm here, you are not going anywhere, and no one deserves support more than you do. You don't have to deal with this on your own anymore.'

Dawn begins to sob and her body sags against Grace as she folds her arms around her. St Jude's has to stay open. It *has* to. Even if Grace has to chain herself to the desk.

'I'm here,' Grace continues. 'And Peter's here, Cara… '

'And Shaun,' she adds, swallowing hard.

Shit.

'Dawn, do you remember what we talked about last night? About Shaun?'

Silence.

'I remember,' Dawn says eventually. 'I just don't think I believe it. It doesn't feel right that he's gone.'

CHAPTER 30

Dawn

'COME ON, DAWN, YOU need to get out of that stinking bed now. We need you,' Cara says, sharpness leaking from her voice.

Dawn sits up and stretches her arms. They feel stiff after three days of being in bed. Taking new medication and letting out twenty years' worth of tears had ensured that she slept for thirty-six hours straight. Her body may be weak, but her mind feels lighter.

'She's not wrong about us needing you,' adds Teardrop Terry as he sits gingerly on the other side of the bed, looking around as if he's not sure if he's allowed to. 'The café's been manic. Sorry. Poor choice of words. It's been hectic,' he amends with a blush. 'Cara's been rushed off her feet and she's been a right stroppy mare. Though I suppose there's no change there really.'

'Oi!' says Cara right before punching him in the torso. 'It's not just the café. We need to get on with the fundraising but it's not the same without you. No one else has your "oomph". I tried my best to ramp people up but apparently I'm too aggressive.'

Something about having Teardrop Terry and Cara in her room makes Dawn want to spring out of bed.

Or at least sit up and crack open a window.

As she props herself up against her headboard, their words begin to sink in. She'd known they'd be kind for a little while – she'd been ill and they're good people. But surely then they'd want her to leave? Now they know she'd lied about Rosie and that she'd given her up? But they're making it sound almost like...

Like they still need her.

'What have people been saying about all... this?' Dawn asks quietly, pointing in her own vague direction. 'Does everyone know?'

'The staff wouldn't be allowed to talk to us about stuff like that,' Terry says, scratching his chin. 'Confidentiality. You know how it is here. But we know the bits and pieces you've told us and we're not going anywhere.'

'I feel like such an idiot.' Dawn pinches the corners of her duvet cover and bunches them tightly into her fists. 'I don't think I'll ever be able to face everyone.'

'At least you're opening your mouth and stringing sentences together today though,' says Cara with her usual lack of tact. 'So, there's that.'

Dawn lets go of the duvet, sits up straight and steadies herself on Cara's bony arm before swinging her legs around until her feet graze the laminate. She looks at the wardrobe and then at the bathroom door, calculating the effort she would need in order to walk to each of them, have a shower and get dressed.

'I'll help you pick some clothes out,' says Cara, more animated than Dawn had seen her for weeks.

'I'll take that as my cue to leave,' says Terry. He gets up and grabs Dawn gently by the elbow as he walks past her. He whispers in her ear, 'It's good to see you making your way back to us, love. You'll get there. I know you will. We all do.'

'Thank you,' she says through a strangled throat as tears sting the backs of her eyelids. She'd often wondered over the past few years – well, twenty-two, to be exact – what it would feel like to have a family again. People in her corner. People who believe her and understand. Turns out it feels pretty bloody great.

Cara turns the shower on, pushes Dawn into the bathroom and proceeds to prattle on about gossip from the café customers as well as keeping her up to speed about what's been going on with the other residents.

'I bought you something to cheer you up,' Cara grins. She picks up a folded T-shirt from the top of Dawn's chest of drawers and shakes it out so that Dawn can see it. It says: *I went to Dover and all I bought was this crappy T-shirt.*

'Oh, Cara.' Dawn thought she couldn't possibly have any tears left after the past few days. Turns out she was wrong. Dawn hasn't been given a present from anyone since before Rob had left.

'I'll treasure it forever.'

Cara chuckles. 'Don't get all sentimental, it was only £4.99 from the market. Thought you'd like it since you like Dover so much.'

'It's a special place.' Dawn wanders into the bathroom and allows the less-than-satisfactory warm water from the shower to trickle over her body with lacklustre force. It still feels amazing though, and it's nice to have her hair sticking to her scalp because it's wet and not because it's thick with grease.

Dawn finally steps out of the bathroom and wriggles into

some leggings and her new T-shirt. Cara is still sitting on her chair, flicking through a magazine. She's about to thank her for her kick up the bum and ask her how Curtis and Kyle are doing. But then she throws her a sentence that sends everything toppling right back down again.

'We need to talk about Shaun,' she says.

Dawn starts gathering up all of her discarded clothes from the floor, folding them up and putting them in her drawers, slamming them closed loudly each time, only to open them again seconds later to shove the next item in.

'Dawn…'

'What?' she explodes, pulling the drawer open so hard that it comes off its runners and lands hard on her little toe.

Cara crouches next to Dawn, pulling the drawer from her grasp. Now her hands are empty, she links them into her own and shuffles forward until she's cross-legged in front of Dawn, her pointed face only inches away.

'You need to sit here, open your ears and friggin' listen. A few weeks ago, I was lower than a badger's arsehole. I'd fallen right off the wagon and I'd ballsed up my kids' meeting. You know what I wanted to do? Give up. Go back to my needles and my burned spoons. You know why I didn't? Because of you. Because I had a mate. A real one, for once in my stinkin' life. You made me carry on, you made me see what's important. And now it's payback time.'

'Wow. I think that's the most I've ever heard you say in one go,' Dawn grins. It almost hurts, and she realises it's a shape she hasn't made her mouth try to make for a long time. 'But the dodgy methadone and the messed-up meeting was my fault. I don't see how *I* was any help, it was me who got it for you.'

'You weren't to know. And you tried. That helped. Trust me.' Cara stands up straight. 'Now you need to help yourself. Face your own shit. Speak out loud about what happened to Shaun.'

'But you saw him,' Dawn whispers. 'Days after I'd moved in. He was here, in this room with all of us.'

'You were always talking to him. Everywhere you went you'd be muttering away. I just got used to it, I s'pose. Didn't think it was worth mentioning. I didn't realise you thought you could see *that* Shaun.'

'But he's still… ' Dawn breaks off as she realises she hasn't seen him since she woke up and glances at the blister pack of new tablets that's lying on top of her chest of drawers.

A tear falls down her cheek and she allows herself to cry on Cara's shoulder as she holds her tight, just like she had for her a few weeks back when she had vomit in her hair.

'I knew Shaun a bit,' Cara says in a gentle voice – gentle for Cara, anyway. 'Enough to say hi to in the park. He was a good kid. Screwed in the head like we all are, but nice. You'd have liked him if you met him. He'd have liked you.'

'I did meet him,' Dawn sobs. 'The night I moved in. The evening before he… was found. He knew I'd got this place over him and I just let it happen. I might as well have killed him myself.'

'Course you friggin' didn't,' Cara says, her no-nonsense tone wrapping itself around Dawn and holding her up a little straighter. 'Shaun was an addict – always in that park or using in the toilets. Didn't like doing it in front of his mum, I respected him for that. It could have happened any time. Even if he'd got the room over you, he wouldn't have just stopped using straight away.'

'But I was helping him.' Dawn's voice cracks and she swallows down the sobs until her throat hurts. 'I was keeping him safe, protecting him.'

Cara stays close and keeps hugging her. 'He wasn't Rosie,' she says after a while.

Dawn doesn't answer that.

'How did his mum take it?' she asks, suddenly.

Cara shrugs. 'No idea. Don't know who she is. Don't know anyone who knows her. All I do know is her boyfriend used to batter her. Shaun was covered in bruises a while back when he'd tried to get between them.'

'I'm going to go see her,' Dawn decides out loud. 'I think Shaun would have wanted me to make sure she was okay.'

Something tells her there wouldn't be a queue of people lined up to do the job.

CHAPTER 31

Dawn

SHAUN'S MUM LOOKS AS if she's been stuck to her chair for several weeks. Greasy strands of greying hair sit flat to her scalp and her eyes are like two black holes. The ground-floor flat smells like it hasn't glimpsed sight of a hoover or dishcloth for a long time, and there are overflowing bin bags in the kitchenette corner.

'Who did you say you were again?' Suspicion burns from her eyes.

'I was a friend of Shaun. Well, someone who really cared about him,' Dawn amends.

'I really cared about him,' his mum says quietly and into the distance. 'I know people probably thought I didn't, Shaun included, but I loved the very bones of him. He was the only good thing I ever brought to this world. And then he was taken from it.'

Dawn waits for her to cry and looks wildly around for some tissues to offer her. She should have brought some with her, Lord knows she's been through enough of them herself that past week.

'I wondered if you needed any help,' Dawn ventures.

'Now that's not something I'm offered very often. People are quick to tell me I need it often enough, though.' She reaches for an almost empty pouch of tobacco and picks up a stray Rizla from the cluttered table beside her, already filled with overflowing ashtrays.

'You want one?' she asks, finally looking in Dawn's direction.

'No thanks. I quit a while back. Love a bit of second-hand smoke, though,' Dawn smiles.

Shaun's mum doesn't answer or look at Dawn as she rolls her cigarette and then puffs away. Dawn starts to wonder if she's forgotten she's even there.

'The funeral,' she announces. 'It's this week. I wanted some stuff to be said but don't know anyone to say them. Don't think I'll be able to get the words out, what with everyone staring. Judging.'

'Why would they do that?' Dawn asks, keeping her voice as gentle as possible without sounding patronising. She knows how it feels when people talk down to you when life starts feeling out of control.

'Let's just say I had a run of bad luck when it comes to men.' She coughs as she flicks her ash. 'Shaun got caught in the crossfire a few times over the years. Never when he was little though,' she adds in a firmer voice. 'But that's not the point. I know that now. I finished with him, the day they found Shaun. If I didn't listen to him before, the least I can do is take notice now... ' She breaks off and then the tears come.

Dawn drops to her knees beside her chair and puts her hand awkwardly on her sharp shoulder blade. 'I've just realised I don't even know your name.'

'Irene,' she sniffs.

'Well then, Irene,' Dawn smiles. 'I'm sure Shaun would be really proud of you. And it just so happens that I have rather a talent for speaking at other people's funerals. Why don't you tell me all about him and what you would like to be said, and I'll see what I can do.'

'Thanks, love,' she says, squeezing her hand with surprising strength given the boniness of hers. 'I'd offer you a cup of tea but I'm pretty sure the milk's off.'

Dawn nips to the shop at the corner of the road then pops by the chippy to collect two extra-large steaming wrappers filled with golden, puffy chips.

'The best in Dover, these are,' she announces brightly as she places them on a plate. Dawn had spent ten minutes washing it up due to the lack of clean ones in the cupboard.

They eat in silence, both of them only managing half their huge portions. It's the most Dawn remembers eating for a very long time. She's surprised by how satisfying it feels to be full.

She washes the insides and outsides of Irene's kitchen cupboards and cleans the windows and the bathroom. She can't find a hoover but makes do with the dustpan and brush she finds on top of the fridge.

Dawn makes Irene and herself a cup of tea and they sit under the open window, breathing in the fresh air as Irene tells her all about Shaun. About her son.

'Thank you,' Irene says before Dawn leaves.

Dawn wants to tell her it's Dawn who should be thanking her. Today's the first day for a long time that there's any light inside her and now she has it, she never wants to switch it off again.

The service takes place in the same church as the funeral of good old Brian. It's a better turn out this time. A couple of Irene's neighbours are sitting at the back and all of St Jude's residents are here. Cara and Teardrop Terry sit in the front row either side of Irene and Dawn. They have been taking it in turns with Dawn to visit her each day this week in the run up to the funeral and they seem to have an extra spark of life in them too.

Dawn's throat closes around the lump lodged inside it many times as she spins slowly and clearly through the eulogy. She may not have known him for very long whilst he was alive, but she owes so much to his memory. She's not only saying goodbye to him along with his mother, she's saying goodbye to the Shaun she'd thought she could take care of for those weeks after his death. In a weird sort of way, Dawn feels as if she's saying goodbye to the years of blaming herself for giving up Rosie.

St Jude's café hosts the wake. Fresh pastries and mini sausage rolls are munched and appreciated by those who had known him, as well as those who hadn't. Dawn picks up a cream cake and scoffs it down in Shaun's memory, remembering their day at Dover Castle. She knows it didn't really happen the way she remembers, but it had been real to her. She tells Irene all about it, and she laughs when Dawn tells her how they'd sneaked into the wedding fayre for the free champagne and cakes, and how he'd stuck up for her in the café when the snooty woman hadn't wanted Dawn to speak to her baby.

'Well, it might've been all in your head – like what happens to you when you've lost your marbles – but I tell you what,' she says as she dabs at her eyes, 'you somehow got him spot-on.'

Dawn is still clearing up after the wake when Peter walks back into the café carrying a bass drum.

'It was Shaun's,' he explains. 'He was in a band a couple of years ago – him and a couple of mates before they all went off the rails and lost touch. His mum had kept it all in her bedroom in case he ever went back to it. She wants St Jude's to have it.'

'Bloody *hell*. Come and look at all this!' Cara calls across the café after Peter has been back and forth from his car carrying various bundles in his arms.

'When did this appear?' Grace asks.

Someone lets out a long whistle. A chipped black drum kit and a dented speaker. A microphone sitting in its crooked stand and a well-loved guitar held together with an assortment of Radiohead stickers.

'Woah.' Teardrop Terry rubs his hands together, both eyes shining at full beam. 'You guys are about to hear some percussive genius once I've put this together.' He grabs the big bass drum and immediately starts fiddling with the pedal.

'I didn't know you played.' Jack sounds excited and Dawn follows his beady stare all the way to the battered guitar.

'Maybe we should clean it all up a bit first… then there's paperwork, risk assessments… ' Grace begins.

'The only risk here is that people might mob us cos we rock so hard,' Terry grins.

Jack has already strapped the guitar around himself and is fiddling with the little knobs at the top while strumming the strings with his other hand, letting out some distinctly untuneful sounds. 'Okay, so it needs a tune-up. It'll sound amazing with a new set of strings though.'

'I had no idea we had musicians living under this roof,' says Grace. 'How come neither of you ever said anything?'

She's asking them both but is only looking at Jack, Dawn notices.

'You never asked,' Terry shrugs.

Ten minutes later, the drum kit is in place and Jack has managed to adjust the strings enough to get something out of them that resembles a tune.

As Dawn listens to the opening chords of 'Wonderwall' and marvels at the rhythm of Teardrop Terry's drumming, another sound catches her attention. The gentle, sweet voice that belongs to Grace who's singing softly next to her.

'Grace. You sound like an angel,' Dawn gasps. 'Get behind that microphone!'

Grace's cheeks blush poppy-red. 'I used to sing sometimes at uni. I was in a band, but Mum told me it was a waste of time.'

Dawn grabs Grace by the shoulders and walks her to the microphone. 'Pretend we're not here,' she says. 'And just sing your heart out.'

Jack does something with the microphone wire, the stand and the speaker and then Grace's angel voice can be heard reverberating around the café. Her hands are shaking, but she keeps going.

It doesn't escape Dawn's notice that Jack is staring at Grace as if she's made of pure gold.

'That was amazing!' Cara shouts and jumps up and down when they've finished. 'Where did you learn to sing like that?'

Grace shrugs, her face still the shade of salmon. 'I always loved singing. Tonight was great, we should make it a regular thing.'

'I was thinking about another regular thing we could do,' Dawn says, crossing her fingers that Grace says yes. 'I was thinking we could put on other wakes – for people who don't have families to do it for them.'

Grace and Peter share a look. 'I think that's a wonderful idea,' Grace says. We'll go over the details tomorrow.'

Dawn is still buzzing from the live music as Cara, Terry and even Grace wedge themselves into number six. They stay up till midnight, grazing on smart-price cola and cheesy wotsits. Dawn's French manicure kit (£5.99 from Savers) catches Cara's beady eye and she insists on doing Dawn and Grace's nails. Teardrop Terry declines the offer.

'Right, I'm off home,' Grace says eventually. 'You should all get some sleep too. We've got our big sleepout coming up in a couple of days – we'll need as much energy as we can get.'

It's only as Dawn's eyes are closing that night that the little niggles begin gnawing at the back of her brain with their tiny, sharp teeth.

This is too good to last. She doesn't deserve to feel like this, to have real friends. Icy fingers of fear squeeze around her heart as she pictures what could happen to each one of them if St Jude's closes down.

CHAPTER 32

Dawn

DAWN IS SITTING ON her favourite swivel chair in the office whilst she has her fifth-ever keyworking session with Grace.

'How do you feel you're coping now you're on your new meds?' asks Grace. 'And how was your first therapy session?'

It's okay to be honest, her therapist had said yesterday. *Looking on the bright side doesn't mean you shouldn't face the darker one too.*

'I'm doing better,' Dawn starts after taking an extra breath. 'But it was bloody hard to start with – talking to a stranger about what happened, but I think it will help, and I know how lucky I am to be offered sessions so quickly when the waiting list is usually so long.'

Grace smiles. 'Only you would find the *lucky* in having therapy after all you've been through.'

'The meds are helping too – I think. Except I still feel a bit groggy in the mornings. What's helping even more though, is knowing that… that scumbag is in prison. Knowing he can't hurt any more women. That he can't hurt me, and he can't hurt Rosie.'

Grace nods. 'I'm glad I told you. I was worried that showing you the article might make things worse.'

'It did in some ways – to begin with. I kept worrying about whether I could have prevented it happening to those other women had I said something sooner, but I wasn't thinking clearly. I am glad you told me, though.' Dawn wheels her chair from side to side.

'There is something else I wanted to talk about – it's that social-and-family networky bit of my file. I think I'm ready to look at the goals on it.'

'Really?' Grace raises an eyebrow and holds Dawn's file a little closer to her chest as if guarding her from a monster that's hidden inside. Perhaps there will be once Dawn has filled that section in.

'It's just that this is your first keyworking session since... '

'I know. But I want to. Meeting Shaun's mum and seeing how much stuff they never got to tell each other; it got me thinking.'

'About your own family?'

Dawn takes a slurp from her mug and her mouth fills with bitterness. Perhaps the milk's off. Must be why her tummy feels so dodgy all of a sudden.

'Mum's obviously non-contactable where she is.' She tries to laugh, but it gets stuck in the back of her throat.

'And your dad?'

Dawn's heart rate gathers speed. Must be the damn caffeine. She takes another gulp of her drink regardless, as her mouth has dried out faster than a cheap perm on a hot day.

She starts the words off but has to swallow and breathe again before they will fit through her throat. 'Now, he... ' *Easy, Dawn. That's it, just blow all that air out in one continuous breath.* 'He was a good dad. Before he left. The best, in fact.'

He'd taken her to school every morning as Mum found it tricky getting up early. He was always the one who put a plaster on her knee, and his shoulder was there to cry on every single time the other kids in the street made her cry.

That's why Dawn had been shocked when that same shoulder was missing, right when she'd needed it the most.

Grace lowers Dawn's closed file onto the desk between them, staring at the label on the back of the shiny purple Lever arch binder. 'I know where your dad is. I've been waiting for the right time to tell you. I needed to be sure you were ready.'

Dawn shuffles down the hill leading away from St Jude's with Grace at her side; her legs still wobbling from the shock. Grace's car is parked in its usual spot. Grace climbs into the driver's side and Dawn stands still beside the passenger door.

'It's unlocked,' Grace calls from inside.

Dawn tries to move her arm to open the door, but her limbs feel like they don't belong to her and her chest constricts with fear.

'It's okay.' Grace opens it from the inside. 'We'll take our time. We can just drive there if you like. See where he lives. You don't even have to get out of the car if you don't want to.'

Dawn stares through the window as they move through the town, watching Grace as she checks her mirrors.

They've reached the top of the hill by the castle before Dawn trusts herself to venture into words. 'I just can't believe he's been so close by all this time. I was sure he'd still be somewhere up north if he was still alive.' Dawn shakes her head, trying to order her thoughts into a neat line. 'I want to see him. However hard it is. I need to know what happened and why he left.'

The rain is pelting down even harder now, and Grace flicks the windscreen wipers up with the twig that makes them go faster. 'I'll be right there with you for as long as you need me to be.'

'Thank you.' Whoever invented the English language should have made more words. Better ones, that are up to the job for conversations like this. 'How did you find him?'

The car radio starts to lose signal as they move past the roundabout and take a slip road to the left. Grace turns the crackly music off.

'I did an internet search. Turns out there are more Brightsides than you might think. I left a voicemail on a few of the phone numbers that came up. A couple of days ago, we had a call from a nurse at one of the care homes I'd left a message with. It was your dad's care home. She said he'd been asking after his daughter. His Dawn-light. With a name like Dawn Brightside, you weren't hard to find once you had the same address for more than week. So, he actually found you, in a way.' Grace slows the car to a crawl behind a minivan as the road starts to heave with traffic. All the cars around them are nose-to-butt.

A huge ball forms in Dawn's throat. 'Why's he in a care home?' she asks when she can trust herself to speak. 'He can only be in his sixties.'

'The nurse wasn't able to tell me very much, but I'm afraid since you last saw your dad, he's been diagnosed with Alzheimer's. Early onset.'

A lorry halts in front of them after the roundabout. Grace slams on the breaks and the back of Dawn's head bounces against the headrest.

'And why is he living in a home in Deal? Why is he so far from home?' Dawn asks once her heart rate has recovered.

'I'm sure the nurse, and perhaps your dad, will be able to tell you more. Nurse Carter says he still has many moments, sometimes hours, of being completely lucid. He may not remember much when you first see him. You might have to be patient.'

The car sways violently from one side to another. Dawn closes her eyes in panic, thinking they're about to come clean off the road. It's only when she opens them again that she sees that they are still moving along in perfect position.

'I thought he'd forgotten I existed,' Dawn whispers. 'I should have looked for *him*. I did when Mum died, and then tried again when I fell pregnant with Rosie. But when he couldn't be found, I just kept remembering all the stuff Mum had said and it kept going around and around in my head. After he left, she told me he wanted nothing to do with either of us – that he wanted to be left alone with his new woman. Part of me hoped he was looking for me but after the psych unit, I was never in one place at a time. He would never have been able to find me, even if he'd wanted to.'

Oaklands Residential Home looks nice enough from the car park. It's just not somewhere Dawn had envisaged her dad ever living. She'd mostly pictured him living in a cottage in the south of France with a glamorous woman and a string of children.

'I can't believe he's been right here,' she whispers.

Dawn and Grace tread the long path through the skinny trees until they reach the door to Reception. The wide hatch reminds Dawn of St Jude's and she finds herself hoping that her dad has found friendships there amongst the staff and the other residents, just as she has at the hostel.

'We're here to see Mr Brightside,' Grace says after Dawn has stood there with her mouth half open for several seconds.

'Of course. Hello,' says the bright smile on the other side. The smile belongs to a smiling nurse with a curtain of auburn hair. She disappears from the hatch and emerges from the door next to it, beckoning for Dawn and Grace to follow once they have signed themselves into the building.

'He'll be in here. The residents' lounge,' she explains. 'Mr Brightside prefers to be in here during the day. We encourage everyone to do this as much as possible. Much better than being cooped up in their room alone each day.'

Nurse Carter carries on talking about the home's policy on structured activities, but Dawn has stopped listening.

He's sitting by the window in an old-dear chair, holding back the edge of the curtain with two fingers. He's watching two birds jumping about on the branches of the tiny apple tree on the other side of the glass. Dad had liked birds when Dawn was little. He'd know what species they were. Dawn wouldn't have a clue.

So maybe not too much has changed. He still likes company, enjoys looking out of the window and watching birds. Perhaps he'll turn his face around and it will melt into a smile the second he lays eyes on her. It would be like the last thirty-odd years had never happened.

'Can I help you? Who are you here to see?' Eyes still the same. Pale blue. Kind. Framed by crinkles that have deepened and joined up with new ones. Same hair, just slightly thinner and flecked with the odd grey speckle. Not too different at all. He stands without too much difficulty. He looks well, healthy in fact. What on earth was he doing in a place like this amongst the ancient Scrabble boards and the smell of stale cabbage?

His eyes are still on Grace.

'Hello, Jim,' sings the nurse. 'I've brought a special lady to see you.'

Dawn's stomach contents begin to argue with her insides. Her dad moves his gaze from Grace's face to hers.

The TV in the corner seems to have got louder; each Loose Woman's voice fighting to be heard in every corner of the lounge over the scratching of pencils on crosswords and the argument by the coffee table about who'd eaten the last custard cream.

Dawn's dad looks her in the eye for several seconds. Then he extends a polite hand towards her. 'Lovely to meet you.'

Dawn clamps her jaw down tight to keep the sob from erupting. She takes his hand with her wobbly one and squeezes it tight. A tear falls from her face and lands on the back of his hand.

'I'm sorry. I need to… I just can't… ' Dawn drops her dad's hand as if it's been in the oven on gas mark seven and scurries back past the lace doilies until she's out through the door.

The reception hall is stifling. Dawn stares across at the green door release button as if she could open it with her eyes. It's only about three strides away but there seems to be several bodies in the lobby between her and the exit. Loud questions from men in hi-vis jackets shout through the hatch. Which drain had been flooding? Had the staff been putting baby wipes and sanitary towels down the toilets again? They'd been advised last time to put a sign up.

Dawn wants to peel her cardigan off but there's no room to

move her elbows between all these people stealing the air from the room. Sweat trickles down her back as the voices get louder and faster, and then the smell wafts through. Old cooking fat mixed with turds made from overcooked vegetables. The room shunts from side to side as Dawn focuses on slowing her racing heart and swallowing back the bile.

A heavy hand on her back. Another one on the crook of her elbow.

'You're okay. You're going to be okay. Come and sit down and catch your breath,' says Nurse Carter as she guides Dawn towards the telephone bench next to the leaflet stand; her very presence parting the waves between the Dyno-Rod experts.

Dawn sits on the lumpy cushion, leaning forward in an effort to suck some oxygen back inside her. A glass of water held inside a hand and a concerned voice appears in front of her nose and she gulps it gratefully, without even looking up at where it came from.

'He gets confused. Forgets,' the nurse says, gently. 'He always comes back, and he always wants you.'

The bodies in the hall begin to file out through the front door closely followed by a staff uniform, leaving a welcome gust of cool but rancid air.

'I wanted him to see me,' Dawn sniffs.

'And he will. I promise. You just need to get back in there.'

Ignoring the wobble in her legs, Dawn puts one foot in front of the other, through the lounge door and back to the chair by the window.

He's looking out of the window again, his stare fixed through the glass. Grace is sitting at his side, speaking quietly and gently into his ear.

Dawn keeps her own words inside and perches on the chair on the other side of him; the deep, plastic-covered cushion squelching all the air out as her butt sinks in.

'But that couldn't have been her. My Dawn-light is only nine years old,' he cries out. 'Lovely girl she is. Always making me laugh. Where is she?'

Dawn looks at the back of his shoulders, willing them to turn. They begin to jerk up and down and a sob reverberates around the room.

Grace continues to speak in a low voice, and he spins around, presenting Dawn with the sight of his face, flowing with tears.

'Oh, Dawn-light,' he gulps, grabbing for her hand.

Dawn and her dad remain in the corner by the window for most of the afternoon. Barely speaking at first, just looking at each other and holding on tight. One by one, the other residents had begun to shuffle off to their rooms and the staff had found jobs to do in other areas of the building.

'Do you like it here?' Dawn asks.

He smiles. 'I think I do. Most of the time, anyway. I just have to keep reminding myself why I'm here. Ironic, really.'

Dawn reaches inside for the right sentence. It feels like an attempt to engineer a bridge that's strong enough to hold up thirty-three missing years.

'I'm sorry it's taken so long to visit,' she says, tutting at herself for the inadequacy. She needs way more material. More steel. Definitely more bricks if she's ever going to reach across to the other side.

'I just thought… I didn't know where you were.'

He takes a long, shaky breath and crosses his slipper-clad feet together. 'I looked for you for years,' he says finally. 'It was my fault. Gave her an ultimatum about the drinking. Next thing I know, she'd upped and left with you, leaving a note saying I'd never find her. She thought I was going to take you away from her.'

It's like a cold sponge has wrung itself around Dawn's heart, holding it still. 'But – she let me think you'd abandoned me. That you went off with another woman.'

Dawn's dad's face goes fag-ash grey. He tries to speak but the words come out in a splutter and he coughs as Dawn pats him gently on the back.

'It explains why we moved house so often after you left,' Dawn says as the pieces of her past begin to slot into place. I tried to find you when… oh. Mum. Did you know?'

'I know she died,' he says gently. He places a hand over Dawn's. 'The staff from here told me. I'm so sorry you were left all on your own, pet.'

You're dad's not here. He's left us. You will never see him again.

'Your mum did love you. She just didn't always deal with things in the best way. Guilt probably. She found it difficult after you were born. Got depressed. None of it was your fault, love.'

Dawn nods slowly at the memories. Her mum's closed bedroom door. Her all-day dressing gown. The empty bottles behind the sofa.

'I fought to get her as much help as I could. I didn't plan to leave, and I never stopped loving you, Dawn-light.'

Dawn releases the ball in her throat and throws her arms around her dad's skinny shoulders. She has so many more questions, but her dad's misty eyes look tired.

'Thank you so much for everything,' Dawn says to Nurse Carter when they arrive back in the lobby. 'There is something

I don't understand, though. What is my dad doing in Deal? Why is he so far from Manchester?'

Nurse Carter gives Dawn a whistle-stop tour of her father's life since she'd last seen him. He'd been diagnosed several years ago and was quickly unable to manage without support. There had been a fire at his first residential home and no next of kin could be found to look after him. The nearest emergency placement had been Birmingham and then that later closed down too.

'Happens more than people realise,' Nurse Carter says. 'So many people are moved from pillar to post and lose contact with their families. I'm sure he would have asked for you many times before he ever arrived here.'

'I wouldn't have been easy to find back then,' murmurs Dawn.

Nurse Carter comes out from behind the hatch and pulls Dawn into an exuberant hug. She's at least six-foot-tall and her puffed-up hair is thick with hairspray. 'Come back soon. I've never seen your dad look so happy.' She tells Dawn she can call her Petunia, but Dawn can already only think of her as Nurse Carter: fellow stranger-hugger. She's pleased her dad has someone so fabulous looking after him.

'I just can't get over the lies,' Dawn says to Grace when they reach the car. 'Why couldn't she just try to stop drinking? She actually let me think he'd *abandoned* me.' Dawn punches the dashboard as she climbs into the passenger side.

'I understand the anger.' Grace places her hand on Dawn's elbow. 'You have so much to process. You need to give yourself some time.'

She turns the key in the ignition. 'There *is* a certain resident who lives in our hostel who would tell you to look for the positives.'

'I suppose I don't need to look very far. And I can't thank you enough for taking me to see my dad.'

'Time to look to the future,' Grace says. 'Early night for us all tonight. Tomorrow, we have our sleepout to look forward to.'

CHAPTER 33

Grace

GRACE LOOKS UP FROM her desk on the afternoon of the sleepout and watches the drops outside the window as they fall from the grey sky, cursing inwardly as they tap against the office window. The very same night they're asking Dover's inhabitants to sleep on the streets for St Jude's would have to mean that huge drops of rain begin limbering up, detangling themselves from the clouds in readiness to flood their sleeping bags and soak their cardboard mattresses.

'It's better this way. Trust me,' Peter says as he looks over Grace's shoulder at the computer screen.

'How's it better?' Grace asks, trying to keep the impatience from her voice. 'Less than half of the participants will probably show up now, meaning we'll make a fraction of the sponsor money.'

'But think of the awareness we'll raise. Sleeping on the ground sucks big-time, trust me, but it's a whole different game of ping-pong when you do it in the wet. It gets right into your bones until the despair has eaten away at every bit of your insides.'

Through the hatch, Grace can see a line of St Jude's residents standing by the door all dressed in waterproof jackets and carrying backpacks stuffed with sleeping bags. Each one had been assured they were under no obligation to take part – they had all been through quite enough on those unforgiving streets to last a lifetime, but almost every one of them had still signed up.

Peter and Grace switch everything off and lock the office door behind them, sticking a 'Closed' notice on the foyer window. It feels odd to empty the building of people, even just for one night, and Grace's stomach somersaults when she looks back at the word 'Closed', hoping it's not a word that's ever there to stay.

The mood is quiet and sombre as the staff and residents of St Jude's march their way as one body down the winding hill and towards the market square, occasionally looking up at the falling sky. Lost in thoughts; perhaps battling memories of days when they'd slept under the raindrops, not knowing when a dry room would next be there to hold them.

Dawn and Cara are already in the middle of the empty market square, erecting the banner lovingly made by St Jude's residents at last week's weekly meeting. It says, 'St Jude's Last Cause: The Sleepout.' But the bright felt-tip-filled letters have begun to run across the page, rendering the words only just legible.

It's only the St Jude's lot so far. 'How many people did we have signed up to this through our Facebook page?' Grace whispers to Peter.

'Quite a few.'

'How many?' Grace repeats.

'Around forty people.'

'But then there should be at least some people here by

now.' Grace's throat feels scratchy and a raindrop hits her in the eye and falls down her face, pulling a tear down with it. 'Then even if forty people and us from St Jude's just raise twenty quid each, that would be... ' She uses her fingers for the simple maths, trying to get her fried brain to operate at its normal capacity. 'Just over a grand. Then it would be worth it. It might be enough to buy us more time.'

Peter's gaze is directed away from the square and up towards the high street where the doorways of boarded-up shops are littered with huddled bodies under assortments of blankets and coverless duvets. 'If you'd ever spent one night having to do this for real, trust me, you'd know this would be worth it either way.'

One by one, the residents of St Jude's drop their bags in place and roll out their sleeping bags so that they lay in a vague semi-circle around the half-hearted shrubbery in the centre of the square.

Cara's pale, slender fingers fumble with the zip on hers, before she opens it and climbs inside, nodding briefly at Teardrop Terry as he follows suit.

Jack has positioned his sleeping bag as far away as he can from Grace's and catches her eye only briefly as he unlaces his trainers. Grace is grateful he understands how she needs to keep things in their different compartments right now, but she feels the loss of his closeness keenly and it cools her quicker than the chill in the air.

'Perhaps we should have hired a marquee?' Grace asks Peter, regretting it when she sees the sudden stiffness in his jaw. 'I only mean so that more people would be prepared to do it in the rain,' she says, folding her arms. 'Plus, I'm slightly worried about people contracting pneumonia.'

Someone sneezes and coughs simultaneously and Peter finally meets her eye. 'It will be fine,' he says quietly but there's a firm edge to his voice. 'We just need to keep everyone's spirits up.'

Heavy grey shutters thunder to the ground behind them, covering the last remaining open convenience store in the town centre.

'That's it, it's nine o' clock,' says Teardrop Terry.

A group of pigeons begin to waddle away from them up the high street as if even they have given up on them. The waterfall behind the shrub stops dead. The water ceases moving as if it's been turned to ice. Grace hadn't realised how much noise it had been making or how much silence it had been hiding.

Cara is sitting up in her sleeping bag and blowing hard on each hand in turn.

'Here,' says Terry as he throws her a pair of balled-up gloves. 'Won't you need them?'

'Nah. Never wear 'em. They don't really work for me. Make my hands colder if anything.'

Grace doesn't feel as if her hands could get much colder. She keeps them scrunched up under the tops of her thighs, lying back to lean on her elbows and stretching her legs out in front of her, forcing herself not to shiver. The rain's getting harder and each available drop is finding its way inside the front of her raincoat. She pulls her hood up higher, but it just slips back down again. She thinks about how it's still July. What must it be like in February, when the air hasn't tasted warmth for several months? When the ground beneath where they are now is not only cold, but frozen solid? When it's not just for tonight but for as many days as she could see in front of her, stretching out with no end, no light and no tunnel?

Grace looks around at each face in their rudimentary semi-circle and feels a renewed respect stir inside her belly for every one of them who has endured this way of life. Day in, night out, amongst ridicule, spit, do-gooder smiles and pity-pennies in otherwise empty upturned hats. How can she allow a single one of them to go back to that whilst she tucks herself in a warm home with hot chocolate and marshmallows?

'Could I please borrow your phone?' Dawn appears next to Grace's sleeping bag. 'Mine doesn't have a camera, it's only a cheap one. £9.99 from Tesco's.'

'What do you need a camera for?' Grace braces herself for Dawn's latest scheme.

'I want to film some of what we are doing. Show people how hard it is.'

Grace slips her phone out from her sleeping bag and hands it over. 'Try not to get it wet. It's not a fancy waterproof one.'

'Grace Jennings?' Dawn holds the phone up to her face. 'My name is Dawn Elisabeth Brightside, one word. Am I right in thinking you were expecting more people for this event?'

Grace nods. 'You could say that. Rubbish weather though. Can't really blame them.'

'Indeed,' Dawn says, looking up at the sky and back at all of them and their drowned state. 'But what would you like to say to the locals, the ones following the story on the St Jude's social media pages?'

'What story?'

'The one you're about to tell me. About St Jude's. About how it's going to close unless people donate to your sleepout and save the place. About how if they don't, it won't be long before lots of people in this group will be doing this for real.'

'There's plenty of people up there in the doorways who are doing this for real,' pipes up Peter.

It gives Grace an idea. 'Don't interview me. Or even him,' she points at Peter. 'Although he knows what this is like much more than I do. Ask them. The people who have done this for real every single night. Any one of them about what this is like. Sleeping out here again after allowing themselves to believe that the future would be better after they'd been offered a room and some support, just weeks or months before potentially having it all ripped away again. There's a reason why people haven't turned up today. Because it's wet and bloody freezing. Dangerous for our health. But that's exactly why we needed people to come down here, just for one night – so these people won't have to do it for many more. No one wants to, not even for one night. And that's exactly the problem.'

Dawn stays quiet, and Grace swallows hard. Of course Dawn knows exactly what it's like to live outside. She should be interviewing *her,* not the other way around. But Dawn is already looking around, considering who to approach next. She turns and walks towards their motley crew, phone in hand, stopping by each sleeping bag, one after the other before visiting the row of doorways up the high street.

CHAPTER 34

Dawn

THE LAST DROP OF rain has fallen on Dover town as the burnt-orange sun sweeps upwards from the sea, bringing with it the first warmth of the day and the faint taste of salt on the lips of each one stirring beneath the ocean of nylon and polyester.

One by one, people haul themselves up to sitting, blowing on their hands and flexing their limbs, many of them amazed they could still feel them after such a night.

Dawn is the first one to peel open an eye and stretch out a numb arm. Next to her, Grace's nose twitches as a clump of her damp hair falls across her face. She sits up with a start, disorientated. Peter turns over and catches Hazel's eye, and her cheeks blush into two perfect round circles. Peter braves a nod and receives one in return, accompanied by the briefest of smiles. It's a start. Nothing like a night on cold concrete to bring people together and leave the past behind.

Dawn lies there a little longer, making shapes with her mind from the clouds above her before scrambling around in her sleeping bag for her linen trousers and flat, ballet-style pumps, £11.99 from Shoe Zone. She needs to get ready quickly today. She has her medical assessment appointment for her

ESA benefit payments. Apparently, claimants are regularly assessed on their health condition and this would be Dawn's first appointment. She checks the pocket of her cardigan and feels for the folded-up letter with the directions on. She's going to need them as she'd spent hours yesterday convincing Grace that she could attend on her own. That she needed to start standing on her own two feet. She's glad she did now; Grace will be shattered today after spending a whole night under the stars, resolutely facing away from that Jack fellow. She'd made it look ever so tiring.

Grace had reluctantly agreed after assuring her if she changed her mind she'd come along with Dawn for moral support. Dawn wasn't sure there was anything moral to support really; how could it be right that the ill and infirm should have to stand on a stage under a spotlight, whilst showing their flaws to an audience who then get to decide if they're ill enough to get the money? They may as well be stripped naked. She's heard they aren't even doctors or nurses. Just people who'd completed a six-week course on being judge and jury.

She rolls up her sleeping bag and stuffs it in her backpack before shuffling off unnoticed to the bus stop.

CHAPTER 35

Grace

EVERY PART OF GRACE'S body aches from sleeping on the ground and she fights to keep her eyes open as she looks through the office checklist. It's almost lunchtime and she hasn't tackled any of the daily tasks yet. After last night's washout, it almost feels like there's no point. If the place closes down, what will it matter if Grace has filled out the health and safety sheets? The first task on the tick list is: *Check emails.*

Damn. Grace feels the blood drain from her face when she sees the message from head office entitled: *Funds Raised for Sleepout.*

Any secret hopes Grace had been harbouring are dashed against the rocks when she looks at the numbers.

She's still staring glumly at the screen when Dawn appears at the office hatch, talking at a thousand miles per hour about her ESA appointment.

'I am so sorry.' Grace gets up from her desk and puts her head through the hatch. 'I should have been firmer about coming with you. Those appointments can be extremely stressful.'

'It's fine, don't worry. It's done. I did fine on my own.' Dawn looks tired but her trademark smile is still stuck firmly to her face. 'I'm not holding my breath, though. The questions were brutal – I felt like I was on an episode of *Judge Judy*.'

Grace should make her a coffee, give her some reassurance about how she could appeal if she wasn't granted the sickness benefit, or a pep talk about how well she's been doing lately; that it might not be long until she's ready to work again and then she won't need the ESA. But the tears are going to fall, and she doesn't want Dawn to see.

'I'm sorry, I need to close the office for an hour. Peter will be here soon. I just need to go somewhere.' Grace rushes the words out and pulls the shutter down before running past Dawn in the foyer and bolting through the front door. Her Fiat is parked at the bottom of the hill and she fumbles with her car keys.

The engine in Grace's car starts just in time for the first teardrop to skid down her face. Had she really believed she could make a difference? She never should have taken the manager's job in the first place; she just doesn't have what it takes. Her mum would never have allowed everything to crumble away like this in her line of work.

She wipes her face dry with the sleeve of her favourite hoody. Cold wind slashes through the car as the passenger door opens.

'Room for one more?' Dawn doesn't wait for an answer, just slams the door shut and buckles up her seatbelt. 'Where are we off to – anywhere nice?'

Grace shrugs but manages half a smile. 'I just thought I needed to be on my own. As you're here though, I'll show you my favourite thinking spot.'

The roads of Dover are quiet with fewer cars than usual.

Raindrops start to fall, splattering against the windscreen. Grace puts the wipers on, and they squeak across the glass.

'I don't know what else to do to keep the hostel open.' Grace hates the sound of her own voice. It's flat. Defeated, with all of the fight sucked out of it.

Dawn places her hand on the gearstick, covering Grace's own.

'Maybe I shouldn't have encouraged the fundraising,' Grace carries on. 'I might have just let you all get your hopes up for nothing. Why didn't I just spent the last few weeks looking for flats for all of you?' She looks in her rear-view mirror as if she's considering reversing the whole way back, rewinding the last three weeks.

'Because some of us aren't ready,' Dawn says. 'Needing a place to stay is the one big thing we all need. But St Jude's is more than that. We need the support, all that other stuff you help us with, so we don't end up back outside again when things go wrong.'

'I think you're almost ready,' Grace says. 'I don't think you realise how far you've come. But the ugly truth is, there's no guarantee that St Jude's will still be here in the winter. All of us will need to start preparing for that.'

'At least we've gone down fighting.'

'I'm so sorry.' Grace's voice gets a dent in it halfway through.

'Not your fault. We'll all be fine, one way or another. And that's all because of the work you and Peter and the others have all done. Besides, it ain't over yet; we've still got two weeks and we don't know how much people will pledge when they see our sleepout video.'

'I love your optimism.' A smile breaks out on Grace's face, taking her by surprise.

She keeps driving forward, shrugging off Dawn's question about where they might be going.

Flint walls and lush green trees fly past the car once they've left the concrete of the town and suburbs and arrived in the car park of Kearsney Abbey.

'I love it here,' Grace says as she pulls up the handbrake. 'The place I told you about is just up there.'

Grace's thinking spot is the left side of a chipped metal bench, on top of the hill that overlooks the lake. The lake that somehow always shimmers, whatever the weather, as it carries around cloud-white swans with their long, proud necks. Grace envies them each time she comes here, for their poise and effortless grace. Pah. She wishes she was effortless.

Everything she'd done up to this point to sculpt herself into what she is now has taken every measurement of energy she has ever consumed. Trying to make her parents proud. Working hard to give her residents the best chance possible. It's all been so exhausting.

'I just don't know who I would be without St Jude's.' Grace lowers herself to the bench and Dawn plonks herself next to her.

'There's a big world out there with a Grace-shaped hole.' Dawn swivels around to face her. 'Perhaps you need to find where it is and slot yourself in. Maybe it's time to remember that you're more than just your job. That there are other things – or people – for you to enjoy.'

A black and white collie runs after a tennis ball and catches it before it hits the ground, wagging his tail smugly all the way back to his owner.

'Time.' Grace turns the word over in her mind as a battle

begins around it. A small frisson of excitement takes hold as she considers a different future for herself. She'd been so busy worrying about what would happen to the residents, she hadn't entertained the thought that there might be more for her waiting around the corner. A life that could hold Jack within it with no recriminations.

'You remember when I asked you what your smart goals were?' Dawn asks, smiling. 'You never did answer me.'

'I did! I told you I wanted to make St Jude's the best place it could be and to help all you lot. For all the good it did,' scoffs Grace. 'Peter's right. Smart goals are a load of shite after all.'

A duck hops out from the water and starts waddling around on the grass, searching for treasures in the ground with its beak. Grace wishes she was a duck. No pressures. No expectations.

'But what else would you like to do if you had to do something else?' Dawn presses. 'What would you want to do most if you could do anything?'

'Channing Tatum,' Grace says without missing a beat, and they both laugh. It feels good, and Grace can feel some of the weight lifting already. 'Okay, I'll tell you.' She holds her hands up at Dawn in mock-surrender. 'There's someone I've got close to. Someone I want to be with. But it's complicated.'

'Does this mystery person know?'

The duck has given up mooching around in the grass and lands back on the lake with a gentle splash.

Grace nods and then shakes her head. 'I'm not sure what he knows to be honest. He's probably as confused as me.'

'Remember that time you told me to remind myself that I was worthy of happiness?'

'That's different – you're… '

292

'Why's it different? Because I'm homeless?' Dawn finishes for her. 'There's a load of people out there going through all sorts of rubbish and not living their happiest lives. What would you tell them?'

'That we can't control everything that happens to us, but that we should grasp onto the positive things as hard as we can,' Grace lets the words flow out, words she has said countless times to residents. 'It's not as simple as that though. There are... circumstances. And besides, I need to focus on the hostel. That has to be my priority. I don't have time to be with anyone else right now.'

'So, you want to be on your own?'

'Not really,' Grace admits. 'I hate making meals for one and secretly detest the happy endings of romcoms.'

'What would make *you* happy? Your happiness is important too.'

Grace's jaw clenches tight as she shakes her head in an effort to dislodge the unwanted pictures that have flooded her mind. Her mum's *I'm-just-disappointed-that's-all* face as she'd rebuked Grace for complaining when her parents arrived home from New York three days late and missed her tenth birthday. *We've been working hard to buy you nice things. To give you a life that will make you happy. You could at least be grateful.*

'St Jude's makes me happy. I love helping you guys.'

'I know.' Dawn reaches across and places a hand on Grace's shoulder. 'I'll always be grateful – we all will. But what's to stop you getting out there and making yourself happy too? Maybe you need to look to your own future – and perhaps that certain other person in Room 4 who always makes you smile?'

Grace looks at Dawn's wide grin and feels the blood rush to her cheeks. 'Does everyone know?'

'I wouldn't know,' laughs Dawn. 'But I've seen the way you look at each other, and if life has taught me one thing it's that happiness can be found in the darkest of places…'

'Isn't that Harry Potter?'

'No idea – I read it on your coffee mug.'

The park side of the abbey has almost emptied by the time that Grace and Dawn make their way back to the car park. The squirrels run and chase and climb, and the trees begin to dance faster as the wind picks up and rushes through their branches.

Grace drives Dawn back to Dover town in silence, but this time it's made from hope and quiet thoughts. She drops Dawn off at the bottom of the hill towards St Jude's before pulling a U-turn and heading home.

When she arrives at her bedsit, Grace pulls her nan's cardigan from the wardrobe. It smells of lavender talc and childhood cuddles.

She bounces across her bed and reaches for her work mobile. Her fingers click on the contacts and scroll to the number she wants. She stares at the screen whilst the smell of beef and onions wafts under the door from the flat next door. Before putting her meal-for-one back in the fridge and pulling a takeaway menu from the drawer, Grace selects Jack's number and types out a message. She adds her address, and suggests he tries to get there in time to help her eat a curry.

After all, what *is* to stop her from grabbing hold of some happiness?

'You're lucky I actually finished work on time, otherwise you would've had to eat this all by yourself,' Jack grins as he helps

Grace unpack the takeaway. 'Bloody hell, how many people were you expecting?'

'Just you,' Grace says, feeling the blush creep across her cheeks.

Jack doesn't answer. He fiddles with the edge of one of the rice containers. He's tanned from working outside all week and Grace is trying desperately to think of something to say to make him smile, just so she can see the dimple by the side of his mouth.

'*Sharknado Two* is on Netflix,' she blurts out. 'Thought we could watch it together, since we enjoyed the last one so much.'

Jack doesn't laugh, doesn't smile. He lets go of the container and turns his dimple-free face towards Grace.

'What is this?' he asks. 'What are we doing here?'

'Just having a curry, watching a film. Doing what friends do. I mean, if you don't want to watch *Sharknado*, there's plenty of other things on. I just thought that… '

'Grace.' Jack interrupts her babbling, turning towards her and walking forwards. He stops close in front, not touching her but leaving only inches between them.

'I can't do this anymore,' he murmurs. His mouth is so near to hers.

Grace's chest squeezes inwards over her thundering heart and her stomach plummets.

'I've tried to keep my distance, tried to be patient,' he carries on without taking his eyes from hers. 'And if you only want a friend, I will be that for you one day. But at the moment, it's too confusing.'

Grace takes hold of Jack's hands, hoping her own aren't too clammy. 'That's why I asked you here,' she croaks. 'I've been confused too. But I know I don't give a shiny shit about the film. Or the curry. And I don't just need a friend. I need you.'

Jack watches her face for several seconds, inching closer until their lips finally find each other. Jack's full lips feel as soft and plump as Grace had imagined they would, and her bare toes curl up as the kiss deepens and his hands move low around her waist, crushing her chest against his.

'Are you still confused?' he asks in a low voice.

'Hell, no,' Grace mumbles.

CHAPTER 36

Dawn

ROOM NUMBER SIX AT St Jude's has become the place to be for friendship, hugs and advice. Dawn doubts it's always good advice that falls from her lips and into the ears of her fellow residents, but they often seem to believe it is and that's what matters. That, and the fact that she usually has a handy stash of Wagon Wheels stuffed under her mattress.

Dawn has spent the last few days after the sleepout, trying to keep everyone's spirits up. This afternoon, though, it's just Dawn and Cara perched on the bed, although Dawn swears to herself that she can still see Shaun's arse print on the far corner of the duvet cover, even if the pills have taken the rest of him away.

Cara's face is shining with the light of a hundred bulbs. She's just got back from spending the day on the beach with her boys. Grace had gone along with her for moral support and Dawn has never seen Cara look so happy or alive. 'You should have seen us,' she says. 'Running about on the beach like a proper family. Curtis even drew me a picture in the café. It's me and him. Look,' she says, pulling out a piece of A4 from her pocket with a few vague squiggles from a felt tip pen that had almost run dry.

'It's beautiful,' says Dawn.

'I suppose I just wanted to say… well, thanks and stuff.' Cara stares down at the paper she's folding into neat squares. 'If you hadn't got on my case and hung around, I don't know where I'd be now, but it wouldn't be with my boys. Grace has been great too. I was so nervous about today; afraid I was going to screw it up. But she made me realise I could do it – be their mum.'

'Thank God for Grace, eh?' Dawn means it. She thanks him for Grace every morning. For all of them, actually. Grace has promised to put Dawn in touch with someone who could give her advice about looking for Rosie. It would be scary, and she'd been warned that it might be a long road but reconnecting with her dad had lent her a glimpse of what the future could look like with family in it.

'I need to pop to the office myself later. Got this in the post.' Dawn reaches over and picks up a brown envelope from the top of her chest of drawers. 'It's the answer to my benefit assessment. Apparently, the computer said "piss off".'

'What? Shit.' Cara pulls out her pouch of tobacco and starts to roll a fag. 'What you meant to do now?'

'It says I can appeal. The staff here said they'd help with it if that's what we need to do. What the hell do people do if they don't have people like that to help? People who get how this stuff works.' Dawn pictures the thousands of people out there who are completely alone.

'Thank God for St Jude's, eh?'

'Yeah. Thank God.'

They both fall quiet whilst Dawn stuffs her letter back into its envelope.

'You heard they've called a house meeting?' says Cara. 'I reckon they're going to tell us how much money we raised.'

'Yup,' agrees Dawn. 'I got everyone Chocolate Hobnobs to celebrate.'

The residents' lounge is crammed full and Dawn is draped across a torn beanbag in the corner. Grace is sitting on an upright chair in front of the TV with Peter next to her. She has her laptop balanced on her knees and although she throws a smile to each person as they enter the room, her eyes keep falling back to the screen and they get wider each time.

'We have news,' she says after a few seconds of dry coughing.

The room sits up a little straighter.

'You all did so well last week,' Grace says, wiping under her eye with the back of her pinkie finger. 'I don't know if you've heard this or not yet, but between the bake sale and the sleepout, we've raised well over a thousand pounds.'

A couple of people clap. Dawn stays silent and watches Grace. She's waiting for more. The main dish.

'We've had a call this afternoon from head office.' Grace bum-fidgets in her seat. 'We've still raised only a fraction of the money we need to cover the shortfall in funding. Unfortunately, despite asking for an extension, that still means that we only have a week to raise the other five thousand pounds, and if not, we'll sadly be closing our doors for good.'

Dawn looks at the plateful of chocolate Hobnobs, untouched in the middle of the coffee table next to the Frustration board.

'We're screwed,' Terry pipes up.

Seagulls screech from outside and a gust of wind carries an empty can of Red Bull across the concrete. Someone should have put it in the recycling bin. Now nobody would, there'd be no point. It will be left there to clatter-clatter, bashing into the plant pots and the garden wall. Trapped. Cold. Freezing during the winter months.

The collective mutters begin from every corner of the room and get louder and louder. Grace sits quietly and Peter attempts to catch the questions from the front and juggle them between his hands before handing them back, regretfully unanswered.

Outside, the dustbin lids rattle in the wind and the waves crash against the chalky cliffs, rattling with the shingle they pull back from the shore.

'I've got an idea,' says Dawn.

One hour and forty-five minutes later, the room is buzzing with words and twitching biros as plans are made and scribbled down. Hazel has arrived as Terry had got his phone out of his pocket to call her as soon as Dawn's great idea had left her lips. Well, as long as they didn't take over the whole thing. This one is Dawn's baby. No. Her project. That's better.

'I must say, it's definitely going to be something different. Will I be allowed to wear my thermals?' laughs Hazel.

'I know it seems a little extreme,' says Grace. 'I was sceptical when Dawn first suggested it, but we have so little time it needs to be something dramatic enough to get people to sit up and take notice. Something that can be shared and spread around quickly on social media.'

'Plus, we don't need to arrange much or collect too many props,' says Peter. 'We just need towels. Well, and swimming costumes, obviously.'

Cara is already tap-tapping away on the communal computer

and Dawn takes her eyes away from the screen as soon as she catches a glimpse of the F for Facebook icon. No time to mope; they have work to do.

'I've added the sponsored swim to our JustGiving page,' Cara says. 'Now people can sponsor us or ask people to sponsor them to join in too.'

Dawn slips away from the meeting before anybody else does. She lets herself out of the hostel and makes her way to the bus stop. It's past visiting hours at Oaklands, so she crosses her fingers that Nurse Carter is on shift. As she gets off the bus and climbs the hill, her soul feels heavy with the weight of the unknown. They *have* to make the swimathon work. But what if it doesn't?

'I'm here to see Mr Brightside,' Dawn says to the man on the reception desk. She hasn't seen him there before. He glances at the clock on the wall behind him and looks pained.

'It's okay, it's his daughter.' Nurse Carter appears behind the Perspex. 'She can come up with me, I was just on my way to his room with his meds.'

He's sitting in his chair, staring ahead. A crossword puzzle book rests in his hands. It's upside down.

'Dawn's here to see you,' the nurse says in a normal voice.

Dawn's pleased. She can't stand it when people shout slowly at older or confused people as if it might make things clearer. It never does.

'Thank goodness,' he says as Dawn kisses his head. 'I've been waiting all week for you lot to come out and look at that boiler. Had to put two extra blankets on my baby's bed last night. Freezing, she was. Freezing.' He shivers and rubs his hands together. 'Do you need any help with your tools? In your van, are they?'

Dawn pulls the spare chair close to him and sits on it. Lucid or not, she needs her dad. 'No thanks, I'll manage fine with the tools. A cup of coffee would be great though.'

The room feels thick with silence when Nurse Carter leaves to get the drinks. Dawn's dad is watching a picture on the wall. A dog with a little girl in a bonnet.

'It's been a rubbish day,' Dawn blurts out. 'Why is it that you can try and try and still things just don't work out how you want them to?'

Silence.

'We worked so hard last week to try and raise some money. It just wasn't enough. We have one more thing to try, but if that doesn't work, we're all going to lose our rooms. The staff will be out of a job.'

Dawn's dad looks away from the picture and back at Dawn. He frowns and opens his mouth as if he wants to say something, but then closes it again.

'That's terrible.' Nurse Carter comes clattering in with a tray of coffees. She puts one in front of Dawn and one in front of her dad. 'Mind if I drink mine in here too? Where is it you're staying?'

Dawn tells her about St Jude's. About the staff and her friends and the help they have given her. She talks about the activities they put on for the community and how she'd taught Bill how to read. She talks and she talks and then she realises the clock has moved a whole hour.

'Don't be daft.' The nurse puts her hands up in front of her when Dawn apologises for still being there. 'What was the thing?'

'Thing?'

'The last thing you want to try to do to raise money.'

'It's a sponsored swim in the sea. Bit silly, probably. It is England after all. It will probably rain and who wants to swim in that? It'll be freezing.'

A smile crosses the nurse's face. 'Your timing is incredible. Last week I took three of our residents for a swim on Deal beach. I've just read about this research piece, you see, in the *Nursing Times*. About cold water and how a quick dip into it is good for our mental health. I'll show you the article on your way out.'

'That will be great, thank you.' Dawn gives the nurse a hug. 'And thank you for listening to me witter on about St Jude's.'

'Pleasure. It sounds like a really special place.'

Dawn's dad looks up. 'So, have you fixed that boiler? Those pipes still don't sound quite right to me.'

CHAPTER 37

Grace

GRACE PULLS OPEN THE curtains of the staff flat and inspects the morning sky with a degree of unease. Grey clouds cluster together, joining forces to keep the sun away from Dover town.

Butterflies shift inside Grace's tummy as she thinks about the day ahead. It's the day of the sponsored swim and yesterday the forecast had promised sunshine. Will people still come if the weather is bad?

Peter insists on taking the minibus for the momentous occasion, even though the walk from the car park is almost equidistant from St Jude's itself. By seven-thirty, all of the residents have climbed aboard, sleepy-eyed and grumbling about the weather.

An hour later, they are all clustered together in clumps across the shingle near the water's edge. Grace watches the scene below from the promenade for a few minutes. Peter has laid out brightly coloured towels in rows across the shingle and is helping Jack to erect the huge St Jude's banner, a result of last Saturday's collective artwork.

Cara stands at the water's edge, pulling a towel around herself and shifting from one foot to the other as the cool morning air blows off the sea and pulls the goosebumps from her arms.

Teardrop Terry picks her up and pretends to throw her into the water.

'I bet I last longer in there than any of you lot.' Cara's howl of laughter mingles with the protests of Dawn and Terry and carries right across to Grace's ears.

They all look so happy, so optimistic that they can make a difference today.

'Grace? Uh-oh.' Peter whistles under his breath once she reaches his side. 'That's not a good face.'

Grace takes a step backwards, wincing as a tiny sharp pebble that had found its way inside her sandal digs into her heel. A seagull squawks, angrily cutting through the sounds of merriment.

'I'm just looking at that sky,' she says. 'And the forecast now for this morning is not good. I just don't want a repeat of the sleepout.'

'People will come,' Peter says. But his eyes are on the choppy grey waves.

'I started looking at jobs yesterday. You know, just in case.'

'Oh, Grace.'

'There wasn't much. A few care home positions. You should probably keep an eye out too, although I bloody hope it doesn't come to that.'

'You are not going anywhere, young lady. We need you.'

'For as long as St Jude's is open. I'll stay till the end. Whatever happens.' Grace plasters a smile on her face and jogs towards the residents. 'Right, you lot – time to warm up,' she yells above the wind. She gets them to stand in a circle facing each other before putting them through a regime of jumping jacks and running on the spot. 'If our muscles are warm and loose before we go in, we'll be able to swim for longer and will be less likely to get cramps,' she says, ignoring the eyerolls from Cara. 'We have ten minutes until we're due to start. Let's use them wisely.'

A man is walking towards them along the promenade. *Thank goodness. People are coming.* The man whistles and a Golden Retriever appears behind him. Man and dog keep walking until they've passed by altogether. No one else is on the beach and there are no onlookers from the promenade.

Five minutes to go.

Grace closes her eyes. Her mind fills with rows of sodden sleeping bags lined up in the doorways of Dover town centre. She pictures people picking up discarded leaflets with St Jude's phone number on and getting the disconnected dial tone when they call.

'They're not coming are they.' Cara appears beside her.

Two minutes to go.

'I think I know why.' Jack is holding up his phone. 'We're relying mostly on our Facebook page to get the word out. But look – the post about today has been deleted. People probably think we've cancelled because of the weather.'

Right on cue, a drop of rain plops onto Grace's forearm, closely followed by another. 'Shit.' Grace sinks to her knees on the stones, the sting from the pebbles lending a welcome distraction from her racing mind. 'It's my fault,' she whispers when Jack plonks himself beside her. 'I edited the post last night. I realised that "swimathon" had been spelled wrong. I must have removed the whole thing by mistake.' She buries her head in her hands. They feel cold against her hot forehead. Nausea hits and she gulps in some air before swallowing it down. 'They deserve better.' She nods towards the residents at the edge of the water. 'You all do.'

Jack places his arm around her shoulder and removes it immediately when Peter turns around and starts walking towards them.

'How do you think we should play this?' Peter asks, his face scrunched up with obvious disappointment.

'They've all got their costumes on,' Grace says. 'And most of them have got sponsors already. We may not be able to make very much, but we owe it to them to go ahead with it.' A tear escapes down her cheek and she wipes it away with her sleeve. 'Where's Dawn disappeared to?' Dawn is running up the promenade and away from them, phone to ear and moving faster than Grace had ever seen her move.

'She said something about meeting someone. She made us promise not to start without her.' Peter chuckles briefly before the lines on his forehead bunch back up again.

The rain continues to fall. The seagulls keep cawing. A group of shivering people in swimming costumes sit down on the pebbles and wait.

CHAPTER 38

Dawn

DAWN LISTENS TO THE ringing tone at the other end of her mobile phone as she walks away from the swimathon and the beach and towards the subway that connects the town to the beachfront. She'd wanted to tell Grace not to worry, that she still has a trick up her George at Asda sleeve, but she hadn't wanted to get her hopes up in case it doesn't work out.

Nurse Carter had promised Dawn that she would bring a few of the staff to join in with the swimming and boost the numbers. Which is great, except that Dawn thought they would be here by now, and Nurse Carter isn't answering her phone.

She stops when she reaches the edge of the subway. She can hear the echoes of many voices and one of them definitely belongs to her favourite nurse. A stampede of footsteps gets closer and closer to the end of the tunnel.

They're on their way.

'Dawn!' Nurse Carter flings her arms around her as soon as she emerges into the light. She smells of Anais Anais and her thick hair almost chokes Dawn as her face is pulled into it.

'I'm so relieved you're all here,' Dawn says when she's finally released. 'And Dad – you made it!'

'Hello, young lady.' He holds a hand out towards Dawn for a polite handshake. He clearly has no clue who Dawn is right now. She swallows the disappointment. At least he called her young. Behind Nurse Carter and her dad are a gaggle of nursing staff from his home and several of their residents.

'I hope you don't mind; we brought a few other people along with us,' Nurse Carter says.

'We've all got our bathers on underneath,' an old lady says in Dawn's ear. 'And we've got lots of sponsors. Our kids, grandkids. Even great grandkids; some of us.'

Dawn feels something lift inside and her face breaks into a grin. Nurse Carter's brought double the amount of people that are already on the beach. Perhaps this could actually work.

'Of course I don't mind! It's just as well you did, there's not quite as many people down there as we'd hoped,' Dawn says.

Nurse Carter fishes her phone out of her tunic pocket. 'It's not quite time yet though – I'm sure in half hour or so loads of people will turn up.'

'But we're already running late.' Dawn dances around, trying to encourage a bit of urgency. She probably shouldn't rush them too much, most of them are at least ninety.

'I thought it was starting at ten.'

'No – nine.'

The nurse gasps and covers her mouth with her hand. 'Damn it. I told the radio station it was ten.'

'Radio station?'

'Yes. Didn't you hear it? I called them yesterday to ask if

they'd plug it this morning. When I told them what was happening with your hostel they said they'd come and interview you before you get in the water – hope you don't mind, Dawn love.'

'Not one bit,' Dawn says slowly.

'And they've already announced it several times today. Everyone in Kent has probably heard it by now, not just Dover. I reckon the place will be swarming.'

'Then we'd better hurry,' Dawn squeaks.

Dawn's mind lights up on the way back to the beach. She links her hand through her dad's arm and imagines people crying in their living rooms when they listen to what Dawn has to say. It will 'go viral' as Cara always says, and eventually, Colin Firth will get wind of it all. 'Who is this Dawn the people speak of?' he might ask. Then he'll Uber it down to Dover, sprinkle millions of pounds over the hostel and then take Dawn out to dinner. He's quite likely to fall in love with her, so she'd better check he's not married first...

'Who are all these people?' Grace is saying. Dawn hadn't realised she'd reached the beach yet.

'Eh?'

'All the people you brought back with you – they're all stripping down to their swimming costumes. A lot of them look very... old.' She mouths the last word.

'I'm Nurse Carter.' A huge hand moves past Dawn's peripheral vision and pumps Grace's fist up and down with the strength of a shot-put competitor. 'I work with Dawn's dad at Oaklands Residential Home. The others are nurses or fellow residents of his. He was very keen to do this – or at least he was at breakfast. He appears to have forgotten since.'

Dawn's dad is speaking to a passing dog walker and absent-mindedly stroking the head of a Great Dane.

'How did you risk-assess this?' breathes Grace, clearly in awe. 'How did you get your managers to agree to it?'

'Same way I got the radio on board to appeal to the people for support,' she says cheerfully. '*Research*.'

Dawn watches Grace's face as she tries to work out what the hell is happening. A car carrying blaring music comes crunching along the road behind the promenade. It screeches to a halt. Four loud door slams echo towards the beach. Four bodies walk towards them. Two cameras and two microphones.

'We're here for the nurse and for a *Dawn Brightside*,' the man with the red hair calls out.

Dawn's chest constricts. Her throat squeezes and her heart thuds. The sudden flash of red she always sees in her mind. *Don't you ever tell. I will find you and kill you.* She clenches her fists, closes her eyes and digs deep, remembering what her therapist had taught her. *You are safe, Dawn. He's in prison and he can't get to you anymore. You can stay where you are. It's just red hair, the same colour as Nurse Carter's.*

'Right here,' she calls back in her loudest, clearest voice.

'Umm… could I please ask what's going on? I'm the manager at St Jude's,' Grace says in her bossy voice.

'We're here about the fundraising – the swim in the sea? We've been telling people about it all morning.'

A swarm of people appear at once on the beach and a din of feet on pebbles reverberates around Dawn.

'Have a listen,' the man says to Grace as he fiddles with his phone.

An advert for a local double-glazing firm blasts out, followed by the familiar jingle of the radio station.

'I don't really get what… '

The man puts a finger over his lips and points towards his phone. Dawn cocks her ear closer to listen to the smooth voice of the radio presenter.

Ten minutes to go, folks, until the charity swimathon gets underway on Dover beach. The event is to raise money for St Jude's, a local homeless hostel that is facing closure due to funding cuts. Over three hundred and thirty thousand people were recorded as homeless in the UK last year, and numbers continue to rise. Recent changes in the benefit system and to government funding have put an unprecedented pressure on local services, bringing places like St Jude's to its knees.

So, what can local people do to help? a second voice asks.

You can start by getting yourselves down to Dover beach. Several supporters will be doing a sponsored swim. There'll be donation buckets at the location or people can give online on the St Jude's Facebook giving page. Why not take a dip yourself?

It does appear to be raining. Do you think this might put people off?

Well, according to local nurse, Petunia Carter, there is solid medical research that suggests a quick swim or submersion into cold water can be beneficial to our mental wellbeing. In fact, she is encouraging her own patients who suffer from dementia and Alzheimer's to give it a go.

You heard it here folks! Come and support your local homeless hostel and have a crack at improving your mental health. See you all in the sea!

CHAPTER 39

Dawn

DAWN LISTENS TO THE chatter around her on the beach as the radio announcement fades into a song from the charts. Spirits are rising and the worry lines have disappeared from Grace's face.

'This is fantastic.' Grace's eyes are glowing. 'And look at all these people!'

Peter is standing between Hazel and Nurse Carter in front of the ice cream stand. People are actually queuing to put their money in the bucket he's holding.

'You going in like that?' Cara asks, looking at Dawn's favourite Dover T-shirt. 'The salt will ruin the lettering if you wear that in the sea.'

'Course not.' Dawn pulls it over her head and wriggles out of her trousers, standing proud in her brand new costume, purchased especially for the occasion.

'Very nice,' whistles Cara.

'£10.99 from Sports Direct,' Dawn says with a grin. 'Fifty per cent off.'

A large microphone appears in front of Dawn's face. 'Could we get a quick interview before you rush into the sea?'

A flash goes off, making Dawn screw up her eyes. A second microphone now, held by a woman wearing a Kent News badge.

'It's not just the radio,' Cara murmurs, rubbing her hands together. 'Local newspaper and TV stations are here. We'll be all over the internet by this afternoon.'

Dawn thinks fast. This is their chance. All of them. It's not just her story to tell.

'I just need one minute,' she says to the crew before pulling Cara towards the waves. 'We need to round everybody up.'

Frantic looks over shoulders and baseball caps. Trying to find her tribe amongst the masses makes Dawn's head spin. With Cara's help, the residents and staff of St Jude's Hostel for the Homeless get themselves in one big huddle, rugby-style. Dawn tells them her plan before looking into the faces of each person present. Collective nods and choruses of *let's do this* echo around the circle.

'We're here to tell you a story,' Dawn says when they reach the cameras. 'Each one of us has one, and we're not going anywhere until you've heard them all.'

'I'll go first.' Jack takes a small step forward. 'Before I arrived at St Jude's, I was a little shit, all alone in the world. I got kicked backwards and forwards more often than a ball in play at London stadium.'

'Hey!' shouts a woman in a West Ham scarf.

'Sorry,' says Jack with a grin. 'But it's true. In and out of foster homes, YOT centres, prison. Now I'm at work on the building site every day, I'm not nicking cars, and I can cook a mean roast dinner.'

'I was sleeping in the park, about a hundred steps from here.

Before that, I was in a squat, getting the shit kicked out of me for refusing to give visitors what they came for,' Cara says, staring ahead at the counter.

Dawn's stomach twists. However awful people's pasts were known to be, there was always more lurking inside them, hiding in the corners.

'St Jude's handed me back my dignity and reminded me I matter. I found people who look out for me. I've not had that in years,' Dawn carries on. 'We all have something to offer the world, we just need a chance.'

Teardrop Terry and the others rattle through their speeches. The woman holding the microphone out asks her colleague to take it whilst she removes her glasses and cleans them with the bottom of her cardigan. She looks up as Teardrop Terry talks about his sixth birthday; the day he found his mum unconscious in a bath filled with red water. 'Everything went to shit after that day. Until I got a room at St Jude's and a key worker who gave one about what happened to me.'

'Okay,' the interviewer whispers. 'I've heard enough.' She clears her throat and places the microphone under her mouth. 'If anyone listening has been at all affected by these stories, please get yourself down here or consider donating online.'

Thunder grumbles in the distance and Dawn looks up at the ever-darkening sky. The rain becomes heavier and instead of running for shelter, people everywhere are peeling off their clothes and moving towards the sea. Loud cheering can be heard to the right and Dawn realises that several others have waded in fully clothed. Close in front of her is her lovely dad, slowly making his way forward over the stones next to Nurse Carter.

'Good luck, Dad.' Dawn gives his arm a squeeze as she walks past. 'I'm going to run right in as fast as I can.'

Dawn looks back when she feels a gentle grip around her hand.

'You go get 'em. My little Dawn-light used to love going swimming.' Her dad's eyes light up with pride.

Dawn kisses him on his soft cheek. 'Thank you.'

The pebbles are sharp and Dawn cries out as she hops across them, the smallest ones sticking between her toes. Goosebumps prick her from top to bottom as soon as her feet find the freezing water. A retreating wave sucks her toes underneath layers of shingle and she heaves them out, striding forward with determination.

'There you are.' Grace reaches for Dawn's fingertips. 'Want to take the plunge together? Ouch, that water's cold on the lady-parts,' she yelps.

Dawn laughs and keeps laughing as the two of them hurl their shoulders under the water and haphazardly flail around. At least, that's what Dawn thought they were doing; Grace is now gliding across the waves with an elegant breaststroke.

Dawn closes her eyes and takes herself back to Urmston Leisure Centre; the shallow pool. Her dad puffing up her bright orange swim bands and the squeak of plastic against skin as they inched up over her arms. *I don't want to take my feet off the bottom. What if I sink?*

'I won't let you drown,' her dad had smiled and pointed to her arms. 'You have those on. You just have to relax and trust you will be held up.' His eyes stayed on hers as she'd kicked and scrabbled her way through the water with wrinkled fingertips and hair slick with chlorine. The pride she'd felt when she managed a width. Afterwards, the scorching hot chocolate in a paper cup bought by her dad from the machine to celebrate.

She narrows her eyes and looks around at the hordes of people splashing about around her. Her dad is nowhere to be seen. Perhaps he'd decided to stick to a paddle with Nurse Carter. Teardrop Terry grins at her as he crashes past and she takes a deep breath in. She may not have armbands on, but the ground is under her feet and she has good people all around her. Dawn springs up and dives under. Cold water gurgles in her ears and carries her weightless body in a wave to her left. Her head breaks through to the surface and she coughs as water hits the back of her throat, filling her mouth with salt. A bubble of joy rises up from somewhere deep inside. Dawn lets out a cheer of pure exhilaration, ignoring her frozen limbs and the seaweed caught around her ankles. She pushes herself back below the waves and focusses on her arms and her legs, moving them the way her dad had told her to, all those years ago. Within a few seconds, she realises that she's gliding effortlessly through the water.

The sky is beginning to clear and the raindrops are fewer and further between. Dawn looks ahead at the majesty of the castle, the green of the hills. She turns towards the shore and sees the crowds waving.

It may have taken forty-two years, but she's finally found a town to call home.

Dawn swims until she can no longer feel her own arms and then wades herself slowly back to the beach. Her eyes sting with salty tears when they glimpse what is happening ashore. The beach and the promenade are covered with people standing shoulder to shoulder. Some of them are holding up makeshift *Save St Jude's* banners. Others say *We Say No to Funding Cuts for the Homeless.*

A fluffy towel is flung around Dawn's shivering shoulders. 'Come and have some hot chocolate,' the stranger says. 'One of the cafés in town has brought down vats of the stuff for all of you.'

Dawn sips the rich, milky drink gratefully from the recycled cardboard cup. Her body feels warmer with each mouthful and the sun is breaking through the clouds. People keep stopping to speak to her and ask her about her interview, but she can't focus on their faces. She's searching for her dad's. Her six-year-old self needs to find him and ask him, *Did you see me, Daddy? Did you see me? I swam. All by myself.*

Teardrop Terry is walking around carrying Cara on his back and Grace and Jack are paddling in the shallow waves. Peter and Hazel are deep in conversation by the ice cream van, but she still can't see her dad.

Nurse Carter has her shoes back on and she's pacing up and down, wringing her hands. Her face pales further when she sees Dawn. 'Oh, Dawn. I thought he must be with you. He isn't, though is he?'

Dawn's stomach whirls and her vision trembles.

'I asked one of the other nurses to stay with him whilst I went to the loo. Now she's saying he wandered off ages ago and she thought he was with me... oh, Dawn.' She gulps and rushes towards the media huddle. Dawn follows on wobbly legs and listens in disbelief to a tannoy announcement. Missing man. Mr Brightside. Tall. Grey jacket. Confused.

A hush falls over the crowd and within seconds people are

putting on shoes and looking around. Dawn moves her head in every direction. The sea is now empty of people, but one thing catches her eye and dread fills her vessels. Floating on the surface of a wave is a cap. A flat cap with a gingham pattern.

Her dad's hat.

The lifeboats and the coastguard are out to sea in record time. People are combing the beach, the promenade and heading towards town.

Dawn's throat is hoarse from yelling her dad's name and her legs keep trying to take her in several directions at once.

'Let's check the hotels along the front, I'm sure he's just gone for a stroll.' Cara throws an arm around Dawn. 'We'll find him. I know we will.'

Faces pass in a blur and Dawn squelches through puddles as she moves along the pavement. All she can see is that hat. Too many voices. Her mum's voice, echoing back through the decades. *He's gone, Dawn. He's never coming back. You will never see him again.*

Dawn holds onto Cara like a grab-rail as they walk into the smart beach-front hotel, their wet hair dripping onto the floor of the dining area. She hears her friend describe her dad to the waiter, but her eyes are drawn to the mirror on the left-hand side of the back wall. The reflection of two men. Both tucking into poached eggs. One in his thirties, the other wearing a gingham cap.

'Dawn-light!' her dad says.

There are so many words in this world. So many. Just none that feel like popping into Dawn's head right now.

'The whole town is looking for you,' Cara says, eyeing up his bacon. 'Dawn's been going off her head.'

'Ah.' He puts his fork down. 'Swimming.' He slaps the table in front of him. 'That was it… we were on the beach. I was looking for somewhere that might sell decent coffee. Then, I walked past this lovely restaurant and couldn't resist the smell of bacon. This young man joined me as all the other tables were taken.' He gestures towards his table companion. 'This is… um… '

'Blake Brown,' the man finishes. 'Lovely to meet you both. Sorry for keeping your dad from you.'

'Blake is down on business from London,' Dawn's dad says as if he's proud of remembering. 'He's a property developer.'

Dawn nods politely at Blake, trying to disguise her impatience.

'Blake and I were listening to you all on the radio. He wanted to know a bit more about your hostel, but I could only remember a couple of things, like the café and something about a writing group. Now you're here, maybe you can tell him the rest and give my old voice a break.'

'But how did you know anything about St Jude's, Dad?' Dawn's voice cracks in the middle.

'You told me all about it, love. Last time you came to visit. I do listen, you know.' He chuckles and rolls his eyes at Blake.

Dawn and Cara slip into the seats next to Blake and fill him in on the many ventures of St Jude's.

'So you also have art sessions, a band *and* you put wakes on for families who can't arrange it for themselves?' Blake is shaking his head. 'I must say, you all sound rather extraordinary.'

Blake offers Cara his last piece of toast and bids Dawn, her dad and Cara goodbye as they leave the hotel and make their way along the seafront.

Dawn's dad looks overwhelmed at the amount of people who mob them when they arrive back at the beach. Nurse Carter is all puffed up, covered in sweat and is as red as a stop sign. She apologises over and over to Dawn and anyone else who will listen.

'It's fine. He's been found and that's all that matters.'

Nurse Carter puts her arm through Dawn's and whispers in her ear. 'You should know that your dad's been like a different person since you started visiting. He sings and he whistles, and he laughs. It's down to you, I know it.'

The door to number six is trickier to open than usual when Dawn arrives back from her eventful day on the beach. She looks down at the small pile of post that Grace or Peter must have slipped under her door, making it stick.

The envelope on the top is plain and brown. Neat, considered handwriting. *Miss Dawn Elizabeth Brightside*. A Manchester postmark.

Dawn takes the A4 sheet from its envelope and stares at each word, trying to trust the ink on the page. It's been a long day and she's been wrong about these things before. She closes her eyes and looks back again at the letter. Same words in the same order. Sentences she's been waiting to see for twenty-two years.

Dear Dawn Brightside,

I hope this letter finds you well. I am writing to you on behalf of the Holding Hands Adoption Agency to inform you that your daughter born on 23/06/1997 has made a request for contact with you.

*Your daughter contacted us several months ago, but we were
unable to trace an address for you until you recently registered at St
Jude's Hostel.*

*As an agency, we have prepared your daughter as fully as possible
for all outcomes. She has stated that she understands you may be
unwilling or not ready to meet her but that she would dearly like to
make contact.*

*Please take the time you need to reach a decision. We are able
to offer support with this if you feel that would be helpful. If you are
happy to receive the letter your daughter has given us for you, please
fill in form 3b (enclosed) to give us permission to send it to you.*

Yours Sincerely,
Louisa Joy
Holding Hands Adoption Agency

Using the closed door to slide against, Dawn lowers herself
to her knees on the floor. She bows forward and presses her
forehead into the carpet, making watermarks on it with her
tears as she weeps through closed eyes. She stays there until the
sobs subside and all the blood has rushed to her face, leaving
her lightheaded and shaky. Dawn gets slowly to her feet, walks
to her chest of drawers and pulls out one of the black biros
she'd borrowed from the office. She pulls out form 3b from the
envelope and unfolds it, looking at the tick box at the bottom
until the image is burned into her mind.

CHAPTER 40

Grace

GRACE PLACES THE CALCULATOR down between the spreadsheet and neatly stacked banknotes on the office table. She stretches her arm out in front of her; it still feels stiff from all those hours of swimming yesterday.

'How do you think we should break the news?' she says. The words in front of her are difficult to look away from. It's as if they are alive and dancing around on the screen of her computer.

'It's great weather.' Peter glances out of the office window. 'How about we get everyone together for a BBQ and let them all know this afternoon?' He looks like a different man this week; like he's had some of the age squeezed out, leaving him lighter without all that worry weighing him down.

'I'll ask Terry and Cara to pop out for supplies. Dawn can run the café on her own for a bit. She's really found her feet there now. The customers love her.'

'Mmm. About that.' Peter snaps the file closed he's been working on. 'Now that we're losing Cara to Francine's and are potentially about to have new residents to train, we could do with a permanent member of staff to oversee the café.'

'Dawn,' Grace and Peter say in perfect unison.

'Love it.' Grace's brain lights up as she pictures Cara and Dawn both doing what they love and collecting pay checks to help them build lives for themselves. 'And while we're on the subject, I was thinking we could have a look at our move-on list. A few of ours are almost ready and our waiting list isn't getting any smaller.'

'Terry is going at the end of the week. That gardening job he landed for himself has accommodation included.'

'Amazing.' Grace claps her hands.

'So that will leave a bed – perhaps for Maisie McDowell? We could send someone to the park to see if she wants to come to the BBQ? And Jack's doing well with his job – he's been saving for a deposit, so it probably won't be long before he... '

'And what about Dawn?' Grace interrupts.

Peter plucks his glasses from his nose and cleans them with the bottom of his shirt. He's wearing a new pair of rimless lenses, not a scratch in sight. 'I'm not sure. She's only just stabilising on her medication. Don't you think she still needs us?'

'Of course. And we need her. We'll always be here for Dawn and if she's up for it, she'll still be around every day in the café. I just think we owe it to her to help her to settle somewhere she can put down roots. She deserves a life she doesn't have to run from.' Grace grabs the interview paperwork from the filing cabinet and pulls on her cardigan. 'Be back in a few.' Her fingers have just glazed the handle of the office door when Peter calls her back.

'Shall I invite Hazel to the BBQ?' Peter's face is straight. Too straight.

'Did you sort things out with her?'

Peter turns swivels his chair around, a grin pulling at his mouth. 'We went out last night. After the big swim.'

'Wonderful. What about the stuff about your drinking, though?'

'She apologised about all that. Apparently, she used to live with an alcoholic who didn't treat her well. Hearing about my past brought some stuff back for her. Just baggage she hadn't realised she was still carrying.'

'Yup. We've all got some. It's good to check each other's arms for it occasionally.' Grace makes her way back to the door.

'Oh, and Grace?'

She rolls her eyes and repeats her step back.

'Well done for all your hard work.'

Terry already has the BBQ fired up and has put the first round of burgers on by the time Grace steps outside. A swarm of residents are crowded around him holding mugs of lemonade.

'Do you want to tell them or shall I?' Grace says in a low voice once Peter is in earshot.

'You tell them, boss. You've earned this moment.'

'So have you,' grins Grace. She claps her hands three times and waits for the residents to stop chatting. 'We have the results from the fundraising,' she shouts across the garden.

Drinks are lowered and several pairs of eyes stare back at her.

'Firstly, I'd like to say a huge well done to everyone who took part, helped with organising or helped spread the word,' Grace continues. 'We couldn't have done it without you, you were all so very... '

'How much did we make?' says Teardrop Terry.

'Just tell us!' Cara is biting her nails.

'Okay.' Grace takes a big breath. 'The proceeds from the swim came to a massive *thirty thousand pounds*. Well over our target and plenty to put towards any shortfalls next year. There's something else,' she adds amongst the cheering and disbelieving squeals. 'On that same day, we were given a sizable donation from a single benefactor, a Mr Blake Brown. It was gifted for the sole purpose of expanding St Jude's so we can help even more homeless people in our community. The planning permission request was made before close of business yesterday.'

The ground below Grace vibrates from the stampede of twenty pairs of feet jumping up and down. Tears are shed. Hugs are given.

'Thank you for believing in us,' Cara whispers in her ear. 'And for giving us a chance when no one else would.'

Jack walks over from the drinks table. He looks behind him before handing her a cup of lemonade, running his finger discreetly across the back of Grace's hand as he does so, sending delicious tingles up her arm.

'Knew you could do it, Miss,' he winks.

Grace's heart has never been so full.

The office phone can only just be heard over the din. Peter kisses Hazel's cheek before rushing back inside and comes out holding the office landline.

'Phone call for you.' He hands the phone to Grace.

Peter is announcing Dawn's acceptance of her permanent job at the café amidst further applause as Grace crosses the lawn and makes her way over the paving slabs near the door.

'Hello?' she cups the phone under her chin.

'Hello, Grace.' Her mum's clipped voice. 'I've been trying

your mobile all morning. I've just seen it. It's all over the internet.'

Grace doesn't speak. She can't. She hasn't heard that voice for so long.

'I can't believe how well you've done, rallying around like that and raising so much money and awareness. Such an important job you're doing. I just wanted to tell you how proud I am.'

Grace looks at the elation on the faces around her. Laughter rings out from the collective conversations in the air from every direction.

'Thanks, Mum. I'm pretty proud of me too.' After hanging up the phone, Grace notices how loose her shoulders feel; how light her chest is.

Dawn is rushing towards Grace, squeezing her own hands when she stops in front of her.

'What's happened?'

'I've been waiting all morning to tell you something.' Dawn is almost dancing on the spot. 'I got a letter yesterday.' A sob comes out alongside her words. 'I still can't believe it.'

Grace ushers Dawn to the drinks corner where it's quiet and pours them both out a cup of lemonade. She reads Dawn's letter three times before looking up at her face and squeezing her with the tightest hug.

'Have you thought about what you'd like to do?'

'I've already written back.' Dawn's eyes are two shining stars on a clear night. 'I sent it first thing this morning.'

CHAPTER 41

Grace

'IF THE EXTENSION GOES on this side of the building, I reckon we could fit around eight extra bedrooms in,' Grace says. It's been a week since they were told about their funding, and Grace wants to move forwards as quickly as possible with the renovations. Sunlight bounces off the front windows of St Jude's and she holds her hands up to shield her eyes from the rays. The warm breeze from the sea behind her blows her hair across her face.

Peter scribbles an outline of the building onto his clipboard, umming and ahhhing before agreeing with Grace.

'Ah, you're out here already,' grins Jack as he walks through the hostel door onto the clifftop beside them. He's wearing a hard hat and has brought two others with him: a man and a woman from his building firm. Both their heads are bare and Grace suspects Jack enjoys wearing his hard hat a little too much. Especially given that no actual work has begun yet.

Jack and his colleagues whip out tape measures and measure windows and doors before giving quotes and discussing time scales.

'Jack has told us all about this place,' the woman says. 'It's a great thing you're doing. We'd like to offer you a lower rate – if you throw in the odd cake from the café, that is.'

'Wonderful,' Grace beams.

Jack darts a look towards Peter, who is inspecting the ground to the left of the existing building. When he's satisfied he isn't being watched, he pulls Grace's arm towards him and murmurs into her ear. 'They said I can finish for the day after this. Meet me at the bottom of the hill in five minutes. There's something I want to show you.' His mouth lightly brushes her earlobe as he speaks, sending goosebumps down Grace's arm.

After saying goodbye to Peter and locking up the office, Grace trundles down Cliff View Hill. Towards the bottom on the left-hand side sits a parked Peugeot. It has an old registration plate and a slight dent on the bumper. 'You bought a car!' she says to Jack as he climbs out of the driver's side. Tears prick the back of her eyes as she remembers his driving lessons over the past month, the wreck that Jack had been on the morning of his test.

'Yup. Needs a bit of work, but still. At least I can drive you places sometimes instead of you taking me everywhere.'

Jack opens the passenger door and Grace climbs in. The seats are worn and the footwell could do with a mat to cover the stained carpet. She smiles at the brand-new air freshener in the shape of an ice cream cone that's hanging from the interior mirror, clearly bought by Jack in an effort to smother the existing smell of damp-dog with lashings of vanilla.

'It's fantastic,' she says. 'What a fab surprise.'

Jack chuckles as he checks his mirror and puts the car in gear. 'This isn't what I wanted to show you. The real surprise is on its way.'

They drive past the harbour and through the town before pulling into the car park by the precinct.

'We're going shopping?' Grace says, feeling a little let down as she pictures trailing around Poundland for windscreen wash.

'Nope. You will see.' Jack gets a parking ticket and pops it in the window before leading Grace across the road and turning right. He stops when they reach the display window at the front of an estate agent and spins Grace around to face it.

Rows of house photos in the rental section with a couple of flats dotted between them. 'What are you showing me?'

'I'm moving out. Leaving St Jude's.'

Grace's arms feel cold and something plummets from her stomach as she pictures her mornings at the office without Jack's twinkling eyes or ridiculous questions he invents just to see her. She'd lost count of the number of times he'd come to ask her what day he needed to put the bins out.

'I see.' Grace feels her voice crack and tries to fix it with a smile. 'Have you spoken to Peter about this? He's your key worker. I'm sure he'll be happy to help you find a flat – I know he thinks you've been ready for a while.'

'It's not a flat I'm looking for.' Jack points at a photo of a pretty thatched cottage. 'It's got two bedrooms and it's right near the beach. It's Kingsdown, so just outside Dover but it's close enough to work now I've got the car.'

'It's more expensive than a flat would be. And it looks quite big for one person.' Why does he want to be so far away from her? Maybe this is his way of telling her that things are changing. He's done with St Jude's, and he's done with *her*.

'My wages have gone up now I've passed my probation period. And there's a reason I wanted you to come with me.

330

I wanted you to choose somewhere with me. Somewhere maybe we'd both like to live one day.'

The roar of the rush-hour traffic on the road behind Grace fades away as she looks into Jack's face. She sees the two of them eating breakfast on the pebbles before work and going for evening walks to the pub afterwards. Notes on the fridge asking each other to buy milk.

'I want us to be together properly.' Jack slips her hand into his and Grace resists the urge to check that no one's watching. 'No more sneaking around. If I move out, I'm no longer a *service user*.' Jack makes bunny ears with his fingers. 'Then, after however much time you are comfortable with, you could move into our new home together.' Jack tucks Grace's windswept hair behind her ear. His eyes hold something new behind them. They're still impossibly green with flecks of brown, his eyelashes still dark. But they're filled with strength. There's a maturity in him that wasn't there before. 'You've always said you hate your flat. We could get our very own pool table and spend our evenings watching shit films. *Sharknado*, even. And then perhaps one day in the far-off future, I'll take you to another kind of window display. The type that has rings in it.'

'Like the one on the seafront that sells buckets and spades,' Grace teases lightly, trying to slow the thud of her heart.

'Not rubber rings.' Jack's face switches to serious.

'Don't you dare propose to me in the middle of Dover town centre. Not when the clifftop and the castle is right up there.'

Jack laughs. 'Don't you worry. We've had enough excitement for one day. Let's go inside, I said we'd meet the agent here at half five.'

'Ready to go?' the agent picks up his keys when Jack tells him who they are.

'Where are we going?' Grace hisses in Jack's ear as they follow Alan out of the door.

Jack's mouth twitches into a grin. 'I arranged a viewing at the Kingsdown property.'

They follow the agent to Kingsdown. Grace's head fills with delight as she looks closely at the stunning village she'd never paid much attention to before. 'It's actual paradise,' she says as she looks at the pretty beach on one side and the rows of well-kept stone cottages on the other.

'Just imagine how peaceful it will be. You work so hard to look after everyone else, Grace. You deserve to have a place like this to hide in at the end of each day.' It's as if he's speaking directly to the disapproval that's trying to break through.

The house is as lovely inside as out. Ridden with character and cute fireplaces, there's no way either of them wants to miss out on it.

'Excellent,' the agent says. 'We just need to do the relevant background checks and paperwork. It's ready to let so fingers crossed, you could be in there by the end of next week if you wanted?'

Jack's brows knit together on the way back to the car and he doesn't say a word as they climb the hill.

'Do you not have the deposit yet?' Grace says, trying to guess the reason for Jack's downturn in mood.

'I've been saving. That's all sorted. It's just the word *background check* that gives me the heebie–jeebies.' Jack turns the key in the ignition and checks his mirrors. 'The thought of anyone looking into my background just reminds me of my past and everything I've done.'

'You're not that person anymore,' Grace reminds him. 'You've got a job – a good one. You've not been in trouble for such a long time. You're no longer on probation and Peter can give you a glowing reference from St Jude's to say that you looked after your room and paid your rent on time. It will be fine.'

'Yes!' Jack slaps the steering wheel. 'I mean, it still might not be fine, but the fact there's a chance it might be is progress, right?'

Laughter bubbles up inside Grace. Even when he's stressed, Jack is somehow still able to make her laugh.

They go back to the letting agent's office to collect the application forms and Grace has a last look at the property details in the window.

'I did look at that flat too.' Jack points to the picture on the bottom row in the middle of the *Flats to Let* section of the display. 'It's near the sea and a great price but it would be better for one person.'

'And I might know just the person,' says Grace before popping back in to request the details.

CHAPTER 42

Dawn

IT'S BEEN ALMOST TWO weeks since Dawn posted her form back to the adoption agency. She still hasn't had a reply yet and has been spending most mornings biting her nails until the post comes. What if Rosie had changed her mind in the months it had taken to track her down? Perhaps Dawn will hear something this week, or the next. If this summer has taught her anything, it's that she should never give up hope.

At least this morning she would be too busy to spend too much time waiting around for the post. Today is a big day: moving day.

'I just don't get how you managed to fit all of this into number six,' Jack chuckles as Dawn hands him yet another box to load into the van.

'Where there's a will, there's a way,' Dawn grins. 'Most of this can go to the charity shop. I don't need it all anymore.'

'Might want to take the labels off some of it, then,' mutters Jack as he heaves past her.

Dawn slips inside the room and looks around at the empty chest of drawers, the stripped mattress. One of Cara's glue-on nails is still stuck to the carpet.

'Well, that's it, then,' she says. Her words echo back at her in the empty room.

Three sharp taps on the door and Grace leans her head around it. 'Could you pop downstairs for a moment? There's something in the lounge I need your help with.'

Grace is quiet as she walks down the stairs beside Dawn. Perhaps she's imagining how lonely she will be in the office without Dawn's interesting stories and words of wisdom.

'No, not there, put it on the table where she'll see it,' Cara's voice travels along the corridor from the residents' lounge.

'Well, if she sees it, it won't be much of a feckin' surprise, will it?' Maisie's dulcet tones.

'Look, lady. I spent *hours* making it and arranging this party. And Dawn is *my* friend. Don't think you can just waltz in here after living here five minutes and tell me how to… '

'Oi. Stop, stop, stop.' Teardrop Terry's voice. 'Dawn will be here any minute. Don't wreck the surprise with your stupid scrawling.'

A sob falls out of Dawn as she reaches the doorway.

'Shit, you're here,' Cara says.

A gaggle of residents let off an uncoordinated display of party poppers that won't pop and Maisie blows weakly on a whistle.

'Surprise!' Teardrop grins.

'I thought you were going to hide first? Honestly, you lot are useless.' Peter tuts as he enters the room. Dawn opens her mouth to speak and then she sees it. Right in the middle of the coffee table is a large cake. The topping is made from the photo they'd used for the fundraising. Dawn's face is smack-bang in the middle and surrounded by piped icing spelling the words, 'Always look on the Brightside'.

'We just wanted to say thanks. For all you did to help us.'

'And to give you a good send-off from St Jude's.'

'Thank you,' Dawn chokes. She clears her throat and stands on a stool. She's always wanted to give a speech to a crowded room but never quite had the occasion to. 'Firstly, I'd like to thank Grace and Peter for inviting me to stay here and for helping me feel like a real person. To Cara, Jack and Terry for showing me what friendship is. And to all of you for coming and making me this beautiful cake. I'll miss St Jude's, but I'll still be around. I'll be working in the café all week.'

'But it's not the same as you *living* here,' says Cara. 'Who will I have my midnight meltdowns with now?'

Someone puts music on, and half the residents start whooping and dancing on the furniture when *Mr Brightside* fills the room.

Dawn dances until her feet feel bruised and Grace reminds her they need to drive over to her new place and start unpacking.

An hour later, Dawn watches Jack and Grace as they argue about where to put the wardrobe they had collected from the charity shop in St Jude's minibus. They look like a couple in love. Looks like Grace has taken Dawn's advice. They will probably be discussing the St Jude's cafe as a reception venue for their wedding before long.

Dawn isn't one for being pushy, but she has drawn up a menu, a table plan and written a maid-of-honour speech just in case she's asked. Which she's bound to be – nearer the time, of course. She's looking forward to telling the wedding guests about how Grace had pulled her from darkness and into the light, and then how she'd returned the favour. There won't be a dry eye in the café when they hear about how she pushed

Grace towards Jack, right before saving the very place in which they're all sitting. Grace will thank her through glistening tears and Jack will publicly promise to name their first child Dawn.

'If she puts the wardrobe there, it will block the radiator,' Grace points out.

'Yes, but if she puts it here then the bedroom door won't open properly.'

Perhaps Dawn could turn the tall cleaning cupboard in the kitchen into a walk-in wardrobe. She could display the clothes on the rails by colour. Grace would love that, and she'd think about what a great influence she'd been on her organisational skills. Then when Rosie visits, she'd be super impressed. *I can't believe you've got a walk-in wardrobe, Mum. Just like a TV star.*

'Dawn.' Grace and Jack chime together. They look like they've been speaking to her for a while.

'Where do you think then?' asks Jack.

Dawn looks at his face for clues.

'The wardrobe!' says Grace.

Dawn look around at the bedroom – *her* bedroom. It has a bay window at the front that is pulling in all the sunlight and dousing every inch of the room with a golden glow. The bed is covered by a yellow duvet with daisies dancing across it. A bedside table stands next to the bed and she's placed her orange notebook on it – the one with the columns that hold details of the shops she's visited and charts what she owes each for her 'bargains'. She is paying them back gradually and anonymously with her earnings from the café.

'Just put the wardrobe anywhere,' says Dawn. Her jaw aches from smiling and her head is pulsing with excitement. 'I just can't believe I have such a beautiful flat to live in.'

'Well, it's clean at least,' Grace says, looking at the walls and the eighties curtains that had been left at the windows. 'And it's definitely the best one we looked at in your price range. Now you've got a job at the café, you could always start saving. Then you could look for something on a… *nicer* road perhaps.'

Dawn links her hand through Grace's and leads her closer to the window. 'Look at that view,' she says, pride leaking from her voice.

'Umm… the skip full of rubbish from across the road or the graffiti on the wall behind it that says "Dave is a twat" next to a pair of badly drawn testicles?'

'Not there. Look up – above all that. Look at the blue sky and those fluffy clouds. That one looks like a baby elephant. I can see the top of the castle from here. And yes, those houses are hiding the sea – but I still know it's right there behind them.'

Dawn had put the tenancy agreement in a frame and placed it on the wall in her new living room before she'd even opened a box to unpack. Grace and Jack had laughed, but it made sense to her. This time, she's moving in without planning her escape. Without feeling like she doesn't belong. 'And look.' She spins Grace around again to face the room. 'Look at the space. My things. I know it's small and you said it needs painting but to me it feels like a palace. It's mine, Grace, and I'm sleeping here tonight in my own bed all because of you and St Jude's.'

'There is something else I need to give you.' Grace hands an envelope to Dawn.

'Is this another surprise?' Dawn wouldn't be surprised – always has a trick up her sleeve, that Grace.

'Umm. Yes. It probably will be.' Grace's expression is hard to read and Dawn's stomach clenches.

'This came in the post today. I recognised the address printed on the back of the envelope. It's from the adoption agency.'

Dawn presses her fingers around her chest of drawers as clouds seem to fill the room in front of her eyes. Someone has turned the music up in the flat downstairs and Dawn can feel the bass vibrating under her feet from below. 'Can you open it please?' she whispers. 'Just tell me… is it from her?'

There's a stain on the wall beside her. It's the shape of Italy. Dawn's always wanted to go to Italy. She traces around the line of it with her eyes as her heart thuds hard and fast.

'It is from her.'

Dawn stares at the sheet of A4 that Grace is holding in front of her. She gets as far as 'Dear Dawn,' before her eyes mist over. Three long blinks and a long breath. She can do this. She has to. She wants to. She's never wanted anything more.

Dear Dawn,

It's so hard to start this letter. Everything sounds like a cliché, and I really hate them. Even my first few words sound too much like this Is the hardest letter I've ever had to write. I used to write letters to you when I was little — mostly whenever I was in trouble with my adoptive parents (often).

I suppose I should start by telling you they were good to me. They never hid the truth from me that I wasn't biologically theirs and always made sure I knew that I was in every other way. Before I came along, they tried to have a baby for seventeen years and always talked about you as the person who had given them the best gift. When I got older, I used to pretend to throw up at how cheesy they were.

I wondered about you often. What your smile looks like. If you laugh much, if you like painting like I do. Lots of times I thought about asking to find you, but I was terrified about what it would do to Mum and Dad (I'm sorry if it hurts when I call them that; it's just impossible not to).

Then Mum got sick — really sick. She's better now but it made me think about a lot of stuff. What if something happened to you or to me and we never got the chance to meet each other. Mum had been thinking the same and I finally told her what I'd wished for every year when I blew out my candles. All I could hear in my head afterwards was 'Don't ever say what you wished for or it won't come true.' That plagued me for days (I know I'm twenty-two now, but I'm pretty superstitious.)

Your contact details arrived from the agency three days ago. Since then, I've mostly been writing versions of this letter and clicking on your Facebook page. I think it's amazing all you are doing for the hostel you live in. And I think we may have the same eyes. In your letter, you said you would like to meet. I'm planning to come to Dover this Friday (29th July). I thought we could meet in the café where you work at half past three? Please let the agency know if this isn't a good time for you, otherwise I will see you there. I have a lot of questions and I know the answers might not be nice or easy ones so I will try not to ask them all at once.

I am so happy you said yes.

Your Daughter.

Dawn stares at the page for a long time after she's finished reading. She holds it close to her chest and looks back at Grace who hasn't taken her eyes away from her. 'The twenty-ninth is tomorrow,' says Dawn.

She is pulled into Grace's arms. Grace's hair smells like dusty furniture and salt and vinegar crisps.

'And tomorrow, I get to see my Rosie.'

CHAPTER 43

Dawn

THERE ARE FEW THINGS more beautiful than watching the sun rise above a choppy sea. It's finally morning. The twenty-ninth of July. The day Dawn will see her baby girl. Not even a second of sleep was had last night, and an early morning walk had felt like the best way to blow away the cobwebs. She walks along the promenade humming 'The Best Things in Life are Free' inside her head. Mostly. The look she gets from a dog walker tells her some of the words may have slipped out. Dawn had spent her first night at the flat both awake and dreaming. Her limbs are heavy from lack of sleep and her heart hurts from changing shape to fit all the different feelings that keep wriggling in.

She reaches the sea shelter and pokes her head around to peer at the benches inside. Bill is already awake, sitting up on the seat, still in his sleeping bag. There's another body on the next bench, still asleep. A shock of purple hair pokes out from the top of a blanket.

'Shhh.' Bill puts a tobacco-stained finger over his mouth before whispering to Dawn. 'This one only got to sleep an hour ago. First night out,' he adds.

Dawn nods, remembering hers. London had felt like as good a place as any to start again that day she first left Manchester. So many people, so many places to hide. It hadn't been as simple to get a room for the night as she'd hoped. Even getting a doorway on some streets was more competitive than she had expected. No matter how bone-tired she was, the cold hard pavements, the noises and the crippling fear made it impossible to drop off to sleep the first few nights.

'Budge up then,' Dawn whispers before sitting down next to Bill on the bench. She flops her rucksack down in front of her and reaches inside it for her flask and two travel cups. She gives one to Bill and balances the other between her knees. 'Can't beat the smell of coffee in the morning.'

'Don't s'pose you got something stronger in that bag of yours,' grins Bill.

Dawn leans back against the cold plastic criss-cross of the bench and warms her hands on her steaming mug. She closes her eyes as she sips her coffee and listens to the crash of the waves, the song of the seagulls. The fresh sea air fills her lungs as she inhales, and she holds it in there for a few moments before slowly letting it all out.

'You're quiet today,' remarks Bill. 'Usually, you won't shut up jibber-jabbering. I don't like to say anything on account of you bringing me my paper and coffee every morning, but you don't 'alf make a right racket sometimes. I'm surprised you don't scare the seagulls off.'

'I just want to save up all the moments from today,' whispers Dawn. 'It's a day I've been waiting for for a long time.'

The body on the other bench wriggles and Dawn checks her bag for an extra cup. 'I'll leave a cup with you for her if she's still asleep when I go,' she says to Bill. 'And if you're coming up to the café later, please bring her with you. We can pop her on the waiting list. She shouldn't be out here.' Dawn's voice cracks. Now she can see the face above the duvet, she can see how young the woman looks – no older than Rosie. She tries to picture her daughter as she usually does in a boardroom or her studio in Milan or Paris, but nothing will come.

'Aye,' Bill nods. 'Long as you don't try talkin' me into putting my name down. My place is out here, amongst the stars. Been too many years now – walls are like prisons to me.'

Dawn pulls a rolled-up newspaper from the inside pocket of her coat and holds it out to Bill. 'It's today's. I can stay another ten minutes if there's any words you need help with, but then I've got to go to work.' A smile sits on her cheeks. She still loves the way that sentence tastes and the knowledge that if she doesn't go in, the scones won't be ready in time for the lunchtime rush and the signs won't be placed outside. It matters that she gets there.

'You should keep it.' Bills eyes hold a sparkle in them. 'You said it was a special day – read every news story and put it somewhere safe. That way you'll remember what was happening in the world around you on the date you want to hold close.'

'Thank you.' Dawn swallows and stares at the front cover. 'Have you ever wished for something so hard and got scared when it was on its way to you? I mean, if you've lost something once, you could just as easily lose it again.'

A German Shephard pants past the shelter, tongue hanging out as he pulls his owner along behind him. A door slams from the houses behind them and a car engine splutters to life.

'Not me. I don't make wishes. Dreams are for other people,' says Bill. 'But you're special. If something finds you, I have a feeling it will want to hang around.'

An image breaks into Dawn's mind. A young woman walking through the café door. She can't see her face yet but that doesn't matter. Her arms are outstretched as she walks towards Dawn and then her hands are inside Dawn's own; right where they belong.

'Make sure you come to the café before three-thirty,' she says. 'We're closing early. There's someone I have to meet.'

'Righto,' Bill says before draining the end of his coffee.

Dawn packs the flask back into her bag and zips up her puffer jacket. 'Oh, and Bill?' she calls back into the wind after she's walked a few paces. 'You're wrong about the wishes. Dreams are for everyone.'

'That's the third plate you've broken today.' Cara appears in the dining area brandishing a dustpan. 'Good thing you're only going to be my boss for a week, or we'd be falling out.'

Dawn brushes up the broken crockery and watches Cara as she whizzes between tables, taking orders and dishing out smiles. She's going to love working at Francine's and Dawn can't wait to see her in action at her first-ever paid job. She'll miss working with her in the café every day. New St Jude's residents will be there to take her place and it will be Dawn's job to train them to be every bit as efficient as Cara.

'Sorry. I'm a bit shaky this afternoon.' Dawn tips the dustpan into the bin. The café is full, and the collective conversations are bouncing off the walls and into her ears, filling her head with noise.

'Of course you are.' Cara sets her tray down on the worktop and grabs hold of Dawn's wrists. 'I know a bit about seeing your kid after a long time away. Not gonna lie; it's weird. It's weird and it's bloody hard seeing how they've grown without you.'

Someone has spilled ketchup on the floor in front of her. She'll need to get a cloth before someone slips on it. A chair scrapes against the tiles, making her jump. Why can't everything just slow down and be quieter?

'But none of that matters when you get to hold them and know they're doing okay.' Cara squeezes harder and Dawn moves her eyes from the puddle at her feet. 'You'll see. She will love you and you will love her. Everything else can be sorted out.'

'What if she doesn't?' The kitchen looks misty through hot tears and the coffee machine is just a blur in front of her. 'What if she can't love me? She might not even like me.'

Something taps Dawn on the shoulder.

'You left a cup behind this morning.'

'Cheers, Bill. Glad you made it.' Dawn pulls her face into a smile. 'Did you bring your new friend?'

'Aye.'

Dawn scans the café for a head of purple hair.

'She's outside talking to that woman who works here,' he says.

'That's good.' At least Grace will be able to fill in a form for her. The new bed spaces will be ready soon, but they will soon fill up and the longer that young girl is out on those streets, the greater the risk to her life.

The café door dings and Grace rushes through it, breathless and flushed pink. 'Change of plan. We need to put the closed sign up now. We'll let everyone finish up but don't let any new customers in.'

'But it's only half past two.' Dawn's heart begins to thud in time with the song on the radio. 'Has something happened? Does this mean I can't meet Rosie here? Oh. That's why. She's not coming is she, and you just don't want to tell me in front of all these people...'

'Dawn.' Grace is using her firm teacher-voice that usually makes Dawn want to laugh. Not today, though. 'I want you to take your apron off and clean yourself up. Cara will put on a fresh pot of coffee and I'll make sure the café is empty and clear. Your daughter is on her way.'

The walls in the café toilets are painted an awful shade of green. Dawn stares at them as she perches on the cold metal loo seat. So strange that the café is decorated so vibrantly but no one had thought to make the toilets pretty. That would be the next job on her list – she'll get one of the new residents to help.

'Dawn? Hurry up in there,' bellows Cara through the wall. 'She'll be here in five minutes.'

A swirling sensation ripples across her stomach. It's just nerves. Butterflies. But just for a moment, it feels like the early flutters of Rosie in her womb. Dawn places her palm across her tummy and a smile falls across her face as she remembers.

'Dawn!' Cara bangs hard on the door.

'Coming.' Dawn stands up and moves her shaking legs towards the sink. She runs cold water onto her cupped hands and splashes it over her face. The face that looks back at her from the mirror is very different to the one she'd arrived at St Jude's with. The sunken hollows below her cheekbones have filled out and the circles below her eyes have disappeared. She removes the smudges of tear-stained make-up and smooths the wild waves of her hair with her hands.

What will Rosie see when she looks at her? What will she see when she looks at Rosie?

The café is empty of people when Dawn returns. Only one table by the window has been dressed with a crisp white table cloth and a vase of fresh flowers from St Jude's garden. A three-tier stand holding two of every cake the café serves sits in the middle. A napkin is folded in half next to it. Dawn's name is scrawled on the front in biro. She unfolds it and reads the note inside.

Once a mum, always a mum. You can do this.
Love, Cara and Grace

Footsteps crunch on the gravel outside the window. A shadow crosses the corner of Dawn's eye. The song falls to a close on the radio, opening up two seconds of silence as the room itself holds its breath. The large bell moves in slow motion from one side to the other as the café door inches open; the joyful *ding* echoing in Dawn's ears.

'Hello, Mum.'

CHAPTER 44

Dawn

GOOSEBUMPS POP UP ACROSS Dawn's shoulders and her whole heart feels swollen, love leaking through vessels and travelling to the parts of her mind she'd kept taped up.

Eyes: wide and dark like hers. They look as if they hold the world inside them, and Dawn can't look away. A splatter of freckles across her nose and a mouth that's used to smiling. Her fingernails are short and clean, and Dawn remembers how tiny her hands were and how perfect her fingers. They'd clamped around her hair and pulled hard before they took her away. It had hurt and she had welcomed the sting to her scalp. She thought she deserved any pain thrown her way.

Dawn looks away from her daughter's pale hands. She's tall – taller than Dawn. Strong-looking too. She's wearing jeans with more holes than denim and a T-shirt with a band on that Dawn hasn't heard of. She wants to ask who they are; she wants to know about every single thing Rosie likes.

'You have purple hair,' Dawn blurts out.

A blank stare takes over Rosie's face and she steadies herself on the back of a chair, blinking fast.

'Are you okay? Do you need to sit… ?'

'Sorry. I need to go outside. I thought I'd be fine, but…
I'll be back.'

Rosie stumbles out of the café and towards the clifftop. She bends over as if trying to get her breath back and stands with her back to the café, looking out over the sea.

Dawn opens the door and pulls it closed behind her. It's the bit after that's hard. The putting of one shaky leg after the other when Rosie's still not turning around. Dawn needs to know she's okay; she needs see that fierce, beautiful face again, so like her own but with the age washed out of it. She stops when she reaches Rosie's side and stands still, seven inches away from her.

'That was a stupid opening line. I'm sure you didn't come all this way for me to tell you your hair is purple,' says Dawn.

A lorry thunders past in the distance along the coast road. BP oil. Flammable. Hazardous. Keep clear.

'Mum… my adoptive mum. She said you weren't coping. That you did what you thought was right for me.' Rosie takes a step back and turns around to face Dawn.

Three seagulls are having a fight over half a cookie that someone's dropped. It has raisins in it. Are birds supposed to eat raisins? Apparently, they're poisonous to dogs.

'I wasn't coping.' *Honesty is the best policy,* Grace always says. 'But I was trying.' *Am.* 'I wanted to be your mum. I loved you.'

The ferry is chugging through the gap in the harbour wall and smaller boats are dotted around the sea as canoes zip their way through the gaps, coming and going from the shore.

'Where were you living?' Dawn has a rough idea already. It's the accent.

The harder questions come next. She wants to know about

her dad. She already knows the story, praise be, so the details can be saved for later. It hurts like hell to hear about a whole load of childhood that has passed in the blink of an eye for Rosie but has taken half a lifetime of horror for Dawn.

Dawn's fingers are itching to touch her daughter's hair. To hold her. To tell her everything will be okay, she'll make sure of it. But she's a stranger, and strangers don't touch.

Rosie takes a tiny side-step and links her fingers through Dawn's. A tear splashes its way down Dawn's face but still she keeps her eyes resolutely on the view in front of her.

'Do you want to come back inside?' asks Dawn. 'There's half a ton of cake with your name on it in there.'

Rosie keeps her little finger laced with Dawn's as they wander across the grass and back to the café. Dawn pours two coffees and shows Rosie around her new workplace before they sit down and tackle the mountain of carbs.

'About the purple-hair thing... '

'You don't like it.' Rosie grins and Dawn gets a glimpse of the cheeky child she'd imagined so often.

'It was just a shock to suddenly realise it was you on the sea shelter bench this morning. I'd sat across from my own daughter – left her a cup of morning coffee and didn't even know it.'

Rosie puts her scone down and fiddles with a napkin.

'Why were you out there?' Dawn asks softly. 'Your letter said you were settled and happy. No mention of losing your home. You can tell me anything, I won't judge, I can't.'

'I have a home. My own flat, a nice one. Hastings.'

'Hastings? That's not even that far!' Dawn has stayed in Hastings before. Lived in a B&B and got a job in a bar. Then a punter had got a bit lairy with her and followed her home. She'd left town the next day, convinced he was the one who was after her. How many times could she have walked past her daughter without knowing? 'If you live in Hastings, how come you spent the night in Dover? You could have left after lunch and still got here in time.'

Rosie picks her napkin back up and starts tearing off the corners, dropping little half-moons of tissue on her plate. 'It will probably sound stupid if I say it out loud.'

'Wait till you hear some of the stuff I come out with,' says Dawn. 'Nothing you say will sound stupid after that.'

'I wanted to know what it was like to be you.' Rosie takes a swig of coffee and looks up at Dawn. 'I heard about what you'd been through. It's all online, all of your fundraising stuff. I know you've lived on the streets on and off for all those years and that some of those nights were in Dover. Silly really,' she shrugs. 'I just knew how brave you must have been to have lived through that and still want to help other people. I thought it might help me feel close to you.'

Dawn doesn't even try to stop the tears falling. One plops onto her arm when she places it on the table. She places her hand over Rosie's. 'It was only ever you who made me brave,' she whispers fiercely. 'Every time I felt like giving up, I thought about this moment. I knew it was worth fighting for even if I never got to have it.'

Rosie smiles and hands Dawn what's left of the napkin. 'I'm glad. So glad you didn't give up.'

'Now tell me,' Dawn says in a rush after dabbing at her eyes. 'Everything you've been up to. I want to hear everything.'

Dawn soaks up every word from Rosie about her childhood

in Liverpool. Her time at uni in London where she'd studied art and met Eliza, who she now lives with.

'You'll love her.' Rosie's eyes shine. 'I'll bring her next time. That's if you want there to be one.'

'I've never wanted anything more. Are you happy together?'

Rosie nods and reaches for a slice of carrot cake.

'Then I can't wait to meet her. What are you doing for work?'

'Well, I'm an artist when I'm not working at the estate agents',' she says through a mouthful of crumbs. 'I got a first at uni and have had a few commissions for paintings but it's slow going. Ideally, I'd like to get some teaching experience – lead some community art sessions.'

Dawn's brain begins to buzz with pictures. Rosie giving classes to St Jude's residents in the corner of the café. Her paintings adorning the walls and being snapped up by collectors who happen to pass by...

'Did you just hear what I said?' Rosie is fiddling with her friendship bracelet.

'Sorry. I was just imagining. Bit of a habit of mine.'

'I hope I'm not too much of a let-down. I'm sure there are all sorts of things you could have imagined about me. Sorry if I don't live up to them.' Rosie chuckles but is still intent on turning the beads around on her wrist.

Dawn leans under the table and reaches for her green hand-bag, £12.99 from Asda. She unzips the front compartment and slides out her most precious photograph. 'This is all I've had to go by. I thought of you every day and there was one thing I knew for sure. That you'd be extraordinary. And you are.'

Rosie takes the photo and places it gently on the table in

front of her. 'I have the perfect place to keep it.' She pulls a startling number of objects out of her rucksack: wet wipes, diary, hairbrush. Then her hands find what she was looking for and she passes Dawn a rectangular folder wrapped in soft fabric. Dawn begins at the back as per Rosie's instructions. A photo of Rosie's graduation and another one entitled, 'moving day'. She flicks backwards to Rosie as a teen; a myriad of style choices.

'My adoptive parents put it together for you.'

A pigtailed Rosie in her school uniform and Dawn is undone. Emotion rises and swallows her whole. 'My Rosie,' she croaks.

'There is something you need to know before you look at the front cover. They changed my name. It isn't Rosie anymore.'

The front of the album is embroidered with neat stitching. The words fill Dawn's chest.

For Dawn,
Thank you for giving us Hope.

'Hope,' whispers Dawn. 'A perfect name. My very own extraordinary Hope.'

ACKNOWLEDGEMENTS

So many thanks to my children, Jack and Emilie, for their unwavering faith in my writing and their patience in those many times when I mumbled, 'Just let me finish this sentence.'

For my awesome husband, Patrick, who hates reading but reads my work anyway, and who once said: 'I've a good feeling about you getting back into your writing again. It makes you happy – what's stopping you?' Thank you for the hugs, the listening and the many packets of sweets!

For my wonderful agent, Sarah Hornsley (The Bent Agency) for taking a chance on me, for believing in my characters, and cheering me on each step of the way. As my daughter has said, 'Sarah has literally changed your life, hasn't she, Mummy?' She is truly the best agent anyone could wish for.

Thank you to my fabulous editor, Charlotte Mursell, for her solid guidance and uncanny ability to see exactly what was needed; for her vision, encouragement and enthusiasm – and for always being kind. This story is all the richer and smoother as a result of her hard work and dedication.

To all the staff and residents from homeless hostels I have worked in – I salute you. I hope this story helps to portray the pressures of funding cuts to vital homeless services. I hope it encourages people to think twice before turning their face away from a homeless person and to consider the circumstances that could lead to someone losing a safe place to call home.

Thank you to my fantastic MA creative writing classmates and lecturers at CCCU – Sonia Overall, Caroline Greville, Danny Rhodes and especially to my mentor and personal tutor, Peggy Riley, who taught me so very much about storytelling and has been a constant source of inspiration and support. Thank you to Charlotte Hartley-Jones for being a wonderful and trusted critique partner.

Hugest thanks to my mum and dad, for always being my biggest champions and checking countless versions of this book in its earliest stages. You encouraged me to chase my dreams and you always believed I'd catch them. Thank you to my amazing in-laws, Anita and David, for the support and help and for looking after our littlies so I could reach my deadlines.

Thank you to the wonderful HQ Stories for being the best-ever home for my story; for taking good care of it and for making it possible to send it out into the hands of my readers.

Many thanks to my new editor, Katie Seaman, for taking me on, for her passion and support and for championing Dawn Brightside so brilliantly alongside my wonderful, hardworking publicist, Lily Capewell and all of Team HQ.

I'll be eternally thankful to my writing buddies, fellow inklings, and to Anstey Harris and Amy Beashel for their support and listening ears throughout my debut process.

At the risk of sounding like an Oscar winner-wannabe – I am also thanking my God (who knows exactly what this book means to me).

ONE PLACE. MANY STORIES

Bold, innovative and
empowering publishing.

FOLLOW US ON:

@HQStories